# A KILLER WEDDING

# A KILLER WEDDING

A NOVEL

## JOAN O'LEARY

WILLIAM MORROW
*An Imprint of* HarperCollins*Publishers*

Without limiting the exclusive rights of any author, contributor or the publisher of this publication, any unauthorized use of this publication to train generative artificial intelligence (AI) technologies is expressly prohibited. HarperCollins also exercise their rights under Article 4(3) of the Digital Single Market Directive 2019/790 and expressly reserve this publication from the text and data mining exception.

This is a work of fiction. Names, characters, places, and incidents are products of the author's imagination or are used fictitiously and are not to be construed as real. Any resemblance to actual events, locales, organizations, or persons, living or dead, is entirely coincidental.

A KILLER WEDDING. Copyright © 2025 by Joan O'Leary. All rights reserved. Printed in the United States of America. No part of this book may be used or reproduced in any manner whatsoever without written permission except in the case of brief quotations embodied in critical articles and reviews. For information, address HarperCollins Publishers, 195 Broadway, New York, NY 10007. In Europe, HarperCollins Publishers, Macken House, 39/40 Mayor Street Upper, Dublin 1, D01 C9W8, Ireland.

HarperCollins books may be purchased for educational, business, or sales promotional use. For information, please email the Special Markets Department at SPsales@harpercollins.com.

hc.com

FIRST EDITION

*Designed by Bonni Leon-Berman*
*Invitations designed by Cheree Berry Paper & Design*

---

Library of Congress Cataloging-in-Publication Data

Names: O'Leary, Joan author
Title: A killer wedding : a novel / Joan O'Leary.
Description: First edition. | New York, NY : William Morrow, 2025. |
   Identifiers: LCCN 2024053839 | ISBN 9780063432215 hardcover | ISBN 9780063432239 ebook
Subjects: LCGFT: Detective and mystery fiction | Thrillers (Fiction) | Novels
Classification: LCC PS3615.L429 K55 2025 | DDC 813/.6—dc23/eng/20250623
LC record available at https://lccn.loc.gov/2024053839

---

ISBN 978-0-06-343221-5

25 26 27 28 29 LBC 5 4 3 2 1

*To my husband, Tom*

# A KILLER WEDDING

PROLOGUE

# GLORIA

August 30, 1974
Charleston, South Carolina

GLORIA BEAUFORT CLUTCHES HER NECKLACE, a gold pendant featuring an etching of Saint Christopher, the patron saint of travelers. *Saint Christopher is also the patron saint of sudden death, but most people don't know that fun fact,* she thinks as she steps out of her lawyer's office and into the snarling Charleston heat.

Everything's changed now. Back in the Smithy & Meyers office, her signature on the divorce papers is nearly dry. A fifty-fifty split . . . of *her* baby. Not her actual baby, of course (though they'll split him too). No, the company *she* grew from nothing, not *John*. Gloria pulls out a silver compact. Her face is an angry red—and shouldn't it be? Sweat drips from beneath her feathery blond hair, down her face, and practically sizzles when it lands on the concrete. Touching her head, she feels her once perfectly coiffed waves sticking up in every direction thanks to the humidity. Apparently, not even a full can of Aqua Net can help her keep it together anymore. She looks how she feels: hot and bothered.

A woman walks out of Berlin's laden with shopping bags and lowers her sunglasses to give Gloria the once-over. *Where is Charlie?* A thump of panic begins in her chest. Did she not say to pick her up at 11:30 a.m. sharp?

The weight of gawking eyes is too much for her right now. She is in no mood to take pictures with housewives doing their weekly errands. Her rage simmers as the company's black Mercedes pulls into view. Finally.

"Good afternoon, Mrs. Ripton." Charlie scrambles to open her car door, as he should. Her eyes flit down to her gold Cartier Tank watch—11:34 a.m.

"Charlie, you know how I feel about tardiness." She climbs into the Mercedes with a huff as he closes the door behind her.

"Sorry, ma'am, the traffic . . ." He expertly lets his excuse fade out, as he's become prone to do in recent years.

"Never mind." She flicks her wrist. She'll let it slide. "And it's Miss Beaufort now." Gloria melts into the cold camel interior of her ride. She thinks back to picking this car out at the dealership, just after they took Glo public. She smiles remembering the shock of the oily car salesman, who smelled like sautéed onions, as he watched her write the check for the full amount. Every time she sinks into one of the car's rich seats, she tingles with pride.

"Right-o, *Miss Beaufort*. I like it. An elegant name, anyway. Suits ya." Charlie meets her eyes with a sad smile. It just about puts Gloria over the edge. Why should anyone feel sorry for her? They should feel sorry for John Ripton! It's him everyone should be worried about. Gloria is the face, CEO, and lifeblood of Glo, the leading beauty brand of the Southeast. If she stays on this trajectory, one day Glo will be the leading beauty brand of the world! And she's done it all as a woman. A young woman at that. Everything she touches turns to gold, and everything John Ripton touches turns out to be somebody else's wife.

The car glides down King Street toward her home on South of Broad. Normally, she'd never be caught dead in Charleston before October 1, but since she and John were married here and their marriage license was filed here, she gets to burn in the hell that is August in Lowcountry. Whatever—the details don't matter. What does matter is the irony. Getting divorced in the Holy City. "Jesus Christ," Gloria mutters . . . and then smirks. A joke just for herself.

She can't run the company with John, she just can't. Their partnership is completely over on all fronts. She can't even look at him. And if Gloria really allowed herself to "go there," to that dark place in the back of her mind that's been starved of vitamin D, she'd admit that she never even wanted to marry John in the first place. He was a convenience. She just needed to get out of her parents' house.

They pass St. Agnes, a beautiful white cathedral. Somehow, even in the maddening heat, it looks tranquil.

"Charlie, take me to church." Gloria closes her eyes and says a prayer.

"Of course, but I don't believe there's a mass scheduled," he says gently. Gloria knows this.

"I need to speak with Father. You can come back for me in an hour." Charlie turns the car around and doesn't press further. This is why she tolerates his occasional tardiness.

"Yes, ma'am. Shall I have Ursula fix Trey's lunch?" Their eyes meet again in the rearview mirror. He smiles broadly, his jolly face working overtime to suppress his clear judgment. Or maybe Gloria's just seeing her own guilt reflected, because she had momentarily forgotten about Trey, her *actual* baby. Naturally, her husband couldn't care less about a fifty-fifty split of *him*. The resentment starts to harden in her heart.

"Sure, fine. Tell him I'll be home for supper." She flicks her wrist again, signaling that the conversation is over. Charlie curbs the car at St. Agnes. The priests have come and gone over the years, but the solid white building has remained perfectly the same as the world changed within and around it.

Seeing her childhood parish puts Gloria at ease. This will be simpler than she thought. Gloria modeled her company after the church; emphasizing the importance of service, community, commitment, and faith to her employees—and instilling a good bit of fear and guilt into them too, for good measure. She steps back out into the heat, but this time she is a part of it. *Hell hath no fury like a woman scorned.* That's what they say isn't it? And sometimes—well, sometimes you have to put a situation in God's hands. She smooths out her black Chanel pencil skirt and marches up the stone parish steps.

A year later, Gloria's young and healthy ex-husband dies suddenly of heart failure. The Lord works in mysterious ways.

# ELLIOT ADLER
E V E N T S

**EVENT:** Ripton/Murphy Wedding     **EVENT COORDINATOR:** Elliot Adler

## BALLYMOON CASTLE HOTEL CONTACTS:

CHERYL CONNOR - *general manager*

DANNY FINNERTY - *head bartender*

NEIL O'MALLEY - *impromptu assistant for the weekend*

## SEATING ARRANGEMENTS
*—Not finalized*

## SWEETHEART TABLE

Graham Ripton and Jane Murphy     *(but this weekend: Gran)*

## TABLE ONE (FAMILY FIRST!)

Gloria Beaufort - *to the world, the iconic G.B.*

Trey Ripton - *father of the groom*   *(CEO of Glo)*

Clementine Ripton - *mother of the groom*

Ben Ripton - *brother of the groom, best man*   *(General Counsel of Glo)*

→ Carlyle Darby Ripton - *bridesmaid, wife of Ben*

Maggie Murphy - *mother of the bride*

*(Lyle)* Father Kenneth - *wedding officiant*

## NEED TO PLACE:

Raquel Williams - *bridesmaid, actress, and Glo fragrance ambassador*

Christine Russo - *Bespoke Weddings senior editor*
*covering the weekend festivities*

ONE

# CHRISTINE

Thursday, October 16
Ballymoon Castle Hotel, Ireland

CHRISTINE'S ENTIRE BODY TINGLES AS her driver slows down in front of a massive wrought iron gate. She's made it—in every sense. She made it through the six-and-a-half-hour flight from New York City to Shannon, Ireland (thanks to the unlimited glasses of red wine); she made it through the arrival terminal with her gigantic and miraculously underweight suitcase; she made it to her personal driver (!!!) idling in a gorgeous brand-new Mercedes sedan. And now she's made it to the wedding venue where she will—for the first time—be the lead editor on *Bespoke Weddings*' biggest feature of the year: the wedding of Jane Murphy and Dr. Graham Ripton, heir to the world's most iconic beauty empire, Glo.

Outside her tinted passenger window, Christine catches a glimpse of a gleaming bronze plaque that reads *Ballymoon Castle Hotel*. She can't help it; she lets a tiny squeal of excitement escape her throat. *This is really happening.* The car chugs along the gravel road as she soaks it all in: the lush green hills, the moody gray sky, the flame-dipped autumn trees that line the bumpy drive. It's all more perfect than she could have imagined. And she's imagined it *a lot*.

Elliot Adler is waiting on the front steps, waving to Christine as the car pulls up outside the grand entrance of the castle hotel. He looks extremely suave in his loose-fitting light-wash Rag & Bone jeans, thick white T-shirt, and green velvet slippers—like he owns the luxury estate himself. Which, for the weekend, he essentially does. For the past decade, the event planner has been at the helm of beauty billionaire and Glo founder Gloria Beaufort's soirees, family weddings included. Christine waves back at Elliot, grinning as his high cheekbones, elfish nose, and signature round glasses come into full view.

The driver puts the glistening black car in park and rushes around to open her passenger door. Christine already feels herself getting used to the royal treatment as she steps out onto the gravel and into the crisp October air. Sure, she's been at many high-profile weddings before, but never in a position of authority—never as the sole senior editor. At the last wedding she attended, in Venice over the summer, she'd actually fallen out of a gondola and into the Grand Canal, because the photographer kept telling her to move so that she wouldn't be in the couple's rehearsal dinner entrance shot. So yeah, nobody was exactly opening private Mercedes doors for her before today. Actually, up until very recently, she'd been the one in charge of door opening . . . if she wasn't already carrying her boss's garment bags.

*Speak of the devil*—Christine feels her phone vibrate in her slouchy Chloé travel tote. She just knows it's *Bespoke*'s editor in chief, Sandra Yoon, "checking in." Christine grimaces. Sandra is not taking it well that Gloria Beaufort specifically requested *only* Christine to cover this wedding weekend, stating that Jane and Graham "didn't need a *Bespoke* army invading the place."

Christine imagines her boss almost snapped the base of her champagne flute when Gloria delivered the news over their lunch at Bergdorf's following the Bespoke Ball last month. Sandra probably had to bite her tongue so hard, she must have drawn blood. Normally, *Bespoke Weddings* was just a blip on the editor in chief's star-studded radar. After all, she had the entire *Bespoke* brand to see to! But when it came to anything involving industry titans like Gloria Beaufort, Sandra liked to be heavily (some might say overly) involved.

She'll deal with Sandra later, though. For now, Christine smooths her shiny strawberry-blond hair (she paid extra for gloss on top of her already out-of-budget highlights, but she thinks it was worth it), checks her teeth on the back of her metallic phone case, and gets out of the car to greet Elliot.

"Here she is! The fabulous Christine Russo that Sandra can't stop bragging about." He grins and wraps her in a quick hug that feels more like he's shaking her by the shoulders. Christine smiles tightly, reading between the lines; she knows Sandra hasn't been bragging to Elliot but more likely bitching to him about Christine representing *Bespoke Weddings* this weekend.

"Hi, Elliot. Good to see you again," she says, looking around. "This place is just . . . wow." They've met dozens of times at weddings over the years, but this is the first time Elliot's ever acknowledged her presence with more than a distracted half smile. Except for one time at that wannabe-ranchers-but-actually-from-Brentwood couple's wedding in Bozeman, Montana, when he momentarily mistook her for the florist and chewed her out about the "horrendous quality of the wild bergamot," throwing his twelve-hundred-dollar custom cowboy hat on the floor for dramatic effect . . . But he probably doesn't remember that encounter.

"Isn't it just *beyond*?" Elliot marvels. "Come on, let me give you a lay of the land." If he felt even a shred of embarrassment at her hint that they've met before, he doesn't show it. The wedding planner trots up the red carpet that coats the enormous castle steps, but Christine finds herself unable to move, completely overcome by the literal fortress in front of her, the castle's green and gold flags flapping in the chilly Irish breeze. Ballymoon is more impressive up close. It's built of serious-looking stone that's been weathered by the many centuries it's stood on this land. Just below the estate, a glimmering lough sits like a perfectly round black button in the middle of the bright green front lawn. The grass is so verdant that it looks like a picture of itself with the saturation turned all the way up.

The main entrance of the castle is flanked by two sharp turrets, puncturing the stormy clouds above them. Christine's mind flashes back to the small, white-shuttered Cleveland town house she grew up in—with its yellow-patched front lawn and slightly chipped red front door—and the familiar beginnings of imposter syndrome bubble inside of her. *You don't belong here,* her subconscious whispers, but she shakes the thought loose with a shudder. She does belong here—she earned this. She has what it takes to pull this off and prove that she's worthy of being a senior editor. Even Gloria Beaufort sees something in her. Christine closes her eyes and tries to clear her mind. She can't afford to be in a bad headspace this weekend.

Elliot stops in front of a large oak door. "Chop, chop!" he calls cheerily. Two castle employees stand on either side of him like modern millennial knights in expensive hunter-green suits. Christine just stares at him, stunned by her own reality. The autumn leaves rustle around her; it's like they're gossiping with one another, and Christine can't quite make out what they're saying, but she just *knows* they're talking about her. She feels goose bumps prickle her skin and pulls her chunky fisherman knit sweater tightly around her as she lets a gust of wind carry her up the stairs and into the castle.

"We've probably got about an hour until the family gets back from pheasant hunting," Elliot muses, checking his cell phone.

"Pheasant hunting?" she asks. "Is that even legal?"

"Does it matter?" Elliot shrugs. Christine ponders this for a moment, slightly startled by his bluntness. But he's right, it doesn't matter. If it's illegal, Gloria Beaufort will just write the check to make it okay.

"Now come on, it's time for the grand tour." Elliot claps his hands together, his assortment of gold bangles clanging as he does. He's got at least five Cartier LOVE bracelets dangling from his left wrist. Christine once heard him joke that it's his signature breakup gift to himself—his way of turning a bad investment into a good one.

"Neil, the hotel attendant—and my impromptu assistant for the weekend—will see to it that your bags are delivered to your suite," Elliot declares. "My assistant, Lizzy, tested positive for Covid literally *minutes* before leaving for JFK. Honestly, her timing is always *impeccable*." Elliot grumbles while typing a text on his phone that Christine assumes is an angry one given the velocity of his finger punches.

She turns around to see a gangly teenager (Neil, presumably), struggling to carry her massive T. Anthony luggage up the steps. The eggplant leather suitcase was her promotion gift to herself—and the most money she's ever spent on anything in her life. Her dad, who's been wearing the same Christmas sweater every year since his high school days, would have a literal heart attack if he saw the price tag. She flinches as the teen drags it unceremoniously along the stone steps. A bellman mercifully joins in to help him.

"Thanks," she calls to them. "Sorry, I'm not a light packer, more of a nomadic hoarder."

Elliot lets out a sharp laugh at her joke, then clears his throat and looks up from his phone as they step inside. "Well, welcome to Ballymoon! This is just reception. Not much to see here," he says dismissively, and starts walking down a hall. Christine's eyes rove over the space that Elliot was so quick to write off. It's a complete work of art. Giant oil portraits of Irish royals grace the mustard-yellow walls, and the hardwood floors are covered in a rich red-and-gold Persian rug that has been meticulously maintained, the crease marks from this morning's vacuum still fresh. And the smell—what is that smell? Christine sniffs the air. Jasmine, maybe?

In the center of the room, she spots a glossy mahogany table that looks like it should be in a museum. At its center sits an ornate vase teeming with the most spectacular floral arrangement she's ever seen: a whimsical array of purple, pink, and orange wildflowers and, yes, jasmine spring out in every direction like a colorful splash of water frozen midair.

"They're all picked right on the property, directly from our very own Foxglove Garden." Christine turns her head toward the front desk, where a stout blond woman watches her admiring the floral feat. The woman's smile is broad and fixed, her lips unmoving as she talks through her grin, like a statue come to life. It's a bit unnerving.

"Gorgeous," Christine says softly.

"We can have our groundskeeper put together an arrangement and send it up to your room," Frozen Smile offers. "Christine Russo, right?"

"Oh no, that's fine, thank you, though. No need to go to the trouble. I can just admire them here!" Christine assumes this woman must be the general manager of the hotel, angling for some sort of favorable review of Ballymoon in *Bespoke*.

"It's not a problem," the woman insists. "Please, allow me. We want your stay here to be as grand as possible. I insist."

Did Christine just see her eye twitch or is the jet lag getting to her already?

"Er, okay," Christine replies. "Thank you, then."

"It's nothing at all! And if you need anything, please don't hesitate to ask for Cheryl." The woman gives her a side-smile and a wink before turning to clack away on her keyboard.

"Great. Thanks, Cheryl." Christine smiles and turns her attention to the front desk itself—which is literally cut out of the gray stone walls. Someone even went so far as to carve an ornate medieval crest directly above where the woman is standing.

"This way, Christine!" Elliot chirps, and she turns to follow him down a long maroon hallway. Ballymoon isn't a dated European castle with drafty halls and musty furniture like one might assume from its ancient exterior. The whole place smells like a fancy department store and boasts impeccable custom furniture in jewel-toned shades and eccentric patterns that somehow work in perfect harmony. And there are modern touches everywhere: a luxury gift shop where a Ballymoon-embroidered baseball hat probably costs fifty dollars, a large (but discreet) flat-screen television broadcasting a golf match, a fitness center with one of those new "mirror" workout things and, of course, multiple Peloton bikes. It's the perfect blend of traditional and modern extravagance.

"When can I move in?" Christine whines longingly as they walk down the hall. She gawks at the pictures that line the walls; this castle hotel has hosted presidents, kings, starlets, and, most impressive, the Beatles.

"I know, right?" Elliot agrees. "And G.B. rented out the whole hotel for a week so we can have complete privacy for the wedding festivities." He claps his hands together again with glee. Elliot doesn't like to share.

"How did the couple decide on Ireland?" Christine asks. The wedding planner takes a sharp left and leads Christine into a large foyer, where a skilled pianist sends soothing jazz music floating through the halls.

"Jane wanted to pay homage to her late father, who grew up in a small village just a few miles away from Ballymoon. Apparently, as a child, he and his friends played on the castle grounds. So sweet, right? A real full-circle moment for her to get married here." Elliot almost sounds genuine, before quickly adding, "And let me just tell you, of all the lavish hotels on the Emerald Isle, Ballymoon is the most iconic . . . and the only one with enough helipads for the Ripton entourage." Elliot pauses and looks down at his buzzing phone. "I need to take this. One sec!" He slides his finger over his phone's screen and strides down the hall shouting into his cell.

As Elliot reems out some poor vendor about delivering napkins in the "completely wrong" shade of ivory, Christine takes the opportunity to look around and let reality sink in. Her cheeks already hurt from smiling. *I'm here. I actually pulled it off.*

For the better part of a year, Christine Russo had been manifesting this exact moment, writing, *I* will *cover Graham Ripton's wedding. I* will *get promoted to senior editor*, over and over in her journal. She recognizes that this kind of behavior is eye roll–inducing at best and borderline psychotic at worst, but she has always been extreme and undeterrable; or to put it in high school terms—an overachiever.

Her parents often recount the story of when Christine was snubbed for editor in chief of her school newspaper in favor of Principal Randall's C-student daughter, Annalise. In response, Christine published a scathing op-ed that she snuck into the paper mere moments before it went to print, accusing the school administration of nepotism and even hinting at the possible misallocation of school funds by Principal Randall to install a pool in his backyard.

She did eventually get the editor in chief position (and a month of detention), but more impressive, her article prompted the school board to start an investigation into Principal Randall. It turns out he very much *was* misallocating school funds. Christine was asked to testify at the trial, which provided an excellent topic for her college essay, and before she knew it, she was a Columbia University student with a highly coveted summer internship at *the* fashion and lifestyle publication: *Bespoke*. Sure, it wasn't the *New York Times*—but it was still within the realm of journalism . . . and plus, it sounded way sexier. Not to mention, the clothes!

Christine loved every minute of learning about the inner workings of the glamorous magazine—but she especially loved the weddings division. *Bespoke Weddings,* aka "The Bridal Bible," was its own beast entirely, a fascinating microcosm of love, wealth, style, and sharp storytelling. Every morning, before inevitably being asked to run some miscellaneous forgotten item to a shoot, she'd steal a moment to click through photos from the most recent *Bespoke Weddings*–worthy affair, treating herself to a dizzying blur of five-star hotels in exotic locations that served fashion icons, celebrities, and billionaires. She'd ogle the six-figure custom gowns, the champagne parties on megayachts, and the floral arrangements that were worth more than five—ten, twenty?—times her intern salary, marveling at the luck of the editors who got to go to these events . . . to cover, capture, and report it all for *Bespoke Weddings*. Literal dream weavers! Christine was desperate to be one of them.

So, after graduation, she clawed her way back into the iconic publication as the second assistant to editor in chief of *Bespoke*, Sandra Yoon, eventually becoming a junior editor at *Bespoke Weddings*, and now, *finally,* as of this weekend: senior editor.

Christine had learned from a young age that getting what she wanted would sometimes require breaking the rules. So she approached landing the Ripton/Murphy wedding the same way she approached getting the editor in chief position back in high school: by pursuing it so aggressively that landing the assignment was not a matter of *if* but *when*. She'd just needed the right opportunity to pitch herself for the job.

And that opportunity had come last month, when she charmed Dr. Graham Ripton's beauty scion grandmother (the one footing the bill for this weekend's lavish affair) at the annual Bespoke Ball. Christine knew that if she could get a few minutes alone with Gloria, she could ensure she'd be the one to cover her grandson's wedding. And she was right.

"Okay, finally that's done with!" Elliot says, walking over to her as he slides his phone back into the pocket of his jeans. "The vendors over here are just"—he chooses his words carefully—"not used to my level of attention to detail." He gives her a conspiratorial look.

"I totally get it." She nods vigorously, as if she too has a very strong opinion on the various shades of ivory napkins.

"Anyway, back to the tour. Here is the castle pub, The Snug." Elliot turns and opens a door to a dimly lit room directly behind them. "It's so adorable and cozy, you'll just want to curl up in it all weekend," he says.

Christine briefly sticks her head in and catches a glimpse of a beautiful tartan window seat overlooking the lough; a near-empty glass of Guinness sits on a shiny wooden table like it's been placed there for a magazine shoot. And maybe it has. The castle is well aware of their upcoming *Bespoke Weddings* feature.

"And over here we have the terrace room," Elliot calls from farther down the hall. Christine rushes to catch up, getting a small glimpse of a beautiful room painted robin's-egg blue, with windows framed by thick cream curtains that overlook the Ballymoon golf course back nine. Just past the course, Christine sees what must be the castle's famous Foxglove Garden, where the wildflowers in reception hail from, and where the family will host Jane and Graham's rehearsal dinner tomorrow night. Elliot breezes out of the room quickly, and again Christine chases after him.

"It's amazing how they've restored this place and maintained each room for their original purpose. Everything is almost exactly the same as when Ireland's High King Brian Boru graced these halls . . . well, besides the spa and fitness center and gift shop and everything, but you get the idea." Elliot turns a corner, and Christine comes face-to-face with a giant taxidermy deer head. The poor animal's eyes bulge in fear and Christine feels her throat dry up.

"Is that real?" she asks Elliot, her heart rate quickening.

"Well, this isn't Disney World, so I'd say so," Elliot trills, unperturbed by the stuffed dead animal. He flings open two large oak doors to reveal a massive library complete with a rolling ladder. A fire blazes in a stone hearth that stretches from the hardwood floor to the cavernous ceiling.

"This is the Queen Gormlaith Library. She was the third wife of High King Brian Boru. Ballymoon was their family home in the early eleventh century. That's her there." Elliot points out a giant oil portrait of a pale woman with a mess of wild red hair that hangs over the fireplace.

"Irish historians say that she was responsible for her husband's untimely death. She was a notorious political schemer and colluded with other Irish kings to take her husband down. Apparently, she was *completely* evil. Totally gorgeous, though. Isn't that how it always goes?" They stand in silence for a moment, staring at the painting and listening to the crackling fire. Queen Gormlaith's almost-translucent green eyes are so intense that Christine feels like she's staring into the sun. She quickly averts her gaze.

"After Brian Boru was killed, the queen just vanished from the castle. Poof! But nobody saw her leave the grounds. A total medieval *Gone Girl* situation!" Elliot's eyes linger on the stone hearth directly in front of them. He lowers his voice. "There's a local rumor that Brian Boru had a secret passageway built into the castle walls as an escape route in the event of an enemy invasion . . . and that the queen tried to use it to flee, but she became disoriented and ended up trapped in the castle walls, never to find her way out . . . her spirit still haunting Ballymoon to this day." He wiggles his fingers like he's telling a ghost story around a campfire.

"I'm sure that story will put all the guests at ease." Christine laughs nervously.

"Come on, Christine, true crime is so *in* right now! Everyone's going to devour the history of this place like the latest Netflix binge." Elliot grins and throws up his hands before power walking out of the room, arms pumping at his sides. Christine follows him, wondering what her step count must be up to at this point.

"On the left here is the Brian Boru Suite," Elliot says as he speeds past an ornate wooden door, "the king's original chambers and, of course, G.B.'s personal residence for the weekend." Christine glances at the door briefly before hurrying after Elliot.

"I love that this venue has some *meat* to it, you know? It was just so much fun researching everything and pulling elements from the castle's history to use for my vision," the wedding planner prattles on.

"All of these details hardly seem romantic," Christine says.

"It's *art*, darling. Would you rather them get married in some Barbie Dreamhouse venue in Palm Beach? Talk about *pedestrian*." Elliot snorts. They continue down the hall, and Christine notices as one of the golden-hued lights above flickers slightly as the wind whips against the castle walls.

"I really hope this weather chills the eff out." Elliot sighs. "I tried to convince Jane to do the wedding next summer, but she had her heart set on autumn leaves." He stops in front of a set of glass French doors.

"This is the drawing room, which will host tonight's welcome dinner." Elliot leads them into the room. At its center is a long, elegant dining table. The perimeter is striped with floor-to-ceiling windows blanketed in rich emerald-green curtains. On one wall stands a glistening oak bar. A flurry of Elliot's staffers scuttle about the place in their signature black *Elliot Adler* polos, toting silver candelabras and lush floral arrangements in preparation for tonight's event.

"I used Queen Gormlaith's portrait as inspiration for tonight—all those *delicious* green hues and that lush navy dress were just too good." Elliot fluffs a floral arrangement that passes by. Then he abruptly stops talking and turns to her expectantly. Probably realizing that Christine hasn't written a single thing down.

"A steel trap," she says, and nervously taps the side of her head. "I won't miss a detail."

"Good," he says curtly. "I'm expecting at least a dozen mentions of Elliot Adler Events in next month's issue. Sandra promised!" He means it as a joke . . . but not really.

She side-steps his request. "Elliot, I must say: you've outdone yourself. I can't wait to see what else you've got up your sleeve this weekend." Elliot files the compliment away without acknowledgment. He then turns to walk the length of the table, on which thick cream-colored place cards are being set out. With a wave of his hand, he motions for Christine to follow.

"As you know, Jane and Graham wanted tonight's welcome dinner to be an intimate, family-only affair before all the wedding craziness begins."

Christine bobs her head up and down. "Of course. I totally get that." She hadn't expected to be invited to tonight's dinner—that was the point of Elliot's little tour, to give her some details and information for her article without her having to intrude on a family moment. She was really just looking forward to a long bubble bath and chicken tenders from room service.

"Buuuuut"—Elliot draws out the word, stopping in front of a place card and picking it up—"Gloria insisted that you join in on the fun. And she's the one footing the bill, so—" He hands her the place card. She looks down and feels an unstoppable smile spread across her face. Forget the bubble bath, she's got to figure out what to wear—because there, etched in glittering cursive, is the name *Christine Russo*.

"Welcome to the A-list." Elliot smirks before prying the card from her fingers. "But if I know Gloria, this seat comes with strings attached, possibly even chains." He adds the last part under his breath as one of his staffers artfully arranges taper candles on the dining table.

"Noted." Christine laughs off the weird comment. Elliot looks at her for a moment, very intensely, his eyes turning a steely gray that matches the looming clouds outside. He opens his mouth to say something else, but shuts it almost as fast as the drawing room doors swing open behind Christine.

"Who knows how to cook pheasant around here?" a deep voice bellows from behind her. Christine turns around to see Ben Ripton, the groom's older brother and Gloria's elder grandson, standing in the doorway in muddy boots and a rumpled wax Barbour jacket. Elliot bristles as the brown sludge from Ben's boots seeps into the pristine handwoven rug.

"Ben," Elliot coos, "this is Christine Russo. She's here to cover the wedding for *Bespoke*. Christine, this is Ben Ripton, general counsel of Glo, and most importantly for this weekend, our best man!" Ben glowers down at her from his six-foot frame. He's textbook handsome, but something about his vibe is disconcerting—like, if Christine was at a gas station late at night and he was the person behind the register, she'd keep her hand on her mace.

"So nice to meet you," Christine says with false bravado.

"Pleasure." He reluctantly extends a large hand toward her. She takes it without thinking . . . before realizing it's wet and sticky. As she pulls away, she sees that her hand is now covered in pheasant blood.

"Sorry about that," Ben says, and grins.

But he doesn't look sorry at all.

PLEASE JOIN US FOR AN INTIMATE

# WELCOME DINNER

TO KICK OFF JANE AND GRAHAM'S
WEDDING WEEKEND

Toast the happy couple and enjoy a
candlelight dinner, starting with a caviar tasting
and followed by a hearty meal of fresh Irish salmon,
County Clare potatoes, a family-style salad
plucked from Ballymoon's organic vegetable garden,
and ending with dessert: the groom's favorite,
apple crumble.

*Thursday, October Sixteenth*

AT SEVEN O'CLOCK IN THE EVENING

THE DRAWING ROOM

AT BALLYMOON CASTLE HOTEL

*Elevated attire encouraged*

TWO

# CHRISTINE

Thursday, October 16, 2025
Welcome Dinner

CHRISTINE SETTLES HERSELF IN HER seat, letting the silky navy-blue Amsale dress she borrowed from the *Bespoke* sample closet trickle down the sides of her chair. The off-the-shoulder dress suits her, delicately exposing her bony clavicle and glowy porcelain skin. She may not have had an unlimited budget when it came to shopping for this weekend, but her petite frame and twenty-eight-year-old skin picked up the slack.

She checks the time: half past six. Elliot flails around the room fluffing pillows and sampling—and sending back—appetizer trays. He told her to arrive at least fifteen minutes early, so she doubled it and arrived thirty minutes early. Christine wants a chance to have her first drink before rubbing elbows with the prestigious heirs to the Glo fortune. Sure, her first interaction with a Ripton didn't go *exactly* how she imagined it would. She shudders thinking of Ben's bloody handshake . . . But she can rebound. She has to.

This is a career-changing opportunity, and Christine knows it. She is here to gather up all the glam and gossip to share with every woman in the world, no exaggeration; from preteens to great-grandmothers, *Bespoke*'s readers are waiting to gawk at the glossy pages she will write to judge, salivate, and dream about being in a seat just like Christine's. It's her obligation—no, her *duty*—to her readers to savor every minute and write a juicy story about how the other half lives that's worth drooling over. It's the moment she's been waiting for since her intern days.

Christine starts by assessing the table where she is currently seated, her eyes taking in every crystal glass and sterling silver utensil, when the place card next to hers catches her eye: *Gloria Beaufort.*

She blinks and opens her eyes again, just to make sure she isn't seeing things. Then her eyes lock with Elliot's. The wedding planner straightens a place setting that's probably already perfectly symmetrical and winks at her—*it's not a mistake.* A high-level perfectionist like Elliot doesn't make mistakes. She is seated next to Gloria Beaufort herself. Before Christine can fully process her excitement, her phone buzzes in her hot pink YSL clutch, a secondhand treasure she found on a thrifting trip when her mother visited her in New York last summer.

Everything going well? texts Sandra, from over three thousand miles away. Christine shoves the phone back into her bag with annoyance, mad at her boss for pulling her out of this glittering moment. Sandra will require an update before the night is over, that is a given—and she'll probably never forgive Christine for securing the get of the wedding season, but it's not Christine's fault that Sandra is losing her touch. *It's time for a new generation to take the reins,* she thinks, smiling to herself, *even if it's by force.*

Christine remembers telling her mom about how she schemed her way into Graham Ripton's wedding behind her boss's back, thus forcing Sandra's hand on her promotion.

"Can you believe it worked?" she'd said, and smiled, slurping down a greasy noodle of beef lo mien from Lin's Gourmet, the perfectly crappy Chinese place on the ground floor of her apartment building. "I am *finally* a senior editor! Isn't it amazing?"

Her mom was silent on the other end of the line.

"What? Why aren't you saying anything?" She put down her takeout box, irritated.

"Honey, really, I'm happy for you—I'm glad your plan went off without a hitch, but that was risky. You could have lost your job if someone caught you."

Christine held the phone away from her ear as the clang and bang of Carol unloading the dishwasher in Cleveland echoed through her studio apartment.

"What was the alternative? Wait another four years for a promotion? I saw an opportunity to elevate my position and I took it. You should be proud of me." Christine took a gulp of Kendall-Jackson white wine (the only thing consistently stocked in her fridge besides Chobani yogurts and under-eye jelly masks) and waited for her mother's retort.

"I am proud of you, of course I am"—her mom sighed—"but if you play with fire, you'll get burned. There's nothing wrong with going by the book, putting in the time—" Christine zoned out as her mom recited her laundry list of self-help quotes for the one millionth time.

"Yeah, if you want a boring life," Christine snorted, and immediately felt guilty. "Sorry—I'm just tired. But I've gotta go pack anyway." She screwed the cap back on her wine bottle.

"I just want you to be careful. Don't you think . . ." Her mother's voice trailed off.

"Just say it," Christine snapped, grabbing a pile of clothes off her love seat and throwing them onto her bed, hoping that somehow counted as packing progress.

"Did you ever think maybe it was *too* easy to get this assignment?"

She frowns at the memory. Christine loves her mom, but Carol is a dental hygienist in Cleveland. She doesn't know the first thing about what it's like to be in Christine's world—and what it takes to stay there.

And tonight, her world is dazzling. She sits up straighter and takes a sip of her drink. It's time to refocus. A seat next to the iconic G.B. will ensure that Christine's editorial coverage of this affair will be perfect. Maybe by next year, she'll have Sandra's desk (and corner office, and Chelsea apartment, and shoe collection).

*Okay, relax*, she tells herself, her heart racing. *Any part of that dream hinges on you absolutely crushing this weekend.* She takes another sip of her drink and looks around, jotting a few notes in her phone. The room is adorned with candle sconces that flicker warmly in front of the hunter-green lacquered walls. On the far side of the space, there is a floor-to-ceiling window overlooking Ballymoon lough. A full moon beats brightly down on the lake with an intensity similar to a spotlight's on center stage. Above her, a crystal chandelier sparkles like a thousand wintry icicles. As Christine looks up, a gust of wind bangs against the window, jostling the chandelier slightly. She winces as she considers the likelihood of one of those icicle-like crystals plunging down toward her. The weather still hasn't let up. It's not ideal for any wedding weekend... even in Ireland.

Turning her attention back to the table, she types a brief description of the room into her phone. *The table is covered in china plates worth more than most life insurance policies and silverware so heavy it's almost like a low-intensity workout just to lift a fork. Giant candelabras with grosgrain navy blue and dark green ribbon line the entirety of the long banquet table, adding a festive, Ralph Lauren–inspired touch. And directly across from the table, a giant fire blazes in the stone hearth, making one rethink ever even considering a summer wedding.*

*The Polo Bar is shaking right now,* Christine adds to her notes before slipping her phone back into her clutch. The first time she heard rumblings that the world's most sought-after bachelor since Prince William, pediatric oncologist and billionaire Graham Ripton, was off the market was actually at the Polo Bar last winter, just after Jane and Graham's engagement was announced. So this is a real full-circle moment.

After a particularly brutal Hinge date that ended with her date sticking his finger in her martini "to taste it," Christine stormed off to the ladies' room, ready to do something drastic like book a last-minute appointment to get bangs, when she heard the first of what would soon be dubbed the "Ripton Rumors."

"I hear she's a drug dealer," an airy voice said from behind a bathroom stall door, the dark lacquer of which was very similar to the one gracing the walls at Ballymoon Castle.

"Wouldn't surprise me. Lucie told me she was an escort that he, like, fell in love with *Pretty Woman* style," replied a raspier voice from the adjacent toilet. Christine took out a lip gloss and started applying it with great care, eager to hear more details about who was being discussed.

"G.B. has to be beside herself." The toilet flushed, and a rail-thin woman in a feathery black top and leather pants walked out to wash her hands. The woman flashed Christine a Crest White smile, unaware of Christine's eavesdropping. She played it cool, acting like she was waiting to use the stall, latched the door behind her, and sat down quietly so she could hear more.

"Gloria's barely there anymore, a shell of her former self, but there's no way her son isn't having an iron-clad prenup drawn up as we speak. That family is not going to risk losing a penny of their inheritance." Christine peeked through the crack between the stalls. The second woman was wearing red-bottomed shoes and, if Christine wasn't mistaken, a silk skirt she'd definitely seen at Zara. A woman who mixed highs and lows was always a reliable source for society gossip.

"There's probably no need," the feathery waif said as she ran her fingers through her nearly butt-length brown hair. "John's friend—you know Matt from Morgan Stanley? Well, you didn't hear it from me, but apparently Glo is in hot water." She smiled at herself in the mirror as she applied a brown matte lipstick.

"Oh my god, really? Somebody better tell Plain Jane before she picks her property out east!" High/Low replied, her haughty laughter floating out of the bathroom along with the click of her heels.

Even though the Riptons hailed from Charleston, like any prominent family in the fashion and beauty business, they spent a majority of their time in New York City and summered in the Hamptons, garnering the attention, and therefore chatter, of Manhattan's elites. Shortly after that night, Christine was hearing the Ripton Rumors everywhere.

"I hear they're filing for bankruptcy," a woman hiding in a giant Canada Goose jacket said while grabbing her flat white at Sant Ambroeus.

"G.B. is ousting her son as CEO—the company stock is going to tank," a greasy-haired guy said too loudly outside Casa Cipriani.

"I hear they're breaking child-labor laws in Indonesia," a robe-clad woman told her friend in a sauna at the Well.

As gossip swirled around New York City during those last gasps of winter, Christine knew likely nothing she heard was true, but what she did know was that Gloria Beaufort's family was at the center of the zeitgeist and Graham Ripton's wedding would be the only thing people would want to talk about for the foreseeable future. And when a wedding date was set for the following October, at a castle in Ireland no less, the society chatter turned into a frenzied scream as anybody who was *anybody* tried to figure out how to finagle an invite.

"Elliot, sweetie, hello!" Clementine Ripton trills across the room, breaking Christine's reminiscence as she barrels toward the table.

"Hi, *gorgeous*, so good to see you." Elliot gives Clementine a kiss on the cheek before turning toward Christine to make the necessary introduction.

"This is Christine Russo. She's here on behalf of *Bespoke Weddings*," he says.

"It's a pleasure to meet—" Christine starts, but she can't even finish her sentence before the mother of the groom locks her in an embrace. *I guess she's a hugger*, Christine thinks, and tries not to let the moment feel awkward.

Clementine takes her face in her hands. "It's great to meet you." She searches for something in Christine's gaze, her eyes shifting back and forth. Eventually—and mercifully—she lets go. "You have good energy. I can just tell these things."

"Oh! Well, thank you," Christine says with a laugh.

A kind way to describe Clementine Ripton would be to say she is eccentric. An unkind way to describe her would be to say she is a whackjob trustafarian with an unlimited budget. She fancies herself an artist and a poet, but she's not particularly good with a pen or a paintbrush.

Any acclaim she's garnered has been bought and paid for with Glo board seats and big donations. From what Christine has heard, Clementine is a patron of the arts who is tolerated by the creative upper crust due to her fat wallet and vast connections, but not actually embraced as "one of them."

"It's hard to have bad energy at a place like this," Christine says, then raises her champagne flute. "Here's to an amazing wedding weekend." She offers her glass to clink as Clementine whisks one off a passing tray, but the mother of the groom ignores her attempt to cheers.

"Were you at the Bespoke Ball?" Clementine asks, and Christine freezes, not sure how to respond, but thankfully Clementine doesn't take a breath. "God, don't answer that, I was tripping on mushrooms, I don't even want to think about that night. I swear I thought Trey had a T. rex head and the whole place was jumping with little green garden gnomes. It was fun, but concerning, you know? Cute little guys, though—the gnomes, I mean. Anyway, if we met that night, I'm sorry I don't remember." Christine doesn't know what to say to this, but luckily Clementine swats the thought away like a fly in her face before continuing.

"Isn't this place just *ah-mazing*? I'm feeling overcome with creativity just standing here." She closes her eyes and breathes deeply. Christine stands awkwardly, waiting for her to reopen them.

The mother of the groom looks, for lack of a better word, bizarre in a long cabernet-colored velvet swing coat, a black maxi skirt, long black gloves, and a small matching fascinator hat with netting flitting in front of her eyes. Sort of like an extra from *Downton Abbey* who is going to a rave, which after the mushrooms comment, tracks.

"You look . . . so chic," Christine says quickly once Clementine's eyelids flutter open. "Love the skirt."

"Do I? Thanks." She laughs. "I wanted to pay homage to the glory days of this outrageous castle, play a part of history, if you will. I think it's a bit like *Gilded Age* meets *Sweeney Todd*, which is exactly what I was going for. It really fits the theme." Clementine does a twirl, spilling her drink on an ancient-looking rug. Christine watches Elliot flinch at the sight before disappearing into the kitchen with another tray of presumably unacceptable lamb skewers. Christine is unclear how the demon barber of Fleet Street fits in with the Ralph Lauren, old-world aesthetics of this dinner party, but she doesn't dare question Clementine's logic.

"Have you seen it?" Clementine picks up a caviar deviled egg, sniffs it, and puts it back on a waiter's outstretched tray. "God, I hate deviled eggs, but Trey devours them. I'm trying to be vegan now. Have you seen *Cowspiracy*? It changed my life." Christine is starting to feel shell-shocked by Clementine's manic energy.

"Seen what, sorry?" She tries to keep up, but Clementine bulldozes on.

"Oh, but back to *Sweeney Todd*. It's marvelous, simply *marvelous*. I've been five times. You know, Christine, you really ought to get more coverage of the arts in *Bespoke*. I've been in Sandra's ear for a while about it. Maybe the two of us can tag team her?" Christine's YSL clutch suddenly feels heavier as she thinks of her boss's unanswered text.

"Where is she, by the way? Sandra?" Clementine plucks a bottle of Dom Pérignon right out of a waiter's hands and fills up a second glass for herself now that a majority of her first is on the rug. *She's fishing*, Christine realizes. Clementine wants to know what Christine's "in" is—or, how on earth she's here.

"Actually"—Christine clears her throat—"Ms. Beaufort asked for me to represent *Bespoke Weddings* this weekend."

Clementine coughs up her champagne. "Sandra isn't coming?" The shift in the air is palpable. "That's too bad. Another one bites the dust then, eh? Oh, let me try one of those." She grabs a vegetable skewer off another passing tray and glides a cube of onion off the stick with her teeth. Christine doesn't have the nerve to ask what she means, but she files the comment away to agonize about later.

"Are you thrilled for the wedding? I know it's going to be spectacular." Christine tries to change the subject, but Clementine is already backing away, her interest in Christine fading faster than the audience's at one of Clementine's notoriously cringey slam poetry happy hours.

"Oh." She stands up a little straighter, pulling down her velvet coat. "Well, I suppose. A bit of a dog-and-pony show, but Elliot is a wizard, so . . ." She smiles, but Christine doesn't miss the clench of her jaw.

"Jane is so stunning. I'm sure she'll make a gorgeous bride," Christine offers.

"Yes, I guess she is quite pretty." Clementine knits her eyebrows as if just considering this for the first time. "I hadn't really noticed, though, until you mentioned it. I feel like everyone pales in comparison to my Handsome Grahamsome." Clementine enunciates the nickname like she's about to pet a puppy, then shrugs. "He just radiates warmth and light. It's that healer energy, I think." She leaves Christine to begin absentmindedly inspecting the china on each place setting.

"Is this the eighteenth-century pattern I picked out? The same ones that Thomas Moore ate off?" Clementine holds up a plate, and in the nick of time, Elliot sails back into the room.

"Of course, darling, the very same." He gently returns the plate to its rightful setting like he's detonating a bomb.

"Good," Clementine chirps. "Do you know what my favorite Moore quote is?"

Elliot and Christine shake their heads.

Clementine clears her throat. "'If honor were profitable, everybody would be honorable.'"

A gust of wind whips through the silence that follows. Clementine erupts into delayed laughter. "So fitting for this crowd, don't you think?" Christine and Elliot chuckle nervously, neither of them quite grasping the joke. Also, it's been a few years since her English major days at Columbia, but she is pretty sure that Thomas Moore never said that. Clementine probably just got that quote from a "Quippy Irish Quotes" Buzzfeed article.

"Elliot, the place looks perfect," Christine says as Clementine twirls around, this time almost knocking over a candle, which Elliot grabs in the nick of time. Christine raises her glass in his direction. The wedding planner accepts the compliment with a tight smile. "You're sweet, but really, the visionary behind tonight's soiree deserves all the accolades." Clementine takes a dramatic bow.

"Wait until you see what I have planned for the cocktail reception after the ceremony." Clementine grins mischievously. "It's just the moodiest, sexiest speakeasy vibe you could possibly imagine!"

"This weekend is going to be *unbelievable*." Elliot stretches the word out like a piece of taffy as he surveys the room for the hundredth time.

"I can't wait." Christine grins. "I am so honored to be here on behalf of *Bespoke*."

"As you should be!" Elliot snarks. "Sandra's leaving big Manolos to fill. Metaphorically speaking, of course. Don't mention I said she had big feet," he adds quickly.

"Oh, Elliot, play nice." Clementine swats at his hand. "It's not the poor girl's fault she got caught in the Venus flytrap."

Christine isn't able to mask her confusion.

"We're talking about Gloria," Clementine says. "Do try and keep up, *Christine Russo*. You're in the belly of the beast now!" Elliot tops off Clementine's glass once more, trying to suppress his smile.

"What do you mean?" Christine starts to ask, but she's interrupted by the swing of the French doors at the far end of the room.

"Look at you, honey! A vision!" Gloria's son Trey whistles from across the room at his wife. For a moment—a fleeting one—Christine watches Clementine's smile curdle in distaste, but before Christine can fully process what she's seen, Clementine brightens and skips over to greet her husband.

The groom's parents share a chaste kiss, and Elliot hands Trey a glass of champagne. Gloria Beaufort's son was summed up recently in the *New York Post* as "a chip off the wrong block." Trey is a pinch-faced, puffier version of his father, with floppy hair that grayed early, leathery skin from a life of too much fun in the sun, and a half-crooked smile that women find "charming" (though the billions in the bank probably don't hurt either). Of all the Riptons, Trey is known for seeking the limelight, and his lavish lifestyle is consistent tabloid fodder.

Christine lets some champagne fizzle in her mouth as Clementine and Trey engage in a hushed conversation by the doorway and Elliot zigzags across the room filling up champagne glasses and fluffing flower arrangements. The candlelit room feels tranquil thanks to the delicate music being played by a world-class pianist situated just outside the drawing room . . . that is, until the record-scratching scream of a toddler erupts the Zen. Little Miles Ripton runs into the room, his chubby paws filled with crushed Cheerios that leave a trail of crumbs on the already-stained rug. His parents, Carlyle "Lyle" Ripton and her husband, John Benjamin Beaufort Ripton IV, who Christine will now internally call "Bloody Ben," follow their son's crumbs into the party.

Lyle is one of those magnetic women whose presence turns heads. Gloria Beaufort's platinum blond, beauty queen granddaughter-in-law is publicly credited with revamping Glo to appeal to the next generation—and she seems to have done so effortlessly, with her cherubic son on one arm and a fun statement handbag slung over the other. She is the woman every *Bespoke* reader wants to be—beautiful, thin, rich, successful but not *too* successful (she's still a mom first!) . . . And the interesting thing is, nobody seems to hate her for it. As the room turns its attention toward the prominent, perfect-looking couple, Christine might as well be part of the castle tapestries. She pulls on her dress, which feels frumpy all of a sudden.

Ben hands Lyle a martini, which she accepts with a quick thank-you before turning her attention back to her son, who has wrapped himself up in the very expensive-looking velvet curtains.

"Hello, honey, did you have a lovely afternoon killing harmless, beautiful creatures?" Clementine says, and fills up a flute for Ben, who downs it in a single gulp. Lyle glares at her husband.

"Hi, Mom." Ben gives his mother a kiss on the cheek, ignoring the barb about their hunting expedition. "You look, uh, interesting." Clementine does a little spin and then leans in toward her son and daughter-in-law. Aware of the family babble bubble forming without her, Christine cautiously makes her way over to take note of their conversation. They carry on as if she's not there.

"I think we should have left him with the nanny." Lyle bends down and wipes some melted chocolate (Christine hopes it's chocolate) off Miles's cheek. She stares at the young mom—immediately recognizing Lyle's taffeta fit-and-flare purple floral minidress from the saves on her Pinterest board. Lyle has paired it with a black micro cashmere flung over her shoulders and strappy black heels—probably from the Row. Christine makes mental notes on how she could possibly re-create the look on her sale-rack budget. The sample closet at *Bespoke* HQ would never offer anything good enough to grace the body of Lyle Ripton.

"Don't be ridiculous. He's fine." Ben takes another glass of champagne from a nearby tray. The rest of the group orbits around them. "Father." Ben lifts his glass in a mock salute. "Where's Raquel?" Ben asks, and his father grunts in response.

Christine notices Trey stand up a little straighter in Ben's presence, which does nothing to distract from the fact that he is a good five inches shorter than his son. Ben and Graham definitely take after their mother in the looks department. And Clementine, despite her eccentric fashion, has perfect bone structure and strong Scandinavian genetics. Ben downs his second drink before grabbing a third from a passing server. The air around the father and son swirls with unsaid words.

"It's family only tonight," Clementine growls, "so she *certainly* wouldn't be included."

"She is a bridesmaid, though," Ben retorts. "Isn't she?"

Christine watches as Trey and Clementine's son expertly pushes their buttons. It's clear everyone is on edge about Raquel. Christine assumes they're talking about Raquel Williams, "it girl," Hollywood actress, the new face of Glo, and apparently, one of Jane's bridesmaids. It's a bit odd, given that the two women must hardly know each other, but rumor has it that Trey insisted she be included.

"She's not flying in until tomorrow, anyway," the groom's father says before reaching for a passing tray of caviar deviled eggs.

"And just how would you know that?" Clementine scoffs in a way that insinuates she knows *exactly* how Trey would know that.

But instead of addressing his wife, Trey turns to Christine. "Can we help you?" He says it with a smile, but Christine immediately panics.

"Sorry to butt in," she says, then makes an awkward throat-clearing noise. "I just wanted to make sure I had the opportunity to introduce myself to everyone before we sit down to dinner. I'm Christine Russo, here on behalf of *Bespoke Weddings* to cover this weekend." The family is silent for a moment—shocked by the sound of Christine's voice, as if one of the candelabras on the table has started talking.

"I thought it was *just family tonight*." Ben sneers in Christine's direction and takes another gulp of his drink. His eyes are already taking on a glassy quality. Christine is unsure how to respond.

"I used to work for *Bespoke*," Lyle says, giving her a cautious smile. "But, Lordy, that just feels like ages ago. You were probably still in college when I was there." She tucks a piece of blond hair behind her ear. Christine does not correct her and say that, in fact, they started at the same time (Christine as an unpaid intern, Lyle straight up the ranks to senior editor of Beauty) and that Lyle is actually only two years older than her.

Instead, she blurts out, "I was at your wedding. I was Sandra's assistant at the time. It was the first *Bespoke* wedding I attended." The crowd goes silent again.

"Oh," Lyle offers finally. "Sorry, I didn't recognize you. I was a bit distracted that weekend." The family chuckles, letting some much-needed air into the room.

Christine blushes. "It was beautiful. Your dress was stunning. Huckleberry Farm is to die for. I'm just itching to get back there." She knows she's word-vomiting now, but she can't stop. She needs the painful awkwardness to end. "That's where I met Miss Beaufort, actually, so I guess it's how I ended up getting invited by her here." Christine stops to catch her breath. It's not necessarily a *lie*. She did technically *see* Gloria Beaufort for the first time at Lyle's wedding . . . "meet" might be a stretch.

Lyle stares at her, mouth slightly twitching. "Is it? Well, aren't you a lucky one." A crack of lightning flashes outside the floor-to-ceiling windows, further illuminating Lyle's blue eyes.

"Ha!" Clementine laughs shrilly. "Anyway, yes, Christine is Gran's guest."

Lyle makes a beeline for her son, who is now trying to find a way into the fireplace.

"Leave it to Gran to invite a reporter to a family dinner to put us all on edge." Ben glowers at her. And now Christine would like to throw herself into the flames as well, but she *has* to soldier through this evening. She turns her attention to Gloria's only child, Trey.

"Mr. Ripton, it's a pleasure to meet you." Christine extends a hand. "I'm thrilled to be covering your son's wedding this weekend."

"Well, that makes one of us." He lets her hand hang in midair and pushes back his unnaturally full head of hair. Christine's mortification must be written all over her face because he quickly adds, "I'm kidding, kidding, sweetie. I'm a big fan of *Bespoke*—and its gorgeous reporters." He winks at her. *Oh my God, is he hitting on me?*

As Christine's cheeks redden, a tiny woman in a modest turquoise shift dress appears. "Christine, I'm Maggie, Jane's mom! Thrilled to meet ya." The woman grabs both of her hands with clownish force. She's dressed like one of Christine's aunts about to attend a local Easter service in Cleveland. Her loud voice cuts through the chatter of raspy rich people with an easy snip. Christine watches Clementine's face contort in annoyance: not only is her son marrying a lowly, trust-fund-less schoolteacher, but to make matters worse, her mother's loud and gauche.

"Hi, Maggie." Christine smiles at the bride's mother. "So nice to finally meet you in person." Her body melts with relief. Finally, someone who actually wants to talk to her.

"Jane is really *such* a big fan of *Bespoke Weddings*! She devours your features!" Maggie enthuses. "I mean, wow, talk about a dream come true. And don't worry at all about being a rookie. We just love a bootstrapper in this family."

Christine beams at Maggie's loud compliment, praying it carries some weight with the rest of the born-on-third-base circle. But nobody seconds the remark. Instead, the rain outside starts to pound with even greater force.

"Oh, I love this stormy weather," Maggie says. "The rain makes everything feel fresh." Still, no one from the family chimes in to follow the mother of the bride's musings. They just stare blankly at her as if they still can't believe she's allowed in the same room as them, let alone the same family. But Maggie doesn't seem to notice, and Christine likes her immediately for it.

"Yes, there's just something so magical about a thunderstorm," Maggie continues, filling the silence as the torrential storm whirls around outside. The mother of the bride's face is kind and inviting. She's got big round eyes and plump pinkish lips and is definitely wearing a bit too much makeup—the creases where she applied her blush are painfully visible—but it somehow works for her. She's charming and at ease, despite the fact that clearly nobody in this room wants her to feel that way.

"I agree. The weather is so cozy this time of year. I love that Jane decided to go with a fall wedding date," Christine says, then swipes an hors d'oeuvre of brown bread and smoked salmon off a silver tray to occupy her mouth while she thinks of something—anything—to say that isn't about the weather.

"I can't even begin to think how much this whole weekend is going to cost," Ben says out of nowhere, and adjusts his perfectly tailored, if not slightly rumpled, suit jacket. Maggie's cheery facade falters slightly.

As if on cue, Elliot makes his way over to the small group.

"All right, people!" He pushes his dark-rimmed Oliver Peoples glasses into place on his nose. "Our couple is en route! Is everyone here?" Father Kenneth, the Riptons' longtime priest, glides into the room during Elliot's announcement.

"So sorry I'm late," he says in a lazy southern drawl. Even though the priest is well into his seventies, he looks vibrant—tall, fit, with chiseled cheekbones and a nice tan. He could be a *Golden Bachelor* contestant, Christine thinks, if he wasn't a priest.

"Hello, Father, thank you for joining us," Elliot says quickly before scanning the room again, looking for anything out of place. His assortment of gold bracelets jingles on his wrist with every turn.

"Not sure where her royal highness is," Lyle sneers. To her right, Christine feels Trey's body tense up at the implied insult toward his mother. Another rumble of thunder vibrates throughout the drawing room.

"I believe Graham is walking Gloria down. She's moving a bit slowly after the long flight," Father Kenneth says with a smile.

"Right. And lovely to see you, Father. It means the world to the family that you made the trip—truly." Trey pats the priest on the back.

"It's a pleasure to be here. I'm sure the good Lord will provide us with a wonderful weekend for the happy couple," he proclaims as another blaze of lightning cracks outside the window. Miles starts to cry and tug on his mother's dress.

"Why don't you let Daddy hold you?" Ben slurs, reaching for his son, but Lyle scoops up the toddler and glares at her husband.

"You can hold him after you mix in a few waters," she hisses. Christine feels her buzzy excitement and anticipation of the weekend start to thicken into something closer to dread.

"It's supposed to be beautiful tomorrow," Maggie cuts in brightly. "I've been obsessively checking my weather app. Not that we mind a little rain—I was just saying how charming it is. It's Ireland after all, right, Father?" Father Kenneth nods and does the sign of the cross, which gets a chuckle from the group.

"Don't worry, we'll be prepared for everything," says Elliot. "And rain on your wedding day is good luck, but more important, it makes for better pictures." Elliot gives the mother of the bride an encouraging look before turning back to his clipboard.

"Okay, back to business. When Jane, Graham—and Gloria—walk

in, we'll start by doing some formal pictures with the family. Everyone please be sure to compliment the bride on how beautiful she looks and express your delight about the weekend ahead. A cheer when they enter wouldn't hurt. I find it's important for the excitement to be palpable." Elliot looks around at the group for some sort of verbal confirmation, but all he gets is a cough from Trey, which Christine doesn't really think counts as "palpable excitement."

"What? Are we going to throw rose petals too? They're not even married yet." Lyle bounces Miles on her hip, an unmistakably sharp edge in her buttery Southern belle voice.

"Rose petals are for Saturday," Elliot answers flatly. "I know everyone is tired from the long flight, but let's remember why we're here, okay?" His smile is thin. Christine has seen firsthand Elliot's ability to navigate delicate situations with difficult personalities, but the Riptons seem like they will prove to be worthy opponents if they're already fighting him on welcoming the couple to their *literal welcome dinner*. The wind screeches outside, and the castle moans.

"Feels like we're in the eye of a hurricane," Christine whispers to Maggie, glancing toward the windowed wall.

"In more ways than one," she whispers back.

"Here they come!" Elliot trills, and two tuxedo-clad butlers throw open the French doors a final time, revealing the dashing Graham Ripton and his flawless fiancée, Jane Murphy. Two camera-strapped photographers follow them into the room, lenses flashing as they contort themselves into crazy crouches to get all the angles.

While Jane has been christened by the internet as Plain Jane, Christine doesn't agree. Really, she is bewitching, with dark brown eyes and long, shiny black hair that could give Cher a run for her money. Her pale skin glows, and though "plain" is not the right word for it, she certainly has embraced a natural, unmanicured beauty. Her face is pretty but not perfect—which somehow makes her even chicer and more alluring. Jane has clearly not fallen victim to a medical spa or the black hole of YouTube makeup tutorials.

A feeble clap trickles through the room. It's the strangest, most unenthusiastic response to the kickoff of a wedding weekend that Christine has ever experienced. Only to be topped by the disastrous wedding welcome dinner she attended this spring in Telluride when a rogue skier plowed into the bride and groom as they entered their après-ski tent.

Eventually, Maggie runs up to embrace her daughter and future son-in-law.

"Wow, Elliot. Everything looks better than I could have dreamed of," Jane says, her voice as light and sweet as the first bite of a macaron. The bride-to-be tiptoes around the room as if she's window shopping at a designer boutique she can't quite afford.

"There he is." Graham gently unclasps himself from his fiancée to pat his father on the back. Trey smiles, and Clementine buries her son in a bear hug. Dr. Graham Ripton, dapper as usual, is dressed casually in green tailored trousers and a crisp white shirt that is just slightly unbuttoned.

"Hello, Grahamsome. You look like Prince Charming." Clementine plants a fat kiss on her son's cheek. Graham's sunny presence already seems to be smoothing things out with the family.

"I don't believe we've met." The groom grins and extends his hand toward Christine, who's momentarily caught off guard at being openly included in a conversation. She's amazed by this lot's ability to cast her out and then pull her back in; it's like experiencing social whiplash.

"Christine Russo. I'm here with Bespoke Weddings," she says. "Thank you so much for having me along for your very special weekend."

"That's right, that's right. Christine! The bride is very excited you're here," he says with a wink. She smiles, letting the hot stares of the rest of the family singe her.

Graham Ripton is one of those people who's even better-looking in person—he's taller than Christine expected, with a warm, inviting face and a blond-haired, blue-eyed look that complements Jane's darker features perfectly. *He bears a striking resemblance to a human Golden Retriever*, Christine thinks. He and his older brother, Ben, look very much alike too—but Ben's hair is a little darker, more of a dishwater blond, and while Graham's blue eyes are bright and cheery, Ben's are pure ice.

After some photos, Elliot urges everyone to sit down for dinner, and as the party shuffles into their assigned seats, it dawns on Christine that Gloria Beaufort didn't make an entrance with her grandson and future granddaughter as promised. The seat on her right remains empty, and the seat to her left hosts Miles Ripton, who is currently slurping applesauce from a silver spoon. Disappointment creeps up inside her as the waiters fill up her wineglass with a vintage Pinot Noir. A night next to two-year-old Miles Ripton is a far cry from sitting next to the iconic G.B. But at least there's wine.

"Well, I guess we'll have to start without her," Clementine huffs, glaring at Gloria's empty seat. With no objections to Clementine's wishes, Elliot claps his hands and a slew of servers appear, each holding glistening silver domes containing their first course. Despite her disappointment, Christine feels her stomach grumble.

The meal is delicious: a caviar tasting that probably costs a thousand dollars a head is followed by seared Irish salmon, potatoes gratin, and family-style fresh greens from the organic garden located just off the property. For dessert, a decadent buttery apple crisp that almost makes up for Gloria's absence. Oddly, nobody at the table brings up the family matriarch. The dinner is eaten around polite conversation, and Clementine loudly gives her compliments to the chef for her "perfect shallot jus." Christine smiles to herself—her father famously never lets anyone in their family buy shallots, claiming they're just "overpriced onions."

Once dessert is almost finished, Christine hears a glass clink from the other end of the table. She turns her head to see the mother of the groom has raised herself to give a toast. Clementine stumbles slightly, hinting that she may have gone a bit overboard on the wine. Christine can't blame her. They're quick with a pour over here in Ireland.

"I just wanted to say—well—life has been a bit stressful lately with finding the new face of Glo. And, God, the Aspen renovation has been taking ages, hasn't it? I know we all crave our mountain refuge. But we're taking a break from all that to celebrate our Graham, who has been a light through it all. So, to properly honor him, and of course the happy couple, I decided to write a poem." Clementine gestures vaguely to Graham and Jane as she pulls out a piece of loose-leaf paper.

"Oh Jesus," Ben groans across the table from Christine. Lyle smacks his leg.

Clementine begins: "A mother's love is all consuming, even if life takes their kids away cruising; far from the nest, on their own quest, and one fateful day they will find their princess, and you'll be left at home bruising." Clementine pouts and laughs sharply, but the line doesn't really land. Christine's eyes dart around the table, her skin crawling from the awkwardness. Jane's face flames as she stares at her half-eaten dessert, not meeting her future mother-in-law's eyes. Graham's smile flickers like a faulty light.

"But the sun, your son, comes from the stars; he will never stray far, even when he finds his new moon. Together they stand, shining on the land, a pair that is sweet, if a little confusing." Clementine continues, flailing her arms for dramatic effect. Ben groans again and grabs the bridge of his nose, as if the poem is putting him in physical pain, but before Clementine can continue, a woman's voice booms through the dining room, loud enough to be coming from a surround-sound speaker system. All heads turn to the back of the room.

"So sorry, am I interrupting?"

There she is: Gloria Beaufort, dripping in diamonds and dressed in a floor-length white silk caftan. That's right: *white*.

"Am I frightfully late?" Gloria makes her way across the room, her elegant caftan swaying with every step. She moves slowly, with the help of a bejeweled cane. Nobody from the table moves to greet her, except the groom, who shouts, "Gran! So glad you're feeling up to joining us tonight." He quickly rises to help his elderly grandmother into her seat.

"Thank you, darling." Gloria pats the groom on the cheek. Her gaze sweeps around the table before landing on Christine. "Hello, *Christine*

*Russo*. Lovely to see you." The founder of Glo grins, shooing away Elliot, who is tripping over himself to help her. Gloria meets Christine's gaze, and Christine feels like she's just jumped into a cold plunge—and not in a refreshing way, more like an "I can't breathe or feel my toes" kind of way. *I see who Ben gets his eyes from*, she thinks. The entire table is silent. Christine is afraid to return the greeting. Clementine crinkles her poem up into a ball and pulls out her chair so loudly that the whole table rattles. Trey whispers something in her ear, but she bats him away, her face puckered like she is sucking on a lemon. So much for "good energy."

"May I have a glass of champagne?" Gloria says to nobody in particular, and a flute appears instantly. She takes a sip. "Ah. That's better. Please, please, continue."

Clementine stares at her with a stormy gaze that mirrors the weather outside. Christine watches the flames of the candles sway, seemingly synchronized with the howl of the wind, wishing she could melt into the earth instead of being the awkward outsider caught in the middle of a family fight.

"It's fine. Forget it," the mother of the groom mumbles, and cuts into the remnants of her dessert with much more force than is necessary.

"You know I hate to miss one of your poetry readings," Gloria says, then laughs.

"I don't appreciate your sarcastic tone, *Gran*." Clementine grips her knife tightly. Elliot motions for the music to be played louder and pounces on Gloria.

"Dinner has already been served, Miss Beaufort, but can we get you something from the kitchen?" His tight leather pants squeak as he takes a knee next to her seat.

"A liquid dinner is perfectly fine for me tonight. Just make sure my glass remains full." She pats him on the hand and turns to Christine.

"Thank you for making the trip," Gloria says.

"I'm so excited to be here," she blurts. "It's an honor to be seated next to you, Miss Beaufort. It's an honor to be here at all. Thank you for trusting me to cover this weekend," Christine gushes, wishing she could exude more of the aloof confidence possessed by this group.

"Call me Gloria." She smiles. And with those words, Christine dies and her spirit enters the pearly (probably Chanel) gates of *Bespoke* Heaven.

"Okay, Gloria!" She beams. Across the table, Lyle stares at them. Maybe she's jealous that the random *Bespoke Weddings* reporter has gotten Gloria's attention.

"I'm so glad you're here. You're the perfect person to cover this weekend. It's going to be . . . quite a spectacle. Quite a story indeed." Gloria guzzles an entire glass of bubbly.

"I'll take another!" she calls, and a waiter instantly refills her glass.

"Anyway, this weather," Gloria continues, "it's just perfect, isn't it?" Her eyes glisten, and she stares at Christine expectantly.

A bit confused, she nods and says, "Elliot was just saying the gloomy gray makes for great pictures." Gloria tuts and shakes her head. Christine's heart sinks—she's somehow said the wrong thing.

"Granny, it's a long weekend. You better pace yourself," Graham says. He laughs just as a tree branch slams into a window. The storm raging outside is getting harder to ignore, but Gloria doesn't flinch, just raises the glass of champagne to her thin lips.

"I'd like to propose a toast." She rises. "To my beautiful grandson and his lovely bride. May you both live many happy and healthy years together. I don't believe in marriage, as you all know, but I do believe in parties. So, let's have a grand one." She attempts an Irish accent, and a few chuckles flutter through the room.

"Here, here!" Trey raises a glass. Clementine's champagne flute sits untouched in front of her, as do Lyle's and Ben's.

"It's a bit inappropriate to say you don't believe in marriage at a wedding, Gloria. Not everyone shares your opinion on the subject." Ben scowls at his grandmother.

"Oh, it's Gloria now? What happened to Gran?" She laughs between sips of bubbly. Christine notices her hand shaking slightly as she holds the glass. But whose hand wouldn't shake under that stack of diamond tennis bracelets, gold cuffs, and a giant sapphire cocktail ring?

"It's all right, we understand the sentiment," Jane says, her voice quivering, and throws a meek smile in Ben's direction. The girl looks like she'd rather have her eyelashes plucked out one by one than remain at this dinner table for a moment longer, and Christine can't blame her. Maggie takes her daughter's hand and squeezes it. Jane squeezes back.

"It's not all right—it's insulting. She can't just—" Lyle says, but she's cut off by a loud crack as a rock smashes through the main drawing room window, crashing onto the candle-laden table, which is immediately engulfed in flames. Everyone screams and scrambles away from the tablescape-turned-hellscape.

But Christine can hardly move. She's transfixed, staring at Gloria Beaufort, who also remains seated, laughing as the dinner goes up in flames. She claps her hands and exclaims, "Wow! Now it's a party!" A shock of cold air rushes through Christine amid the fire and smoke.

THREE

# GLORIA

One Year Earlier
Charleston, South Carolina

"SHE'LL NEVER LAST." LYLE PLUCKS an olive off the toothpick in her martini, balancing it in between her teeth before clamping down on it with a hard bite.

"What makes you say that?" Gloria puckers her thin lips in amusement at her granddaughter-in-law. The family is enjoying predinner drinks in the study, as Gloria calls it, before meeting Graham's new girlfriend, Jane, for the first time. The study is Gloria's favorite place in the house. The bright coral walls and raffia carpet provide a modern and feminine take on the classic old-world man's study that used to occupy her mansion on Charleston's South of Broad. It was the first room she redesigned when she bought the stately home over fifty years ago, and she likes to give it a refresh every few years to help her stay young. Most recently she's added a pair of vintage leopard-print wing chairs. She jokingly says that her constant interior design changes are her version of a facelift.

"Jane is just"—Lyle chooses her words carefully—"not Graham's perfect match."

"I have to agree," Clementine chimes in. "Her energy's just all over the place. And she's an Aries... Not good." She fidgets uncomfortably in the leopard-print chair in between Gloria and Lyle, which is a little small for her larger frame. Gloria rolls her eyes. She feels a cough coming on and grabs a handkerchief off her end table. Her family looks on as she wheezes as if they've never seen someone with a cold before.

"Do you need a glass of water?" Clementine offers.

"I'm fine," Gloria says crisply, and takes a swig of her martini. "That astrology stuff is nonsense. Just another way for people to explain away their unattractive qualities." Gloria tuts.

"Spoken like a true Taurus," Clementine mumbles under her breath as she picks and prods at the elaborate cheese board in front of them. The piles of Brie, Gruyère, and truffle goat cheese are enough to make anyone who's lactose intolerant pass out on the spot.

"Are you going to eat any of that?" Gloria asks. "Or just make it inedible for everyone else?" The older she gets, the more unbearable she finds her daughter-in-law's eccentricities.

"It's a new diet," she says, and sighs. "I'm just sniffing it and letting my senses decide if it's worth the calories or not." She closes her eyes and breathes in deeply, her nostrils flaring over the fifty-dollar French Gruyère, her unkempt beige locks falling in her face—and more unfortunate, on the charcuterie. Gloria feels her blood pressure rise.

"Graham has historically dated career women. You know, ambitious, outgoing girls with big ideas," Lyle continues, unfazed by Clementine's antics. "Families who *get it*. Our situation is unique. She's pretty as a peach, but I'm not sure sweet little Jane is *the one*. Not just anybody can dive into all this and come out unscathed." Lyle nods her head subtly toward Clementine during this proclamation. Clementine doesn't notice, still contemplating the cheese—but Gloria gets the point: *Graham's girlfriend does not come from our world—and look what happens to that sort in our family. We don't need another cheese-sniffer.*

"What does Jane do?" Gloria asks, before finally swatting Clementine away from the cheese board and cutting herself a hunk of gooey Brie.

Lyle sips her martini. "I think she runs a charity daycare or something."

"She's an elementary school teacher," Clementine corrects her, "molding the minds of America's youth."

"Well, that's noble, if not a bit fiscally irresponsible," Gloria muses. "I say let's give her a chance."

Lyle is unwilling to let this go. She leans in closer. "She's sketchy, Gloria. There's like . . . a heaviness to her, a darkness even." Gloria squints at Lyle. She can't tell if the girl has had yet another round of Botox or if her vision is just blurry from too many martinis. Either way, Lyle's face is expressionless as she voices her concern—as smooth and spotless as Gloria's Mercedes.

"She's a brunette," Clementine whispers, as if she's translating what Lyle is trying to say. Clementine sits back and readjusts her turquoise-and-yellow headband that matches the Emilio Pucci muumuu that billows around her. Gloria doesn't understand why her son's wife always feels the need to dress like a county fair tarot card reader.

"That's not what I mean," Lyle snaps. "This has nothing to do with her appalling lack of warm highlights—which, believe me, she needs. I just worry that she might be taking advantage of Graham." Lyle flails her arms in the air to express the discontent her face cannot, knocking her cherry red Hermès Kelly bag onto the floor in the process. She scrambles to pick it up.

Gloria laughs. "Graham is not an idiot. Frankly, he's smarter than you." Lyle looks momentarily jarred by this, sitting up a little straighter, like she just stepped on a thumbtack, but ultimately she doesn't say anything. Nobody says anything to Gloria. It's not worth the headache; she's always right. Or in other words: she never apologizes.

Ursula, Gloria's house manager, as the family calls her, comes into the room smiling. "Trey and Ben are in from New York and just unpacking. So as long as the new couple is still on track to arrive at seven, dinner will be served shortly." She wipes her hands on the dish towel hanging off the belt loop of her khakis. Ursula is pushing seventy now, but Gloria has no plans to encourage her retirement. Plus, Ursula *likes* working for Gloria. Or at least she's professed it enough times when Gloria has had one too many tumblers of Macallan Eighteen and started demanding Ursula tell her how she really feels about working for her.

"Thank you, Ursula." Gloria nods in her direction. "Could you bring us all another round of drinks, please?" Lyle and Clementine ready themselves to protest, but Gloria knows that they can never stand the sight of their near-empty glasses. Clementine shouldn't be drinking at all on her medication, but Gloria suspects she's stopped taking it again. She sighs. *A battle for another day.* Ursula turns to fulfill the request and runs right into Graham.

"Surprise! We're early!" Graham envelops Ursula in a hug, and she laughs, thrilled to be reunited with "mi favorito" as she calls him. Behind her grandson, Gloria sees the shadow of a slender and elegant brunette with haunting eyes and a giant but tasteful arrangement of Gloria's favorite flowers: pink peonies. Of course Lyle was being bitchy—she's threatened.

"Hi, Gran." Graham leans down to kiss his grandmother. "This is the famous Jane. I've been dying for you two to meet." Gloria stands up with the help of her cane to survey the girl.

"Thank you for having me tonight, Ms. Beaufort. It's a pleasure to meet you," Jane says with a smile, and holds out the flowers. She doesn't rush to fill the silence that follows. Gloria appreciates this.

"These are just lovely, thank you," Gloria says finally, but she makes no effort to take the bouquet, merely nods her head toward the glistening coffee table expertly arranged with two-hundred-dollar coffee table books not meant for reading. Jane tries to place the slightly damp bouquet of bright pink flowers somewhere on the table where they will inflict the least amount of harm. Her presence has sucked the air out of the room as everyone waits for Gloria's assessment. She can feel her family's eyes on her, reading into every move she makes, every word she says. It's a waste of their time, though, as she hasn't decided anything about Jane—and when she decides—when Jane does the small, almost unnoticeable thing that will cement Gloria's opinion of her forever—none of them will be paying attention. They'll be three martinis deep, fighting with one another or loathing themselves. All she knows at this point is the obvious: Jane is charming, Graham is smitten, and they're both incredibly nervous and desperate for her approval.

"Well, we're all here. Let's eat." Gloria picks up her cane and leads the charge into the dining room.

DINNER IS AN ASSORTMENT of clanking cutlery and giving compliments to Ursula for the delicious steak and comparing calendars about who will be in Southampton for the Fourth of July and who will be using the Aspen house Christmas week. Collectively, Gloria's family attempts to drown out Jane's presence. But Graham is hell-bent on inserting her into the family dynamic.

"Jane, you'll love Southampton. Gran's property is teeming with natural beauty, just like you," he faux swoons, and winks at her. Jane blushes.

"God, you're so cheesy," she says, and laughs. "But I'm sure it's gorgeous."

"I'd imagine you'll spend a lot of time there this summer," Lyle quips. "Don't teachers have the summers off? Must be nice."

Gloria takes a large gulp of the Argentinian wine that Trey has had shipped back from his latest trip to Mendoza. It's not very good—the shipping cost was more than the wine itself—but her son has never been good at discerning value. He's much better at lighting money on fire.

"I usually waitress in the summer to make extra money," Jane offers. "The tips are great."

"I used to do that," Clementine says, perking up. "That's how we met." She gently touches her husband's hand. "I was saving up money to move to New York to become an actress." Jane's face breaks into a relieved smile.

"How cool. I could never act. I get terrible stage fright. Did you ever get any fun parts?" Jane takes a small bite of her steak, clearly eager to turn the spotlight on someone else.

"No." Clementine looks wistful. "In the end, I felt more called to poetry." Ben stifles a laugh that he tries to pass off as a cough, and his father glares at him.

"Jane is a fantastic teacher—and a real renaissance woman herself, Mom. You've not lived until you've walked through the Met with her. She knows everything there is to know about art."

"I didn't realize you were so into art, Graham," Ben says loudly, bits of wedge salad flying out of his mouth as he speaks.

"I wasn't until Jane opened my eyes to it," Graham shoots back at his brother before cutting into his steak.

"I'm sure that's not all she's opened your eyes to," Ben sneers. Graham puts down his steak knife in a way that symbolizes the beginning of a war, but Jane cuts in before he can respond.

"I don't really know that much," she says quickly. "I just grew up going to a lot of museums with my mom. I'm an elementary school art teacher, so hardly the next top Picasso scholar." She laughs nervously. Graham seems even more hell-bent on gaining everyone's approval now. Gloria notices a ferociousness in him that she's never seen before. He *loves* this girl.

"Jane's also very good at chess, Gran. She beats me literally every time." He takes a swig of his wine. Gloria puts down her fork—this gets her attention.

"Really?" She raises an eyebrow. "Who taught you?" Gloria leans back in her chair, daring someone to comment on how little of her dinner she's finished, but nobody says anything.

"My mom works as a nurse at a retirement community. Oak Bluffs near Folly Beach?" Jane blushes immediately, realizing that, of course, none of them know it. "Anyway, I would go with her—and chess is quite popular with a lot of the residents there. So they kind of collectively taught me." Gloria is delighted by this development.

She pushes out her chair with force. "Well, then, I believe it's time for a match." The rest of the group dutifully follows Gloria back into the study (after they all refill their wineglasses to the absolute brim), where she takes out her prized possession—her bright orange Hermès chessboard. Graham watches the game intently, Ben with muted interest, looking up every few minutes from scrolling on his phone, and Lyle with pursed lips. Clementine and Trey don't even feign interest. Instead, they retreat onto the balcony to have a five-star fight about Trey extending his trip to Argentina and missing Clementine's fundraiser for her poetry scholarship at Williams College.

Jane's first move is good: the King's Pawn Opening. It allows her to either pursue aggressive or positional play. She's gauging Gloria's style, but Gloria is nothing if not highly aggressive. She makes her move.

"The Budapest Defense," Jane whispers. "Nice choice." The girl studies the board, cracking her knuckles.

Gloria cringes. "Don't do that." She *hates* when people crack their knuckles.

"Sorry," Jane says, blushing. "Bad habit." She moves another pawn.

Eventually, Gloria's family loses interest in the chess match. Lyle leaves when Miles's wails ring through on the baby monitor, and the boys turn to entertain themselves with whatever sports match is muted on the flat-screen. But for Gloria and Jane, the world blurs and there is nothing but the silent bloodbath happening on the chessboard.

It becomes clear that Jane is playing the long game, grabbing weak pawns and strategically placing her pieces in exposed squares. *It's a smart strategy, if a boring one,* Gloria observes. She watches her step, trying to resist her tendency toward splashy showmanship on the board. Her antique grandfather clock ticks loudly in the corner. It's the longest match Gloria's played in a while, and soon they each have just a few pieces left. Graham hovers over them to watch their final moves.

And then Gloria sees it. Jane can checkmate her. Her winning move, Gloria realizes, was advancing a pawn to promote it to a queen, trapping Gloria's king on the back line. She didn't think anything of it then—but now Gloria is unable to stop the pawn. Her heart rate picks up.

# A KILLER WEDDING   49

Jane cracks her knuckles again . . . but Gloria doesn't say anything this time. Is she going to lose this match? She never loses. But then Jane moves her queen. She had Gloria in checkmate . . . and she bungled it. Gloria looks up at Jane in shock—noting the focus in her eyes, the tenseness of her shoulders.

"You won," she says tightly as Gloria moves her own queen, putting Jane in checkmate. Gloria drums her ring-encrusted fingers together, grinning.

"You moved too quickly in the end," she muses. "You had me right there." Gloria demonstrates what Jane should have done on the board.

"How did I miss that?" Jane groans and runs her fingers through her hair.

Graham walks over grinning and kisses the top of her head. "Gran is a formidable opponent, but you put up a good fight." Jane beams at her fiancé, and Gloria studies them.

"Well, the good news is I still love you," he says tenderly as they stare into each other's eyes. Something feels off-kilter. Gloria won, but somehow it doesn't feel like a total victory. She can't marry the image of the shy schoolteacher at her dinner table with the prowess of the woman opposite her on the chessboard.

"I'm going to get a glass of water," Jane says hoarsely. "Great match." The two women shake hands. Gloria watches her leave the room. Once she disappears, Graham immediately turns to her and starts whispering frantically.

"Gran, while we have a minute alone, I want to tell you something." His eyes flit toward the doorway that Jane just walked out. Ben has followed her, presumably to check on Lyle and the baby. Gloria knows exactly where this is going.

"I know we've only been dating a few months, but as the saying goes, when you know, you know. And I *know*, you know?" he babbles nervously. When Gloria doesn't say anything, he pauses and takes a deep breath, before dropping his voice to a whisper. "What I'm trying to say is . . . I intend to ask Jane to marry me. If I have your permission, I'd like to gift her the emerald ring." Gloria smiles and nods absentmindedly at her grandson as the gravity of his decision sinks in. Her mind is still on the board . . . trying to make sense of it. The way the girl played, her carefully calculated moves, just to throw it all away with that stupid blunder in the end? It doesn't make sense. Then reality slaps her in the face. She gasps.

"Are you okay? Is everything all right?" Graham grabs her arm.

"Yes, of course—I'm just so happy for you," she says, trying to recover from her shock. "You can give her the emerald ring. You have my blessing." Her grandson's face breaks into that dopey grin she loves so much. Satisfied at having gotten her approval, and clearly worried Jane might walk in at any moment, Graham promptly changes the subject. As he drones on and on about some new initiative that he thinks would benefit her nonprofit, Grow 2 Glo, Gloria silently seethes.

The girl *let* her win. Jane knew she had her—a player who is skilled enough to checkmate with a pawn in the eleventh hour has remarkable foresight, an uncanny ability to see the board from a bird's-eye view, an extraordinary talent to discern her opponent's weaknesses. Gloria was playing checkers, while Jane was playing 3-D chess.

And really, it was Jane who captured the king at the end of their match. Gloria sees that now.

The king, of course, being Graham.

This girl is a master strategist on and off the board . . . and it's obvious that she's playing the long game. Gloria feels her body shake with the desire to *really* win now.

"Gran, are you okay?" Graham asks, taking one of her shaking hands.

"Yes, yes." Gloria bats him away. "I am just so excited for you, for all of us. Jane is really . . . something, isn't she?" She hesitates on the word "something," because what she really wants to say is "hiding something."

And Gloria intends to find out what it is.

FOUR

# CHRISTINE

Thursday, October 16, 2025
Welcome Dinner

"QUICK, SOMEONE, DO SOMETHING! WHY are y'all just standing around?" Lyle bolts toward the door with Miles clutched to her chest. The only person who heeds Lyle's request is one of the photographers, who decides to snap a photo of the flaming table.

"That's not what I meant!" Lyle shouts, as Neil, Elliot's impromtu assistant, stumbles into the room, a blur of red hair and uncoordinated limbs, and blasts a fire extinguisher at the table. The immediate danger is gone, but the aftermath is scarring. The table is covered in smashed glass, bloodied with red wine, and the (Christine is assuming priceless) antique oak dining table is charred to a crisp. The bride bursts into tears.

"What on earth was that?" Ben demands of Neil, who, upon closer glance, Christine surmises can't be more than sixteen.

"It—it must have been from the storm—it's quite nasty out there." He's clearly still in shock himself.

"The storm didn't *hurl a rock* through that window," the brother of the groom spits out.

"This is completely unacceptable," Elliot says, masterfully stepping between the two. He turns to Ben. "We'll get to the bottom of this, I assure you, but in the meantime, let's get everyone out of here. We'll have nightcaps sent to each room to help soothe the nerves."

Once in the calm of the lobby, the dinner guests murmur with discontent as a mass of Ballymoon and Elliot Adler staffers go in and out of the drawing room in a tizzy. Lyle hands her wailing son to a nanny who has suddenly materialized and helps her slurring husband steady himself.

"Why don't you go relax and spend some time in your suite? Honestly, just try to forget the whole thing," Elliot says, coaxing the bride and groom toward the staircase to their room.

He adds, "I'll send up enough champagne to drown yourself in." He laughs nervously. "Let's all get a good night's rest. Big day tomorrow! Most of the guests will be here by noon!" The wedding planner claps his hands, his face contorted into a forced smile. Christine watches a single bead of sweat drip down his waxy face. She is about to head for her room to try to process what she just witnessed when she sees Lyle grab Gloria's hand.

"Where is Sebi, Gloria?" Lyle whispers. "What did you do?"

"I don't know what you're talking about." The elderly woman rips her hand from Lyle's grasp.

"Fine, don't tell me. But just know, you don't control us anymore," Lyle whispers, her voice trembling. She holds Gloria's gaze, the two of them frozen in the doorway, the table smoking behind them. Christine takes a few steps back. If either woman notices her presence, they don't say anything.

"Whatever that was back there, I hope that's the end of it," Lyle finishes.

*Is she referring to the rock? Does Lyle think Gloria arranged the disaster herself? Who is Sebi?*

"Lyle, like I said, I don't know what you're talking about, but I can assure you I'm the least of your problems." The matriarch gives Lyle's swaying, hiccuping husband the side-eye before turning from Lyle with a thud of her bejeweled cane. Gloria doesn't seem at all rattled by Lyle's outburst, or by the fire they just all narrowly escaped; instead she calls to Jane, who, with Graham, has slowly made her way to the top of the staircase.

"Jane, please stop by my room early tomorrow morning. I know we'll both be up at the crack of dawn." She laughs sharply and waves her cane in the bride's direction. "I want to give you a little something before the wedding festivities kick into high gear."

"That's sweet of you, Gran," Graham says, kissing his bride tenderly on the top of her head. Jane nods, her face still ashen. A slow smile untwists on Gloria's face, drawing attention to her sallow cheeks and sagging skin. It's known in the industry that Gloria Beaufort chose the "aging gracefully" route, but she looks significantly worse than the last time Christine saw her, which was only a few weeks ago at the Bespoke Ball. Gloria disappears down the hall as the rest of the group scatters, leaving Lyle and Christine standing alone in the lobby.

"I could sure use a stiff drink. How about you?" Lyle turns to Christine, who looks over her shoulder to make sure some other family member hasn't just walked back in.

"Yes! I'd drink rubbing alcohol at this point. Anything to chill me out after *that*," Christine answers, before Lyle can change her mind.

Lyle snorts. "Great. Same. I'm a mess . . . as you can probably tell." Lyle shifts her blue gaze in a way that implies she knows what Christine's just overheard and then starts off down the hallway, presumably toward The Snug, and Christine follows.

She hadn't noticed from a distance, but under the unflattering overhead lighting in the hall, there is no mistaking that Lyle looks like the cheap knock-off version of her former self. The fashion world's golden girl's purple minidress looks a bit tight around the hips. Her blond hair is frayed at the ends and her eye makeup is smudged . . . not in a sexy way.

"Two Guinness please," Lyle orders from the bartender as they enter the castle pub. The Snug is the kind of place you'd find in the pages of an Agatha Christie novel. A fire burns in the hearth and a fluffy nest of green-red-and-gold tartan pillows lines a banquette beneath a beautiful large bay window that lets in wisps of moonlight. The storm outside seems to have subsided for the moment. Lyle sits down on one of the rich burgundy leather barstools, and Christine joins her.

"Here we are, ladies." The bartender sets down the drinks.

"Didn't peg you as a beer drinker," Christine says as Lyle lifts a pint of Guinness to her lips.

"Normally I don't allow myself the calories, but when in Rome, as they say." She smiles. "A Guinness in Ireland will be worth it. Plus, I think they have vitamins or something, right?" A slight lull in the conversation follows as they sip their drinks and assess the pub.

The antique shelving behind the bar is filled with porcelain dogs of all different breeds and sizes. Christine rushes to fill the wordless void yet again. "Is this bar dog-themed?" she asks the back of the bartender's head. He turns around and replies, "It's an old bar joke." The bartender's eyes crinkle; real-life Irish smiling eyes, in Ireland, nonetheless. *He's cute*, she thinks, smiling as she takes the first sip of her drink.

"What's the joke?" Lyle asks.

"If you're in here, you're probably in the doghouse," he says, and winks.

"Ha!" Lyle laughs and momentarily loses her footing on the barstool. Christine grabs her arm to help her avoid the fall, but she pulls herself away with a cool "I'm fine."

"If you ladies can tell me how many dogs there are in this room, you'll win a free drink." The bartender leans over the bar toward them, and Christine can see flecks of navy in his gray-blue eyes.

"I know for certain there's an old bitch upstairs—what does that get me?" Lyle asks. Christine blinks twice, stunned by her direct hit at Gloria, and the bartender expertly turns back to the glasses he was polishing, clearly not wanting to get involved.

"Sorry," Lyle says on an exhale, turning to Christine. "That must have sounded a bit harsh to you." She takes a large gulp of Guinness.

"Every family comes with its baggage," Christine says as she fiddles with her coaster. She thinks about her family's baggage (student loan debt, expensive health insurance, needing a new roof) and how different it is from what Lyle is dealing with. It feels weird even trying to relate to her.

Lyle takes another sip of her beer and lets out an exaggerated "Ahhh." "This is actually pretty good!" She takes another sip, her shoulders slumping with relaxation.

# A KILLER WEDDING   55

"It's a known fact that Guinness is better in Ireland," Christine says. The bartender carries a tray of drinks out of the pub. Once he's gone, Lyle swivels her barstool to face Christine.

"Listen, honey," she says in a low voice, "the reason I asked you to get drinks is because I want to warn you"—she takes another sip before continuing—"about Gloria." Christine's mind cuts to Gloria laughing at the flames at the welcome dinner.

"If she's being nice to you, or includes you in any way, just rest assured, she wants something from you. That woman's meaner than a wet panther. You being invited here this weekend means you are a pawn in her game. Trust me." Lyle is talking in such hushed tones, it's almost like she's afraid Gloria is in the room with them. Her eyes move around the bar as if she's an animal being hunted, which makes sense given her panther comparison.

"What do you mean?" Christine feels her heart beating in her chest. "Are you talking about the rock? You think she did that?"

"Gloria likes a visible show of force." Lyle sighs. "But I saw her talking to you in there, making you feel like you're *so* important and she is *so* impressed with you and your UGG boots, Starbucks-cup, earnest Midwestern energy. No offense," she offers lamely. But her words sting with the truth. How could Christine have believed, even for a minute, that Gloria Beaufort of all people was impressed by her trivial career at *Bespoke Weddings*? She still had so much to prove—it's why this weekend is so important, why she can't afford even one misstep. She also makes a note to throw out her UGGs immediately upon landing at JFK.

"Just . . . just don't trust her, okay?" Lyle pleads. The bartender breezes by them again with his tray of empty glasses.

"Could I have another, honey?" Lyle points to her already-empty pint glass. The bartender nods and starts to pour another drink.

"I'd assume mixing family and business has its issues. It must be complicated working in her shadow at Glo," Christine says. She knows enough to gather that Gloria Beaufort is a controversial player in the business world.

"Sure, you could say that," Lyle responds, snark dripping from her voice.

*What did Gloria do to this woman?* Christine thinks. *And what could I possibly offer Gloria Beaufort other than the splashy cover story in* Bespoke Weddings *that's already promised?*

"Lyle," a familiar deep voice rumbles from the doorway, "it's time for bed." The two women turn their heads to see Ben scowling by the pub's hostess stand. Christine looks away, not wanting to be intertwined in another family squabble, but she can feel Ben's gaze zero in on her, and it feels very different than the bartender's earlier gaze.

"Sorry, lost track of time." Lyle takes a last sip of her Guinness before sliding off her barstool. "Good night, Christine. Just—keep your wits about you, okay? You're not in Kansas anymore," Lyle calls back over her husband's shoulder.

Christine turns back to the bar, resisting the urge to put her head down on it and groan audibly.

"Rough start to the wedding weekend?" The bartender hands her another beer with a sheepish grin. It's just the two of them now. She knows that she needs to go to bed. That she should *not* intertwine herself with this cute and possibly interested castle employee—she needs to try to figure out *what the hell just happened with Lyle Beaufort*—yet her butt stays glued to her barstool against her better judgment.

"Just what I need, more alcohol," she says, and laughs.

"I'm Danny." He sticks out his hand. A few fine-line tattoos on his biceps stick out from under his black T-shirt. Christine clenches her stomach in an attempt to kill the butterflies. She's got work to do, and it doesn't involve *I'm Danny.*

But she shakes his hand and says, "Christine."

"Your friend seems upset." Danny raises an eyebrow. "It's not cold feet, is it?"

Christine laughs and takes a small sip of her drink.

"No, not the bride . . . just typical family drama," she offers. "Er, I guess not typical, though. Given the family." She's probably already said more than she should, but Danny barely acknowledges the comment.

"True," he says with a sly smile. "What I'd give for some of *her* family problems."

"Honestly, same." Christine smiles back. She can tell he's about to take the opening, about to invite her to linger a bit longer, engage in some harmless hotel bar flirting—but she can't. Not this weekend.

"Thanks for the drink, but I'm going to have to call it a night." She stumbles off her barstool. Her feet are killing her—the Christian Louboutin heels she snagged at a sample sale a few weeks ago are definitely a size too small, but for under a hundred bucks, she couldn't say no. Now she's wishing she had.

"Rain check," Danny calls as she exits the pub. She smiles to herself but doesn't reply. They both know the forecast shows nothing but rain this weekend anyway.

JET-LAGGED AND SLIGHTLY DRUNK, Christine slips off her heels for the walk back to her room. The castle is quiet except for the occasional crackling of a fireplace or creak of wood—until she gets to the guest wing. As she rounds the corner toward her room, she hears Elliot's unmistakable snarl. She pauses, not wanting to walk into yet another argument.

"This is the last straw. I'm done, do you hear me? Absolutely done. You've crossed the line." She peeks her head around the corner to see Elliot shouting outside the open door of a hotel room. "You can't treat people like this. It will come back around one day, trust me!"

He slams the door, and Christine continues her walk down the hall, pretending to answer a text on her phone in an attempt to avoid eye contact with the enraged planner, but Elliot hurtles past her without a second glance. Once he is down the hall and out of sight, Christine continues toward her room, and her eyes linger on the room that bore the brunt of Elliot's tantrum. She remembers the intricately carved wooden door from his tour earlier.

The Brian Boru Suite—Gloria's room.

# FIVE

## JANE

Friday, October 17, 2025
Morning of Rehearsal Dinner

DREAD SLOSHES AROUND IN JANE'S stomach as she winds down the creaky castle hallway . . . but on second thought, maybe it's the salmon from last night? Either way, she feels like garbage this morning. She wraps her oversize cashmere sweater around her. It was a gift from Lyle for her birthday this year, the first and only kindness extended toward her by her future sister-in-law.

It's early, just past 6 a.m., but Gloria told her to come by whenever she woke up, and she would have gone over to speak with her at 4 a.m. if she could have. Jane is ready to get this over with. The hallways are still hidden in shadows when a gust of wind blows open one of the castle windows, sending her heart into her throat. This place is supposed to feel elegant and regal, but honestly, it just feels haunted. The gothic atmosphere is impossible to ignore in spite of Elliot's best efforts to make everything festive.

She passes a slightly dusty portrait of a young Irish royal with untamed reddish-orange hair. There are homages to this particular woman all over the castle. Jane can't remember her name, something almost Greek-sounding. She had a hard time focusing during Elliot's opening tour, but the woman's glowing apple-green eyes are unforgettable. They'll be sealed in her memory forever. The picture light blinks overhead. Or maybe it didn't? Is her mind playing tricks on her again? It does that sometimes. She tries to take in the painting, to momentarily lose herself in the art.

The woman is trapped in a heavy velvet dress, complete with a suffocating collar. *A physical representation of the stifling patriarchy,* the art history student in her thinks. Then their eyes meet again, and Jane jumps back in shock. She can feel the woman in the painting practically begging her for help.

"Same, girl," she whispers under her breath. Oil paintings have always moved her. Jane used to make her mother spend hours at the Met every time they went to New York to visit her aunt Laura. She would study every brushstroke and listen to the audio guide about the artist over and over again. She's not exactly "living the dream," as an elementary school art teacher, but hey, that's what a delusional sense of artistic capability and no bank account will do to a girl.

Jane rubs her giant emerald engagement ring for good luck, which is ironic, because getting that ring (Gloria's, of course) marked the beginning of her really, really bad luck.

Even though it is undeniably stunning—a one-of-a-kind vintage ring featuring a cushion-cut emerald surrounded by a halo of flawless diamonds—she's never been comfortable wearing the piece; according to a quick Google, its worth is in the *seven* figures, the thought of which makes her nauseated again. Reaching into her pocket, Jane pulls out two white pills. Just a little something to ease the nerves. The floorboards moan under her green velvet flats, and she jumps a little with every step. She feels like one of her students on the way to the principal's office.

Gloria wants to see her under the pretense that she's going to give Jane her "something borrowed" for her wedding day, but Jane knows that is just a facade. She knows it in her bones, the way animals know a tsunami is coming hours before it actually strikes. Gloria looked right over the flames and into her soul at dinner last night, and Jane felt . . . well, honestly, she felt absolved. She can't live like this anymore. She'd rather be dead.

Her feet stop in front of Gloria's room: the Brian Boru Suite. The premiere room in the castle. She takes four cleansing breaths. Melody, her psychiatrist, told her to do this before entering a combative situation. If only she could have been honest with Melody about what she was really up against. Instead, she nodded solemnly at her advice, shed a tear or two about her mother not understanding her, and at the end of the hour collected her Xanax prescription. After one more breath, Jane gently raps on Gloria's door. No answer. Maybe she fell back asleep. She knocks again, this time with a bit more force. To her surprise, the door opens with a slow squeak.

"Gloria?" Jane calls out. She hears Kevin O'Leary's unmistakable voice on the television. *Shark Tank*, Gloria's favorite. Gloria was a guest judge once. Jane remembers watching that episode, before she even knew Graham existed, completely enamored by the woman. Gloria has always been confident, funny, and whip-smart. Everything Jane is not.

Jane teeters in the doorway, unsure what to do. Gloria's cream pashmina wrap is flung carelessly over a gold dressing room chair. On the carpeted floor lies a giant diamond stud earring next to her signature bejeweled cane. She'll never get used to how careless Graham's family is with their expensive things.

Her body refuses to move itself into the suite. Instead, she clutches the crystal doorknob for support and listens to *Shark Tank* blare on the television, unable to face the end of her life as she now knows it. But something else is stopping her from entering the room; something is off. A change in cabin pressure. Her heart rate quickens, her mouth dries up, and the false bravado of her internal pep talk fades to a whisper inside her pounding skull. She can still turn around, go get ready for brunch, see how long Gloria will let her get away with it. *You don't have to do this. You can just keep going*, her subconscious shouts. Jane is confused; she can't tell what part of her is urging her away. Is it the devil on her shoulder or the angel? Is there any *right* way to get out of her predicament?

But then she hears his laugh, echoing from somewhere deep within the castle, and she jumps, her whole body jerking itself forward, away from him at all costs, and into Gloria's orbit.

# SIX

## CHRISTINE

Friday, October 17, 2025
Morning of Rehearsal Dinner

THANKS TO JET LAG, CHRISTINE'S sleep cycle is off, and she is awake early. She sits up in her canopied four-poster bed, stretching out her legs in the buttery sheets, and immediately lets out a long groan. One of the most horrific parts of a hangover is when the night before comes rushing back in clear, jagged pieces like a shattered wineglass. She remembers Trey making a pass. She remembers Lyle's warning. She remembers texting Sandra a selfie of her and Miles Ripton at the welcome dinner. She covers her face with her pillow and groans even louder.

Finally, after a few minutes of self-loathing, she takes the silky pillow off her face and lets her eyes adjust to the morning light, properly surveying her suite for the first time since she arrived. Even in her slightly hungover state, she must admit staying at places like Ballymoon is the best *Bespoke Weddings* work perk. Her room is totally gorgeous, ornately decorated in shades of pale green and soft cream. Everything is delicate and detailed; she feels like she's nestled inside a porcelain teacup. The flower arrangement the slightly creepy woman at the front desk sent up to her room wafts the delicious scent of jasmine her way, and Christine regrets ever protesting her kind offer.

She stretches her arms above her head and grins. Despite the less-than-stellar first night of the weekend, Christine is determined that today will be a great day. The rehearsal dinner has evolved to be an event almost as important as the wedding itself, and she will be on her A game. She will write the most eloquent, observant, and flattering piece that *Bespoke Weddings* has ever published, and it will catapult her career to new heights.

Continuing her manifestation, she puts on a fluffy Ballymoon embroidered robe and pads over to the espresso machine that sits on the suite's cherrywood desk, fit for the Oval Office. Christine is thoroughly convinced that the best part of life is coffee, and she grins as the smell of the freshly brewing black nectar lifts her spirits even higher. Maybe after enjoying her morning beverage in bed, she'll drag herself to the gym.

Her work for today mercifully does not begin until later this morning, as everyone adjusts to the new time zone. Her first wedding-related event will be the bridal brunch at eleven, where she should get a little time to talk to Clementine about her involvement in the wedding-planning process. Then in the afternoon, she'll have her first "official" interview for *Bespoke Weddings* with the mother of the bride, who'll share the inspiration behind tonight's rehearsal dinner—and hopefully a few juicy details about the bride herself. And finally, Christine will have a short window to interview the wedding officiant, Father Kenneth, at the church, before returning to the castle for the rehearsal dinner itself. So, come to think of it, there might not be time for the gym.

Christine unplugs her phone and scrolls through her notifications as the coffee machine prattles on. She's relieved to see Sandra hearted the selfie from last night, which causes a pang of guilt. Her mind flashes back to the moment she met her now boss, how enamored she'd been of the woman she is now actively trying to replace. College Christine would be appalled by her disloyalty to Sandra. But then again, College Christine didn't really know what she was getting herself into. She was just a twenty-one-year-old with no forehead wrinkles and seventy-four dollars in her bank account who was quickly running out of student loan money. It turns out those one-dollar pizza slices added up quicker than she thought they would, and unlike her classmates from fancy towns like Greenwich and Larchmont, which sounded more like celebrity baby names than actual places, she knew she couldn't ask her parents for help. She needed a job.

Which is how, during her senior year at Columbia, Christine found herself working three mornings a week before class at Blue Bottle Coffee in midtown Manhattan—a coffee shop where she made lattes with foam hearts for fabulous people who could afford to spend eleven dollars on coffee every day. She absolutely loved it—the free artisanal coffee and the people watching. One day, the little bell above the coffee shop entrance tolled, in walked Sandra Yoon, and Christine's fate was sealed.

When she saw Sandra for the first time, her now boss was probably in her early sixties and not trying to hide it. Even her face itself was immediately interesting to College Christine. Her severe black bob and strong Roman nose were still striking. When Sandra came to the cash register and handed over her thick gold Amex credit card, Christine zeroed in on her loud red lipstick. It somehow looked both refined and bold, two qualities Christine hoped to hone in her post-graduation life. She'd later learn it was Chanel Rouge Allure in the shade Pirate. She'd actually brought a tube to wear during the Ripton wedding weekend.

Every day, Sandra would come in and smile, order her nonfat no-whip extra-hot latte, and bark away on her cell phone. She was never rude, but she was never polite either. She just seemed genuinely and glamorously busy. Sandra was always shouting tantalizing tidbits into her iPhone.

"Tell Georgia to ship the sample sizes from the latest Markarian collection straight to their Nantucket property. Overnight it or have her fly them there herself.

"I don't care how much it costs, we need every yellow tulip in Holland, do you hear me? I don't *care* that they're out of season. The entire runway must be lined with them. No, they need to be lemon yellow not golden yellow.

"I can't say for certain, but I think Leo will be there. Of course, *that one*. Are there any other Leos? God, no, don't seat him next to me."

Christine would hang on every word and memorize every outfit. Eventually, her intrigue got the better of her and she googled the name printed on the Gold Amex she swiped every day—Sandra Yoon. It turned out that the chic lady who frequented the coffee shop was *a big deal*. The editor in chief of *Bespoke*! A living fashion legend! Which explained her seemingly endless supply of amazing coats: long belted trenches, beat-up leather jackets, and, on occasion, a fur.

One day, Christine was busy heating up a breakfast sandwich for another customer when Sandra walked in. So her colleague manning the register, Deryl, got to take Sandra's order. Given that a Sandra sighting was usually the highlight of Christine's day, her heart dropped a little at missing out on their usual exchange. But then—

"I'd like her to make it," Sandra said, pulling out one of her earbuds and pointing at Christine. "She knows how to do it the right way." Deryl looked back at Christine, shrugged, and let her make Sandra's order.

Brimming with pride, Christine handed her the coffee. "Here you go."

Christine came to New York City determined to be a journalist, but after a few months at Blue Bottle Coffee, she just wanted to be Sandra Yoon.

Worlds collided when Christine went to a Columbia internship seminar and, lo and behold, Sandra was being interviewed in a three-part series about her tenure at *Bespoke*. Christine's whole body pulsed as she learned more and more about the publication considered the world's pinnacle of style, luxury, and sophistication. She knew about *Bespoke*, of course. Even in Cleveland, Ohio, women gobbled up each monthly issue. It just never occurred to Christine before that moment that she could possibly get a job there—that there were jobs to be had at the magazine besides being rich and gorgeous. On the last day of the seminar series, she took in a deep breath, mustered all the courage she could find, and marched up to her icon.

"Excuse me, Miss Yoon?" She smiled. "I'm Christine Russo. Do you have time for a coffee? Possibly a nonfat no-whip extra-hot latte?"

A KILLER WEDDING 65

Sandra grinned from gold hoop earring to gold hoop earring. Christine started her internship the following month.

The hotel room coffee machine starts screeching and blinking red. Christine shakes her head, dislodging the memory and grabbing a mug. The idealized version of Sandra from the coffee shop isn't the Sandra she's worked for these past four years. Certainly not the same woman who barked at her in her office only a few weeks ago.

"I don't know what you did, or *who* you did, but Gloria Beaufort wants *you* to cover her grandson's wedding," Sandra had yelled at her. "I practically choked on my endive salad at lunch." Sandra crossed her arms over her chest, the metallic Manhattan skyline gleaming behind her like the city itself was on her side. Christine quickly tried to force her face into an expression of utter bewilderment.

"Well? What did you do?" Sandra scowled, her carb-starved body vibrating with barely bridled rage.

"I'm sorry, I'm so confused." Christine crinkled her nose. Sandra rolled her eyes.

"I tried to talk her out of it. You're going to be eaten alive by that crowd, and I don't know if I'll be able to do anything with whatever scraps are left of you when it's all over." The *Bespoke* editor in chief tapped a pen on her clear glass desk as if ruminating on what to have for dinner and not on the future of Christine's career.

"Not to mention," she continued, "this is way too big a story for one person." She folded her arms over her silky Balmain blouse, waiting for Christine to process what she'd said.

"Wait, she wants *just* me? What about you?" Christine never dreamed Gloria would trust her enough to cover the wedding solo. Sandra's reply was a slow smile, clearly taking pleasure in her bewilderment. *Bespoke* was like that; the world's most elite haute couture and lifestyle publication lived off eating its young.

Sandra nodded. "Gloria is very taken with you, apparently. It's you or no coverage at all. I'm not sure what she's playing at, but my hands are tied. I have to promote you to senior editor and *Bespoke Weddings has* to cover this—if we don't blow it out of the water with this story, there will be budget cuts . . . and then jobs on the chopping block. Understand?" Sandra was clearly trying to imply that *Christine's* job would be on the chopping block, but everyone at the company knew the truth: her boss was the one who should be sweating. After twenty-five years of Sandra Yoon's reign, there were rumors going around that people at the top were looking for someone younger and fresher to head up *Bespoke*. The revenue of *Weddings* was just a small piece of Sandra's growing problem.

"I totally understand," Christine said, and nodded solemnly.

"A Ripton family wedding is not an opportunity we can afford to squander. I don't need to remind you how lucrative Lyle and Ben Ripton's wedding issue was. The highest numbers we've seen since Meghan and Harry."

"I know. I promise, I won't let you down," Christine insisted.

"Good." Sandra redirected her attention to her laptop. Christine recognized this as her cue to go.

"So, what did you say to her?" Sandra asked again as Christine opened the office door, a faint hint of desperation in her boss's voice.

"What do you mean?" *Shit, shit, shit.*

"At Lyle Ripton's wedding." Sandra sighed. "You must have said something to make her so besotted. Where else would you have chatted with Gloria Beaufort?" her boss scoffed.

Christine's shoulders slumped in relief. Sandra still didn't know.

"We just made small talk for like a minute," Christine said, hovering in the doorframe.

"Well, you should consider becoming a snake charmer, then, especially in those boots." Sandra smirked. Christine shrugged off the barb about her beat-up Rag & Bone snakeskin booties, numb to her boss's snide remarks, closed her office door, and promptly signed the NDA sent over from Gloria Beaufort's office.

Christine has nothing to feel sorry about, she tells herself now. Sandra had it coming. "Karma is my boyfriend," Christine sings softly, and flips to her Spotify app to play the Taylor Swift jam as she gets ready for the day.

She pours herself coffee, then scurries back into her giant bed, clutching her hunter-green Ballymoon Castle Hotel mug. Maybe she'll "accidentally" put it in her suitcase before she leaves. She's settling back into her nest of fluffy pillows, bringing the warm cup of coffee to her lips, when a blood-curdling scream sends the brown liquid straight onto her eight-hundred thread count sheets.

"Damn it," she whispers, jumping out of the mess. The scream continues. It's a woman's voice—and it's close. Just down the hall, if she had to guess. She checks the time on her phone—seven a.m.—and pokes her head out of her room just as Elliot whizzes past her, the groom's parents following in his jet stream.

"Well, don't just stand there!" Clementine calls as she breezes by in a priceless-looking maroon kimono. "There's clearly an emergency." Christine quickly pulls on a fuzzy sweatshirt, then races down the hall after them. Elliot and Clementine are stopped in front of a door, listening to what have turned into guttural sobs, just as Maggie emerges from down the hall, her face slathered in overnight cream. "That's Jane," she says breathlessly before running past them and through the open door. Everyone shares a look before plunging in after her.

Nothing could have prepared Christine for what she sees next.

Her mind moves quickly, taking blurry mental snapshots of the scene in front of her: Jane on the ground, doubled over, Maggie kneeling next to her, rubbing her back. Lyle sitting in a wing chair, face buried in her hands. Ben hovering over all of them, stony and serious. Father Kenneth, eyes closed, praying. Graham kneeling by his grandmother's side, taking her pulse . . .

Because there, in the center of the room, lies Gloria Beaufort, splayed out on an ornate rug, pale and lifeless. . . . her head framed by a halo of her own blood.

Christine covers her mouth in horror.

"Oh Jesus," Ben groans as the newcomers take in the scene. "Elliot, please shut the door." The wedding planner blinks a few times, confirming the reality of the situation, then does as he's told.

"She's gone," Graham says stoically, dropping his grandmother's wrist. Christine is momentarily stunned by how clinical his words sound . . . but then remembers that he is a doctor and wonders how many times he's given families this horrific news.

Clementine stands stunned and statuesque, her eyes glued to the family matriarch's body. Trey starts crying silent tears, unable to take his eyes off his dead mother. Nobody moves. Finally, Father Kenneth takes it upon himself to cover Gloria's bloodied body with a nearby top sheet, while whispering a Hail Mary. Ben is about to say something, anything, when there's a knock on the door. Everyone's eyes widen. Clementine puts her finger up to her lips as if to shush them, while Ben points at Elliot and cocks his head at the door. Christine feels her heart start to race.

Elliot mouths, "Me? Are you serious?" with exaggeration, but the brother of the groom just stares at him. With no other obvious choice, Elliot begrudgingly goes to the door as the knocking grows louder.

The wedding planner clears his throat. "Who is it?" He presses his ear against the door.

"It's me, uh, Neil, mate. We heard a scream—just making sure everyone's all right." Christine sees Elliot look through the peephole to confirm it's the ginger teen.

"Fine, thank you, Neil, just a bit of a jump scare—thought we saw a mouse." Ben glares at Elliot as if to say, *Seriously, is that the best you can do?* Elliot throws up his hands in response.

"Oh, a mouse, eh? I'll let management know. We can get someone to do a sweep of the room. Call an exterminator," Neil says from behind the door.

"Not necessary," Elliot snips. "It was just a shadow. No mouse. All good here."

"Grand. Well, I also wanted to let you know that breakfast is being served shortly and—"

Elliot interrupts him: "Thank you, we'll be there in a bit. Bye now." Silence.

"Okay. Grand," Neil finally says. "Let me know if there is anything else ya need, fresh towels or linens—"

"Yup, everything is *just grand*, we're all *grand*," Elliot says through gritted teeth. "Bye now."

Christine can practically see Neil's dopey, baby-faced smile through the door and feels a swell of jealousy. He gets to walk away while Christine is trapped in some sort of billionaire-murder nightmare. The group listens to the sound of Neil's footsteps fading. Elliot quickly opens the door to throw the *Do Not Disturb* sign on the handle, before closing it again with a slam.

"Oh God, I think I'm going to be sick," Jane yelps. She looks like she's on the verge of a full collapse. Leftover mascara runs down her face, and her once-glossy hair is slick with sweat.

"Did she . . . did she take her own life?" Maggie asks quietly, staring at the bloodied sheet.

"No, no, it's impossible. Mother would never do that. She loved her life—she loved her family," Trey asserts.

Ben rubs his temple. "It's not like we don't have enemies," he mumbles. Everyone squirms at the implication: that somebody might have murdered their matriarch.

"Mom was beloved," Trey sobs.

"Dad, of course she was—but you know as well as I do, you don't get to our position in life without . . . well." Ben doesn't finish his sentence. He doesn't have to.

"But nobody heard any gunshots?" Maggie whispers. "Weren't you staying just across the hall?" She looks to Ben and Lyle.

"We didn't hear a thing. There must have been a silencer on the gun, which, by the way, is nowhere to be found, so that doesn't bode well for the suicide theory," Ben says.

Everyone lets this sink in. Ben rubs his forehead again as if all of this is just too much for his brain to process. Christine doesn't blame him. In fact, she doesn't *want* to process this. She wants to walk back to her bed, pick up her coffee, scroll on Instagram, and continue living her life, in which things like this *don't happen*.

"We have to call the police," Lyle says, and rises to her feet.

"No," Ben, Elliot, and Trey say in unison, and then freeze, stunned by their agreement.

Ben takes the floor. "No, that is not wise, given the current circumstances."

"What do you mean 'the current circumstances'? Your grandmother was shot dead. We could *all* be in danger," Lyle says breathlessly. She looks beyond tired, yet somehow still put together in a hot pink silk sleep shirt and shorts, with a matching silk eye mask resting atop her head. Christine, however, is not surprised by Ben's callousness, unable to shake the memory of their bloody introduction just yesterday.

Ben closes his eyes and takes a breath. "Think about it. We cannot be in the press. Especially for something like this. *A murder?* We'll never recover. It would be the final nail in Glo's coffin . . . Oh God, sorry, poor choice of words." He cringes.

"Wow." Lyle looks at her husband, mouth agape, her eyes a wintry mix of anger and sadness. Christine's ears perk up. *What did he mean by that? Could there possibly be any truth to the Ripton Rumors?*

"It will just . . . It will create a frenzy," Trey says. "It's not what Mom would have wanted—not on Graham's big day." Trey's voice quivers as he agrees with his eldest son. He leans against the wall for support.

"The guests are already on their way," Elliot offers. "They are *in the air*. Wait, no." He looks at his watch. "People that took the red-eye from New York are actually landing as we speak." His eye twitches. "And not just people! *Three hundred and fifty people!* Staying on the property!" The wedding planner looks like he might pass out.

"Well, what do you all propose we do? We can't just go forward with the wedding as if nothing has happened," Graham chokes out, his voice faltering as reality sinks in. He points at the now crimson-colored sheet.

"Gran might have been murdered by someone at this hotel. Maybe by someone in this room. We don't know—"

"Graham!" Clementine gasps, and turns to Elliot. "Elliot, will you get some coffee and tea delivered? And maybe some scones? Nobody is thinking clearly . . . Graham must have low blood sugar, to say something like that." She throws herself into a plush indigo chair.

Elliot nods, then reaches for the phone to call room service, thinks better of it, and exits the suite in search of coffee himself. *It's weird*, Christine thinks, *to see Elliot being treated like one of their servants*. He's a star in his own right, running an exclusive event planning company, yet he's getting coffee for these people like a desperate *Bespoke* intern. Then, with a start, she remembers seeing him last night outside this very room. The fight. The venomous words.

Ben runs his hand down his face and sighs. "Okay, all we know for sure is that Jane was the one . . . who discovered the body." Everyone looks at the bride-to-be, still a puddle on the carpet, the charred remains of last night's fire smoking behind her.

"Gloria wanted to give me my something borrowed," Jane says. "She told me to come this morning—you heard her say that last night, right?" The bride looks toward her fiancé, who nods solemnly. Christine also remembers Gloria's instructions to Jane from the night before.

Jane continues. "And, and, well—the door was ajar, I heard *Shark Tank* on, so I figured she was up. I knocked, waited a minute, then decided to just pop my head in. When I rounded the corner, she was . . ." Jane trails off and collapses back into tears. Graham holds his fiancée tightly.

"I know how it must look," Jane sobs, "but I could never—I would never . . ."

"Well, it doesn't look *good*," Clementine observes, saying what everyone surely must have been thinking since entering the suite.

"Mom!" Graham hisses, wrapping his arms tighter around Jane.

"I was just stating the obvious! *You're* the one who said someone in this room might have committed murder," Clementine whispers.

"Let's all remember our faith," Father Kenneth says, voice trembling. "Perhaps a shared prayer would be in order—to let God guide us . . ." But the group ignores him, their attention still squarely on the bride.

"I can't believe this is happening," Jane says. She curls up in the fetal position, and Maggie takes a turn to console her.

"It's all right, honey. We all know you had nothing to do with this." Maggie strokes her daughter's hair.

"God, Clem. Would you have some empathy for once?" Trey snaps at his wife. "Clearly the poor girl is beside herself, as we all are." The groom's father stands panting before her, eyes bloodshot, face soggy with tears. His wife is silent for a moment, eyes closed.

Clementine tries to take a steady breath before responding. "You are going to lecture *me* about empathy? I have so much empathy, it's practically coming out of my eyeballs." She bulges out her eyes for dramatic effect. "Did you not just hear me order breakfast for everyone, worried about how they're all handling this on an empty stomach? And by the way, where were *you* last night, Mr. Have Some Empathy? You never came to bed." The accusation hangs in the air like a guillotine blade.

"Dad," Graham demands, "is that true?" Trey looks cornered, his eyes fliting around the room until they land on Christine. She stumbles backward, knocking over a chinoiserie lamp. For the first time since she entered the suite, the family is acutely aware of her presence.

"Excellent, just excellent," Ben scoffs. "Please tell me you haven't already written up Gran's obituary to leak to the press."

"Relax, Ben, she works for *Bespoke Weddings*, not CNN. Christine won't be telling the media anything." Lyle's calm voice doesn't distract from her frosty gaze.

"Of course not," Christine says quickly, picking up the lamp. "I am so sorry for your loss." She sounds awkward, and she feels awkward. She should not be here among this grieving—potentially murderous—family. Come to think of it, why *is* she here? Her career-changing opportunity has morphed into a one-way ticket to Rikers Island, or whatever the Irish equivalent is, before her very eyes.

"You know what, I'm just going to leave. This is clearly a very personal family matter. So sorry I intruded." She tries to make her way toward the door.

"I'm sorry, Christine," Ben says quickly, "but that's not an option at the moment." Nobody, not even Lyle, comes to her defense. Christine blinks but doesn't move. She feels in her gut that she should cooperate with them. Something is not right here, and now is not the time to go against the wishes of her rich and powerful overlords.

"Everyone, let's take a pause," Ben says with severity. "We need to think this through." His tone has shifted, and Christine gets the sense that this is Ben's general counsel persona—the voice he uses when addressing the legal team at Glo HQ that reports to him.

"You were the first one to find Jane in here, Ben. Tell us what you saw." Clementine puts a hand on her son's shoulder.

His mouth twitches. "We woke up to a scream. Our room is just across the hall. I got up to see what the commotion was, and Lyle went to check on Miles. I saw Gran's door was half open—"

He chokes on his own voice before continuing. "I, uh—so I walked in and the first thing I noticed was what a wreck it was, clothing and jewelry everywhere. A mess of broken room service dishes on the floor. I immediately thought there could have been a robbery." The family seems to accept this, potential robbery clearly always top of mind.

"Then I saw *her* kneeling over Gran's body." He cocks his head in Jane's direction like he's saying "'sup" at a party.

"I don't like what you're insinuating," Graham says in a stern voice. "Again, Jane had no reason to hurt Gran." Nobody questions him, their perfect golden son. It's clear to Christine, whatever Graham wants, he gets . . . even if it's getting his fiancé off the hook for murder.

Ben sighs. "I don't think it could have been Jane either, for the record. What does she have to gain from this? They're not even married yet." Maggie gives an offended huff at his words, but the bride doesn't seem to register them. She just continues to cry on the floor.

"I bet it has something to do with the rock from last night. That was very alarming. We should have flown in more security," Trey grumbles.

They all stand in silence, listening to the thump of raindrops hitting the pavement outside. The storm is unrelenting; any beginnings of daylight are completely hidden by gray clouds. The door squeaks open, and everyone's heads snaps toward it, only to see Elliot reentering with a tray of coffees. He passes them out silently.

"It's just so awful." Trey is now completely blubbering. "My poor mother. *Murdered.* It doesn't make any sense." He uses all his bodily force to blow his nose into a tissue.

Graham stands next to his father. "I know this is unbearably difficult, but we need to do the right thing . . . for Gran. We need to call the police." His voice catches.

"Like I said"—Ben opens Gloria's mini fridge—"calling the police is not an option at the moment." He cracks open a bottle of white wine. Nobody questions the early morning glass of Chardonnay, given the circumstances.

"Boys, let's remember to be good and faithful servants of God, even in this perilous situation," Father Kenneth tries again, steadying himself. "We must honor Gloria's memory."

"Thank you, Father," Graham says. "We all certainly need that reminder." The groom throws his brother a dirty look.

"Not to butt in," Elliot says, "but it's almost eight a.m., and we've got a body on our hands and some decisions have to be made."

"Elliot is right. Whatever happened to Gran—it doesn't matter right now," Ben says.

"Actually, that's not what I meant—" Elliot tries to say, but Ben continues. "What matters is that nobody finds out about this. We just have to keep it quiet until the wedding weekend is over. Then we'll find who did this and make them pay, but we'll control the narrative. We'll keep it quiet and out of the press," Ben says. "Until then, nobody says anything. If anyone asks, Gran is sick. Keep it vague."

Ben looks directly at Christine. "And you—look, I'm sorry you're involved in this." He throws up his hands again, not really seeming very sorry at all. "But since you are, you need to know that the NDA you signed prior to coming here prevents you from speaking a word about what's happened. You too, Elliot. Understood?" Elliot's head bounces up and down like a bobblehead.

"Christine?" Ben asks. If Christine hadn't gotten laser-hair removal last winter, she's sure every hair on her body would be sticking up at this point.

"I'll continue with my coverage as I normally would," she says quickly, the words coming out of her mouth before her brain has a chance to catch up. "It's my job to deliver a story about a gorgeous destination wedding and that's what I plan to do. Nothing more, nothing less." She is in this now, whether she wants to be or not.

"Good answer," Ben growls, and turns to Father Kenneth. "And, Father, just to bolster us with some good press before we navigate this weekend, let's send out that press release about Grow 2 Glo's latest initiative with the, the"—Ben snaps his fingers, trying to find the words—"the youth centers, or whatever." Father Kenneth doesn't acknowledge the request; his eyes are still shut. *He's probably still praying this isn't real*, Christine thinks.

"Don't drag Gran's charity into this," Graham snaps. "This is not how a murder investigation works, Ben. You can't try to distract the public. You can't threaten witnesses. Days can't tick away—key evidence will be lost. Aren't you a *lawyer?*" Graham shouts at his brother.

"I have to agree. This is not what our Lord—" Father Kenneth tries to say, but Ben cuts him off.

"Damn, I guess my track record of following in Jesus's footsteps is finally coming to an end." The best man almost laughs. "Father, consider this a confession—which, *as a lawyer*"—he side-eyes his brother—"I understand you are obligated to keep between you and your parishioner, right?" Father Kenneth shuts his mouth and doesn't respond.

"Right, that's what I thought. Okay, Graham." Ben clears his throat. "Here's the alternative if we go to the police right now: your wedding is ruined, our reputation is incinerated, the company stock tanks, we're all implicated in a murder investigation, we lose control of the empire our grandmother spent her life building—which is currently hanging on by a thread—we're disgraced and ostracized from every person of means and power in the world—"

"Benjamin, that's enough." Trey puts his hand up. "Obviously nobody wants that. Graham, be reasonable. It's just for the weekend. Then we'll properly honor Gran. We will give her justice. This is just a slight delay."

"Graham," Jane says softly, taking her fiancé's face in her hands. Everyone turns to look at her. "Gloria wouldn't want this to stop us. She'd want us to get married." A moment passes. Graham's eyes are teary, but he nods at Jane, wrapping her tighter in his arms. Christine finds herself thinking the moment is almost a sweet, if not painful, reminder of her single status, until she realizes that the bride is essentially asking her husband to aid in covering up a potential murder so she can have her dream wedding. It takes being a bridezilla to another stratosphere. Nobody says anything for five seconds, which is all Ben needs, apparently, to consider an agreement reached.

"Good. Elliot, we need to keep the body on ice and hidden until the weekend is over and we decide what to do. Can you find us a lock-and-key freezer situation?"

"You're kidding—I can't *move a body*—"

"Can you do it for a million dollars?" Ben offers casually. That shuts Elliot up. Seconds tick away while he weighs the pros and cons of Ben's proposal.

"I'll see what I can do," Elliot says finally. "How do you want me to . . . transport her?"

"She's only like five feet tall. You should be able to think of something," Lyle says unhelpfully, stealing a sip from Ben's wine bottle. Christine is struck by how unfazed Lyle seems by all of this . . . almost like she's not in the least surprised to have woken up to discover Gloria's been murdered. And maybe she isn't. After all, last night she told Christine exactly how she felt about her husband's grandmother.

"What about that giant suitcase?" Clementine points to the Louis Vuitton luggage sticking out of the closet. Elliot shivers.

"Great, that should work." Ben claps his hands. "Now we clean this room up . . . ourselves. *Nobody* comes in and out of here. Elliot, we'll need security or someone trustworthy to stand outside at all times." The wedding planner nods, his ghostly white face going back and forth between the blood-soaked sheet and the suitcase, trying to wrap his brain around what he has to do next.

Ben flexes his hands. "Let's get to work." The family surveys the disheveled hotel suite, which looks like it housed a rock star instead of an elderly woman. Timidly, they start moving around the space, fluffing pillows and fixing crooked paintings. It's clear none of them have cleaned a room in a while—or ever. Christine folds Gloria's pashmina while Elliot gets rid of a broken dish. Everybody is trying to busy themselves with any task that can be completed without having to go near the real mess . . . the pool of blood in the center of the room. Finally, Lyle marches over, removes the sheet, and with her hands on her hips asks, "Now, which one of y'all has a good stain remover?"

SEVEN

# LYLE

Two Years Earlier
Lyle and Ben's Wedding Day

THE SUITE IS IN FULL swing. Lyle closes her eyes and takes in all the celebratory sounds, committing them to memory: the fizzle of champagne, the sound of dresses shedding their dry-cleaning skins, the high-pitched flurry of her nine bridesmaids. She takes a deep breath and reopens her eyes, blinking carefully in order not to disturb her newly set false lashes. It's a perfect day at Huckleberry Farm, just as planned. Birds chirp on cue, proving that even the wildlife knows how much it costs to rent this venue and feel pressured to live up to the hype.

"It's too bright over here for photos. I think we better do them in the sitting area off the bedroom," Lyle's mother commands. Carrie "Could Have Been the Next Cindy Crawford" Darby (as she's known in the Atlanta society scene) gives her daughter's shoulder a squeeze before gliding into the next room to assess the lighting, her loyal flock of vendors and their respective assistants trailing behind her. Lyle's mother doesn't walk—*she glides*. Despite her towering six-foot frame, Carrie's presence is delicate and ethereal.

The bride-to-be takes a pearl drop earring off the vanity table, where her wedding day jewelry has been laid out with military-grade precision. Everything in Lyle's life has been measured, calculated, and planned to perfection, and her wedding is no exception. It's their mother-daughter Super Bowl, Carrie often jokes. While other girls might find Carrie's level of parental involvement stifling or aggressive, Lyle loves the path her mom has paved and continues to pave for her. She is and always was, for lack of a better expression, a chip off the old block.

But to be honest, it's not really the right expression, because nothing in Lyle's life ever chips; not the Waterford crystal in her Restoration Hardware dining hutch or the gel manicure on her fingernails. Never. And now here she is, the bride of the year. First a *Bespoke* editor, then a Bergdorf brand strategist, and most recently VP of brand marketing for the beauty conglomerate Glo. And now that she is marrying Benjamin Ripton, the handsome heir to the company that cuts her paychecks, she'll reach the pinnacle of her professional life: becoming a rich housewife or, as it's now called, a lifestyle influencer.

This is it, the crescendo of both Lyle's and Carrie's careers: a wedding for the ages that will grace the glossy pages of *Bespoke Weddings* and be worshiped by brides-to-be for years to come. Ben is exactly the kind of guy Carrie and Lyle always dreamed of (minus the drinking, but they're working on that). Carrie put it best: "You find the best piece of stone, and then you chisel away." Lyle is more than ready to chisel away at Ben's drinking habit. The word "problem" or (gasp!) "alcoholism" being far too uncouth.

"Ladies." Carrie claps. "Let's gather for Una and Adrianna over there." She points to a lilac cushioned window seat with a gorgeous farm backdrop. Una Neary, leading *Bespoke Weddings* photographer and Annie Leibovitz prodigy, shuffles the girls into position. Her colleague for the weekend, Adrianna Roccato, an up-and-coming film videographer sporting an ill-advised choppy black haircut, bounces behind her, grinning. *Good, she should be grinning,* Lyle thinks. She's about to put Adrianna on. The. Map. This wedding will be a huge get for her, and Lyle only gave her the job as a favor to a, um, dear friend.

"Simply gorgeous," says Sandra, the editor in chief of *Bespoke*. "I mean, there are just going to be too many shots to choose from for your feature." Sandra, who's wearing a fabulous linen blazer, scribbles furiously in a little black notebook, her spritely strawberry-blond assistant hovering behind her like a shy toddler. Normally, the editor in chief of *Bespoke* would have better things to do than micromanage a wedding editorial, but Sandra is a friend of Gloria Beaufort—and she knows Lyle joining the family is an opportunity for *Bespoke* to get even closer to the illustrious Glo founder.

The morning continues according to plan. Carrie directs Lyle in a series of poses to highlight her best features: long neck, glacial blue eyes, and old Hollywood figure that Lauren and Chan of the Pop Apologists podcast claim "is only rivaled by Marilyn Monroe." Her bridesmaids, all veterans of the fashion and society worlds, know exactly how to cock their heads and beam their professionally whitened smiles for the camera.

"Are you sure we don't want to do a first look?" Una asks between flashes. "There's still time."

"No. I want Ben to see me for the first time walking down the aisle," Lyle asserts.

"I love that," Adrianna gushes. "I can't wait to capture it. *Bellissima*." Una rolls her eyes. A first look is better for the photographer; a live shot of the groom crying is unbeatable for the videographer. Lyle doesn't care about any of that, though. The truth is, she's not ready to see Ben yet. Every time she lets herself envision that moment, she sees *his* face instead. And Adrianna cooing Italian phrases like "bellissima" certainly doesn't help.

"I think I've got what I need," Una says, and swings one of her three cameras over her shoulder. "Ready to put on that gorgeous dress?" Carrie squeezes Lyle's hand. She knows about *him*, of course. Lyle had to tell her. Her mother of all people would understand.

"It was just puppy love. You were in Italy, for God's sake," Carrie had said between bites of her seared tuna poke bowl. "You needed closure. It's okay, Ly." *Ly*. How ironic her pet name sounded in that moment. Carrie held Lyle through the tears. "Ben doesn't need to know," she had whispered. "It doesn't mean a thing. Ben is the man someone like you is meant to marry." That was a month ago. Carlyle Darby never disobeyed her mother, and she wasn't going to start now.

Carrie zips up Lyle's lace gown with a bit more force than was needed a few weeks ago. Lyle stands in front of the mirror, heart beating in her ribs. She's a vision, but in moments like this—the picture-perfect ones—a cold stream of worry trickles through her blue-blooded veins. Could they all find out? She adjusts her breasts in the corset. They're peeking out of her form-fitting dress, teetering on the edge of poor taste.

"Oh, honey," Carrie gushes, "you're radiant." Monique Lhuillier designed this dress specifically for Lyle; it features a full ball gown skirt and a dramatic train. Monique pinned the fabric on her directly so that every inch of the dress would be perfectly sculpted to her body. It was definitely worth the trips to Los Angeles for fittings over the last year. The gown is, factually, stunning, but it doesn't feel like Lyle. She feels like she's in a costume, or worse, a disguise.

"You're glowing," Una says, as her camera flashes around the room, capturing the dress from every angle. Every snap further securing her spot among fashion's top photographers.

"Brava, brava. Let's bring in the bridesmaids, sì?" Adrianna is perched on a sofa arm ready to pounce on the bevy of blondes waiting outside for their entrance. The suite doors fly open, and the hysterics begin.

"Lyle!" "A princess!" "Gorgeous!" "I'm crying!" The bridesmaids shine in various shades of green, meant to match the wildflowers and greenery of Huckleberry Farm.

"You're just breathtaking," Alison, her maid of honor, chirps. The bride tries to respond but can offer only a lukewarm smile. She feels like she's being buried alive under a pile of compliments she doesn't deserve.

"I need a minute," Lyle whispers to Carrie. Her mother nods and addresses the troops.

"Okay, everyone, let's give our bride some space. We'll meet her down in the garden for photos. Who wants some more champagne?" Carrie holds up a fizzing bottle of Dom and leads the way out of the suite. Alone again, Lyle closes her eyes and tries to breathe. Her head throbs, and a bead of sweat mercilessly cascades down her airbrushed face. There is a knock on the door.

"Sorry, do you mind coming back later?" Lyle calls, but the door opens anyway and her soon-to-be grandmother-in-law, Gloria Beaufort, walks in. She looks effervescent in a blush-colored gown with elegant oversize sleeves that ripple, creating a waterfall effect. Her makeup is, well, Glo-ing, and her eyes are perfectly dewy, probably thanks to their new product, Gloss Drops, that would be hitting the market the following week if all went according to plan. Which, of course, it wasn't, and that seemed to be only encouraging Ben's drinking.

Lyle had been, and would continue to be, loud about the possible use of butyl benzyl phthalate—a chemical linked to developmental and reproductive toxicity—that was being used in the Gloss Drops formulation. The scientists in the Glo lab had raised several red flags about the use of this ingredient. Not only was the chemical dangerous, but a cheap shortcut like that was also bad for the brand—it would make them look unwilling to change with the times, thus making Lyle's job as head of brand marketing even more difficult. Her efforts to stop the use of this chemical were proving futile, though. Trey continued to bulldoze ahead despite her pleas, but she couldn't bring herself to let it go. Her own mother had struggled with infertility before Lyle was conceived.

"Oh, Gloria. Sorry, please come in." Lyle twists her face into a smile. She quickly rearranges her vanity, grabbing all her non-Glo products and shoving them into the top drawer. Lyle may not be obsessed with all of her company's formulations, but she is obsessed with Gloria Beaufort. After all, she's the one who introduced her to Ben at Paris Fashion Week in 2020, just after Lyle signed on to work at Glo. Nancy Meyers herself couldn't have written a chicer meet-cute. Gloria looks the bride up and down, eyes pausing briefly at her chest. Lyle's heart beats loudly, heat creeping up from her polished toes to her sculpted cheekbones.

Gloria doesn't say anything but rather seats herself on the pink toile vanity chair. She smiles at the pile of Glo products that covers the marble vanity. Even after so many years, the billion-dollar beauty empress is giddy to see her products in action.

"All Glo, I see. It's no wonder you're luminous, hm? But don't think I can't spot a Westman Atelier contour stick from a mile away. We really need to crack that code." Her eyes crinkle. Lyle tries to laugh, but it sounds more like a cat being run over. She needs to relax.

She finally meets Gloria's eyes, and it's game over. A twitch of the lip, an awkward cough, a shift in the air—it's instinct, but Lyle can read Gloria's body language. She's seen the way she sits up in a chair before she delivers a fatal blow to someone's career, the way she shakes out her wrist before leaving an exorbitant tip. Gloria knows about him. She knows everything, and Lyle has been naive to think she wouldn't. They're playing poker now, and her only option is bluffing.

"Since we're using exclusively . . . ish"—Lyle winks—"Glo products for the wedding, the company will get a full page in *Bespoke* next month in addition to the *Bespoke Weddings* feature." She reaches deep within and flashes her former Miss Georgia Teen smile. "I'm so proud that I get to represent the brand y'all built on my big day." Lyle prays that the sentiment sounds sincere.

"Today is just the beginning, isn't it?" Gloria says. The family matriarch picks up a blush brush and touches up her face. Lyle admires that she's let herself age gracefully; wrinkles are proof of wisdom, and that's the problem: Gloria is not an idiot.

"I have a little something for you." Gloria rummages through her gold Chanel evening bag that Lyle has always coveted. Gloria's closet is like a fashion museum.

*Maybe it's just bridal jitters*, Lyle thinks. *Maybe she really just wants to give her grandson's future wife a gift.* She needs to get a grip.

Lyle gives the perfunctory response. "You shouldn't have. You're already doing so much." Ben told her to expect something exorbitant as a wedding present. It's Gloria's way of marking big occasions. Now a box appears on the vanity table. It's unmistakably Cartier red. Lyle gasps and embraces Gloria, soaking in her warm vanilla scent.

"I have a lot of respect for you, Miss Carlyle Darby, soon to be Ripton," Gloria says while gently putting a hand over the box. "I think you will be a perfect addition to our family. A wise investment, one might say." She chuckles.

"Thank you. I feel the same. I have—" Gloria lifts her other hand to cut Lyle off. Lyle looks around and grabs a rogue glass of champagne and takes a sip, the bubbles burning her throat on the way down. She feels like she's going to be sick.

"But, Carlyle," Gloria continues, "I was disappointed to come across this." She produces an envelope from her glittering bag and slides it toward Lyle, who feels her stomach somersault at the sight of it. She slowly picks it up with shaky hands and opens it just enough to see the bottom of a printed-out photo of her on *his* balcony, in *his* shirt, *his* arms around her waist. Lyle shoves the picture back inside the envelope with force. She doesn't need to see any more.

"I can explain." Her voice cracks.

"I'm not interested in the details. I'm just here for some housekeeping business. First, you'll sign the prenuptial agreement. Naturally, given the circumstances, you understand that. There is a copy in there." Gloria motions toward the envelope, and Lyle nods meekly. This cannot be happening, but it is and it's her fault.

"Second, you'll break it off. Immediately. If I ever hear his name, this will all come to an end. That seems fair, doesn't it?" Lyle notices the slight upward snarl of Gloria's thin lips, and everything finally crystalizes: this is how Gloria Beaufort has built her empire. This is who she is. Lyle had been ignorant and frankly sexist to assume Gloria forged a billion-dollar business on good taste and goodwill alone. She's a razor-sharp businesswoman, and she's working an angle. She wants something from Lyle in return for not telling Ben about *him*. Lyle is being blackmailed.

"Why are you doing this? Why not just light the match and send this whole day up in flames?" Lyle cries.

Gloria shrugs. "I like you," she says. "You're smart and good at your job. Brilliant, actually." The compliment is confusing in the context of their standoff.

Gloria sighs. "Believe me. I don't relish this, but I need someone in this family who can actually work. Someone who knows the business. Someone with integrity. I've watched you build your career, and truly, I'm impressed. I see a lot of myself in you. I need to know that you'll take care of Glo when I'm gone. Think of this as my insurance policy." Gloria shifts her gaze toward the envelope again.

There it is. Behind her eyes, Lyle sees the vision board she's spent years imagining being ripped up; the multiple homes, the exotic vacations, the brood of perfectly dressed children—it will never be like that for her, she knows that now. She'll be running Glo. Sure, it'll be glamorous, but it'll be a slog. Lyle will never get out of the board meetings. She'll be at every fashion week event, schmoozing for contracts, partnerships, and features. Constantly dieting, pulling and prodding at her skin in the never-ending quest to be younger, thinner, more relevant. The world will call her "impressive, a hard worker, not one to rest on her laurels," but really, in the game of life, she'll have lost. But that's not even the worst part: she'll be living under Gloria's thumb. She'll be a shadow king, unable to make any of her own decisions, beholden to Gloria at all times. She thinks of her efforts to reformulate Gloss Drops, her futile efforts to try to bring Glo into the next century—and feels a hard knot start to form in her stomach.

"I see." Lyle folds her arms.

"Chin up, darling. Think of it like this: you're getting a promotion! You're the future CEO of Glo." Gloria pats her cheeks, and Lyle has half a mind to push her into the wall.

"What about your son?" Lyle asks. Gloria had *just* named Trey CEO last year after her eighty-second birthday, deciding it was finally time for her to take a more "passive role" at the company—as chairman of the board.

*Passive role, my ass*, Lyle thinks.

Gloria spins the blush brush around on the vanity table. "We both know Trey's not really cut out to run a Fortune five hundred company. I have to find the right moment to speak to him about an early retirement, but it's comforting to know you'll be ready in the wings when I do."

Lyle feels a pounding start inside her skull.

"You are a beautiful bride." Gloria slips the Cartier box into Lyle's hand. "Welcome to the family."

Lyle opens it to reveal a sapphire-and-diamond tennis bracelet. In another world, the world she envisioned, this would be the cherry on top of a perfect day, but now she just feels as though she's been handed her handcuffs.

"Thank you—it's stunning," she manages, then immediately puts the box down. Suddenly she can't breathe. The dress is too tight.

Gloria takes it upon herself to reopen the box and clasp the bracelet around her wrist.

"There we go. That's better. Don't worry, there is no judgment on my end." Like that's what Lyle is worried about at this point—*Gloria's judgment.* The bracelet catches the sunlight just right, and for a moment she is brought back to the beaches of Positano. She can almost see his face, backlit by the golden sun, leaning over her for their last kiss ... *I'll never see him again.* Her eyes well up as she lets her heart ache for the first time in months.

"You're not marrying into a family of angels by any stretch," Gloria says. "If anything, I was relieved to find a few skeletons in your closet. I like to have something to work with. Some parts of this business are grizzly, but you already know that." Lyle stares at her blankly.

*Is she referring to Gloss Drops? Does she know about butyl benzyl phthalate?* Lyle wonders. She doesn't listen as Gloria drones on about her future plans for Glo. Instead, she looks at the wall, waiting for numbness to replace her pain. There are no words left. At least Gloria doesn't know everything. She doesn't know about—

"And won't you make a wonderful little future heir," she says, patting Lyle's belly. "I hope you have a nice head of Italian hair." With that,

Gloria smiles sweetly and leaves the room. Lyle sees stars and then everything goes black. Wedding day nerves, not enough water, she'd later tell the gaggle of bridesmaids hovering over her with looks of shock and concern.

Her *Bespoke Weddings* feature opened with the line "Carlyle Ripton can't believe her luck."

At least that part was true.

*Jane loves Graham  
a whole brunch!*

LADIES, PLEASE JOIN US FOR
A BRUNCH TO CELEBRATE OUR BRIDE
HOSTED BY CLEMENTINE RIPTON

an assortment of...
dainty sandwiches, scrumptious scones,
and petite sweets will be provided

FRIDAY, OCTOBER SEVENTEENTH
AT ELEVEN O'CLOCK IN THE MORNING
THE DUCHESS OF CUMBERLAND PARLOR
BALLYMOON CASTLE HOTEL

*Pastel attire and fascinator hats encouraged!*

EIGHT

# CHRISTINE

Friday, October 17, 2025
Bridal Brunch

"CAN YOU PASS THE CLOTTED cream, please?" Clementine asks, but Christine doesn't hear her. Her mind is still in Gloria Beaufort's suite, replaying the image of Lyle on her hands and knees using a toothbrush to scrub bloodstains out of the carpet. What is Christine supposed to do now? Does she tell Sandra what happened? Does she go to the police?

"Hellooo, anybody home?" Clementine taps her spoon on her teacup. She is wearing a couture fascinator hat with a swirl of purple and blue feathers that make it look like a baby peacock has taken up residence on her head.

"Sorry." Christine shakes herself out of staring and passes the clotted cream to Clementine, who plops a large scoop of it onto her plate. The rest of the group—Jane, Lyle, Maggie—sit in silence, trying to ignore the symbolism of the empty chair at the end of the table.

"Isn't anybody going to eat? We need to keep our energy up!" Clementine urges. "The scones are amazing. Like little bites of heaven." She bites into one, crumbs landing in the crevices of her purplish lips. Everyone blinks at Clementine, who seems to have completely forgotten about the events of this morning.

"Just so you know, that's not vegan," Lyle says, pointing at the pile of clotted cream on Clementine's plate.

The mother of the groom considers this for a moment, but ultimately shrugs and says, "Oh whatever. I think I'm over that," and takes another big bite of her scone.

"Christine," Jane asks timidly, "what's on your schedule for today? Is there anything I can do to help with the article?"

"Oh," Christine says, shocked by the reminder that she still has to write an article about this disastrous weekend. "That's so kind of you, but honestly unnecessary. I know as the bride you've got your hands full today. Elliot has my day planned down to the minute." She smiles. "I'll get a run-through of the rehearsal dinner from your mom after brunch, and then I'll do a quick sit-down with Father Kenneth this afternoon before the rehearsal." Jane starts to say something, but Neil interrupts, approaching the table with a tray of individual green-and-white chinoiserie teapots.

"Top o' the mornin', ladies," he grins. "Everything to your liking so far?" He fills up Jane's cup with steamy Irish breakfast tea.

"Thank you. Everything is just beautiful." Jane smiles. It's not a lie, even though it certainly feels like one now. The Duchess of Cumberland Parlor is the sort of place you'd imagine Kate Middleton would take her breakfast every morning: tasteful, classic, and incredibly posh, adorned in various hues of blue and soft white. The room sits perched on the very edge of the castle, overlooking a grassy knoll and golf course, where Trey and Ben are currently attempting to play a casual eighteen holes. Christine flinches as she watches Ben whack one of the balls, sending it flying out into the abyss of gray clouds overhead.

"The weather is supposed to clear up for this evening," Neil remarks. "A little bit of luck for the big day. The forecast said there would be no sun for weeks." He fills up Lyle's cup next.

"*So* lucky," she snorts. Christine feels the group tense up.

"Are you waiting for Ms. Beaufort?" Neil asks.

Everyone looks at one another in panic. A sea of bulging eyes trapped under ridiculous fascinator hats. They are certainly a group of unlikely-looking criminals. But their silly European cosplay doesn't take away from the gravity of the situation. If one of them breaks from the plan, they're all done for.

Finally, Jane clears her throat and responds. "No, she isn't feeling well, but we are waiting for one of the bridesmaids who may be joining us. I believe she just arrived this morning. Raquel Williams?"

Neil's pasty white skin turns pink. "Yes, she's here. Quite exciting for us, a real American movie star." His eyes glisten with excitement.

"More like a glorified porn star," Lyle snarks, and the young waiter's face falls at his misstep. Clementine tries to suppress a smile as she takes a sip of tea. Christine is shocked to hear Lyle so openly criticize Raquel Williams, the new face of Glo's iconic fragrance, Jolie Chose Jaune. Even though Raquel has been splashed across the tabloids for her scantily clad bikini pictures and laundry list of playboy boyfriends, she is solidly among the top and most highly paid actresses in the world—a huge get, even for a company as established as Glo.

"This castle has hosted more notable people than Raquel, for God's sake. Neil, you mustn't make her feel more important than she is. This is a haven for artists, leaders, people of cultural importance . . . she's lucky to be here, among us," Clementine says with the flourish of delivering a Shakespearean sonnet. Neil looks like he wants to evaporate into the air.

"Well, I just loved her in *Amongst the Treetops*," Maggie says, and smiles sweetly. "My patients adore that movie. Such a fun one."

Neil lets out a sigh of relief. "A classic, for sure," he says, then practically runs away from the table.

"Do you work in the medical field, Maggie?" Christine asks, adjusting her teal-blue fascinator hat, which she borrowed from her British friend Rupa. It matches her fun, silky pantsuit perfectly, which she thought looked glamorous when she tried it on at Nordstrom a few weeks ago, but now thinks it kind of makes her look like a flight attendant.

"No, no," Maggie replies quickly. "Well, sort of. I'm just an LPN—licensed practical nurse. I work in a nursing home. Anyway, the plan was always to go back to nursing school full-time, but then this one came along." She smiles at Jane, who is clearly not paying attention, typing away on her cell phone.

"God, those homes are so depressing, aren't they?" Clementine says. "I'd rather be dead than in one of those soul-crushing places." She slurps her tea absentmindedly.

"Good Lord, Clementine," Lyle snaps. "*Really?*" She puts down her butter knife with a loud thud. "Do you think that's an appropriate thing to say? After what happened?" Christine's breath catches, waiting for a confrontation to explode, but Clementine looks genuinely embarrassed. This woman is the living definition of "speaking before thinking," Christine concludes. Mercifully, a voice rings out from the drawing room doorway, distracting the group.

"Don't tell me you ladies started without me!" It's Raquel Williams, in the flesh. Christine doesn't feel the familiar bubble of anticipation in her stomach upon meeting a celebrity; it's more of a weak gurgle now. This morning's events have left her senses wrung out.

Raquel struts toward them, an almost-blinding smile on her flawless face. "I just cannot contain my excitement! The wedding is happening. It's all so *magical*!" Raquel's eyes pop against the shimmer of her flashy green sequin minidress. "Can you believe this thing?" She does a spin. "I know it's a little much for brunch, but Ireland needed a sparkly emerald moment, you know?" There is no denying Raquel's beauty: glowing skin, sharp cheekbones, and curly chestnut hair that bounces with every crystal-coated stiletto step she takes. Christine tries not to look at her for too long; she doesn't want Raquel to think she's a gawking fangirl.

"Hello," Clementine says tightly, refusing to comment on Raquel's outfit. "Won't you take a seat? We don't want a scene." A few Ballymoon staffers linger in the doorframe of the parlor, clearly hoping for a glimpse of the actress. It's hard to ignore the entrance of a star as recognizable as Raquel Williams, especially when she's dressed in an outfit better suited to meeting Taylor Swift at Zero Bond than to eating tiny plates of Michelin-star canapés with industry titans like the Riptons. A celebrity as big as Raquel knows how to dress to blend in and be unassuming, but she has pointedly chosen to go in the opposite direction with her look this morning. Her outfit is essentially begging for a Deuxmoi feature.

"Of course, of course. Hello, gorgeous bride." Raquel gives Jane a kiss on the cheek. "Oh, those look delish." She takes a seat, eyeing the homemade lemon bars on the top level of the tiered serving tower. Jane smiles awkwardly. The two could not look more mismatched, Jane in her simple ivory corseted Emilia Wickstead midi dress fit for lunch with the First Lady and Raquel in her sequin mini sheath—fit for a strip tease in the Broadway production of *Chicago*. Christine is well aware that Raquel's presence in Jane's bridal party is more of a press power play between Raquel's team and Glo, and not a reflection of their actual friendship.

"God, honestly, I feel so well rested after that flight!" Raquel says as she helps herself to Jane's teapot. "I guess that's the beauty of a private jet. So nice of Trey to send it for me."

Clementine's eyes grow wide. "He sent the jet for you?" For all her talk about "good energy," Clementine looks like she wants to flip this table and smash her tiny teapot on Raquel's head.

"I was on set, so it just made the most sense. It was literally the only way I could get here in time. Those sheets in the bedroom—deliciously silky," Raquel says as she sips her tea. Clementine's face is tomato red, and Christine watches her grip her knife. She closes her eyes and takes a deep breath. Raquel quickly turns her attention toward Christine, baring her teeth in an eager smile. "Anyway, have we met? I'm Raquel."

Christine always finds it funny when celebrities introduce themselves. As if everyone in the room doesn't know everything about Raquel, down to what smoothie she ordered at Erewhon last Tuesday. Almond Butter Blast, if anyone was wondering.

"This is Christine Russo. She works for *Bespoke Weddings*," Lyle answers for her. "She's covering this weekend."

Raquel beams at Christine. "Ah, give Queen Sandy a big kiss for me, please! Love her!" Raquel squeezes her arm.

"I will," Christine lies, imagining giving Sandra a big kiss and then promptly being carried out by security.

"Good." Raquel takes another sip of her tea and closes her eyes in satisfaction. "Mm, that first hit of caffeine in the bloodstream—there's nothing like it, is there?" Nobody comments on this, so Raquel continues. "Anyway, how's G.B. doing? Adjusting to the time change okay?"

A flurry of panicked stares ping-pong across the table.

It's an innocent enough question on Raquel's part, but Christine feels herself buckling under the weight of it. The gravity of what she's been a part of and the implications it holds for the future of her career—*her life*—come crashing down on her. She starts to feel nauseated.

"Gloria is resting," Clementine says.

Lyle takes a big bite out of her scone. "This is delicious. Have you tried the blueberry, Raquel?" The starlet ignores her, turning toward the bartender, who is approaching with a tray of mimosas.

"Good morning, ladies," Danny says in his cheery Irish brogue. "I believe we have a bride to celebrate—slainte!" He smiles, revealing a dimple that Christine didn't clock the night before, as he puts the drinks down on the table.

"How thoughtful—thank you," Maggie responds, as everyone silently accepts their mimosa. The mother of the bride is doing a good job holding it together, but Christine notices how her once loud and lively presence has become more muted. Once Danny is gone, the silence at the table grows louder when only Raquel reaches for her mimosa.

"What's gotten into everyone?" Raquel laughs. "Is the jet lag really that bad? If I didn't know any better, I'd think I was at a funeral."

Christine feels bile in the back of her throat.

"Excuse me," she says quickly, scooting out of her chair and making a beeline for the powder room before anyone can interject. Once she's in the comfort of the closed stall, she puts her head in her hands and lets her first tears fall, her body expelling all the pent-up anger, sadness, and stress of the morning. Then the door to the ladies' room opens, and someone turns the lock. She chokes on the sudden rush of fear that interrupts her sobs.

"Christine," she hears Lyle snap. "You need to get it together, sister." Her voice is firm, but breathy, betraying a small trace of anxiety.

"I can't do this. I am not cut out for this. I did not sign up *for this*," Christine sobs.

"Neither did I," Lyle snips back, her limited-edition key lime–green Manolo Blahniks hovering at the base of Christine's stall door. "Yet here we both are."

"I wish I never stepped foot in this castle. I want to go home," Christine sniffles.

"Well, people in hell want ice water, but that doesn't mean they get it!" Lyle snaps.

"What does that even mean?" Christine sobs, her brain too foggy to demystify Lyle's wild array of Southern phrases.

"You just—" Lyle pauses and lowers her voice. "You need to be careful now. I'm not sure if you've fully processed what's going on, but none of us are safe. This family . . ." She trails off. "They make their problems disappear." Lyle's voice wobbles. "So don't become a problem, okay? Become an asset."

"How do I do that?" Christine knows she sounds like a whiny teenager now, but she can't help it—that's how she feels. She's due a moment of self-pity after all the work she did and sacrifices she made to get here. And for what? To be implicated in a murder investigation? It's all too much. She lets out another long sob.

"Not crying in the bathroom would be a good start," Lyle says. "But I don't know, just . . . try and figure out what's going on—get any information you can and hold it close. That's what I've done. You need leverage, you need to be one step ahead of them, always. That's the game, that's always been the game with Gloria, now more than ever, I guess." Her voice drops into a faint whisper. "That's how you get through this weekend in one piece."

Christine lets her words sink in, forcing herself to process the reality of her situation.

"Okay." Christine sniffles, rising off the toilet seat. "Okay, I'll try." She hears Lyle unlatch the lock on the bathroom door.

"Good," she says. "And just . . . be careful, okay? Don't trust anyone."

Christine's body tenses up. She sits on the toilet, unmoving, listening to the *click-clack* of Lyle's heels as she exits the bathroom.

Eventually, Christine pulls herself out of the stall, pats her face with a soft hand towel, and looks in the mirror. As she fixes her mascara and reapplies her lipstick, her mind works through her options. She could try to flee, but even if she makes it to the airport, she doubts the family will let her leave the country. They have powerful friends everywhere, many of whom are descending upon Ireland at this very moment.

For argument's sake, say she does make it back to the United States—that will just delay the inevitable. At the very least, they'll ruin her career like Ben threatened, and at the most . . . Well, she doesn't want to think about that. She feels herself breaking again remembering the risks she took to get here, to secure Gloria's attention—but through the sadness and anger, one of her mom's tried-and-true inspirational quotes reaches her: the only way out is through. And Christine has to get through this—she *can* get through this.

Taking a shaky breath, she plunges back into the party. The brunch table has been cleared of teacups and scones, replaced by more mimosas and a chilling bottle of Dom Pérignon from the hotel's seemingly endless supply of high-end alcohol.

"I think that's enough champagne for me," Jane says sullenly. "I'm going to go have a nap and try to unwind before it's time to get ready for tonight." The bride's eyes flit around the room. The brunch has come to an end, and the first wedding guests are beginning to trickle into the parlor to say their hellos. Jane's gloomy presence is certainly enough to raise eyebrows, so nobody fights her on leaving.

"That's a good plan, honey. It's been quite the morning," Maggie says, and warmly rubs her daughter's back.

"I suppose we'll stay here and greet everyone for you, then?" Lyle sneers as Jane leaves the table.

Raquel has already taken it upon herself to be the first to start mingling with the new arrivals. Leaning over the table next to theirs, she laughs loudly, speaking with a dapper balding man who, if Christine's not mistaken, might be a member of the British royal family.

"Christine," Clementine says, "would you mind tracking down that bartender? I think he trotted off to the pub down the hall. We'll need more drinks circulating here as people continue to arrive." Now that Elliot is . . . *otherwise engaged* . . . Christine realizes she is the closest thing the family has to hired help.

"Sure," Christine agrees, eager for any excuse to leave this table. As she gets out of her chair, she watches Trey waltz into the room and Raquel's eyes light up. Christine is almost knocked down as the blurred vision of dark curls and sequins rushes to embrace the father of the groom.

The laughter and chatter of the guests fade as Christine makes her way down the corridor toward the pub. The wind outside causes the castle to creak and moan, almost making it feel like they're all stuck on a ship. Relieved to be alone, Christine takes her time walking down the hall, assessing the antique knight's armor and the moody oil paintings that line the castle walls. After this morning, everything looks much less *luxury hotel* and much more *haunted mansion*.

She's just about to reach the pub doors when she hears whispers coming from the library on her right, so she decides to take a quick peek into the mahogany-paneled room. Below the large windows under the darkening sky, she sees Ben and Graham speaking in hushed tones.

"Graham, you have to trust me on this. It's the only way we can get out of here unscathed," she hears Ben say. Graham doesn't face him; instead he stares into the flames in the stone fireplace.

"I just don't think I can make it through this weekend acting like everything is fine when everything is so . . . fucked," Graham says, his voice breaking. "We've just lost our grandmother. She was possibly, well, *you know* . . . And I'm supposed to just go through with this wedding like everything's normal?" Graham flings himself into a burgundy leather armchair. "I know Jane thinks it's what Gran would want, but I don't know if I can do it."

"If you don't, we all end up broke or in jail, or likely both," Ben snaps. "Don't worry about the legality of it all. You can still change your mind. The marriage needs to be filed in the US anyway—this is all just a show."

"You're such a dick," Graham groans. "My apprehension about going along with your plan to *withhold information from the authorities* has nothing to do with my love for Jane," Graham grunts at his brother.

"I didn't mean it that way—I just wanted to take some of the pressure off. If certain things come to light . . ." Ben trails off. Graham gets up, his face frozen in a frown.

"You think she did this? That's quite a statement coming from you, Ben. Your rap sheet would be longer than the Bible if it wasn't for Gran's money." Graham narrows his eyes at his brother. Ben doesn't say anything.

Graham continues. "Maybe whoever *actually* did this is trying to do just what you're doing . . . trying to stop Jane and I from being together." Graham mutters to himself as he walks to the window; a crack of lightning illuminates the dark sky as rain starts to pour. The castle lights flicker.

"Graham, you know I just want what's best for you. You can't blame me for not fully trusting her. She just kind of popped up out of nowhere, your central casting dream girl, and then you guys, like, immediately got engaged. Did you ever stop to think—"

"Enough," Graham growls.

"Okay, okay," Ben says. He tries a softer approach. "Listen, Jane aside, you've been on edge since we got here. Since before any of the shit this morning. What's going on? You know you can tell me." He walks toward Graham, and Christine leans in closer, straining to hear the conversation as they move farther away. She can barely make out their two forms in the shadows of the stormy sky.

"You know exactly why I've been on edge," Graham snaps. "Are you going to tell me what really happened that night, Ben? Why you showed up to the hotel blackout drunk with—" Graham's voice shakes.

Ben starts to say something, but he's interrupted by another crack of lightning. All the castle lights go out. Christine hears a few faint screams from down the hall.

"What the hell was that?" Ben curses. "What's going on?"

Christine senses that the brothers are moving toward the door. She turns to leave, but her eyes have not yet adjusted to the dark. When she turns around, the lights flicker on, and she realizes that she's stumbled right into Trey Ripton.

NINE

# TREY

Five Months Earlier
New York City

PEOPLE SAY THERE IS NO way Trey can possibly remember the moment he was born, but they're wrong. He wishes he could forget his eyes opening in shock under the bright fluorescent lights of the hospital on that July morning in Charleston, but the memory is visceral. He remembers being placed into Gloria Beaufort's arms, the two of them looking at each other, and thinking: *There must have been some mistake.* It was the first of many times he shriveled under his mother's gaze. The most recent being this morning, during their legal briefing with Chase & Brown after receiving a class action notice. Trey always knew that he wasn't cut out to inherit the Glo empire. Now everybody else knows it too. Including his own son, who also happens to be general counsel of Glo. He grimaces, thinking of the look Ben gave him on the call this morning—like he wanted to jump through the screen and choke him. But his son remained silent, letting their defense attorneys take the lead.

Trey puts his head in his hands, running his fingers through what used to be a thick head of brown hair but is now a thick head of very expensive hair plugs, and curses his bad judgment. He should never have signed a contract with Broadway Manufacturing. If he'd done just a little research, he'd have known they were slimy and untrustworthy.

It was their idea to cut corners on the formulation to make Gloss Drops more profitable, not his. But to admit that would be to admit he didn't do his due diligence as CEO. Ultimately, it was still he who put his mother's company in peril.

Of course, he could blame the person who connected him with Broadway Manufacturing in the first place . . . but that is too embarrassing to even fathom. And what would it matter anyway? If he pointed the finger and said, "But they introduced me to this bad company!" he'd still be legally liable. He is still CEO. All he'd do is alienate someone he admires and respects dearly. Trey sighs, gazing out the window of his West Village brownstone as his gardener trims the hedges that line his perfectly maintained courtyard. As it always is with his life, everything looks absolutely perfect—and he's had nothing to do with any of it.

Trey sighs again and looks at his Rolex—his father's before it was his—to check the time. John Ripton II: another man who couldn't live up to Gloria Beaufort's expectations. He wonders, for the thousandth time, what his life would have looked like if his dad had lived. If he hadn't died so suddenly when Trey was just a small boy, leaving him alone with a mother more interested in her own success than in her son. Would he still be in this position?

He hauls himself out of his leather swivel chair, trots down the sisal runner on his spiral staircase, out into his sparkling black-and-white tiled foyer, and straight into his idling Lincoln Town car. Trey doesn't fully grasp the extravagance of his life—and how could he? It's all he's ever known. For him, the multiple properties, private jet, celebrity friends, and exotic vacations are merely the backdrop of what he considers an utterly lonely and rudderless existence. Cue the tiny violins.

His phone buzzes nonstop as he inches uptown. It's mostly missed calls from his son, Ben, and texts asking where the hell he is. Trey types back, On my way. He still has to go through the motions of his job, even though his days are numbered—and that requires being on set for the shoot of Glo's new fragrance campaign with Raquel Williams. Which started an hour ago and was also his idea.

The car inches uptown toward the Rainbow Room, where he's sure the cameras have already started rolling, where people are probably whispering about him being late *again*. He doesn't care though, and with good reason this time. All he can think about is his own impending doom. He could tell trouble was brewing soon after Gloss Drops hit the shelves. Several Glo employees—including Lyle—told him they needed to pull the product from the market and reformulate, but he ignored every appeal. Business was booming! He wanted to continue riding that wave as long as possible; his impulse always toward what feels good in the moment, no matter the long-term consequences.

And Trey would never admit it, but deep down, a part of him wanted this to happen; the small, boyish part of him that wanted his mother to *finally* pay attention to him. His therapist says he tends to engage in self-destructive behavior. He's starting to think she might be right. Maybe he shouldn't have fired her after she suggested family therapy. But honestly, the last thing he wants is to spend more time with his dysfunctional family.

The driver blares his horn at an e-biker who cut off their car, and Trey curses under his breath as the minutes tick by. In some ways, the meeting this morning had been a relief. It was finally out there, what Glo—and by proxy, he—had done. They were poisoning people for profit, and now there was proof. It was looking like people would be willing to testify—and not just disgruntled customers: doctors, scientists . . . possibly even former Glo employees. The "situation," as he'd called it in the last few meetings with legal, had become a class action lawsuit the company could no longer ignore.

Trey would step down as CEO by November 1, just after Graham and Jane's wedding. Honestly, he's surprised it took his mother this long to oust him from the C-suite. She never thought he was capable of making a sandwich, let alone running a billion-dollar company—it's like she wanted this to happen too. Though her stony glare this morning on Zoom certainly insinuated otherwise.

The real question that remains is who will replace him? From Trey's perspective, it looks like Gloria has been grooming Lyle for the job ever since she married into the family. Trey's heart aches momentarily for his son; not being named CEO will be such a blow to his fragile ego. Ben is so bright, so passionate about his role as GC. He'd graduated from Harvard Law with honors. When did it all go wrong for him? When did he start drinking so much? Now he is just another failure to add to Trey's growing list of shortcomings.

The car comes to a halt outside 30 Rockefeller Plaza, and Trey grunts a thank-you at his driver before lurching out of the car and into the building. He buries his head in the top of his jacket, his body already preparing itself to hide from cameras that might be watching him; he's afraid the news of the class action lawsuit could break at any moment even though the plan is to try to keep it quiet and settle out of court privately.

According to Tania Abdullahi from the legal offices of Chase & Brown, their defense would be to claim ignorance, to lean into the angle that even though Trey is the acting CEO of the company, he is essentially a dunce who signed off on things he didn't understand, which isn't entirely untrue—but it doesn't seem like much of a legal defense when the prosecution has witnesses ready to spell out just how the company ignored that certain chemicals in their Gloss Drops are directly linked to infertility.

Trey waltzes over to the private Rainbow Room elevator door that's being held open for him by someone from Glo's security detail. His ears pop as he is catapulted to the top of the building, and he thinks, fleetingly, of how quickly the elevator levers could snap and he could hurtle toward the center of the earth. Would that be such a bad thing at this point?

The elevator pings, and he arranges his face into its usual unbothered, easygoing appearance. They'll have to settle the lawsuit, and it will be catastrophic for the company. The question will be: Can they survive it? The doors open, revealing his son, Ben, looking as stressed and unhappy as Trey feels himself.

"Where have you been? You're over an hour late and now we'll have to pay the crew overtime. Taylor is going to be pissed," Ben hisses.

Trey rolls his eyes, already dreading another conversation with their CFO, Miriam Taylor, about cutting costs. Look at where cutting costs has gotten them so far.

"I'm here now," he says, and claps his son on the back. He walks past him and into the shoot.

The Rainbow Room is one of those places that takes your breath away, no matter how many times you've been lucky enough to step into it, but on this bright spring morning, it's nothing short of spectacular. The floor-to-ceiling windows reveal a sea of silver and gray buildings glittering like polished knives under the bright blue sky. Trey is convinced there is a shade of blue sky that is only visible in New York; it's a sky fueled by ambition, jacked up on coffee, heading to a make-or-break job interview or audition. It's a sky that's a league above the rest, untouched by rejection or self-doubt, a sky that gives the people who live under it the audacity to unapologetically pursue their dreams.

It's the same color blue as Raquel's bralette.

"Hello, gorgeous!" Trey feels his heart swell, his mind mercifully muddled with lust for the model turned actor (who recently turned twenty-seven) in front of him.

"Oh my God, hi," Raquel squeals, and runs over to him, enveloping him in a huge hug. He looks into her young, beautiful eyes. Ben marches toward him, determined as ever to ruin the moment.

"Dad," his son cuts in, "you remember Giovanni, right?" Trey reluctantly releases Raquel and shakes hands with the hunky photographer who'll be shooting Raquel for their perfume campaign.

"Pleasure." Trey shakes his hand and the man smiles.

"Thank you for this opportunity, sir. I'm, ah, very excited to be here," the photographer says in an Italian accent.

"Of course, of course. Our marketing team just raves about your work," Trey says. "Now let's get started."

"Brava, brava." The photographer claps his hands, and people spring into action.

Trey can't keep his eyes off Raquel. He loses himself in her beauty, happily letting the worldly problems of this morning float up into the clouds above 30 Rock. Whenever something bad happens in his life, instead of looking within, or leaning on his family—Trey prefers to lean on a beautiful young woman he barely knows. So, when the shoot is over, he takes Raquel to dinner at Carbone for the world to see. He won't remember, until the dessert course, that today is his thirty-second wedding anniversary.

# TEN

# CHRISTINE

Friday, October 17, 2025
Afternoon of Rehearsal Dinner

"WELL, WELL, WELL." TREY SMILES devilishly. "You can't just throw yourself at me, Christine. I am a married man." He laughs, his grip on her wrist tightening. Christine is still in such shock—surprised she didn't see even a glimmer of Trey approaching her—so much so that she doesn't fully register his inappropriate comment. It's as if the father of the groom just appeared from out of nowhere. She thinks back to the rumors of a secret castle passageway that Elliot mentioned this morning, which obviously is a crazy jump to make, but still. Everything is starting to feel spooky.

"I—I—" Christine falters. "I was—looking for Danny, the bartender. I got turned around. This place is a maze."

Trey's eyes shrink into tiny black slits. "You weren't eavesdropping on a private conversation, were you, sweetie?"

"Everything okay here?" Danny suddenly materializes in the hall, his tone upbeat. "We're just about to set up a little cocktail bar in the parlor for the arriving guests, if that's what you're checking on, Mr. Ripton." His eyes briefly land on Trey's grasp on Christine.

"Right," Trey says as he lets go of her. She feels the blood rush back to her wrist. "We just got a bit turned around in the dark—didn't we?" He smiles, and Christine tries not to wither under his gaze.

"Ah, yeah, sorry about that," Danny says. "This place may be equipped with all the modern luxuries, but at its core, Ballymoon is still a medieval castle. Eleventh century, to be exact. It's amazing they figured out a way to wire electricity here at all." Danny balances a tray of Guinness pints in the air and cocks his head to the side to knock his shaggy light brown hair out of his face.

Trey ignores the bartender. "Boys," he calls out to his sons in the library. "Hannah Sibel just arrived. She's a new board member at Glo and I want to introduce you." Ben follows his father down the hall, and Graham trots after them. Christine's heart is still thumping as if she's just finished a 5k—or it's what she imagines that might feel like. She's more of a Pilates girl, which, come to think of it, probably won't be much use to her in her current situation. She should have taken martial arts at the YMCA like her dad suggested when she told her parents she'd be moving to New York City for college.

"Are you okay?" Danny asks, lowering his voice as the three Ripton men make their way down the hall.

"Yeah, thanks," she says, trying to sound casual. "Just got turned around in the dark." She rubs her wrist where Trey grabbed her.

"Got it," Danny says, clearly not believing her. "Are you a part of the family?" He shifts his tray of drinks to his other hand, his eyes drifting toward her reddened wrist, clearly confused about how she fits into all of this—which is fair, because so is she.

"No, no, definitely not," Christine says. "I'm writing an article about the wedding." She never leads with *Bespoke*—always finding it's cooler when someone pulls the information out of her. This way, she's able to pretend to be low-key, even though she's never been low-key one day in her life.

"Ah, so you're a journalist, then?" Danny asks. "For what publication?"

"I'm an editor at *Bespoke Weddings*," she replies, waiting for him to look impressed.

"Wow." Danny whistles. "Can't say I'm surprised you have such a glamorous gig, though. Has anyone ever told you you're a dead ringer for Emma Stone?" He smiles. She can't tell if he means it as a compliment or is merely making an observation. Either way, she feels awkward.

"Ha! No, that is a first for me." Christine laughs a bit anxiously. "Well, anyway, you're just the man I was looking for. I am here to relay the message that they need more drinks in the parlor."

"Message received, madame." Danny gives her a mock salute.

"Thanks." She smooths down her silky trousers with a shimmy before walking away, just in case his eyes linger. Then, impulsively, she turns back around.

"Actually, one more thing. You seem to know a lot about this castle. Have you heard of a hidden passageway that runs through Ballymoon's walls?" she asks. If there really is a tunnel system, she figures, then it's definitely a clue to how a murderer could get around the castle unnoticed. Danny stares at her for a moment, his mouth hanging open slightly. Is she crazy, or did she see a millisecond of recognition cross his face at her question? But then Danny knits his brow in confusion, hand slightly wavering under the heavy tray of Guinness.

"Sorry, what?" he asks, and Christine is flushed with embarrassment.

*Great, now he thinks you're a lunatic.*

"Oh, never mind," she says, and tries to laugh it off. "Just some local gossip Elliot mentioned this morning that I was going to include in my article. Just wondering if you'd heard anything about it. Thought it would be fun to add a quippy line like 'a castle complete with a secret escape tunnel . . . perfect for brides who get cold feet' or something, if the rumors had any truth to them." She takes out a lip gloss to occupy her mouth and keep herself from saying anything else stupid.

"Secret passageway." Danny rubs his chin stubble with his free hand, smirking. "Can't say I've come across it yet—but let me know if you do.

I'd be keen to check it out." He smiles, and his eyes do that crinkly thing again.

"Danny, mate, I'm dying over here. Some help, yeah?" Neil groans as he passes by, carrying two trays of dirty plates and glasses through the swinging bar doors. Another auburn-haired waitress breezes by them looking equally stressed, balancing a tray of what look like spicy margaritas. She shoots Danny a dirty look.

"Coming, coming—and honestly, who orders spicy margaritas in Ireland?" Danny shouts as he walks back toward the pub, before turning to Christine and saying, "Hope you'll stop by later for a pint, yeah? If it's Ballymoon lore you're after, I can definitely help with that."

Christine doesn't make any promises, but instead offers him a friendly wave and a quick "Thanks!" before trotting down the hall, heart racing, Lyle's words, "You need leverage," echoing in her ears.

Danny hesitated when she asked about the passageway—which could mean something. And if there's any truth to these whisperings about the secret tunnel system inside the castle walls, Gloria's murderer could have used it to get around invisibly last night . . . and could use it to strike again.

As Christine makes her way down the hall, she stops to look at a portrait of Brian Boru hanging precariously on a stone wall. The king's vibe is definitely giving the eleventh-century equivalent of "drives an obnoxiously loud Porsche and won't stop talking to you about crypto." So she kind of *gets* why the queen might have helped kill him. Just as she leans in to see if the king has a unibrow or if it's just the shadowy lighting in the hallway, the stone wall behind the painting caves in, revealing a door that sends Christine stumbling backward in shock.

"Oh! Sorry, love! Didn't mean to give you a scare," Cheryl from the front desk says brightly, registering the bewilderment on Christine's face. "Back office has a bit of a fun entrance with this hidden door. This place is full of funny little nooks and crannies." She knocks on the portion of the wall from where she's just appeared. Christine tries to steady her breathing after yet another unsettling interaction with Cheryl.

"No problem," she whispers, and then scurries past before the woman can say anything else, more convinced than ever that the passageway *does* exist.

Christine pauses outside the parlor as a deep roll of thunder vibrates through the castle, causing various silver and china and crystal (and Christine) to clamor and shake.

The crisp sheets and the fancy champagne and the fluffy hotel robes and sweet-smelling jasmine are no longer able to mask the overwhelming sensation that Ballymoon has witnessed unspeakable darkness.

. . . and that Gloria Beaufort's blood was not the first spilled within these castle walls.

ELEVEN

# GLORIA

### Five Months Earlier

GLORIA ENDS THE ZOOM CALL with Chase & Brown by slamming her laptop shut, because she's eighty-five years old and she couldn't care less about learning how to properly use this new technology—and why should she? Plus, slamming the laptop felt more dramatic, and more appropriate given the circumstances.

Trey, her only son—*her heir!*—has put her life's work in jeopardy—and for what? Gloss Drops? Some trend for teens who want their eyes to look dewy . . . What happened to getting misty-eyed the old-fashioned way? *Through tears.* Gloria is certainly ready to make some people cry. She picks up the landline in her office and dials Jeremy.

"You have access to every employee's email, right?" she barks at Glo's Chief Technology Officer—his title itself another techy thing Gloria doesn't fully care to understand.

"Theoretically, yes, but company policy—" Jeremy starts to say, and Gloria cuts him off.

"Jeremy"—she breathes heavily into the phone—"*I am the company.*" She may have made Trey CEO on paper, but she's still chairwoman of the board. And everybody at Glo is well aware of who calls the shots . . . though apparently not when it came to Gloss Drops. Her body shakes with rage.

"Right." Jeremy sighs on the other end of the line, resigned to losing the battle before the war's even begun. "How can I help?"

Gloria leans back in her swivel chair, seething. "I need you to go through Trey's email inbox," she says, "and find out who he's been conversing with about the Gloss Drops over the past two years. Find out who connected him with Broadway Manufacturing. I want every email—printed out and in my office by end of day. And this is very *sensitive*, Jeremy. Don't delegate. Do it yourself."

Gloria has a hunch. She knows her son is not exactly winning any prizes in the morality department, but she also knows he's . . . well, not a mastermind either. And this Gloss Drops formulation—the way it was concocted, planned, and artfully hidden from her—she knows it was not Trey's doing. Someone put the idea in his head, someone helped him pull this off behind her back—someone he is now trying to protect.

"I'm looking right now," Jeremy says, dragging out the words as he speaks. Gloria can hear him typing in the background. She cocks an eyebrow, impressed. She still hasn't gotten used to the speed of modern technology.

"There aren't that many emails about it—a few with Lyle, voicing her concern about phthalates on the record, and . . ." He trails off, and Gloria's heart sinks. She should have just made Lyle CEO right after she married Ben, but Gloria just couldn't bring herself to disappoint her son. She couldn't find the right moment. She had been a bad mom to Trey. She knows that now, fifty-three years too late. Promoting him to CEO, if only in title, felt like an appropriate consolation prize. Clearly, that was a massive mistake on her part.

"Oh!" Jeremy says, perking up. "I found a few in his recently deleted files from someone else . . . That's weird—" Jeremy mumbles, but Gloria cuts him off.

She lowers her voice to a growl. "From who?"

TWELVE

# CHRISTINE

Friday, October 17, 2025
Afternoon of Rehearsal Dinner

CHRISTINE HURRIES DOWN THE COBBLESTONE path in front of Ballymoon Castle on her way to meet with the mother of the bride. It feels wrong to continue conducting interviews given the circumstances, but, well, it's still her job, and probably the only way she can try to figure out what happened to Gloria Beaufort. She stops briefly to gape at the lush landscape in front of her. The walkway is lined with tall oak trees that are clearly meticulously maintained; Christine wonders what the path might have looked like during the reign of Brian Boru and Gormlaith, a time when the trimmed-back branches were welded together, a wild, dark blur of various shades of green, like a watercolor painting.

She checks the time on her phone again and picks up the pace. Her little aside with Danny has her running behind schedule. Luckily, she switched into her Adidas after the bridal brunch so she's able to crank up her power walk. Sandra would become physically ill if she saw Christine's outfit—beat-up running shoes, silky trousers, and an oversize hoodie covering her lightweight top—but again, there wasn't time to do a full outfit change. The outfit is almost weird enough to look purposeful—and she's grateful to the fashion world for the current "ugly is in" trend. Lost in her own thoughts, Christine is caught off guard when a scruffy man emerges from the bushes at the base of the castle and steps right in front of her. She stumbles back.

"Sorry if I scared ya, love," he says, observing the shock on her face. "I'm the groundskeeper—just trimming back some of these calendula. They grow like weeds!" He laughs and rubs a hand on his heavily patched jeans. He has a kind, creased face and the lean frame of someone who spends his days working the land.

"No problem," she says, trying to keep her voice even.

"You have a lovely day now," he says, and tips his cap to her.

She picks up her pace. *It was just the groundskeeper,* she tells herself. *Relax.* Christine takes a deep breath and tries to calm her nerves, but the truth is, anyone she comes into contact with at this point really *could* be a murderer. She can't completely spiral, though—that won't help anything. She needs to do what she does best before deciding who is worthy of her fear: some serious digging.

A chat with Maggie will be a good palate cleanser after brunch with the Riptons. Jane's mother can offer an outsider's perspective on what it's been like to be thrown into these ... less-than-ideal ... family dynamics.

At the end of the path, Christine is met with an archway constructed of wild and unruly olive branches leading into the Foxglove Garden, nestled at the base of the Ballymoon lough. Beyond the branches, Elliot's staff members buzz around in preparation for tonight's rehearsal dinner. Christine walks through the curve of the arch, as if she's stepping into the pages of a Brothers Grimm storybook. Even in mid-October, and probably thanks to the heavy rain, the garden still looks lush. Set against the autumn trees, purple and white wildflowers stretch toward the sky. Hot pink gardenias coil around each other and spill out onto the path. The beauty is so otherworldly, so vivid with swirling colors, that Christine momentarily thinks she might still be a little drunk from the mimosas. She reaches out to touch a flower but is stopped by a shout.

"Don't touch that!" Maggie waves to her from a folding table near the back of the garden.

"Oh, sorry, I—" Christine blinks, pulling her hand back from the rose she was admiring.

"You've got to be careful of thorns, hon. The most beautiful ones are always the most dangerous, aren't they?" Maggie puts her gardening shears in her apron, her simple pink shift dress from earlier at brunch still on underneath. She strikes Christine as the type of woman who finds an affordable dress that she likes and buys it in five colors—like her own little personal uniform. Maggie walks over to Christine and exposes the thorny side of the beautiful rose she had almost picked.

"Thanks," Christine says, and relaxes. "I don't think I could stomach the sight of even one more drop of blood," she whispers. The mother of the bride gives Christine a bear hug that makes her feel right at home—the kind of hug her mom would give her when she'd come home from college for the summer.

"How are you doing, sweetie? I hope you're trying to enjoy yourself despite everything." Maggie gives a sad pout. Her comment strikes Christine as being a bit off, but she can't think of what a normal thing to say would be given their current situation.

"It's been a lot. If you want to talk—"

Maggie cuts her off. "I've been better, but chin up, buttercup, right? The show must go on!" Her voice pitches up an octave as she tries to make herself sound cheery. She waves Christine to follow her as she returns to her workstation, where she is currently arranging primroses in mason jars. "Anyway, we better change the subject to something a bit more festive." The mother of the bride's eyes rove around the garden, reminding Christine that they're not alone.

"Elliot!" Maggie calls as she clips the ends off a few flowers. Christine looks up to see the wedding planner and a handful of his staffers overseeing the bar setup near the Greenhouse Restaurant entrance. It's a beautiful, verdant event space made entirely of glass—and a perfect backup venue if the weather doesn't cooperate tonight to hold the rehearsal dinner outside in the garden.

"Do you have any extra scissors up there?" Maggie shouts.

"Yes, one second," Elliot calls, and trots toward the ladies holding an extra pair of shears. Christine can hear the hint of annoyance in his voice. The wedding planner is *not* used to having one of his MOB's be so . . . *involved*.

"Time to get snipping," Elliot says as he hands Christine the scissors. His face betrays nothing about the events of this morning, only adding to Christine's unease.

"I'm a bit of a novice when it comes to flower arranging," Christine says with a smile. "My mom didn't exactly have a green thumb growing up. We could barely keep a basil plant alive for more than a few days." She picks up her shears anyway, ready to give it a try.

Maggie laughs. "It's not as hard as you think!"

Similar to Elliot, Christine's never covered a *Bespoke* wedding where the mother of the bride rolls up her sleeves on the big day. She appreciates that Maggie is making a very pointed effort not to let the Riptons change her.

"You can start with the roses—just cut them at an angle. That helps them absorb more water—and remember, be careful of the thorns." Maggie winks and snips the stem off a pink rose with force, handing a bunch of sweet-smelling flowers to Christine and Elliot.

Christine glances at Maggie, and realizes, up close, the woman looks a bit shipwrecked—dark circles under her eyes and deep worry lines etched on her forehead. But that doesn't take away from her natural beauty. Christine marvels at Maggie's thick wavy hair and golden skin, even though both are a little worn from years of tanning and bleaching. She's the kind of woman about whom people would say, "In her day, she was a knockout," and that beauty still radiates from within her. For a moment, they work in silence, Maggie and Christine snipping and Elliot organizing the fresh cuts. Until Elliot squints his eyes, judging his staffers' cocktail table placement.

"Neil, Felicity—I said *on the right*," he snaps. "Be right back." Christine bristles at Elliot's tone, her mind conjuring up images of his temple throbbing as he shouted into Gloria's suite.

Alone with Maggie now, she clears her throat and says, "So tell me about Jane. What was it like raising our bride?" She dusts the discarded flower stems off her notebook. Maggie eyes it warily.

"Oh my . . . how do I sum up twenty-eight years of Jane Murphy?" She laughs. "She's got that *special something*, my daughter. People are just drawn to her, like fireflies to a lantern." Maggie fluffs some flowers in a jar and sets it to the side. Christine admires the tiny array of pink cowslips and delicate white Easter lilies that looks like it would cost at least one hundred dollars from an overpriced florist in the concourse of her office building back in Manhattan.

The mother of the bride takes a noticeable pause before continuing. "It wasn't always easy, though. The teenage years were challenging," she chuckles. "Do you have to write down the conversation? I sort of thought our 'interview' would be more like pictures of the flowers and links to my favorite gardening tools." She laughs again, louder and more frantic this time. "Sorry, I'm just afraid of saying the wrong thing." Maggie clips a bright purple flower and plops it in a jar, but she's made it too short and it looks odd among the other flowers. She pulls it out.

"Oh, it just helps me remember all the details," Christine says. "Don't worry, anything that goes to publication will have to be fully signed off on by you first." It's a bit of a fib on Christine's part, but there's some truth to it. Sandra would never send anything to print without Gloria Beaufort's approval. And then an icy splash of reality reminds her that Gloria Beaufort does not exist anymore.

"The photographers will grab some gorgeous shots of this garden, which will be the bulk of the rehearsal dinner spread anyway. And send me any links to gardening tools you have! We'll include them in the article. But for now, back to Jane if you don't mind." Christine slaps on a smile and hopes Maggie doesn't notice her hands shaking as she picks up her notebook.

"Okay, great. Um, well, anyway, I raised Jane on my own. We lost her dad in a car accident before Jane was even born. Seamus and I had just gotten engaged . . . I was only eighteen at the time. It was a terrible start on my road to motherhood, to say the least." Maggie adjusts the white grosgrain ribbon on one of her jars, making the bow a little fuller.

"I'm so sorry to hear that." Christine's heart goes out to the young single mom.

"Thank you. It was a long time ago, though that pain never really leaves you," Maggie says sadly. "But Jane was such a beautiful, bright child. Always really shy, but so sweet." Maggie travels back in time, eyes welling up at the thought of her young daughter.

"What was she like as a teenager? You mentioned those years were challenging," Christine presses.

"Just the usual high school stuff that we don't need to get into. Stolen bra from Victoria's Secret—hardly anything noteworthy." She fluffs a beautiful yellow flower in the jar she is working on. Elliot huffs back toward them after giving Neil a stern talking-to, probably returning just to micromanage Christine's interview. She tries not to let his presence bother her.

"Right. Typical teen stuff." Christine doesn't press her again. "When did you first meet Graham? What was your initial impression of the couple?"

"Let me do those ones." Elliot takes over Christine's flowers, straining to be polite. She happily relinquishes the dahlias she was butchering.

"I didn't meet him until very recently. Just last week, actually, if you can believe it." Maggie snorts, and Christine detects a note of hurt in her voice.

"Wow, really? You just met your daughter's fiancé a week before the wedding? Why the holdup?" The words tumble out before she can fully process how impolite she sounds. Elliot glares at her, but Maggie doesn't seem to take offense.

"Jane is very . . . independent." She sighs. "And we've had a history of fighting about her choice in boyfriends. Lots of not-great guys who

I wasn't crazy about. After a couple of big arguments, she said, 'Mom, I'm not going to introduce you to anyone else until I'm sure it's the real thing,' and I respected that. It was better for our relationship." Maggie doesn't look at her, but instead focuses intently on her next floral arrangement. It's almost as if she's talking to herself. Afraid to interrupt her unfiltered thoughts, Christine just nods.

"And the minute I met Graham I was just like—*wow*." Maggie grins. "He is just so lovely, even though it happened a little fast for my liking, I'm relieved Jane ended up with someone like him. He's a dream, right?" Maggie puts down her scissors suddenly. "Wait, you won't put that in the article, will you? About the ex-boyfriends? That was off the record," she says quickly. The blood drains from her face, diluting her complexion and taking it from a tan leather to more of a muted honey.

"Oh, of course not," Christine says. "I'll just say it was a whirlwind romance. When you know, you know—that type of thing."

"Good, yeah, that's right. That's what I meant." Maggie smiles shakily and fiddles with the chain around her neck. "Sorry, I didn't realize how nervous this interview would make me. I thought that the article would be more about the wedding itself and less about . . . personal stuff." Elliot narrows his eyes and looks directly at Christine as he pointedly snips the head off a rose.

"Oops," he says. Christine ignores his warning for her to stop prying and start asking questions about his tablescapes.

"And how has it been planning a wedding with the Riptons? I'd imagine it's all a bit overwhelming," Christine presses.

"Oh, it's been such fun!" Maggie says tightly, though Christine doubts this is true. "They're a beautiful and successful bunch, aren't they? But what I really love is their relationship with God. Make sure that's clear in your article." Maggie nods toward the notebook as if she wants Christine to write that down.

"Sure, of course. So, would you say that you connected with the family over your shared religious beliefs?"

Maggie puts the finishing touches on her jar before answering. Her arrangement is eccentric and whimsical, while Christine's and Elliot's look choppy and off-kilter.

"Yes," Maggie says finally. "A close relationship with God is very important to both families." She clutches her gold Saint Christopher medal for a moment as if to say a prayer. This seems to be Maggie's go-to move when she gets nervous. The irony of her statement that both families have "a close relationship with God" is not lost on Christine. *Now Gloria is even closer,* she thinks.

"I feel like I don't have much else to add, hon," Maggie says, and puts down her shears. "I know people say that Jane and Graham are a bit of a Cinderella story—single mom, busy nurse, kid who practically raised herself—but Jane had a great childhood. For the most part, we were happy. It was a rich and full life, before all this glitz and glam." Maggie picks up another jar and fills it with water from a glass pitcher on the table.

Christine nods her head. "How did you and Jane end up deciding on Ireland for the wedding, again? There is a family connection, right?" She pretends to forget Elliot's mention of Jane's late father from yesterday, curious what the mother of the bride has to say on the subject. Maggie hands off a few vases to one of Elliot's people, who have started circling the table.

"That was all Jane, actually. She wanted to have it here in honor of her father, which I was surprised by, because we never really talked about him growing up. Guess it was my way of processing the tragedy. But when she said Ireland, I didn't fight her. It's her day. And who wouldn't want to get married in a castle?" Maggie jokes, and Christine smiles warmly in response.

"Maggie, I'm sure Christine is dying to hear about your vision for the rehearsal night. Can you tell us a bit about what you have planned?" Elliot asks tersely, plopping a bright red flower into one of the jars. He shoots Christine a look.

"I figured the whole wedding weekend would be so ritzy, and I always thought we'd have a backyard wedding for Jane." Maggie lights up talking about her plan. "I love my garden and Jane does too . . . so I wanted to bring a little bit of that homey feel to the event. I even brought my own mason jars that I'd been saving for years—you know, just in case. Jane said it was silly to ship them all the way over here, but I insisted. I prefer doing things myself. I'm a doer." Maggie puffs out her chest with pride.

"I love that." Christine smiles. "And what's on the menu tonight?" Her stomach starts to grumble as something delicious wafts into the garden from the Greenhouse Restaurant kitchen.

"We're going with a classic American backyard barbecue . . . with an Irish twist. You'll have to wait and see, but I guarantee you won't leave hungry." Maggie puts the final touches on a jar by tying a bright pink ribbon around the top of the glass. Christine notices Jane stroll into the garden to assess the progress. Maggie waves to her daughter, who drifts toward them.

"Mom," Jane calls, "it's almost time for your hair appointment. I figured we could walk over together." The bride looks a bit more relaxed now in a matching white yoga set that highlights her lithe frame, but her eyes remain proof that the events of this morning actually happened—puffy and red-rimmed, with dark circles underneath.

"Perfect." Maggie gives her daughter a quick peck then looks back at Christine. "Any other questions? I've got to finally deal with this!" She points to the messy bun that sits on the top of her head and laughs, taking off her grass-stained apron and folding it over the table.

"I think I've got enough for now. Looking forward to tonight!" Christine closes her notebook, and Maggie gives her a hug.

"Thanks for squeezing this in, Christine." Elliot scoops up a handful of jars. "I hope your other interviews go just as well even when I'm not around to supervise." He means it as a joke, but Christine hears the edge in his voice. Maggie puts her arm around her daughter, and they turn to leave.

"Oh," Christine says quickly, "just one more thing for my notes. What did you say Jane's father's name was? I want to make sure we honor him appropriately in the feature."

Maggie's smile shrivels up. "Seamus. It *was* Seamus," she whispers, then turns her attention to the bar setup at the far end of the garden.

"Make sure you use the edible flowers in the Murphy Margarita. They're behind the cases of Merlot," she calls over to the barkeep, who is notably not Danny.

"Come on, Mom," Jane says. "We're going to be late." The bride successfully pulls her mother toward the exit, and they disappear down the path leading toward the castle. Christine closes her notebook, ready to follow them out through the garden's archway, but Elliot blocks her path.

"Christine, just a minute, please," he says through pursed lips. "The nature of your questions for Maggie were quite personal," he huffs, and cocks his hip. "I was under the impression that the focus of your article would be on the actual wedding events . . . not the private lives of my clients. Our team has worked tirelessly to make every detail of this weekend magazine-worthy and we deserve our moment." Elliot scowls. "Not to mention, I believe the family made their wishes for your article's subject matter *quite clear* this morning, don't you? Let's keep that all top-line."

Christine folds her arms over her chest. "Well, Elliot, *Bespoke Weddings* wants readers to get to know the people behind the party. That's what sells magazines." Sure, maybe she didn't need to ask *such* personal questions, but this is now about more than getting coverage for her article. She needs to know who she's dealing with here. She needs to protect herself.

"Right," he snorts. "Well, if you end up needing more information about the actual events you're here to capture, just give me a jingle." They glare at each other while Christine waits for Elliot to move out of the way, but he doesn't. She takes a step into his personal space.

"If *you* want to tell me what you were doing slamming the door to Gloria Beaufort's suite last night, why don't you give *me* a jingle?"

Christine finally reenters Ballymoon after navigating the maze that is Foxglove Garden—where she got lost not once but twice trying to find her way out. Eventually a hotel staffer took pity on her and led her back to the castle, and (unfortunately) right into the clutches of the overbearing front desk woman, Cheryl.

"How was your time in the garden? Isn't it beautiful?" Cheryl asks, rushing to greet Christine before she is able to make her way to the elevator bank.

"So gorgeous," Christine says quietly, still a little shaken. "It will photograph beautifully tonight." The woman smiles proudly, pulling down her too-tight hunter-green blazer as it rides up slightly over her stomach.

"I should think so. Voted most beautiful hotel garden in all of Ireland, three years running," she declares. Christine slowly inches backward toward the elevators.

"I can see why." Christine grins even though "most beautiful hotel garden in Ireland" seems like a pretty niche competition. She presses the elevator button repeatedly as the woman prattles on.

"Would you like to have a quick look at our spa?"

"Actually, I'll see it on the morning of the wedding," Christine says quickly. "Thanks though!" She gives a small wave as Cheryl disappears behind the sliding gold elevator doors.

When she finally reaches her suite, Christine slams the door and sinks down behind it. Heart pounding, the graveness of her error sinks in. *Did I seriously threaten Elliot Adler?* Groaning, she leans her head back against the door. She'll need to try to smooth things over with him before he gets in touch with Sandra. *Why on earth would Elliot kill Gloria Beaufort?* she chastises herself.

All she witnessed last night was an ill-timed argument with a disgruntled vendor. It happens all the time. Her phone pings with another text from Sandra—just a series of three question marks. Christine quickly responds: Sorry. All good here, working hard to soak up everything I can! MAGIC. She prays that the three question marks have nothing to do with her outburst at Elliot.

Good, Sandra responds instantly. I don't need to remind you that the stakes are VERY high.

Christine gives a sad laugh and thinks, *You certainly don't.* She sends a thumbs-up and closes her eyes. Naturally, Sandra is referring to her own job security and the fate of *Bespoke* now that upper management is sniffing around and saying things like "The magazine needs to appeal more to Gen Z" and "Have you considered getting *Bespoke Weddings* on TikTok?"

Christine pinches the bridge of her nose and closes her eyes. Her head hurts with the delayed hangover she knew was bound to hit after the amount of champagne she's consumed so far on this trip. There's no time for a nap—not that she'd sleep anyway. She has to head over to the church in just over an hour so she can interview Father Kenneth before the rehearsal begins. Hopefully her conversation with him will shed more light on the family and help her navigate this nightmare. Her meeting with Maggie was a bust. Besides Jane stealing a bra, and Maggie not wanting to talk about her dead fiancé, she didn't come across any useful information. All she did was ensure that Elliot will never want to work with her ever again, which will *not* be good for the future of her career. Christine feels her body tense up, already envisioning an enraged call from Sandra demanding she fix her relationship with "one of the elite wedding industry's most powerful players."

She pulls herself up off the floor and walks over to her bed, looking at it longingly. The hotel suite is pristine after a visit from housekeeping. On the edge of her crisply made sheets, she notices a tented piece of cream-colored paper. She picks it up, hoping to devour the chocolate that is surely underneath, realizing she's barely eaten at all today, but there's nothing. She knits her brow in confusion and opens up the note. Instead of the usual *Enjoy your stay! Turn down service will begin at whatever-o'clock*, it reads, *LOOK INTO SEAMUS O'REILLY* in an exaggerated block font.

Instantly, her fingers release the note like it's laced with poison. She watches it flutter to the floor, her heart now beating with the fervor of six hangovers.

## THIRTEEN

# MAGGIE

Summer of 1996
Folly Beach, South Carolina

"MARGARET MARY OLSON, WILL YOU do me the great honor of being my wife?" Seamus asks in his Irish brogue, his eyes teary.

Maggie looks at him, down on one knee in the sand on their favorite beach. It's early. The sun is just rising. The horizon is the pink hue of a new day, a fresh start.

Maggie thinks she's going to be sick.

Before he can even open the ring box, she runs toward the ocean, falls to her knees, and pukes. She cries and laughs as the salty waves lap against her. She feels Seamus behind her. She quickly turns around, swatting his hands away from the small of her back. He stumbles, a bit confused.

Quickly, she grabs his face and says, "Yes, of course I'll marry you, you idiot." They both laugh. He even kisses her in that moment, post-puke, and if that isn't love, Maggie is convinced she'll never find it. *This is it*. She tears up. Hopefully throwing herself into the water hasn't ruined everything. That wasn't planned.

"Not exactly how you pictured it, eh?" Seamus's eyes crinkle as he wraps her in a tight bear hug. She can hardly breathe.

"I wouldn't change it. I wouldn't change a thing." Maggie puts her hand on her stomach. But that isn't entirely true . . . She would change a few things if she could. Starting with the unplanned teen pregnancy.

"You've got that special something, darling." He gives her a big kiss. They're standing now, the water tickling their legs, soaking their clothes. A couple walks by with their dog and smiles. A happy engagement, they must think, as Seamus slips the tiny diamond ring onto Maggie's finger. She doesn't ask where he got it, or how he could afford it, or if it's even real, or the million other questions running through her mind.

All she says is "I love it." Seamus admires her hand with pride. Maggie always thought she would get married. She just didn't think she'd be eighteen and already pregnant. It doesn't matter, though; she just got accepted to nursing school. She hasn't told Seamus yet, but she will start in the fall as planned. She will have this baby, and she will take care of them. She's a doer.

"Should we celebrate properly, then?" Seamus asks. The gulls caw above them. Gulls always unsettle her. They sound like a warning from above.

"I think we might want to change first." Maggie shivers in the cold water.

"Ah, come on, let's at least have a glass of champagne soaking wet to mark the occasion." He puts an arm around her. He's not a big man, actually quite the contrary—he's around five seven and a little gangly. She knows she shouldn't drink—she's pregnant!—but just a sip can't hurt, can it? She walks with him toward the small downtown. She also needs to give up smoking. For God's sake, she's going to be a nurse.

"Okay, but just a sip." Maggie smirks. They make their way toward the boardwalk, and Seamus grabs her hand. Maggie likes how his rugged palms feel in her soft hands. The sand is warm between her toes, and the ring catches the sun just right. The moment looks perfect.

"We've come a long way, haven't we?" Seamus smiles. She has to agree—they *have* come a long way. Well, Seamus has come a long way to begin with—all the way from Ireland, actually, to start a new life in the American South. He'd grown up lapping up the promise of the

American Dream, and as soon as he saved up enough money from driving his taxi in Limerick, he headed over. His knowledge of the South was thin, though—and instead of ending up among the cowboys of Texas like he planned, he ended up on the beachy shores of South Carolina.

"A happy accident in the end," he'd told Maggie, "because of you." But she knew he was just saying that . . . Life in America hadn't really gone according to plan for Seamus.

"That place looks perfect." Maggie points to a diner just off the boardwalk. The restaurant has a faded turquoise sign that reads *The Ritz Diner.*

"Taking my girl to the Ritz!" He laughs.

"Perfect. Mom's hungry." Maggie rubs her stomach. They probably can't afford much on the menu, seeing as Seamus has just started his first "real" job as a Coca-Cola delivery truck driver and they are living solely off Maggie's grocery-bagging salary. Her parents kicked her out after they found the letters. They didn't even know she was pregnant. Not that it would have changed anything. She and Seamus had been planning this already. Okay, not the baby, but running away together . . . once Seamus was able to. The couple settles into a worn leather booth at the diner. Their wet clothes squeak against the red vinyl.

"What'll it be?" an unenthusiastic waitress asks as she jabs her pad with a pen.

"We're celebrating," Seamus says, grinning. "So have your sommelier bring us the finest bottle of champagne." The waitress doesn't even crack a smile.

"Seamus—" Maggie knows better than to finish her protest. He knows well enough they can't afford whatever bottom-shelf champagne this diner has. Not that she wants—or is legally allowed—to drink.

"All we have is André," the waitress says, exasperated with them already.

"Fine, we'll have that, then. And a full Irish breakfast." Seamus winks.

"And for you, sweetie?" She turns her tired face toward Maggie. The waitress's bright blue–dusted eyelids are not having the youthful effect that she was probably hoping for when she got ready this morning.

"Oh, I'm fine. We'll share." Maggie sips her water and avoids eye contact. She can feel Seamus scowling at her.

"Catch yourself on," he snorts. "She'll have a triple stack of pancakes, bacon, eggs, and, oh—an ice cream sundae." He closes the menu with a smack. The waitress pauses, waiting for the punchline.

"She's in the family way," Seamus says, and grins.

"Ah. Congratulations. I'll put everything on the griddle. And don't believe everything you read, honey—Guinness is good for the baby." The waitress jots down their order, and Maggie thanks her.

"Right you are!" Seamus claps in agreement. Once the waitress disappears from view, Maggie groans, "Why'd you order all that? We don't have the money." She crosses her arms over her chest.

"Who said we don't have the money?" His smile unfolds slowly, like a magician about to display the winning card. All of a sudden, Maggie feels particularly freezing in her wet dress.

"What did you do?" she whispers, and looks around. The diner is pretty much empty besides the two of them.

"You leave the family finances to me"—he sips his coffee—"and enjoy your fecking breakfast." Seamus's Irish accent is always a bit more pronounced when he's agitated. She reaches across the table and touches his arm.

"Hey, I'm sorry. It's really nice to be out together. Think of all the times we dreamed of going out like this." She knows this will only push him further into his anger, but she has to.

"This place is shite. In a couple weeks, we'll be eating at the real Ritz." The waitress brings their André and pops it ceremoniously at the table.

"This one's on the house," she says. "Food will be out in a minute." Seamus beams at the waitress, and she laps it up. It still baffles Maggie how he can flip his switch like that—how he can turn an unenthusiastic waitress into his best friend within ten seconds of meeting her—how he can go from seething to smiling in a mere moment.

"See, I told you our luck is turning around! Slainte!" He extends his glass of champagne for a toast. Maggie hesitates, then reluctantly clinks her glass to his. The alcohol tastes warm and gross as it slides down her throat. Overcome with regret and the need to protect her baby, she discreetly spits the bubbly liquid into her napkin.

"I almost forgot." Seamus reaches into his denim jacket pocket. "A little something for the missus." Maggie feels her heart fall deep into her stomach. She hopes the baby will catch it and hold it tightly.

"You're back with them?" Maggie already knows the answer, but she has to ask.

"On a temporary basis, yes. The boss just landed a big new client. Loads of cash—a proper fortune." He keeps his voice casual as he looks around the room, assessing it like he's ready to case the joint. Maybe he is.

"But—but you promised . . . You said you'd get a *normal* job." The words aren't coming to her. She feels the involuntary lurch of vomit in the back of her throat.

"That was before I knew about the baby," he snaps.

"That doesn't change anything." She swallows down her sickness with a shudder.

"It changes everything. My little love's going to have anything she wants." Seamus bends the end of his menu, ensuring that it can never be used again.

"Not if her dad is in jail," she whispers. Seamus slams his hand on the table. Across the room, an old man whispers something to the younger man he's with, who could be his son. Seamus is causing a scene.

"I didn't ask for your permission. Actually, I didn't ask for any of this, did I? You reached out to *me*." He swats the champagne glass off the table. Maggie can feel the tears welling up behind her eyes. She had been stupid, hadn't she? One too many crime shows. It started as a joke, really. A dare from a friend at school to write a letter to Seamus O'Reilly, the cute new Irish guy in town . . . who just got arrested. *You wouldn't*, she'd said. But she did—and he had been charming. And he was getting on the straight and narrow after this, he promised.

"I thought we were in love." The tears stain her face.

"Love don't pay the bills, sweetheart," he says sarcastically through clenched teeth, his knuckles white from gripping the tattered menu.

The waitress comes back and drops off their feast, her eyes lingering on the shattered champagne flute.

"Sorry about the glass," Maggie mumbles.

"Uh-huh. You let me know if you need anything." The waitress knows Seamus's type. The charm has worn off, as it always does. She gives him a dirty look as she puts the pancakes down in front of Maggie.

Maggie would never admit it, even to herself, but Seamus is sort of a dunce. She's surprised that the gang he's working for hasn't gotten rid of him already, since he's proven to be such a liability time and time again. Seamus is quick to anger, and it gets him in trouble. A life with him would mean bringing the baby to supervised prison visits.

"Promise this is the last gig and then you'll quit," she says. "You'll get a normal job, and we can live a normal life." She cuts into her pancake even though she has no intention of eating it.

"Promise. Cross my heart, hope to die." Seamus smirks as he chews a piece of bacon. "Now open your gift."

She puts down her butter knife and picks up the gift. Inside is a small golden Saint Christopher medal. She stares at it. She knows what it means. Seamus wears the same one. It's a symbol that he has recommitted himself to the gang and, by association, so has Maggie.

"Soon we'll buy a house, and you won't have to work. This new client is serious dosh, Mags. We're going to be rich." Seamus crunches away, bits of bacon flying from his open mouth along with his lies.

Maggie knows this isn't true, because, well, not only is Seamus a criminal—he is a *bad* one. He's sloppy and brash—he doesn't think things through. That's how he ended up in jail in the first place.

"But I want to be a nurse. I've already been accepted to school." Maggie brings her fork to her mouth, forcing herself to take a bite of her pancake. It tastes like a damp sock, but she needs to eat for the baby.

"Sure, sure, but soon we will be so rich, we can do whatever we want."

They finish their meal in silence. Maggie stuffs the pancake into her already full belly to avoid talking to him about their future further.

"My beautiful bride-to-be, why don't you head on back to the motel? Get yourself out of those wet clothes."

The ticking of the diner clock thumps loudly in the silence that follows. Maggie meets his eyes directly and holds contact. His beautiful brown eyes, his dark luscious hair, his scratchy wool-blanket stubble, his dimples at the crevices of his mouth. She drinks him in, trying to memorize every piece, every tic, every detail. She puts on the Saint Christopher medal. Maybe she can sell it for something. Maybe she'll keep it and wear it like a battle scar.

"Sure, see you in a bit." She hopes the words sound casual, that her voice doesn't catch. She waves goodbye to the waitress as she walks out of the restaurant. *Poor woman*, she thinks. The moment Maggie's feet hit the sidewalk, she starts to run, desperate not to hear the sound that will inevitably follow her exit . . . but she hears it anyway. The gunshot, the shriek of the nice waitress. The old man and "his son" are probably up now; they've probably got him.

Her legs carry her through the beach town, past the seedy motel they'd been staying at and straight to the train station. She'd stored her bag there in the women's room. A wig, a change of clothes, a one-way ticket. It isn't until she is safely on the train that Maggie allows herself to cry. Because she did love him. And she is sorry. She's sorry for their baby too, who will grow up without a father.

"Got all that, then?" Maggie says a bit too loudly as the train starts chugging. Her seatmate gives her side-eye. But she doesn't care. They're finally finished.

Maggie is on her way to a new life, and Seamus is going to prison. She rips the mic off the inside of her blouse and doesn't look back.

FOURTEEN

# CHRISTINE

Friday, October 17, 2025
Afternoon of Rehearsal Dinner

SOMEONE WAS IN MY ROOM.

*Who is Seamus O'Reilly?*

Christine's mind races as she slowly leans down to pick up the piece of paper. She opens it again to confirm that it's real and that she is not in fact having a full psychotic break. With shaking fingers, she types *Seamus O'Reilly* into Google on her phone.

The first few results that come up are for some guy who writes for the Cut and, apparently, has a children's book coming out next year. This is followed on the results page by the Instagram account for a Seamus O'Reilly who works as a personal trainer in Dublin. After scrolling through just a *few* of the personal trainer's thirst traps, Christine decides to refine her search. She types in *Seamus O'Reilly Ballymoon*. Maybe this person works at the castle. Nothing fruitful comes from the search, though—just more press about the first guy's children's book. She lies back on her bed, thinking.

What about *Seamus O'Reilly criminal*? It's a bit of a reach, but whenever someone says to "look into that guy," it kind of implies that they're shady and up to something. It's worth a shot.

She tries to keep her breathing steady as the news articles pop up.

*August 1996—Seamus O'Reilly arrested in Folly Beach, South Carolina.*

*November 1996—Seamus O'Reilly refuses to take a deal in exchange for information on a crime syndicate with ties up and down the Eastern Seaboard.*

*January 1997—Jury finds Seamus O'Reilly guilty of aggravated assault, armed robbery.*

There's only one image accompanying the news articles, and it's of a young man with inky-black hair, wild eyes, and an intense snake tattoo slithering up the side of his neck. He has chiseled cheekbones and delicate features that makes him look like a gothic fairy—or maybe a character from *Twilight?* Actually, now that she thinks about it, he kind of looks like—

*Holy shit. Maggie's dead fiancé. Seamus.*

Christine rushes to her desk, pulling out her laptop and googling images of Jane and Graham, zooming in on Jane's face. There is a sea of pictures to choose from, but Christine clicks on a high-quality Backgrid photo of the couple at last year's Grow 2 Glo Gala. She stares at Jane . . . at her dark brown eyes, her jet-black hair, her lithe frame and hollow cheekbones. With shaking fingers, she opens up another browser and reenters Seamus O'Reilly's name.

Except for the plethora of tattoos, Seamus O'Reilly's resemblance to Jane Murphy is . . . uncanny. But Christine is sleep-deprived, and scared, and a little jumpy from too much caffeine this morning. It's possible she is just imagining the similarity between this man and the bride-to-be who sat across from her at brunch. *Sometimes people just look alike. It doesn't necessarily mean anything*, she tells herself, tapping her fingers on the desk, thinking. Then she has an idea.

Christine googles *Seamus Murphy* and *Seamus Murphy car accident.*

After clicking through ten pages of search results, she finds no record of an apparent untimely death, not even one small local story about the tragic car accident that Maggie claimed killed Jane's dad. All she finds is the LinkedIn page of a Seamus Murphy who runs an insurance brokerage firm in South Florida. And then it hits her: Maggie and Seamus were never married. Maggie must have given her daughter her own last name, which means Jane's dad's surname could be anything . . . it could be O'Reilly.

"Shit." She runs a hand through her hair. It's clumpy and greasy and in desperate need of a shampoo. The weekend she spent FaceTiming her mom, painstakingly packing and repacking her suitcase with all her overpriced skincare products and best shoes seems so stupid now. She wonders if she'll even have time to shower today.

Christine clicks back to her Google search of Seamus O'Reilly, refreshing it to make sure she didn't miss anything, and her breath catches in her throat, because *somehow* in her frantic googling, she failed to read the top search result:

*Arrest Warrant for Seamus O'Reilly*

*. . . failed to show up to a parole hearing . . . considered armed and dangerous . . .*

"Oh my God," she whispers. Her whole body is shaking. Christine slams her laptop shut and closes her eyes. *Do not jump to conclusions,* she tells herself again. *There is probably a reasonable explanation for all of this. Or it's just two people who look alike. Maybe distant relatives or second cousins—a 23andMe nightmare the Murphys don't ever need to know about.*

But jump to conclusions she does—the alarm bells in her brain are ringing, and coupled with her hangover and exhaustion, she is on the precipice of a full-blown panic attack. The snippets of information she's found so far are damning.

Christine pulls up yet another web page and searches Jane Murphy. She needs to find out her birthday. And there it is on her fan (or troll) created Wikipedia page, just under her outdated sorority photo headshot. Jane was born on April 3, 1997. She would have been born when Seamus was behind bars, where he stayed up until two years ago. The math is mathing.

She closes her eyes and lets the puzzle pieces slide into place. Maggie was a teenager, newly pregnant; she was probably scared of her unborn child's father, a known gangster who'd already been arrested before they met. She probably decided it would be better to never tell Jane the truth about her dad. It made sense. *Even if I'm right—which I am probably not—there might be nothing sinister about it*, Christine thinks. *Maggie could have just been a young mother trying to get out of a dangerous relationship and protect her daughter. There might be no need for me to bring up my discovery of this criminally inclined Seamus O'Reilly to anyone—the person who left this note might just be someone trying to ruin Jane's wedding by embarrassing her in the press. They might just be hoping I take the bait.* Christine runs her fingers over the note.

*But what if this guy was somehow involved in Gloria's murder? Who would want me to know that . . . and why?* She thinks back to the events of this morning. Could she have been the only one in that room with Gloria's dead body who was a true outsider? The only impartial person who can be trusted by this mysterious note-sender?

At this point, all Christine knows for sure is that somebody, potentially somebody dangerous, has access to her room and that Maggie might have lied to her about what really happened to Jane's dad.

Elliot's castle lore tumbles around in Christine's brain; she thinks of the hidden passageways he mentioned and the weird hidden door Cheryl popped out of this morning. She has to do something; she can't just sit down now. She needs to find out who sent this note, and how they got in here. Pacing her hotel room, she feels along the walls for clues. She works her way over to the closet, feeling for a hidden lever, something, anything . . . But all she finds is cold castle stone. She needs to get a grip. Realistically, whoever got in her room did so by getting a copy of her keycard. It could be someone who works here . . . But how does she figure out who was in here without drawing attention to herself, especially in front of the Riptons?

No, she can't say anything without fear of the family silencing her for good. Closing her eyes, Christine tries to think. For now, she'll keep the note to herself. She leans against her closet in defeat, throwing an engraved wooden hanger on the floor in frustration. There's a loud knock on the door.

"Christine," Elliot's voice trills from the castle hall, "I know you're in there. I come in peace—and with coffee." She rushes for the door, desperate for human interaction and a distraction from her mental spiral. *Maybe I can still make things right with him before it gets back to Sandra,* she thinks as she swings open the door.

"Oh my God." A look of shock registers on his face. "What happened to you?"

Christine touches a piece of her crusty hair and realizes what she must look like. A raccoon-eyed bride of Frankenstein who stuck her finger in an electrical socket would be an apt comparison.

"Ah, coffee, you're a saint." Christine brushes off the comment, takes the warm to-go cup, and ushers the wedding planner into her room. "Come in before anyone else sees me."

"Listen," Elliot says apprehensively, "I just wanted to apologize for our little tiff earlier, but I can come back later if it isn't a good time . . . You're kind of giving feral cat energy right now." He makes a window-washing motion with his hands as if trying to physically erase her mess.

"No, now is good." Christine takes a sip of coffee, letting the black liquid soothe her from the inside out. "I'm just sleep-deprived. You're a lifesaver for this, thank you. And please don't think anything of the 'tiff'—it's already forgotten."

Elliot pauses, looking her up and down with a wary expression. Christine feels her face working overtime to appear at ease, but she knows her forced fake smile often makes her look a little manic.

"Right . . . well, I shouldn't have snapped at you about the questions you asked Maggie. But I don't have to tell you, it's been *a morning*." He says this like he overslept and missed a yoga class and not like he woke up and discovered the dead body of a famous billionaire. Elliot settles on the velvet love seat in the suite's sitting area and motions for Christine to sit opposite him.

"That's an understatement," she says as she flops down on the plush pillow-lined window alcove. Elliot surveys her room; his eyes roam over the clothes thrown out of the closet, the dresser moved into the center of the room, the framed black-and-white photos of the castle slightly wonky on the walls.

"What are you doing here? A one-woman renovation of this hotel room?" He raises one of his perfectly manicured eyebrows. Christine cringes.

"Sorry—I . . ." She almost mentions the note and her theory about Jane's father and her hunt for the secret passageways, but it sounds too insane to bring up at this point. Elliot already thinks she's nuts. She takes a long sip of coffee while thinking of an excuse.

"I couldn't find my laptop charger," Christine lies. "Obviously, there's no Apple store within fifty miles of this place, so I panicked. Found it, though." She smiles and feels her left eye start to twitch.

"Rightttt." Elliot draws out the word skeptically. "Listen." He clears his throat. "About what you heard between me and Gloria—"

Christine rushes to cut him off. "Really, I shouldn't have said anything. I'm sorry too. I totally didn't mean to insinuate anything about, well, uh, whatever was going on between you two last night." Her mind flashes back to the bloodied sheet from this morning. "I know how heated these sorts of weddings can get."

Elliot's body relaxes. "Good. Let's just remember we're on the same team here. But if you must know, Gloria was withholding my advance. I lost my cool. It wasn't my finest moment. I'm not proud of it, but this is what they do. They try to bully you, take advantage of you . . . until, eventually, you snap." Elliot snaps his fingers, and Christine flinches. She knows that Elliot is speaking from ten-plus years of experience catering to society's upper echelons. She's seen the way people like the Riptons behave firsthand too. She's not sure if she totally believes him, but the story's believable *enough*.

"I know. Rich people don't like to part with their money." Christine offers her best sympathetic smile. "And I agree, we're on the same team. The goal is to just make it through this weekend." She sifts through the curated snack basket on top of her suite's mini fridge for something salty. The coffee has made her head hurt more, but everything in the basket is expensive and healthy and unappetizing. It's times like this that she misses her mom's snack cabinet—filled with Cool Ranch Doritos and Fruit Roll-Ups and every other unhealthy, soul-nourishing gas station snack you can think of. She keeps digging.

"Exactly." Elliot smiles. "We're still professionals here. We have a job to do." Christine can't tell if Elliot is talking to her, or if he is just trying to hype himself up.

"Right. And if we make it home, we can add 'avoided murder' to our résumés." Elliot stiffens, and she immediately regrets the joke.

His face twists into an expression of disapproval. "Don't joke like that. Don't even let that *word* leave your mouth again. Let me correct you: An elderly member of the family tragically passed. We kept it under wraps in order to avoid a media frenzy that would disrupt a high-profile wedding. And that's all we'll ever say about it. Ever. Capisce?" Christine nods, producing a candy bar that looks like GOOP's take on a Milky Way from the basket, but she's lost her appetite.

"Now, you were hired to cover a glamorous and exclusive affair with your outlet's signature witty punch and glittery Instagram spread—and that's what you plan to do, right?"

Christine watches Elliot's nails puncture his cardboard coffee cup.

"Of course," she says, and gulps. "Sorry, it was just a bad joke. I would have asked Maggie those questions regardless, for what it's worth.

They were preprepared. Sandra approved." Christine takes a bite of the bar and immediately spits it into her hand. It tastes like cacao powder mixed with chalk. Elliot watches her with disgust.

"Good." He rubs his hands on his leather pants and stands up. "I'll see you at the rehearsal in"—he checks his iPhone—"well, look at that—in less than an hour."

His eyes glide up and down her body. "You've got your work cut out for you." Christine's eyes drift to the pile of clothes she needs to sort through to find her outfit for tonight.

Elliot makes his way toward the door. "Really, Christine, I can't stress this enough—don't try to outsmart the Riptons. You'll lose every time. Trust me." The door closes behind him with a thud.

With less than thirty minutes to get ready for the rehearsal and make it to the church in time for her interview with Father Kenneth, she doesn't have time to consider Elliot's cryptic threat. Instead, she dashes around the room, throwing on her trusty Alice + Olivia black dress (very Audrey Hepburn), her go-to vintage pearl earrings (very Gloria Beaufort, RIP), and grabs a black patent leather Chanel micro handbag (very out of her budget, from a bag rental company). Christine has almost successfully made up for lost time, when there is another knock on her door.

"Hello," Christine says, opening it up to reveal Cheryl. *My God, it's like this woman is following her!*

"Hello, dear," the woman replies, her frozen smile still firmly in place. "I was just checking in to see how you're liking everything so far." She takes a step closer to Christine, craning her neck slightly, as if she's trying to peek past her and into the hotel room. It feels intrusive.

"Great, thanks!" Christine says, trying to keep the irritation out of her voice as she fastens the clip on one of her pearl earrings.

"Do you need anything else? Fresh towels or a cup of tea or anything at all?" the woman presses, taking another step even closer to Christine, who can now smell the coffee on her breath. She backs up slightly, starting to feel uncomfortable in Cheryl's presence.

"No, everything is lovely, thanks again. Sorry, but if you don't mind, I'm running late for an event—"

Cheryl flushes red and seems to get the hint.

"No problem," she says quietly. "Sorry to keep you. Have a lovely evening."

Christine closes the door, slightly unnerved once again. Maybe this is just normal treatment for senior editors at weddings of this level, but she can't shake the feeling that there was something loaded and menacing about that interaction. *Could Cheryl know something about Gloria? Could she somehow be involved?* She tries to shake it off. If she starts reading into every little interaction she has this weekend, she'll go insane. Turning in front of the mirror, Christine checks her outfit one final time before slipping a lip gloss and portable phone battery into her purse. *Cheryl is just a thirsty hotel manager jockeying for her property to get a mention in* Bespoke, Christine tells herself as she grabs her purse off the bed.

It's not until she is about to dash out of the room, her taxi idling in the castle drive, that Christine realizes she isn't wearing any shoes. *Keep it together,* she mutters, slipping on the emerald slingbacks she sourced from Poshmark. But now, instead of thinking about how chic they'll look in her Instagram photo roundup, she worries if the heel is sharp enough to use as a weapon if needed.

## FIFTEEN

## ELLIOT

Friday, October 17, 2025
Afternoon of Rehearsal Dinner

ELLIOT CLOSES THE DOOR TO his suite, his pulse elevated, the underarms of his favorite Tom Ford T-shirt slick with sweat. Was he convincing enough? Did she believe him? The sun shines through the window of his room, momentarily blinding him before the inevitable roll of clouds buries it again. His suite overlooks Foxglove Garden, which is great, because he can keep a close eye on the rehearsal dinner setup, but he can't help but be a smidge bitter that *Christine* somehow got a waterfront view.

*He* has seniority here. While that little nobody was taking cheap tequila shots in some third-rate sorority house in God Knows Where, Ohio, he was making the Riptons' wildest, most nonsensical events come to life. From Lyle's *Yellowstone*-themed bachelorette party in Bozeman (Elliot had to beg and *bribe* Paramount to delay shooting on season five so they could rent out the actual ranch) to Clementine's fiftieth birthday party on a yacht charter through Greece *during Covid*! He could write a book about what this family has put him through. The events of this morning? *Moving a body!* The cherry on top. Maybe he will write that book one day. But for now, he has his hands full.

He throws himself on his bed, his body relaxing into the feathery duvet. It's moments like this when Elliot Adler thinks: *How did I get here?*

He left rural Texas on his eighteenth birthday in search of total freedom in New York City, where he could be himself, where he could date freely, where he could wear whatever he wanted, be whoever he wanted to be. He remembers being on that Greyhound bus, rattling through New Jersey as the skyline came into view, brimming with pride. He was finally taking charge of his own life. Now, he realizes, he's trapped himself in a different kind of cage. It happened slowly, but at this point it's undeniable that the Riptons call all the shots in his life. He has to be whatever or whomever they need him to be at all times. Elliot might as well be back in his family home again, playing a part, just trying to make it through the day, his freedom a fleeting illusion.

If he could just close his eyes for five minutes . . . He nestles his head into one of the mustard-colored throw pillows that line the king-size bed, and his phone immediately starts buzzing.

The groom's cake is here and it's the wrong shade of green.

A bridesmaid forgot her shoes. Can we overnight a pair of Jimmy Choo Etana 95 sandals in gold from London? Size eight is in stock at Harrods?

The lead hairstylist went into early labor. I knew we should have flown Sergio in.

Before Elliot attempts to put out even one of the numerous fires that have broken out in his fifteen-minute absence, he clicks on his J.P. Morgan banking app one more time to check his balance.

It's still there—and it's a *lot* of zeros.

He drops his iPhone 16 Max right on his nose: the reality of his new money quite literally hitting him in the face. It looks . . . suspicious. But what he told Christine is true. Gloria Beaufort did owe Elliot a lot of money. She hadn't even sent him the final payment for Ben and Lyle's wedding over two years ago until last night. Elliot let it slide, because, well, *it's G.B.*—any event he did for her would result in fifteen more on his already-full calendar. He couldn't say no to her. The cage was locked, and she had the key.

His brain won't stop rehashing every detail of their fight and fallout. He squeezes his eyes shut, trying to force the thoughts out of his head. He didn't want it to end the way it did between them. He tried to be polite about it, following up promptly but not too often. *Her people will get back to me*, he told himself, *it's just a matter of time*. But weeks turned into months that turned into years, and the sheer cost of Graham and Jane's wedding was too much for his company's bank balance to bear. By the time the week of the wedding rolled around, he was physically ill with stress. If she didn't pay him soon, he wasn't going to be able to make payroll for his twenty-plus employees. He might have to remortgage his farmhouse in the Hudson Valley. He might need to cancel his two-week trip to St. Barth's. That was *not* happening.

So, after a brutal call with his financial advisor, he picked up the phone and called Gloria directly. The conversation was terse and tense. Gloria insinuated that Elliot should be doing Graham's wedding for free given the sheer press his company was going to get from it. The gall of that woman! Something inside of him ruptured and an uncontrollable rage washed over him. Even now, he can't remember the full extent of how their conversation went, but it ended with Elliot threatening not to come to Ireland. When he hung up the phone—or rather, when he chucked his phone against his two-thousand-dollar Restoration Hardware standing mirror, which shattered upon impact—he could not believe what he'd done.

Thirty agonizing minutes later, he got an email from Gloria. It simply read, *Come to Ballymoon. You'll get your money after the welcome dinner.* At first, Elliot was relieved to not be fired. Then he was excited to finally get paid. And then anger set in again.

Not paying him had been a game. It was always a game with Gloria. She liked pushing people's buttons, seeing what made them tick so she could use it against them. How could he have fallen for it? He let her see the chink in his armor; he let her know with absolute certainty that Elliot Adler Events needed her business more than anything. The emotions sloshing around inside him were like a bevy of cocktails that did not mix well. He ran to the bathroom and threw up, trying to physically purge his body of Gloria's hold on him.

What choice did he have? He went to Ireland to finish the job he started and get his long-overdue paycheck. After the welcome dinner, he went to Gloria's room as instructed. When she opened the door, he immediately noticed how frail she looked. She struggled to hold a glass of scotch; her bony fingers wrapped around the heavy crystal glass like spider legs. No spectacular jewels, no overlined lip, no ravishing designer gown. Instead, Elliot saw a tired elderly woman in a rumpled (albeit Turkish silk) nightgown and felt, for the first time, a spark of empathy. Then she opened her mouth.

"After that incident with the rock, you know that I cannot in good faith possibly give you another cent," she said. Her voice was even and unbothered. With those words, their small spark of shared humanity was snuffed out like a candle in the wind. Elliot lost it.

"You will pay me what I'm rightfully due or I'm leaving. I won't be toyed with anymore, Gloria," he remembers shouting. "This is the last straw. I'm done, do you hear me? Absolutely done. You've crossed the line." He couldn't help it; his body would not listen to his mind's pleas to take it down a notch. When he finally shut his mouth, Gloria just stood there staring at him. She took a long sip of her scotch, letting the silence stretch out between them. Finally, she put the glass down on the small table by the door and coughed lightly into her handkerchief.

"Good." She smiled. "It's nice to see you've grown a pair after all these years."

*She smiled* and he couldn't help it—he shut the door right in her face.

Picking his phone up off the bed, he looks at his banking app one final time, unable to process that she really did pay him, and handsomely. Or somebody did. The wire went through last night—and it's unclear when Gloria, um, well, *left the party*. But one thing is certain: money left her account and slid into Elliot's. It's significantly more money than all Gloria's owed invoices put together. An uncharacteristically generous bonus for someone who was so notoriously stingy. So now Elliot has to grapple with the fact that the payment he needed—the money he was rightfully due (mostly)!—makes him look incredibly guilty. And . . . *he moved the body*. The Riptons might try to pin it on him. Christine saw the fight. She heard Elliot's rage-filled monologue. He's basically handed everyone a motive on a silver platter.

*Stop*, he commands himself, sitting up. *Nobody is going to find out about the money. Nobody is going to find out about the murder. She was an elderly woman; she was bound to die soon.* He breathes deeply and opens his eyes. His phone buzzes again. It's time to pour himself into work. His email icon flashes red with over fifteen new notifications, so he decides to start there. Clicking on it, his eyes are immediately drawn to the first unread message in his inbox. He doesn't recognize the sender, but the subject line makes him freeze.

Gloria Beaufort-Funeral Arrangements.

SIXTEEN

# CHRISTINE

Friday, October 17, 2025
Afternoon of Rehearsal Dinner

RAIN DROPLETS PELT THE BLACK taxi as it rattles down the gravel drive toward St. Frances of Clifden Cathedral. Peering out the foggy window, Christine notices a glow of warm light from inside the white rectory cottage and feels herself relax slightly. The humble abode now seems infinitely more inviting than the glamorous Ballymoon Castle.

"It's nasty out there, love," her taxi driver murmurs from the driver's seat.

"I know," Christine groans. "I hope it clears up before tomorrow."

"Ah, I wouldn't fret about it. Part of the joy of Ireland is whatever the weather is, you shouldn't get too attached because it'll change in an instant." He gives Christine a toothy grin, revealing a mouth of yellowish teeth, and tips his cap. She has half a mind to ask this sweet, scruffy man to turn around and drive her straight to the airport, but she just bites her lip.

As her taxi driver chugs along carefully through the torrential weather, Christine takes a moment to check her Instagram feed—the portal into her previous life. Sandra has posted a series of photos from the Carolina Herrera fall bridal collection, followed by a slew of snaps from her annual birthday bash, which Christine presumes she purposely planned for this weekend, so she'd have an excuse as to why she wasn't at Graham Ripton's wedding. Sandra's actual birthday isn't until mid-November.

Christine clicks through the photos of her colleagues holding expensive cocktails in the private dining room at the moody West Village hotspot Via Carota and is surprised by the swell of anger that rises inside her. She should be there, blissfully unaware of the Ripton family underbelly, sipping an extra-dirty martini and mainlining cacio e pepe in an oversize Khaite sweater as the autumn leaves gently fall outside, as is her God-given right as a *Bespoke* employee! Instead, she's cold and wet and jittery from too much coffee and too much murder—completely out of her element in every way—about to do an interview in a stuffy church rectory. This was *not* how this weekend was supposed to go. Her mom was right. She shouldn't have forced this. The universe is punishing her for breaking the rules and pushing herself into Gloria Beaufort's sphere. She feels her eyes well up. The car comes to a halt on the sidewalk in front of a simple white structure across from the grand and Gothic cathedral.

"Here we are," the cabbie chimes.

"Thanks for the ride," Christine mumbles, reaching to open the car door. As she's about to step out of the car, her phone vibrates with a new email . . . from an unknown sender. The subject reads: Trouble's Brewing Among the Angels. Holding her breath, she opens the email.

It contains just one sentence: *Ask Father Kenneth about the new executive chair*, followed by a link that Christine immediately clicks on. After twenty seconds of buffering purgatory, the link finally loads to reveal a press release from the annual Grow 2 Glo Gala that took place just two weeks ago.

Quickly skimming the write-up, Christine gathers that at this event Gloria made a speech announcing the vast majority of her fortune would be left to her nonprofit, Grow 2 Glo, an organization that financially supports South Carolina's underserved youth. She also announced that her grandson, Graham Ripton, would be taking over for her as the charity's executive director. In other words: Graham Ripton is now fully in charge of the nonprofit and, by proxy, the lion's share of Gloria's money . . . And whoever sent this email seems to think Father Kenneth might have thoughts about it.

But why?

Pulling the press release up on her phone, her eyes quickly dissect every word, comma, and semicolon. It's a lot of fluff . . . mostly just variations of "Gloria Beaufort is 'confident her grandson has the prowess and passion to bring Grow 2 Glo to new heights'" blah, blah, blah . . . And then, finally, in the last paragraph, something interesting:

DR. GRAHAM RIPTON HAS NOT BEEN HEAVILY INVOLVED IN THE DAY-TO-DAY OPERATIONS OF GROW 2 GLO, BUT MS. BEAUFORT REMAINS FULLY CONFIDENT IN HER CHOICE OF SUCCESSOR. "FAMILY COMES FIRST, AND GRAHAM HAS PROVEN TIME AND TIME AGAIN THAT HE WILL BE A CHAMPION AND THE ADVOCATE GROW 2 GLO NEEDS IN THE YEARS TO COME," MS. BEAUFORT ASSERTED AT THE GROW 2 GLO GALA LAST EVENING.

*So, there must have been some whisperings that Graham wasn't the "fan favorite" for this role,* Christine thinks. *Why else make a point to justify Gloria's decision?*

Below the final paragraph is a link to a media kit with pictures from the event. Christine clicks on it and scrolls through photos of celebrities and millionaires enjoying a ten-thousand-dollars-a-ticket night in the name of charity.

One photo in particular catches her eye. It's of Gloria and Trey, both of them smiling tightly. Trey tries to put his arm around his mother, but they're standing just far enough apart to make it look awkward. This is not the noteworthy part of the photo, though—what Christine has zeroed in on (and zoomed in on)—is the scene behind them.

It's Graham Ripton and Father Kenneth hovering by the bar. Graham's face is locked in a scowl, and the priest's face mirrors it exactly, each of them gripping empty whiskey glasses like grenades they're about to throw on the floor. Christine's eyes widen at the photo.

She immediately thinks of the subject line from the email:

Trouble's Brewing Among the Angels.

"Everything okay, miss?" The cabbie's voice startles her.

"Totally fine! Sorry—thanks." Christine pays him and shuffles herself out of the car and into the rain, shoving her phone into her purse as Father Kenneth opens the rectory door.

SEVENTEEN

# FATHER KENNETH

Saturday, October 4, 2025
Grow 2 Glo Annual Gala

FATHER KENNETH FEELS THE WEIGHT of the entire ballroom's eyes on him as Gloria says the words, "I am thrilled tonight to announce my successor for Grow 2 Glo's executive chair . . ." He forces his fake grin to stretch even bigger, feeling the edges of his mouth almost disappear behind his earlobes, his cheeks aching. He knows what's coming next, but it won't make it any less painful to hear it announced so publicly.

"Someone I deeply admire, whose integrity, passion, and commitment to helping others is unmatched." Gloria pauses, avoiding eye contact with him before she twists the knife.

"My grandson, Dr. Graham Ripton."

There is a millisecond of confused silence before the Guggenheim erupts in applause. Even after the clapping dies down, and Graham has embraced his grandmother, the echo of everyone's cheers vibrates through the museum for minutes, taunting him.

"Sorry, Father," Trey whispers in his ear. "You know how Mom can be." The priest nods and pats Trey on the shoulder.

"The joy is, and will always be, in the good work I get to do on Gloria's behalf." He smiles. It's true—mostly. He inhales deeply, calming himself, thanking God for his good fortune, for his ability to navigate difficult times like this.

*It's okay to get jealous. It's okay to feel wronged. It's what you do with those feelings that matters.* Father Kenneth feels the beginnings of his next homily taking shape. So, at least there's that to cling to. But it's more than petty jealousy that he's concerned about... It's the future of Grow 2 Glo. Father Kenneth is genuinely concerned that Graham is, er, not the best fit to run the charity—to put it mildly.

Out of the corner of his eye, he sees Gregg McDowell, president of Broadway Manufacturing, approaching their table, probably hoping to have a moment with Trey to salvage his contract with the company.

Trey tenses up. "Not this guy again. Who even let him on the list this year?" he whispers to Ben across the table.

"McDowell bought this table months ago. I didn't think he'd have the gall to show up." Ben shrugs. "But I guess if he's willing to shell out fifty grand for a table, I'll happily take his money given what he's cost us."

Across from him, Lyle rolls her eyes, and Ben throws his hands up. "What do you want me to do? Kick him out? This room is full of hungry sharks waiting for their chance to take a bite out of us. It's not like we'll ever work with the guy again. He'll be ruined soon enough."

McDowell is momentarily intercepted by Raquel Williams, who stops him to chat just before he gets to their table. Now Trey is even more enraged.

"Honestly, the nerve." He seethes as a spunky pink-haired photographer snaps a picture of McDowell posing with the starlet.

"Let's get one more," the photographer says brightly. "Scooch a little closer together, you two. There, that's perfect." Raquel squirms as McDowell pulls her closer by the waist, his hand hovering dangerously close to her butt.

"And where's Sebi? Wasn't he contracted for tonight? Who is that pink-haired idiot?" Trey demands, narrowing his eyes at the photographer. Ben lets out a loud laugh before throwing back the dregs of his vodka tonic.

Father Kenneth sighs. He used to find these events invigorating; he loved working the room, making connections with powerful people who could make a real difference in the work they were able to do at Grow, but now he just feels drained, defeated. Retirement can't come soon enough.

"Father." He hears Graham's voice behind him. "Let's have a drink." The priest turns around and looks up to see Grow 2 Glo's newest executive chair hovering over him, his expression stern.

"Of course," the priest says, rising—happy to join Graham and avoid a conversation with the man responsible for his, and all of Glo's, increased workload and headaches over the past year. "And many congratulations, young man. I look forward to working together."

Graham smiles at the gesture of goodwill as they walk toward the bar. He orders two whiskeys neat and hands one to the priest.

"To new beginnings," Graham says, and they clink glasses. Father Kenneth lets the whiskey slide down his throat, warming his bruised ego. He doesn't say anything; years of listening to confession has taught him never to say the first word.

"I just wanted to say that I am, um, I'm sorry." Graham frowns. "I tried to talk Gran out of this. It's obvious to everyone that you're the best equipped to run Grow—that you're the most natural choice . . . but she wouldn't budge." Graham takes a swig of his drink, and Father Kenneth feels his fingers tighten around his whiskey glass despite himself.

"Please, don't worry," Father Kenneth insists. "The only title that matters to me comes from the man upstairs." The priest laughs, relaxing his grip, making room for the Lord to come in, to free him of this hateful jealousy, to show him the way—to remind him of his greater purpose.

"Good." Graham swirls his drink on the bar. "I'm glad to hear that." He pauses before continuing. "Then you won't mind that I'm looking to make some pretty significant changes to how Grow 2 Glo operates." An eerily familiar expression appears on the young doctor's face.

"I think there's some room for improvement. Don't you?" Graham frowns and a cold wave of shock runs through Father Kenneth. "The organization is not where I'd like it to be financially." The priest doesn't reply, so Graham clears his throat and continues. "I hope you'll be an asset to me, Father. I'd like us to work together to make Grow 2 Glo the best it can be, for all of us," he concludes with a smile. Father Kenneth stares at his empty glass in shocked silence. Despite his gentle tone, Graham's words feel loaded.

All he can muster in response is "Of course. We're in this together."

"Good." Graham pats him on the back. "That's what I was hoping to hear."

But when Father Kenneth finally works up the nerve to look Gloria's spawn in the eye . . . the priest is surprised to see the reflection of his own steely gaze in the young man's eyes.

EIGHTEEN

# CHRISTINE

Friday, October 17, 2025
Afternoon of Rehearsal Dinner

"CHRISTINE," FATHER KENNETH SAYS WITH a smile, holding open the door to the rectory. "Come in, come in. I've put on a pot of tea. I feel like we could all use an extra splash of warmth today, don't you?" His eyes glisten with tears, the skin around them wrinkling as he gives her a sad smile, and she returns it. Behind him, the crackle of a newly lit fire illuminates his kind face. The whole scene reminds Christine of the final days with her own grandfather, who passed away just a few years ago.

"I hope you're doing okay," she says softly, and the priest's eyes fill up again.

"I'm afraid not." His voice cracks. "But I am turning toward prayer, and recommitting myself to sharing Gloria's light amidst all this darkness. It's all we can do in times like this." He clears his throat as the kettle starts whistling behind them.

"That's the tea. Please, make yourself comfortable." Father Kenneth motions to a small sitting room just by the front door as he disappears into the rectory kitchen. Christine nestles into a faded pink-and-white pin-striped chair in the small living area and waits for the priest, her mind still reeling from the weird email.

Could Graham not be the perfect prince everyone seems to think he is? Is there reason to suspect that he might not be the best person to handle Grow 2 Glo in Gloria's absence? Or is Father Kenneth jealous of Graham's being named to head up the charity? Did he expect to be left in control of the nonprofit, given he has been so involved in the organization over the years?

Outside the sitting room window, the cathedral where Jane and Graham will be married tomorrow is being pelted by rain. The giant gargoyles perched at either end of the entrance make it seem like a better place for a pagan ritual than a wedding.

"Here we are." Father Kenneth returns and places a tray with a small teapot and two mismatched cups on a rickety coffee table, then perches on the edge of a sagging salmon-colored sofa.

"It was so kind of Father O'Donnell to let us use the rectory for our little chat," he says.

"Yes, it's uh, charming," Christine musters, and takes out her notebook. "You don't mind if I take down a few notes, do you?"

He blows on his tea before replying. "Not at all. Whatever you need. I'm here to help. And I'm certainly happy for the distraction . . . But I must say, I'm surprised I made the cut. Imagine me, featured in *Bespoke*." He chuckles softly.

"I always like to talk to the officiant. They have the best insight into the couple in my opinion." As Christine observes the priest up close—in his expensive suit, with his perfectly gelled hair—she feels his similarities to her grandfather, who rarely wore anything but his beat-up Levi's and an oil-stained shirt from his auto shop, fade away. Truthfully, she has never seen a less priestly-looking priest in her life—and she went to Catholic school, and she's Italian, so she's met a lot of priests.

"So," Christine says, smoothing out the open page in her notebook, "Father Kenneth, you've been an honorary member of the Ripton family for many years now, correct?"

"Yes. Gloria Beaufort—may God bless her soul," he adds quietly, "was a member of my congregation for many years. She was my first friend when I was placed in Charleston. I was just twenty-five. Gloria was a new mother and already a successful businesswoman. We were an unlikely match for fast friends." His upper lip quivers as he brings the cup of tea to his lips.

"I'm sorry," Christine offers. "I know talking about her under these circumstances must be incredibly difficult." Christine crosses her legs, giving her other shoe a moment of reprieve from the shaggy rectory carpet. "How did you two meet?"

"Gloria came to me after her marriage ended, seeking forgiveness from God. Divorce is a sin in the Catholic church. She wanted to be absolved." Christine briefly stops taking notes. Even though she only met her briefly, she can't imagine Gloria Beaufort "seeking forgiveness" from anyone.

"Ms. Beaufort was a great patron of the church, right? How much money did she donate over the years exactly? I've heard it could be in the millions." Christine tries to make the question sound off the cuff, but Father Kenneth sits up a little straighter, hesitating before he responds.

"Gloria's donations did countless good for the church, on many fronts. But it's really her nonprofit Grow 2 Glo that will be her legacy," the priest asserts. Christine perks up—the opening she was hoping for.

"Can you tell me a little about Grow 2 Glo?" she asks before quickly adding, "I'd love to give the organization a mention in my article."

"Yes," Father Kenneth says, brightening. "It's become my life's work, second to God, of course." He winks. "Our mission is to support South Carolina's youth through funding scholarships, sponsoring community centers, and any other initiatives the brilliant team can come up with."

"And what's your role at the organization, exactly?" Christine asks. "I understand you're very involved."

"Chief Operations Officer," he says, and smiles. "But I am also head coach for the Grow 2 Glo beach volleyball team—a position I take very seriously. We are two-time defenders of the Charleston Champions for Charity League Cup." He grins and Christine clocks his long legs, his broad shoulders—even in his seventies, you can tell Father Kenneth is athletic.

"I'm sure Gloria is immensely grateful to you, Father," Christine continues, "given all the good work you've done on her behalf over the years. I understand that you will carry on her legacy with Graham Ripton at the helm of Grow 2 Glo. I'm sure you're happy that the organization will remain family-run." Christine casually reaches for her mug of tea, keeping her eyes trained on the priest. She takes a sip of the warm liquid and watches his face closely, catching the subtle clench of his jaw. He takes his time before responding, considering his words.

"Graham and I . . ." he starts. He stops and shakes his head before continuing. "Well, we have different visions for the future of Grow 2 Glo. We're from different generations. But I'm confident we'll sort it out." His words are kind but firm. "The focus right now is on his marriage to Jane." Father Kenneth's smile crumples, his expression now stern. "And that's what we should be discussing." Christine is momentarily caught off guard by the frostiness.

"You're right, sorry." She quickly tries to shuffle the conversation along. "I got a little side-tracked. Could you tell me about the hymns that the couple picked out for their ceremony?" Father Kenneth looks at her skeptically for a moment but ultimately launches into a speech on the history of "Ave Maria," followed by a dissertation-level analysis of the readings Graham and Jane selected for the ceremony. As he talks, Christine's mind drifts. There is no mistaking that the priest is not thrilled about Graham's being tapped to run the charity. There is something going on there.

"Anything else I can tell you, my dear?" Father Kenneth says, jolting her back into reality.

"Just one more question for you, Father, and then I'll be out of your hair," she says quickly, glancing at her list. "What would you say was your first impression of the couple when you started seeing them for Pre-Cana?" The priest smiles warmly, eyes dewy with happy tears.

"I could tell from the moment that they started preparing for the sacrament of marriage that they were made for each other. A perfect shining example of God's love and plan for us all. That's what I love about Pre-Cana, it really—"

But before Father Kenneth can give Christine a lesson on the history of Pre-Cana classes (aka the practice where old unmarried men give young couples relationship advice), the interview is interrupted by a woman's scream. The high-pitched cry echoes through the thin rectory walls, and they both leap to their feet to look out the window. A bus that is shuttling members of the bridal party to the church has pulled up outside the cathedral, and a group looks on as Clementine Ripton stands screaming in the middle of the street.

NINETEEN

# CLEMENTINE

Clementine and Trey's Wedding Day
May 1993
Charleston, South Carolina

COLLEEN CLEMENTINE FITZGERALD STANDS AT the back of St. Agnes church in Charleston, South Carolina, trying not to throw up. Black spots creep into her vision as she feels her father's grip tighten on her arm. Bobby Fitzgerald is not a man to be toyed with, and everyone knows that. Especially Clementine. Well, apparently not everyone. A flower girl tugs on a bridesmaid's lavender puffy dress and says, "Can we go already?"

The bridesmaid, Clementine's sister, Madeline, hurries to shush her, but the bride has heard enough. She runs outside the church and into the snarling heat. It's an unseasonably warm day for May. It's been over an hour—an hour—that guests have been waiting for her to walk down the aisle and marry Trey. Who, by the way, is nowhere to be found.

Clementine's eyes blink rapidly as if she's just waking up for the first time since meeting her fiancé last year. Ever since the day Trey walked into Sully's BBQ and into her life, everything has been blurry and buzzy with new love . . . until this moment. Now Clementine's earliest memories of meeting her fiancé are coming back too vividly—and they're about as unforgiving as the overhead lights in a Macy's fitting room.

She remembers the moment Trey walked into her bar with a pack of salty, swearing guys: a bachelor party. The kind of bad luck that only comes at the end of your shift. But the tips would be great, and she was just a couple of grand away from finally being able to move out of her parents' house. Maybe soon she'd even have enough to move to New York. The shining city lights of Manhattan were getting brighter and brighter—they were almost within reach.

"Hi, y'all, what can I get you?" She smiled at the table, and they all smiled back. She held her head high as ten separate gazes looked her up and down.

"A round of Miller Lites please, Clementine. Beautiful name," Trey said, eyes lingering on the name tag just above her right breast. She hadn't noticed him at first, but when he said her name, a light switch somewhere deep in her heart turned on and a current ran through her. Even after it all started crumbling down, Clementine would always feel confident that what she had experienced that night was love at first sight.

But now, on her wedding day, (sans groom) she feels faint at the memory. Her veil feels more like a heavy blanket than a Ripton family heirloom. A church door slams and out marches her future mother-in-law, Gloria Beaufort, looking strong and confident in a navy Chanel suit. Gloria could have just as easily walked out of a boardroom instead of a church, but that's just Gloria—always business. Clementine stands up a little straighter in her presence as she always does.

"I'm so sorry." Gloria embraces Clementine, her voice like honey. "Don't worry. He's here. We got him." It feels more like Clementine is being told that police found her attacker and not that her mother-in-law found her fiancé.

"What happened? Where was he?" Maybe there's an excuse, maybe there's an explanation.

"Don't worry about that now. I talked some sense into him. Trey's not about to disgrace this family. Not again." Gloria dabs sweat off Clementine's brow with a handkerchief, nearly scratching her face with a giant aquamarine cocktail ring. It's not exactly what Clementine was hoping to hear, but Gloria has never been one to put things delicately.

"Under-promise, over-deliver. It's the first and most steadfast rule of business," she'd said to Clementine the first time Trey brought her back to his family home on South of Broad.

*Not again.* The words drip with bad memories. Clementine thought she was different, but she wasn't, was she? She thinks back to that first night she met Trey. They stayed at the bar until 5 a.m., her completely sober, him nursing a beer. They talked about everything, neither of them allowing the conversation to end, even as the pink and orange-sherbet hues of the next morning creeped in through the windows.

Trey canceled his plane ticket back to New York that morning. He spent the week with her, rediscovering his home city. Long walks on King Street, hazy beach days on Sullivan's Island. Laughing, kissing—like the opening scene of *Grease*. Trey loved that she was carefree, that she was into yoga—which was not mainstream at the time. He listened to her poetry. She shared her dreams with him; he joined her in breath work and meditation, unironically. When she was with Trey, Clementine was launched into a sparkly new reality where she was a queen whose every quality was to be admired and worshiped. With Trey it was different—it was intoxicating. But looking back, she wonders if it was *him* that made her feel that way, or all the pot they were smoking.

It wasn't until his last day in town, idling in her Jeep at the airport terminal, ready to send him back to business school, that she even thought to ask, "Whose bachelor party were you in town for, anyway?" He squirmed away from her, avoiding eye contact. And that was her answer.

"I can't do this," Clementine whispers to Gloria. "I'm sorry, but if Trey could do this to me for no reason, no excuse . . ." She trails off, a sad slideshow of happy memories flashing through her brain.

"He just overslept," Gloria snaps. "Too much drinking—or God knows what—last night. I warned them not to go back to that seedy bar." Clementine bristles at the mention of Sully's. It's not seedy. It's the kind of bar that would host the likes of Hemingway or Steinbeck; artists, writers, and poets all flock to Sully's. It's perfect—with its thin screen door that blows back and forth in the ocean air and its well-loved stools etched lovingly with the initials of its past patrons; it's as close as someone can get to the beating heart of humanity. Of course Gloria wouldn't understand that.

"Really? He overslept on his wedding day?" Clementine reaches up to take off her veil. Gloria grabs her arm.

Clementine yelps. "Ouch—what are you doing?"

"What are *you* doing?" Gloria's eyes blaze. "You broke up my original match for Trey and now you seem intent on setting fire to whatever's left of his reputation." Clementine knows she's never been Gloria's favorite, but the bluntness of the comment catches her off guard.

"I thought we loved each other, but, but—" Clementine bites her fingernail, and her thumb starts to bleed, staining the cuff of her lace sleeve.

"Don't be so naive. I'm helping you here. I dragged him down here, didn't I?" Gloria yanks on the veil and reinforces the pins. Clementine winces in pain.

"Dragged him?" Trying not to pass out, she steadies herself against a magnolia tree. She feels the familiar sensation of fury building deep inside her. *Deep breaths, one, two, three* . . .

"It's a figure of speech." Gloria takes out a cigarette and offers one to the bride. Clementine refuses, still focusing on her breath.

"Listen." Gloria shrugs and lights up, blowing a ring of smoke that quickly melts into the humid air. "I can't force you to do anything. But I'll just say this: if you walk away now, you'll never get out of this town. You want to be an actor? A writer? An artist? A rodeo clown?" Gloria laughs, and Clementine feels her jaw clench. "Well, this is your chance. Trey can provide you with a one-way ticket to that life." She takes a long drag of her cigarette.

"Gloria, he tried to . . . leave . . . me . . . at . . . the . . . altar!" Clementine enunciates each word for clarity, her voice dangerously close to a scream.

"Ah, ah, ah." Ash floats down from Gloria's burning cigarette. "He overslept. Just sage him or whatever it is you do."

Clementine has the primal urge to lunge at her but she focuses on her breathing. She can control this—*innnnn, outtttt, innnn, outttt.*

Gloria sighs. "Look," she says more gently, softening her approach. "I think you're good for Trey—I do, really. I have *also* had it up to here with his antics. It's time for him to settle down with a nice, simple girl and stay out of the press. He's embarrassing me too."

Clementine shouldn't be shocked that Gloria is somehow making this moment about *her* relationship with Trey, yet she is. She stares at the woman, mouth agape.

"And for what it's worth," Gloria goes on obliviously, "I think all that yoga mumbo jumbo you're into will be good for him. Maybe he'll finally lose that flabby belly of his."

Clementine balls her fists at "yoga mumbo jumbo." Gloria is always diminishing her.

Maybe if Gloria ever thought to ask Clementine about her life—maybe if Gloria tried to get to know her future daughter-in-law *at all*—Clementine would tell her about her ongoing mental health battle . . . the one that had brought her to her knees and to the practice of yoga; she'd tell her about how the art of meditation freed her to *feel* and write her poetry again, allowing her reprieve from the mind-numbing drugs prescribed to her by her psychiatrist. But, no, Gloria is too wrapped up in herself to care about anyone else.

Gloria continues as Clementine glares at her. "My son is not perfect. I know this—but now, thanks to me, he's here, you're here, we're all here." Gloria puts out her cigarette. "A word of advice on your wedding day," she says, and gives Clementine a mean smile. "Life is long, and life is hard. It's best you learn now that people will constantly disappoint you. In my experience, the saying that if you're going to cry, you might as well cry in a Mercedes rings true. Come to think of it," Gloria says, pulling the giant glittering aquamarine off her finger, "here. Have a cocktail ring to take the edge off." She places the ring in Clementine's palm, and her hand is immediately weighed down by its heft. "See? Things are better already."

Clementine closes her fist around the ring and imagines throwing it at the back of Gloria's blond head as she walks back into the church. After ten deep breaths, she finally opens her palm, revealing puncture marks and tiny drops of blood from her intense grip on the stone. She stares at it, still under the shade of the magnolia, trapped in time.

She has two futures laid out before her, and she has minutes—no, probably seconds—to make a choice. The ring burns in her hand, while the possibility of a future with Trey burns in her mind. Does she even love him anymore? Can their relationship recover from this blow? But either way, Gloria is right—he can help her make her dreams come true. Instead of slumming it in some Harlem walk-up, she can leave for auditions from the comfort of Trey's West Village brownstone, keys to the Mercedes in hand. She could be connected with anyone and everyone in his high-profile Rolodex. If she gets homesick, she can come back to Charleston and stay at his family's gorgeous (and virtually always empty) mansion. Even if she fails, if she crumbles under the pressure, succumbs to her demons . . . she can still live a life of immense comfort and luxury.

But if she marries Trey, will everything be too easy? Will she ever *truly* "make it"? Or will all of her accomplishments be diluted by her association with Gloria Beaufort? It's an impossible decision; both roads lead to regret, and she's already angry about the impossibility of it all. She feels her breath catch, wrath wriggling into her bones. But a few minutes later, she stands at the back of the church again. When the organ starts playing "Here Comes the Bride," she walks into her new life, eyes wide open. Her engagement ring to Trey is on one hand, her aquamarine consolation prize from Gloria on the other.

At the altar, she trembles as she slides the wedding band onto Trey's finger. Looking out at the sea of smiling guests, she sees herself from their perspective: a bride trembling with emotion on her wedding day. But what they are really seeing is a woman vibrating with anger . . . that she now feared might never go away.

It turns out she was right about that. You can't yoga your way out of a cheating husband, or "om" your way out of a mental health crisis.

TWENTY

## CHRISTINE

Friday, October 17, 2025
Afternoon of Rehearsal Dinner

"YOU GAVE HER THAT RING?" Clementine howls at Trey. "At our son's wedding? Shame on you!"

Christine follows Father Kenneth outside as Graham leaps to restrain his mother, lifting her off the ground and carrying her to the far side of the coach. Suspended in the air and kicking her feet in her elaborate gold cape dress, Clementine looks like she's playing Wonder Woman in a community theater play, and in lieu of an expensive rigging system, the director opted to have Graham carry her across the stage.

"Get that ring off her finger," Clementine shrieks. Her face is blotchy, wet with tears. Trey whispers something to Raquel. He places his hand on the small of her back, but the starlet shrugs him off, motioning for him to go to his wife.

"Clem, sweetie, I just lent it to her for the evening... See how it matches her dress so beautifully?" He cautiously approaches his wife like she is a wild animal. "And you *hate* that ring. I've never seen you wear it—"

"She needs to leave—now." Clementine trembles, closing her eyes and inhaling deeply. She steadies herself on Graham's arm. The groom's expression is blank as he gently helps his mother put her shoe back on. *It's almost like he's used to this,* Christine thinks. *Maybe he is.* Christine remembers Clementine's white knuckles gripping the knife when Raquel spoke about the jet this morning and gulps.

"What on God's green earth is going on?" Father Kenneth turns to Raquel, who throws up her hands in exasperation. Her pillowy lips mouth, "She's crazy."

"She thinks we're having an affair!" Trey insists. "But we're not, Father. I promise, we're not! I truly didn't think you'd miss the ring for one night, darling." Trey tries to grab his wife's hand, but Clementine yanks it away.

"She tried to come at me with her shoe!" Raquel exclaims, pouting and crossing her arms over her very revealing low-cut navy dress.

"And then I thought better of it. You're not worth the dirt under my feet," Clementine scoffs bitterly, then, hands trembling, reaches into her purse and pulls out a bottle of pills. She rattles them in her husband's face and throws two back. "Happy now?"

Christine doesn't know what to think in this moment; she feels sorry for Clementine on so many fronts—sorry she married someone like Trey, sorry she's clearly in the throes of some sort of mental health crisis, and sorry that Raquel had the audacity to come to this wedding at all, let alone be a bridesmaid. *Could Clementine have snapped? Perhaps it was she who killed Gloria in the heat of an argument about Trey's philandering?* Christine shudders. It doesn't seem out of the realm of possibility.

"Okay, everyone." Elliot claps his hands, smiling maniacally. "Let's get into the church, move it, move it!" Christine watches Jane squeeze Graham's hand tightly as they walk toward the cathedral. At Elliot's coaxing, everyone reluctantly trickles into the church after them. Christine doesn't move from her place on the gravel drive—and neither does Ben.

"Not you. A word?" Ben grabs Raquel's arm, spinning the bridesmaid around. Momentarily, it looks like they're doing a dance; Raquel's shimmering blue off-the-shoulder cocktail dress swishes beautifully as he turns her around. Then Christine clocks her perturbed face.

"I have nothing to say to you," she says bluntly, and tries to wriggle out of his grasp.

"I wasn't asking." He pulls her toward a small cemetery behind the rectory. *Am I the only one seeing this?* Christine thinks as she watches the last of the bridal party disappear into the church. Not even Trey turns around to check on his alleged mistress.

Ben's tight grip compels Christine to follow them. As the best man pulls a hobbling Raquel away from the cathedral, Christine walks in the opposite direction, planning to sneak around the other side of the rectory to listen in. She takes off her heels, hanging them from her wrist as she tiptoes around the little white building.

"Whatever is going on between you and my dad, it ends now," Ben demands. The wind whips around, ruining Raquel's fresh blowout, her dark curls fly all over the place, making her look like Medusa. Their backs are to Christine as they face the cathedral opposite the small graveyard. She struggles to hear exactly what's being said, so she hunches down, using the tombstones to shield her body so she can get closer.

"Your father is an adult. He can do as he pleases," Raquel retorts. She tries to hold down her thick brown locks to keep them from getting any more windswept.

"You can keep the ring. My mom will forget about it," Ben offers. "But that's it." He releases his grip on her arm. Raquel takes the opportunity to take a few steps back from him. Christine zeros in on her finger, which now boasts what must be a ten-karat aquamarine cocktail ring.

"Don't try to *negotiate* with me." She scowls at him and pulls a cashmere shawl off the strap of her black Bottega bag, wrapping herself in it.

"All right. How much, Raquel? How much for you to just get the fuck out of here after this weekend?" Ben's shouting now, the vein on his forehead throbbing. Christine feels herself start to sweat. Raquel just laughs.

"A million? Two?" Ben asks . . . And even though it sounds like a joke to Christine's broke ears, she knows he's serious.

Raquel takes a step toward Ben. In her six-inch Jimmy Choos, she meets him at eye level. "What I want can't be bought—it has to be earned," she snarls.

"In my experience, there is not much my family can't buy," Ben sneers. There is a pause as the autumn leaves swirl around them on the wind, almost as if their standoff is creating some sort of vortex.

"I don't want Gloria Beaufort's money. I want *to be* Gloria Beaufort," Raquel says crisply. Christine feels goose bumps spread across her body.

Raquel continues. "Your dad and I have business together. He's made promises to me and I intend to see that he keeps them."

"And what could possibly make you think that my dad's a man of his word?" Ben scoffs.

Raquel shrugs. "I just have a gut feeling that he'll give me what I want." She admires her cocktail ring briefly. "Gorgeous, isn't it?"

Raquel turns to leave, but Ben grabs her again before she's out of reach. The wind is relentless now, blowing up Raquel's dress and revealing her shapewear underneath. *Stars, they're just like us!* Christine thinks as she struggles to hold down her own dress with her free hand.

"I'm not joking, Raquel. If you don't end things—it will get very bad for you."

"Are you *threatening* me? Is that why Sebi isn't here? Did you threaten him too?" Christine's heart races. She remembers Lyle asking Gloria the same question last night: *Where's Sebi?*

"I have no idea where he is, and frankly, I don't care. This isn't about him—it's about protecting my family from *you*." The wind is howling now, and Christine worries that the dark clouds overhead are on the verge of dumping rain again.

"Frankly, Ben, I'm the least of your problems. Now get away from me." Raquel frees herself and heads for the iron gates that lead out of the cemetery. Christine notices a figure loitering by the cathedral door, watching the scene unfold. She squints but she can't quite tell who it is. It was a flash of white—possibly Jane? Before she can blink again, they're gone.

"I know you got in last night," Ben shouts desperately. Raquel pauses by the cemetery gate.

Ben keeps talking. "I have access to the jet log, Raquel. So, if you're not sleeping with my dad, what were you up to all evening?" The wind whips through the silence that follows, carrying an array of colorful leaves with it. Raquel's mouth opens, her body twitching with the words she wants to say, but ultimately, she walks through the gate toward the church without giving Ben the satisfaction, leaving him alone among the dead. He watches her disappear up the cobblestone steps and into the cathedral before sagging to the ground, sitting on the edge of an unmarked tombstone, running his hand through his hair, texting on his phone.

Christine moves closer to him. She wants to know more; she needs to know more. *Are Trey and Raquel actually having an affair? What did Raquel mean when she said she wanted to* be *Gloria Beaufort? And her whereabouts last night . . . is it possible she could be the murderer?*

Christine slinks across the wet grass, hiding behind a large tombstone for a man named Gary Finnegan (sorry, Gary) when her phone shrieks with a *PING!* She rushes to silence it, as the words NEW VOICEMAIL FROM SANDRA YOON light up her screen, but the high-pitched chime rings through the air. She holds her breath and hopes the loud weather muffled her phone. After a few agonizing seconds, she dares to peek her head out from behind the tombstone to see if Ben heard the notification. His head is cocked, his eyes narrowed. *Shit,* she thinks. *He heard it.* But ultimately, Ben just shakes his head, pulls a flask out of his jacket pocket, and takes a swig.

TWENTY-ONE

# BEN

Two Months Earlier

BEN SHOULD NEVER HAVE AGREED to go to Paris for their anniversary. But when Lyle asked him months ago, her face struggling to contain her extreme excitement, he didn't have the heart to say no. He hadn't seen her face light up like that in so long.

"I have to go to Italy for work the following week anyway! Come on, honey, Paris is always a good idea!" she pressed. And Ben loves his wife. He loves her so much, he agreed to go even as their company navigates what will surely be a massive, damaging lawsuit.

Now here he is, standing on the balcony of the Four Seasons looking at the Eiffel Tower, inhaling his Juul like that viral picture of Ben Affleck smoking cigarettes mid-breakdown. Nothing hopeful stirs inside of him as he gazes out on the City of Lights—unless you count the bottle of Jack Daniel's he finished an hour ago. Lyle hasn't been herself recently and Ben fears the worst. That maybe she's . . . being herself with someone else. Ben has kept the thought at bay for as long as possible, but here in Paris, it's hard to ignore. After all, this is the city where he first found out about his dad's numerous infidelities. It's the city where he and Lyle met.

A warm breeze wafts away the banana scent of his e-cigarette. Does he confront her? Does he start reading her texts? How did they get to this point? He sits down on a patio chair and puts his head in his hands. Everything is starting to become too much.

When his grandmother introduced him to Lyle, Ben knew she was the one. It's almost as if Gran handpicked her for him, plucking her from *Bespoke* and dropping her off at his door. He still remembers shaking her hand for the first time, the shock he felt when their fingers touched as he said, "Welcome to the team."

He loves everything about Lyle. The way she throws her head back when she laughs, the mole on her lower back, the way she bites her lip when she's thinking. She's razor-sharp—a force in the fashion and beauty worlds alike. Yet she's also incredibly warm and thoughtful. Always humming and making delicious egg sandwiches with avocado and tomato on a Sunday morning just the way he likes them. And fun! She's the first at the party and the last to leave.

*She was perfect*, he thinks. Wait, what is he saying? *She is perfect*. It's his family that's the problem. They ruin everything. Deep down, he knows that if his wife has wronged him in any way, they're at the root of it. He hears laughter on the city streets below; he looks down to see a young couple embracing under one of the dim streetlights, lost in the lavender haze.

Ben used to love Paris. He loved coming here with Gran for the company parties, meetings, and of course fashion week. It's a vibrant, artistic city. A city for lovers. And a city for cheaters, apparently. That's what he found out when he caught his father kissing a woman who was not Ben's mother in this very same hotel. Of course, Lyle doesn't know that—he tries to shield her from as much as he can when it comes to his family dysfunction.

Ben peeks his head through the balcony door. Lyle sleeps soundly in their sprawling king bed, blissfully unaware of his emotional turmoil, and he wants to keep it that way. He just has to keep pushing it all down. He walks back out onto the balcony and looks at his phone. There's an update from Chase & Brown on the status of their pending class action lawsuit—and it's not a good one. The unraveling of his family's company has been gradual and seemingly purposeful on his father's part. Trey is an incompetent businessperson, and he seems hell bent on destroying the company Gran built from nothing.

When Lyle recommitted to being a part of the family business after their wedding, despite her pregnancy, everyone breathed a collective sigh of relief. Ben was thrilled to continue to work with her to bring Glo to new heights. But of course, this coincided with his father's ramped up self-sabotage—starting with the godforsaken Gloss Drops that led to this lawsuit in the first place. Something nags at him, though; his dad has insinuated that the Gloss Drops fiasco wasn't his brainchild. But when Ben pushed for more information about this, Trey just shut down.

Closing his eyes, he takes another drag of his e-cigarette. Ben has tried to make it work with his family—he really has tried. They just seem to make a point of doing the opposite of what he advises. The door cracks open behind him. Quickly, he shoves his Juul into his pocket. He told Lyle that he quit.

"Hey, what are you doing up? It's late." Lyle wraps her arms around his waist. The feel of her silky pajamas instantly puts him at ease. She sniffs the air but doesn't say anything. They're in Paris; she'll let it slide.

"Jet lag, I think." He pulls her in tightly, taking in her subtle citrus scent. Being married to a woman like Lyle is the best thing in the world. She nestles into his chest.

"Why are *you* up? I just saw you sound asleep," he says, and kisses her forehead.

"I got a text from Isabelle Arnold's rep. They're pissed we didn't sign her for the next campaign." She yawns.

For a while Ben couldn't understand why his dad refused to sign Isabelle Arnold as the new face of Glo's fragrance. She's a rising Hollywood star with a stellar reputation who for some reason (or thanks to some talentless manager) was interested in partnering with them. Instead, they signed Raquel Williams. Ben's blood boils at the thought.

"Are you stressed about work?" Lyle rubs his back just the way he likes. How could he doubt her faithfulness? She loves him.

"When am I not stressed about it?" A wave of guilt washes over him. He's ruining their trip.

"Let's stop talking about Glo. It's our anniversary," he says, and smiles. "We'll deal with all of that when we get home." Lyle's iPhone lock screen flashes to life with a new notification, briefly showing a picture of their ruddy-cheeked toddler, Miles—but when Lyle clicks on it, she groans.

"What is it now?" He kisses her neck.

"It's her." She shoves her phone in his face, and there it is—Raquel Williams taking a shot of tequila in a thong bikini on the cover of *Page Six*.

No, they couldn't hire Isabelle Arnold. They had to hire Raquel Williams: Hollywood's hottest mess. Sure, she was always in the press . . . for all the wrong reasons: partying too much, public fights with her ex, and now, it seemed, semi-pornographic bikini photos! Ben snorts. Of course this is who his father wants to hire. Probably because he wants to sleep with her.

"Another brilliant decision by Dad," he says with a sigh. The dazzling Eiffel Tower light show fizzles to an end.

"Look on the bright side," Lyle says. "At least her ass looks well-moisturized." They both giggle. The laughter slowly grows into a belly laugh and then descends into a full-on howl. Ben hasn't laughed this hard in a long time. He wipes the happy tears from his face and looks at his wife, only to realize that she's now crying real tears.

"Hey, hey—what's wrong?" He pulls her close again. Her warm body shivers in his arms.

"Sweetie, I have to tell you something." Her voice is distant. She pulls away from him.

"You can tell me anything. What is it? Is everything okay?" He takes her face in his hands and looks at her, really looks at her.

"It's bad. It's very bad." She's sobbing now.

Ben's heart thumps in his chest.

"I made a big mistake."

Ben waits for her to open her mouth and say the words that can't be unsaid.

Lyle continues talking but Ben can't hear anything. He watches her lips move. All his worst fears and deepest insecurities are morphing into his reality: the failed relationships, the women who just wanted to be with him for the money, for his name. Lyle wasn't any different. She loves someone else. Nobody loves Ben; everybody just uses him.

"It didn't mean anything." The words flow out of her now like water from a dam that has finally broken, drowning everything in its path, everything that they built just washed away. Pushing his wife aside, he grabs the railing, part of him hoping that it also gives up on him and that he can be smashed to bits on the streets of Paris.

"Gloria found out," Lyle sniffles. "And she's been blackmailing me—since our wedding." She sobs at the admission of her *years* of infidelity. "She intimidated me into agreeing to work for Glo in exchange for not telling you about the affair, said if I didn't do as she instructed, she'd tell you."

Lyle's heaving now. "I can't live with her lording it over me anymore. I can't—I'm so sorry. I had to tell you; it was eating me alive. But . . . but I want to fix this. I want to work to put it behind us. I want to be free of this awful mistake. And that's what it was Ben—a huge *mistake*." The city buzzes around him. A car horn, a rogue drunken laugh—he's jealous of everyone in the world that isn't him right now.

Why is everyone in his life so broken? It's not fair. His father's a liar and a cheater. He's married to a liar and a cheater. His grandmother is a manipulative narcissist who knowingly let him enter a fraudulent marriage. What is he supposed to do with all this? Just sit here and take it like a schmuck?

"Please tell me you can forgive me. We're a family. I love you. It's been killing me. I don't want it to poison our future. I needed to tell you so we can begin healing . . . so we can move on." Lyle's body is seizing now, physically ridding itself of the dirty secret.

"Who is he?" Ben whispers.

"It doesn't matter." She sighs. "It's over now."

"Who is he, Lyle?" Ben says with a growl. "You at least owe me that." She waits a beat and then says *his* name. Ben's heart breaks.

"Convenient you're going to Positano right after this," he says finally, still staring at the concrete of their patio, unable to look at her.

"Ben, look at me." Lyle takes his head in her hands, forcing him to face her. "I promise you it's over. It's very, very over. It could not be more over. You have to believe me." She starts to cry again. "I want nothing more than to never think of it or speak of it again. I love you. It was a stupid mistake. And it felt like a mistake from the beginning. And I don't know, Gloria's threats, her holding it over me—it made it so much worse." She covers her face with her hands, her giant princess cut engagement ring sparkling in the moonlight.

"I'm not sure I can get past this." He buries his face in his hands. "But I want to try. For us. For Miles—" Their baby.

Suddenly an image of his dark-haired, olive-skinned son flashes before him and Ben asks, "Is he even mine?" *My grandfather was Sicilian!* his mother-in-law had proclaimed when Miles was born. Oh god, he is such a fool.

"I—I don't know genetically," Lyle blurts, "but he is our son in every sense. Miles is your son." Lyle curls up on a pin-striped chaise lounge, the Eiffel Tower glistening behind her, illuminating her tears even more.

With this final reveal, Ben lets himself split open. He cries, a guttural, exorcist-level sob—for everything. For his father, his wife, for the son who isn't really his. And it feels, honestly, really good. Another drink wouldn't hurt either. Ben makes his way through the balcony doors to the high-end minibar. Anything to numb the pain he feels at this moment.

He cracks open a bottle of Grey Goose and drinks it straight. Shuddering—only partially from the vodka—he thinks of his grandmother. She let him marry a woman who was actively cheating on him and then proceeded to blackmail her. It doesn't even make sense. Why did she want Lyle in their family so badly? Didn't his Gran think *he* was competent enough to manage Glo when she was gone? The lack of faith that Gran apparently has in him stings almost as bad as the infidelity.

There are no clear answers, just clear alcohol. He takes another sip. The vodka burns everything in its path. For a brief moment, his mind leaves his body, and he watches himself smash the bottle against the gilded hotel wall. Lyle shrieks from the balcony. A framed print of two Parisian lovers smiling at each other in a café lies shattered on the floor in front of him, glass glittering on the carpet. He admires his own destruction. It feels good to be the destroyer. *Yeah, how about that?* Maybe he gets to break something for once.

The door slams on his way out of the suite, and when the elevator doors open, he takes it all the way down. Before he can forgive, he needs to go low. As the numbers ding with each floor, he can't help it . . . he goes on Instagram and types in the name Sebi Giovanni . . . the guy his wife has been sleeping with. Clicking on stupid picture after stupid picture, two things become clear: 1) Sebi photoshops his abs; and 2) He has a hideous collection of tacky hipster scarves.

Ben watches the little pink circle around Sebi's profile picture glow with a new story and quickly clicks on the icon. It's a repost from the tequila brand Lumina, which is apparently collaborating with some sneaker company, Shoo, to make an . . . ugly pair of neon-green sneakers? Honestly, all of these ridiculous collaborations need to stop. Sebi captions the repost *Can't wait to shoot this insane launch party! September 6—see you at Gusto's!* Ben snorts. This guy thinks he's a serious photographer? What did Lyle ever see in him? The elevator doors open and he struts into the lobby, fists clenched. He has an idea. Ben is going to *finish* this loser.

He texts his assistant: Block my calendar next Saturday, September 6. Ben's not going to be the one getting—*literally*—screwed over anymore.

*Garden Greetings!*

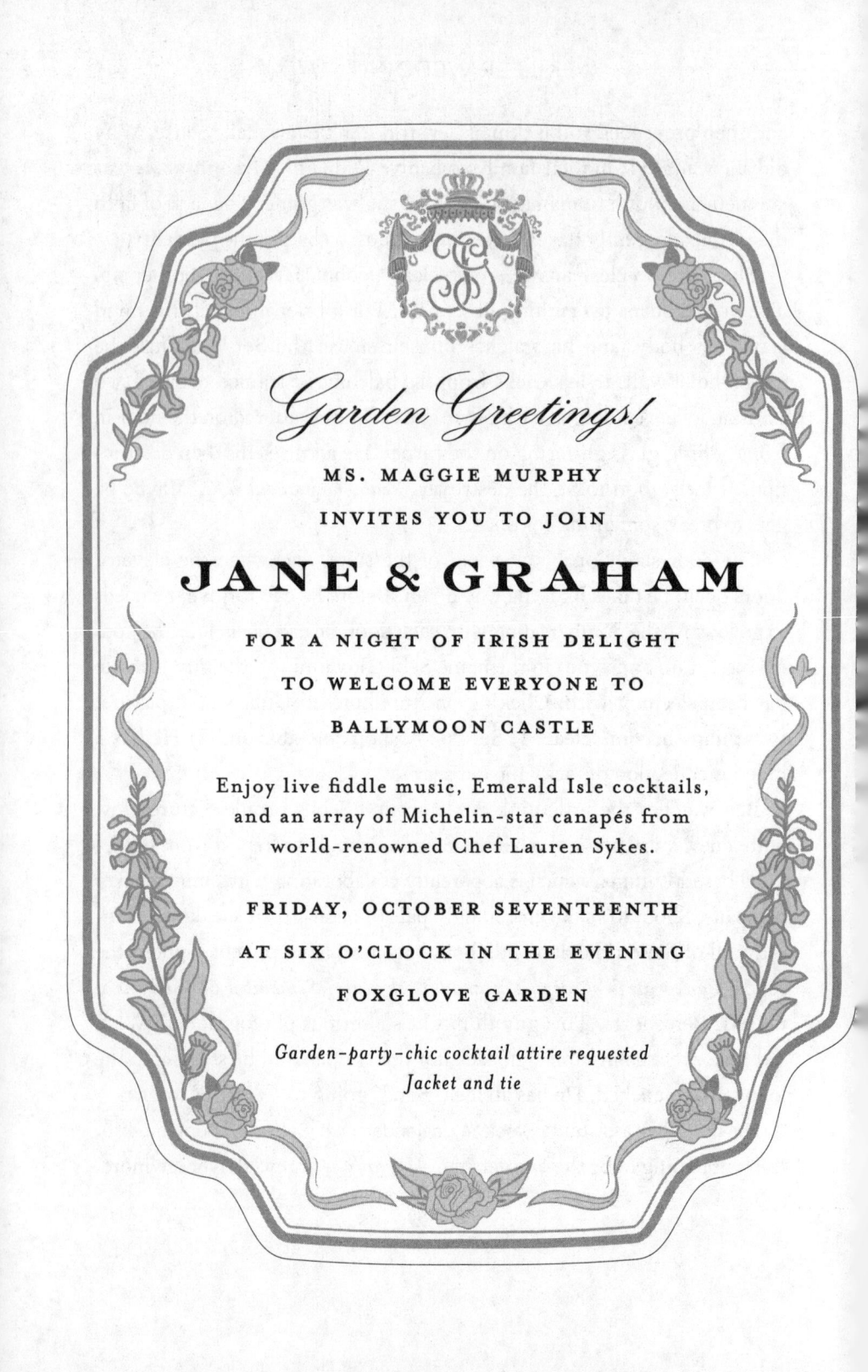

MS. MAGGIE MURPHY

INVITES YOU TO JOIN

# JANE & GRAHAM

FOR A NIGHT OF IRISH DELIGHT

TO WELCOME EVERYONE TO

BALLYMOON CASTLE

Enjoy live fiddle music, Emerald Isle cocktails, and an array of Michelin-star canapés from world-renowned Chef Lauren Sykes.

FRIDAY, OCTOBER SEVENTEENTH

AT SIX O'CLOCK IN THE EVENING

FOXGLOVE GARDEN

*Garden-party-chic cocktail attire requested*
*Jacket and tie*

TWENTY-TWO

# CHRISTINE

Friday, October 17, 2025
Evening of Rehearsal Dinner

ON THE RIDE BACK TO the castle after the church rehearsal, Christine googles the names Sebi and Raquel Williams together just to see what might come up. Once again, the Google gods do not disappoint. Her phone is immediately flooded with numerous GETTY-watermarked pictures of a man named Sebastiano Giovanni and Raquel Williams taken in the Rainbow Room this past spring at what appears to be a party celebrating the launch of Glo's latest fragrance campaign.

From what she can tell, it looks like Sebastiano, who apparently goes by Sebi, is an acclaimed fashion photographer who has worked on numerous high-profile campaigns, including, most recently, Raquel's fragrance campaign for Glo. Christine pulls up Instagram, the next phase of any online-stalking mission, and types in *Sebi Giovanni*. He has around thirty thousand followers—a lot, but not celebrity level. He's one of those people who hovers just on the edge of fame; connected just enough to get invited to all the big parties, but not noteworthy enough to be accosted by the prying eyes of the press and public. He's in the best (and most underrated) class of humanity: he has money, connections, and anonymity.

She zeros in on photos of Glo's Jolie Chose Jaune fragrance campaign. A half-naked Raquel is covered in yellow rose petals; her red lips open in a wide O-shape as she spritzes a Glo perfume bottle onto her neck. The caption reads, *Such a dream shooting this beauty for another iconic Glo campaign. Thanks to the gorgeous Raquel Williams, her team, and everyone at Glo for making this possible #choosejoliechose #raquelwilliams.*

So, Sebi was the photographer who worked on Raquel's infamously risqué Glo perfume ad. *Who cares? Why does everyone keep asking where he is? Was he invited to the wedding and didn't show up? What does Ben have to do with it? Did the two have a falling out?*

Christine tries her Google strategy again—this time typing in the names Sebi Giovanni and Ben Ripton. A bunch of new photos pop up from a Lumina Tequila brand event last month . . . it looks like both Ben and Sebi were in attendance. But there are no pictures of them together. *Did something go down between them at this party? And how do Seamus O'Reilly and Grow 2 Glo fit into all of this?* Christine tries to work through possible scenarios in her mind as the taxi pulls into the castle entryway.

She needs to talk to somebody, someone who can help her make sense of all these mismatched clues and complicated family dynamics. The only person Christine really feels comfortable going to at this point is Lyle—the one who warned her about this family to begin with. Lyle also mentioned Sebi last night to Gloria—maybe she can shed some light on what's going on with the mysterious photographer.

Christine puts down her phone and looks out the window. Ballymoon is perched on the rolling green hills in the distance; it's an impressive sight to behold, especially under the orange flush of the setting sun. The dark clouds have been chopped into small chunks of pink fluff that float around the orange glob like stuffing ripped out of a pillow.

It's hard to tell if they're in the aftermath of the storm or the eye of it. Soon the car rounds the bend, and the twinkling lights in Foxglove Garden come into view. A few guests filter through the archway entrance, signifying the beginning of the rehearsal dinner.

Her cabbie puts the car in park outside the entrance. "Have a nice evening," he says. Christine thanks him before jumping out and walking up the path toward the garden. Her phone starts vibrating, and she groans, remembering her missed call from Sandra. She can't ignore her any longer. Sliding her finger over the unlock button, she plasters on a smile and answers the call.

"Hi," she says sweetly. "So sorry I missed you earlier, we were in the church—"

"You have been off the grid in a way I can't say I appreciate," her boss snaps. Christine feels her stomach twist into knots.

"I know, I know. I'm sorry—it's just been . . . a lot." Christine cringes as the lame excuse leaves her lips.

"Well, it *is* a lot, Christine. There is *a lot* on the line here," Sandra says tersely. The rumors about Sandra's imminent replacement must have some weight to them, because her boss is starting to sound even more desperate.

"Trust me," Christine says, "I've got it under control. Everyone is thrilled with the weekend so far." She almost laughs at her lie before quickly adding, "The pictures are going to be stunning."

"Well, I just got off the line with Cheryl Connor—Ballymoon's general manager—and she seems to think you're a bit stressed and in over your head," Sandra says, and Christine stops in her tracks.

The annoying front desk lady. Sandra asked her to *spy on her*. Christine feels her blood boil. The last thing she needs is that woman sniffing around this mess.

"Well, respectfully, I don't think *Cheryl* knows what she's talking about. In fact, I'd go so far as to say *she* might be in over her head. You should see the flower arrangement she had sent to my room . . . horrific. And I think there might be poison ivy in it." She hears Sandra's voice catch on the other line.

"Luckily I was able to intercept the one going to Jane's room before it was too late," she lies. *Whatever. Sorry, Cheryl.*

"God. Honestly, is anyone even remotely capable anymore?" Sandra groans. Christine relaxes. From Sandra, this is essentially an apology.

"Well, anyway, try to get some comments from Raquel Williams," her boss says. "Her agency just called. They're looking for *Bespoke* to do a feature on her. Apparently, she has a new business venture launching soon," Sandra scoffs. "We'll see if she can get it off the ground. But regardless, Raquel could clearly use some good press based on what I've seen."

Christine feels her mouth dry up a little at the mention of Raquel, her mind replaying her cold words to Ben in the cemetery earlier, but she just takes a deep breath and replies, "I'll see what I can do. I've got to run, the rehearsal dinner is starting and I don't want to miss a minute of it. More content coming soon! Ciao!" She hangs up before Sandra can protest, shoving her phone back into her purse, positive the calls will keep coming. But at this point, Sandra's concerns are the least of her worries.

ONCE SHE'S ASSIMILATED INTO the party, Christine grabs a well-deserved chilled flute of champagne from a passing tray. The night is perfectly crisp, and the party looks almost mystical with its wild array of bright flowers, shimmering tea lights, and crackling fire pits. Christine watches as Clementine and Trey share a brief hug at the end of the path, and a small army of photographers leap into action to capture the moment. The mother and father of the groom pose for the camera, Clementine's pink pumps securely back on her feet, her visible rage from earlier replaced by a medically induced glaze.

Christine searches the sea of silky Net-a-Porter designer dresses and custom Italian suits for Lyle. Everyone looks perfectly lovely, chattering away, enjoying their gin martinis with a twist and caviar-topped canapés. She is stunned momentarily by the normality of it all. To these people who just arrived, tonight must seem like your average million-dollar destination-wedding kickoff. Christine listens for any murmurs about Gloria's absence between snippets of conversation about how the "sea scallops with vadouvan are to die for" and who just got back from St. Barth's, while Irish fiddlers pluck their strings in the background, but she doesn't hear a word.

That's when it hits her; she finally realizes the power of the people she is dealing with. The Riptons can truly make a murder go away—they already have. They can make *her* go away too. She grabs one of the high-top tables for support, the realization physically winding her.

"Evening, madame! Canapé?" Danny sticks a plate of assorted appetizers under her nose, grinning at her. She stares at him for a moment, jarred by his lightheartedness cutting into her death spiral.

"Those look great." She smiles, trying to pull herself out of it. "But I'm worried about the quality control of the Guinness pours without you behind the bar."

"Never fear, I'll be back to it shortly." He laughs. "I threw Neil a bone for a few minutes." Danny nods in the direction of the bar, where Neil is pouring a glass of white wine to the brim while ogling at a tipsy wedding guest in a skintight Hervé Léger bandage dress.

"I see." Christine takes a sip of her drink.

"You have to try this goat cheese and heirloom beetroot thing—the balsamic drizzle Chef puts on top is insane," Danny insists.

"Thanks, but I don't like cheese." Christine smiles.

"What do you mean you don't like cheese?" Danny thrusts the plate closer to her face, adding to her annoyance.

"It upsets my stomach," she says.

"It upsets everyone's stomach . . . *It's cheese.*"

*Well, I don't like feeling bloated and groggy.* Christine doesn't have time to waste defending her position on freaking *cheese*. But she looks down at the goat cheese snack and sighs—it does look good. And honestly, shouldn't she indulge in something at this point?

Christine grabs an appetizer off the plate and shoves it in her mouth. It's delectable. "Delicious!" she says with her mouth full. She now realizes how hungry she is.

"Have another. It's not that Kraft crap they make in America." Danny smiles.

"Do not speak ill of American junk food," Christine says as she humbles herself before the appetizer tray and puts a few more bites on her green *Jane & Graham*–imprinted napkin.

"Sorry, I assumed you were raised on caviar and lobster like this lot," Danny jokes, motioning to the party around them.

"Hardly—except for when I'm working weddings like this." She smiles. "Thank you, though. This is bringing me back to life."

"It's good, yeah? Enjoy. I'll see you later for that pint you promised." Danny grins and turns to let another guest take a few appetizers off his tray.

"Not sure I'll have time," she calls after him, but he's already heading for the bar, where Neil is being swarmed by guests looking for another one of his signature fish-bowl wine pours. Christine tries to keep a satisfied smile at bay by stuffing her face with her appetizers. Danny is into her, she thinks, but the thought is rudely interrupted by three hundred and fifty loud cheers as the happy couple makes their grand entrance.

Jane and Graham must be made of Teflon, because if they are at all rattled by what's happened this weekend, they're not showing it. Jane glows in a pale rose Oscar de la Renta midi dress embroidered with sequin hibiscus flowers. The dress looks like it was designed specifically to mimic the blooms of Ballymoon's garden—which, honestly, it probably was. She absolutely nailed the look: casually elegant, flirty, and perfect for the setting. Graham looks equally dashing in a navy blue suit and subtle shamrock tie. Momentarily, Christine slips into her old life and decides to take a few videos and photos on her phone to send to Sandra as proof of life.

Then Christine makes herself comfortable at the frayed edge of the party, lingering with the spare staff and the smokers. She scans the crowd, but there is still no sign of Lyle. She likes the nook she's chosen for herself, though. This is always her favorite part of covering weddings: observing all of the interactions and details, unnoticed from the sidelines. Every wedding tells a different story—and not just a love story, but a story about friends, family, setting, and style. Except tonight is different. Instead of Christine surveying every detail unnoticed, it feels like all eyes are on her.

Every few minutes, she makes eye contact with another one of her coconspirators. First Clementine, then Elliot—even Jane. Everyone is watching each other, making sure nobody breaks. It's like the prisoners' dilemma in real life: if one of them comes clean about what happened to Gloria, they're all in trouble.

Sandra replies to Christine's text with Plain Jane looks gorg. Don't forget one single detail. Christine's mind instantly replays the events of this morning. The bloodied sheet over Gloria's body, the hotel room in disarray, the family all pointing their fingers at each other. Christine takes a long sip of her champagne; the details she remembers so sharply are not the ones Sandra wants on the pages of *Bespoke Weddings*. Christine wobbles slightly in her heels as a server pushes past her with a tray of martinis, and she bumps directly into the guy behind her, who promptly spills his Manhattan down the side of her dress. Elliot's eyes narrow at her from across the party.

"I'm so sorry," Christine mutters, spinning around—only to be met by Ben's unforgiving hypothermia-blue stare.

"Everything okay, Christine?" He smirks. She stumbles back again, nearly knocking into Clementine this time, who snaps, "Watch where you're going."

"Sorry, sorry," she says, but the Riptons turn away from her, and the party starts to spin; colors blurring, manic laughter growing louder, the smell of sizzling lamb from the barbeque making her nauseated. A photographer's camera flashes in her face. It's all too much. She forces her way through the crowd toward the bathroom for a moment of reprieve.

At the vanity, Christine splashes water on her face, her hands trembling. *Keep it together*, she mumbles to herself as she takes a hand towel and blots her dress. Luckily, the thick black fabric is very forgiving and has pretty much hidden any signs of a stain from Ben's drink. Raquel breezes into the bathroom just as she's about to brace herself and head back into the party.

"Ah! Tell me it wasn't red wine," she groans as she parks herself in front of the mirror next to Christine, looking at her slightly damp dress.

"No, thank God," she replies weakly. Christine grabs another towel to continue blotting her dress. She wants a minute with Raquel, given what happened in the cemetery—maybe she'll say something useful.

"Good." Raquel smiles and pulls a tube of lipstick out of her purse. "I just needed a breather. God, being a bridesmaid is exhausting. I feel like I'm on a press tour."

Christine nods, like she also understands how draining a press tour can be, even though the closest thing she's ever experienced to one is probably when her nana died, and they had to traipse all over Cleveland to scatter her ashes in random locations, because her aunts and uncles couldn't agree on where she wanted her final resting place to be. Christine was fairly certain Nana didn't even want to be cremated, but she kept this to herself.

As Raquel puts her lipstick back in her bag, Christine hears sniffling from behind one of the stall doors. Their eyes meet, both Raquel and Christine wondering what would be appropriate to do in this situation. Raquel, of course, takes the lead.

"Everything okay in there?" the starlet asks gently. The sniffles quiet down and after a few moments the toilet flushes and out walks Maggie.

"Oh, hi. Sorry. Yes, everything's fine. Just a bit emotional." Maggie smiles through her tears. "It's been a lot." Despite her teary eyes, she looks lovely in a soft orange dress with a subtle floral pattern.

"Come here." Raquel opens her arms to give Maggie a hug. The mother of the bride falls into the movie star's embrace. Christine wants to warn Maggie to be wary of Raquel. After what she overheard at the church, she definitely doesn't trust her.

"I've been to a lot of weddings, and this is about the time the mother of the bride has a little well-deserved breakdown," Christine offers, feeling obliged to interject with something positive. Maggie laughs, but then her sobs grow louder.

"It's not just that," she says. "It's my necklace. My Saint Christopher medal I've had since before Jane was born. I lost it." She grabs at her chest, where the necklace used to hang.

"Oh nooo," Raquel pouts. "I'm sure it will turn up. Where did you last see it?"

"That's the thing." Maggie leans against the bathroom sink. "I distinctly remember putting it in the little dish in my bathroom last night. In the moment, I even thought: Oh, isn't that lovely? They've thought of everything here, even a little dish for jewelry—but when I woke up this morning, it wasn't there."

"So odd," Raquel murmurs. "You know, I weirdly had a similar thing just happen. I could have *sworn* I put my earrings on my nightstand when I got in last night, and poof! This morning, they were gone. My favorite Fewer Finer Daily Diamond hoops," she whines. "Anyway, I chalked it up to me being a scatterbrain but . . . I don't know. It's probably just a coincidence." Raquel lets Maggie go and shakes her curls out in front of the mirror. "I'm going to get back out there and see if our bride needs anything. I'm sure it'll turn up, love." She blows a kiss and struts out of the bathroom, leaving Christine and Maggie alone. The mother of the bride blots under her eyes with a paper towel.

"Do you think maybe there could be someone on staff stealing jewelry?" Christine asks. "I don't want to blame housekeeping, but we could bring it to the manager's attention. I know Raquel doesn't seem concerned, but I think it's more than fair to let management know if you both happen to be missing things."

"I don't want to cause a scene after, well, you know, everything that's happened. It was an old necklace. It could have fallen off, or I could have misplaced it." Maggie clears her throat. "It's just a little unsettling." Maggie's eyes meet Christine's, and she senses that now is her opportunity to ask about Seamus O'Reilly, to ask if Maggie needs to tell her anything, but just as she opens her mouth, an influx of tipsy guests barge into the bathroom.

"Enjoy the party," Maggie says quietly before slipping out.

After that, the night slips into a boozy, blurry haze. Christine chats briefly with a young (but already heavily Botoxed) guest who begs her for an internship at *Bespoke*, followed by some small talk with an older woman who attended Columbia fifteen years prior to Christine's birth. She's about to excuse herself, still desperate to find Lyle before the night is over, when a glass clinks at the far end of the party. Graham stands on the patio steps holding a microphone in one hand, his other arm wrapped around Jane's waist. The party dips into a quiet murmur and, after a few seconds, complete silence. All eyes are on the couple.

"Hi, everyone." Graham taps his glass again with the side of a knife. "We just wanted to take a moment to thank you all for coming to celebrate with us. We know that all of you traveled to be here and it means so much, truly." Christine watches as the groom gets choked up, his bottom lip quivering. "And to our family—thank you for everything. It's so special for us all to be here together tonight." Tears are streaming down Graham's face now, his hands shaking so much that he could drop the mic at any moment. People are starting to chatter... Weddings are emotional, but it's very obvious Graham doesn't seem overcome with love. He seems overcome with grief.

Jane takes the mic from him quickly. "This is very emotional for both of us. So, we'll keep it quick. We want to thank my mom, Maggie, for hosting this beautiful event. Mom, come say a few words, please." Jane motions for her mother to join them on the steps, and everyone starts clapping. Jane hands her the mic.

Maggie blots her eyes with a handkerchief. "Thank you, angel. This is just... wow. I am so honored to host this event for all of you tonight. Thank you for joining us here in beautiful Ireland to celebrate Jane and Graham's love." Maggie pauses briefly and smiles. A few guests clap and raise their glasses, and a woman shouts, "We love you, Mags!" Christine turns to see a taller, bonier version of Maggie, presumably her sister, standing at the far end of the garden.

"Love you too, Laura!" The mother of the bride laughs, and for a second everything feels normal.

Maggie continues. "Graham is the man every mother hopes her daughter will marry. Kind, loyal, caring." Her voice catches, charged with emotion. Christine looks to Jane just as a fat teardrop rolls down her cheek. Graham puts his arm around the bride, but Jane tenses up under it, subtly pushing him off her. Christine's gone to enough weddings to clock this as odd. In these intensely emotional moments, the bride and groom tend to melt into each other, not pull away. She looks around to see if anyone else noticed the slight, but all the guests have their eyes glued to the mother of the bride, obligatory wedding-guest grins slapped on their faces just in case the photographer happens to turn a lens toward them for a candid shot. The garden is overcome with that forced, unnatural silence as everyone thinks, *God, please, can this speech be over so I can get another double gin and tonic?*

Maggie continues. "I sleep so much better at night now, knowing that Graham is taking care of my daughter. She is my most precious gift." Behind her, two gas lanterns flicker, casting her in a burnt-orange glow.

"And one day, when I'm gone, I'm so glad that Jane will have a big, happy family—"

A gust of wind blows through the garden, and Maggie pauses, pulling her wrap tightly around her shoulders. Something has caught her eye. She looks to the far end of the garden, squinting, but says nothing. Seconds go by that feel like minutes. Somebody coughs. Christine tries to see what Maggie's looking at but has the unfortunate luck of standing next to a group of guys Graham used to play basketball with who all seem to be at least seven feet tall.

Maggie's eyes dart back to her loose-leaf paper, zigzagging across it in a panic. "Sorry, let me just—I lost my place," she says breathlessly, but she never finishes her speech.

Toward the back of the garden, guests start to shriek. Christine only has about ten seconds to wonder why before she herself is drenched in water. Her eyes immediately look up at the sky, the usual culprit of an unexpected shower, but it's cloudless, glowing a rich navy blue in the moonlight. For once, the rain is not to blame.

"It's the sprinklers!" she hears Elliot shriek into his headset. "Turn them off!"

Christine joins the rest of the guests and jogs toward the greenhouse for cover, watching as Neil sprints to a small thatch-roofed garden shed where the sprinkler knobs are located, frantically attempting to turn them off. But the damage is done. The entire place has turned into a frenzy of drenched dresses and soggy suits making a beeline for dry land.

Except for Christine. She lingers behind to have a word with Maggie . . . because the mother of the bride looks as if she's seen a ghost. And Christine can't help but think that maybe from her perspective, she has.

ELLIOT HANDS OUT TOWELS to everyone along with his profuse apologies. Luckily, the guests seem to have found the entire thing *hilarious*, despite how completely mortified and unmoored the family looks.

"Find out who did this," Christine hears Ben spit into Elliot's ear.

"Of course. I've already reprimanded the security guards who were supposed to be stationed outside the garden. Apparently, the only person who came in was the groundskeeper to grab something from the greenhouse, but management is insisting that he left hours ago." Maggie stands behind Elliot, completely silent, shaking under the Ballymoon golf towel Elliot threw over her shoulders.

"Obviously, it must have been somebody impersonating him. I don't need to remind you how *serious* this situation is, do I?" Ben tries to keep his anger to a low simmer. Elliot merely gives a tight nod and continues to hand out the towels. Christine is unsettled by the mention of the groundskeeper, immediately thinking of the man who stumbled out before her on the path earlier in the day.

"Maggie," she asks gently, "did you see anyone? Maybe the groundskeeper during your speech? It looked like something startled you."

Maggie shakes her head vigorously. "No, no. I just got a little bit of stage fright." Christine can tell she's not telling the full truth but doesn't push the issue. Honestly, if Maggie did see Seamus O'Reilly, like Christine suspects, she probably doesn't even believe her own eyes. Christine feels Ben glaring at her, clearly unappreciative of her input.

"I'll sort it out. But for now let's keep things moving." Elliot tries to manage a smile. "And enjoy the after-party. We've got a karaoke stage set up and everything down at Shenanigan's Pub. It's a bit of a hike to get there so let's get a move on so you guys don't miss out on the fun!" He shuffles Ben and Maggie down the path toward the garden's exit as Christine finally sets eyes on Lyle, emerging from the women's room, towel-drying her damp blond hair.

Christine approaches her. "Can I talk to you for a minute?"

"What is it?" Lyle says in a low voice. Christine pulls Lyle aside to a shadowy corner of the garden, trying to shield them from the view of the guests as they make their way to the after-party or, more likely, to change out of their damp clothes.

"Who is Sebi? And why does everyone keep asking where he is?" Christine is shocked by the authority in her voice, but Lyle only responds by looking at the ground.

"What happened between him and Ben? Did they have a fight at that Lumina event? Is that why he isn't here?" Lyle's head snaps up.

"What are you talking about?" Lyle demands. "Ben wasn't at that event. He was with Graham that night. They had tickets to a Yankees game." Christine pulls up her Google search and thrusts it in Lyle's face. Lyle studies the photos, her face contorting with confusion. She snatches Christine's phone, zooming in closer on the photos of Ben at the event, as if she doesn't believe they're real.

"Lyle, please, if you know something, tell me. Leverage, remember? Let's help each other get through this," Christine pleads softly. After a full minute of deliberation, Lyle looks up, tears pooling in her doelike eyes.

"Sorry, I— This has caught me completely off guard." Her voice sounds like someone's who's just been punched in the gut. "I'll tell you everything I know."

TWENTY-THREE

# LYLE

Two Months Earlier
Amalfi Coast, Italy

LYLE ROAMS THE STREETS OF Positano, already feeling more relaxed thanks to the Aperol spritz she consumed immediately after landing in Naples. Despite the warm weather, she finds herself shivering, her body probably still ridding itself of the exorcist-level meltdown she had in Paris.

Glo is doing a collaboration with a darling little shop on the Amalfi Coast that makes a limoncello-scented sunscreen. It's all the rage on TikTok, apparently. She is supposed to be meeting with the owner, Lorenzo, at his shop, but she sent her assistant instead. Victoria is very discrete—if the sweet twenty-four-year-old suspects what her boss is up to, she's smart enough not to give herself worry lines about it.

Lyle would love to meet with Lorenzo and dream up their collaboration together, but she has more important things to tend to. In a progressively messy series of events, her personal and professional lives have fused together, and although she's technically here on business, she has to get some private affairs in order before she can get back to Glo.

She stops in front of a weathered turquoise building overlooking the sparkling water and takes a good long look at the view. She watches children play in the water, their mothers lounging, laughing, drinking cool drinks under the hot Italian sun. Why couldn't her life look more like theirs? So enjoyable, so uncomplicated. She hikes her bag up on her shoulder, the contents of her severe leather work tote feeling even heavier in the lazy haze of Italy. After allowing herself one more moment of self-pity, she tucks a chunk of blonde hair behind her ear and rings the doorbell.

Sebi must have been waiting eagerly on the other side, because the door opens immediately, and he pulls her in by the waist. Her brain sounds the alarm, but it's too late, her body melts into his arms.

HOURS LATER, THEY SIT on his small balcony, drinking wine and watching the sunset. He's grinning at her dumbly, his eyes heavy with chianti and lust. She puts her drink down on the edge of the balcony railing and clears her throat. Her mother's voice plays on loop in her brain: "Don't be afraid to ruin a perfect moment. That way he'll know you're serious."

"Sebi," she says, and sighs. "You know why I'm here. We can't do this anymore." She feels resolved. In this moment, she knows she truly is ready—ready to be with Ben and live the rest of her life aboveboard. There will be no more skeletons in her closet after this. He twirls a lock of her hair, the finality of her words clearly not registering.

"You always say that." He takes a sip of his drink. "You don't mean it."

"I do," she says, becoming annoyed. "I told Ben about us. I apologized—it has to be over now. I need to work on my marriage. I have a family. I have a son to think about."

"Divorce him. We are a family now," Sebi says casually. "You and Miles can move here, live with me. We can make love every night, we can teach him Italian, it will be *perfetto*." He leans back, and she notices his camera is perched next to him. "You look bellissima in this light. Don't move." He scrambles to get his camera into focus.

"Stop." She puts her hand in front of her face, but she hears his camera click. She used to love it when he took her picture, but now she just feels violated, like he's taking pieces of her without permission.

"I don't want a divorce," she snaps. "I love my husband. It's over between you and me. This was the last time." Lyle watches the sunset over the Amalfi Coast. She'll miss this view.

"I don't believe you," he says, but his eyes give him away. Her words are starting to sink in, and she sees the panic in his face as he puts down his camera. "You love me. We are in love."

"No, we're not. This was a mistake, and now it's over." She rises from her seat on the tiny balcony.

"It's because of them, isn't it—that family of ah—" He searches for the word. "Sharks. They're forcing you to do this. This isn't you." Sebi has not been shy about his distaste for Lyle's in-laws, especially after she (unwisely) told him about the lawsuit that was brewing. He's a passionate and empathetic person—she always found the Riptons cold and unfeeling. Sebi had been an outlet, someone she could release all her pent-up emotions to, a shoulder to cry on. But she doesn't need that anymore. She's stronger now.

"They're not forcing me to do anything," she says. "If anything, Gloria tried to make me end things with you sooner and I didn't listen. I should have, though. This has gone on for far too long." Lyle wonders if the words she's saying are true. Her lip quivers as she struggles to keep tears at bay.

"Bullshit," he spits. "This has Gloria written all over it. Don't do this, Lyle, don't let them own you like this. They don't own *us*. This isn't fair." He clutches his heart in an exaggerated display of passion that at one time she would have found irresistible. Now she just rolls her eyes and says, "Fair's a place where they judge pigs." Sebi always found her Southern phrases adorable, but right now he just looks horrified. She wonders briefly if the Riptons influence on her has chilled her to her core, if the warm, mushy parts of her are forever frozen solid now.

"I've already made my decision. I choose my family." Lyle goes inside and starts getting dressed, peeling off Sebi's worn blue dress shirt for the last time.

"I'll go to the press. I'll tell them about us." He follows her into his tiny bedroom, frantic. She looks around the room she once found charming, with its patchwork quilt, nightstands covered in magazines and photography books, the small window that looks out onto the sea. Maybe she can integrate some of these warmer touches into her sterile beige master bedroom at home.

"Fine," she says. The freedom she feels no longer harboring the momentous secret of her affair outweighs the fear of any personal negative press she might have to deal with.

"I'll tell them about Miles— I'll demand a, ah, eh"—he searches for the words—"paternity test." He slams his fist on the dresser. Lyle freezes. He wouldn't do that. He doesn't know for sure about Miles, does he? Sebi has always made it clear that he does not want to be a father. He's never expressed any interest in meeting Miles until today. Whereas Ben has always doted on their little guy. He loves her son. Lyle decides not to acknowledge the threat, instead slipping on her sandals and heading for the door.

"I'll leak the lawsuit. I know what's happening. I'll go on the record. The Riptons aren't getting away with that too. They just take, take, take. There will be consequences for them. I'll make sure of it." He tries to block her from leaving the bedroom, his chest heaving.

"God, Sebi, you sound so pathetic. You owe your career to them. That fragrance shoot put you on the map and you know it—they've given you everything. I am the one thing that you can't have. Stop acting like a spoiled child." She sidesteps him.

"But you're all I want, Lyle. You're all that matters. I won't let them win—I won't, *amore mio*." He's crying now, and her heart pounds. He's threatening a scorched-earth campaign, and he just might be heartbroken enough to follow through with it.

"I have to go," she whispers as she reaches for the doorknob. He tries to grab her, but she runs out and immediately spots a taxi. "Drive please," she says as she slides in. The leathered old man behind the wheel leaps into action.

"How you say, eh—crazy boyfriend?" He chuckles, but Lyle isn't in the mood to joke. She watches out the rear window as Sebi chases the car down the street, but eventually, he stops, his body fading from view. In the safety of the car, she allows herself one small squeal of distress, then dials Gloria.

"We have a problem," she says, immediately launching into her problem. "He's threatening to go to the press. I'm worried he just might, and he'll be in New York next week. He knows about everything. The lawsuit, even Miles." Her voice cracks as she says her son's name. He can't be dragged into this, he just can't. She'll kill Sebi if he goes that low.

"This is why I told you to end it years ago." Gloria sighs. "I'll handle it," she says after a moment, and the line goes dead. Lyle tries to steady her breathing. Gloria will pay Sebi off, she'll make this all go away.

*It's all for the best,* she tells herself over and over again as she walks into Hotel Caesar Augustus. *I could never live in Italy. He could never give me the life I want.* The lie has become her mantra, and she repeats it to herself as she enters her suite, dons her hotel robe, and completes her skincare routine. Once she's nestled in the velvety sheets of her luxury hotel room, Lyle closes her eyes, thoroughly convinced that she has properly handled the situation and turned the page on her years-long affair, blissfully unaware that she has just started a chain of unfortunate events that cannot be stopped.

TWENTY-FOUR

# CHRISTINE

Friday, October 17, 2025
Evening of Rehearsal Dinner

"I REPORTED SEBI MISSING RIGHT before we left for the wedding," Lyle tells Christine through her tears. "He hadn't answered my texts since I ended things close to a month ago, but I wasn't really concerned. The last time we broke up, he iced me out for *five* months. But he was contracted as one of the photographers for the Grow 2 Glo Gala and didn't show up, which was so unlike him. That's when I got worried." Lyle doesn't take a breath, and her body shakes as she purges this secret. "So the next day I called the hotel in New York where he was staying, and they said he was supposed to have checked out already but he hadn't and his stuff was still in the room. It seemed like the last place he was seen was that Lumina event and—" Her voice cracks. "Gloria was just supposed to make sure he didn't go to the press about us. She was just going to pay him off," Lyle continues. "But then he went dark." Christine's mind flashes back to Lyle grabbing Gloria's wrist after the welcome dinner, demanding, "Where is Sebi?"

"And then Gloria acted like she didn't have anything to do with it. I truly never thought that Ben— I mean, I know he was angry, but he would never—" She can't finish the sentence.

Christine stares at her, dumbfounded. Sebi being Lyle's scorned ex-lover was not on her bingo card.

Lyle squeezes her eyes shut, trying to stop her tears. Damp rehearsal dinner guests trickle out of the garden, and a few necks crane in their direction, Lyle's distress illuminated by bright lanterns that frame the women's bathroom door. They need to wrap this up.

Christine pulls Lyle out of the unforgiving light of the lanterns, dropping her voice to a whisper. "Do you think Gloria got Ben involved? Do you think they might have conspired to . . . ?" She doesn't need to finish the sentence.

"I don't know. I didn't think it was possible. I thought Gloria would do what Riptons do: throw money at Sebi and make him go away. That's it." Lyle grips Christine's phone so tightly, Christine's afraid she might snap it in half.

"I need to get out of here," she says suddenly. "I need to be with my son. Don't show these photos to anyone else. I need to think." She hands Christine her phone back.

*Did Ben kill Sebi because of the affair? Or did Gloria have Sebi killed to prevent him from going to the press? Is Lyle even telling the truth?*

"Christine." Danny's voice cut through her tumbling thoughts. She turns to see him approaching her from behind the bar setup. Annoyed to miss even a second with Lyle, she turns back without acknowledging him. But she's too late. Lyle has evaporated into the herd of guests. Danny's standing right next to her now, hands pushed deep into his pockets like a shy teenager.

"Can we still have that drink?" Danny pulls a beat-up leather jacket over a very soft looking white T-shirt. He looks more like James Dean about to get on a motorcycle than a hotel bartender out of his uniform.

Christine sighs and looks over his shoulder, trying to see which way Lyle went. If she doesn't look at him, she doesn't have to be reminded that he is very attractive.

"You deserve a break." He looks at her, his perfectly chiseled chin dotted with stubble, his kind eyes, his clean woodsy scent . . .

"Trust me, I would love to, but I really can't." She crosses her arms over her chest and gives him her best "I wish I could" smile.

Danny throws his hands up. "Okay fine. What if I told you I had some pertinent information that might interest you . . . for *your article*." He says the words "your article" while his fingers make air quotes.

She freezes. "What is that supposed to mean?" She feels her heart lodge in her throat. *What does he know?*

"Well, well, well—would you like to find out?" He smirks, tosses his keys in the air, and catches them. Christine hesitates, so Danny tries again.

"C'mon, let's get out of here and have a wee drink, yeah? I know a local spot that pours a great pint. I'm rather sick of The Snug if you can believe it." He smiles, and she sighs in defeat. Christine knows that she should be investigating this new information about Sebi and Lyle, but she feels overwhelmed and, frankly, exhausted. Maybe a brain break is just what she needs in order to make sense of these new clues. Plus, the idea of leaving the Ballymoon property—even if only briefly—sounds too good to pass up.

"Fine," she agrees, "but only one."

After a Guinness, Christine feels her edges start to soften. Merry Irish music and laughter twirl through the air, making the local pub buzz. Eventually the dark thoughts about what is happening under the stony surface of the castle will come rushing back; eventually, Christine will have to coax Danny into telling her what he knows. But for now, she allows herself the small indulgence of *not* thinking about what happened and enjoying a charming local bar with a charming local.

"So, tell me about *Bespoke*. Have you always been a fashionista?" Danny takes a sip of his drink, followed by an audible "ahh" like he's in a beer commercial.

"Don't say 'fashionista.'" Christine contorts her body into an exaggerated shudder.

"What if I say it with a Spanish accent? *Fashionista*." He grins, baring his teeth in a mischievous smile.

"No, that's worse. Please, stop." Christine puts her elbows on the bar, laughing.

"All right, let me rephrase: How did you decide on a career in the fashion industry, Ms. Russo?" Danny sits up straighter and folds his arms like he's conducting a job interview. She pauses for a moment, stunned that she actually doesn't know what to say. It's a simple question. She should have a canned answer ready, but in light of everything that's happened this weekend, she's questioning everything she ever did to get herself here.

"It just kind of happened," she says finally. Danny gives her a quizzical look.

"I don't believe that. You don't seem like the kind of person that things just 'happen' to," he observes.

"What makes you think you know anything about me? We just met." She winces at her own harsh-sounding words.

"I'm pretty good at reading people," Danny says, thankfully unoffended. "Part of the job."

"What kind of person do I seem like, then?" Christine asks, her thoughts swirling with a mix of mild offense and intrigue.

"The kind who always knows *exactly* what she wants and how to get it. Who doesn't care what it takes or who she has to bulldoze to get it. A real *wagon*, as we say over here." He laughs.

"Charming. *A wagon*—every woman's dream comparison." Christine takes a sip of her beer to hide her smile. Maybe he does get her a little.

"You should take it as a compliment! Now, come on, tell me about how you landed every girl's dream gig," he presses.

"Okay." She takes a sip of her drink and decides to start with the facts, proceeding to tell Danny about how she met Sandra in the coffee shop and then approached her at the seminar.

"So yeah, I put every ounce of energy I had into trying to become some version of the glamorous woman from the coffee shop, and now here I am." Danny nods, absorbing this information. Christine rushes to fill the wordless void, to defend the immaturity and impulse that apparently got her here.

"But truthfully, at the core of it all, I was just chasing the feeling of going home to Cleveland for Christmas and looking like the rom-com success story. Big city, amazing job, fancy car, cool-girl clothes, hot boyfriend. I guess I've always just like . . . wanted to win?" Christine is shocked by the truth in her own words as they tumble out of her. It feels cathartic. "But this wedding—my first as a senior editor—it's changed something in me." She chooses her words carefully. "These people, this weekend, this *level* of wealth, it's just . . . not at all what I expected, and I already feel a paralyzing bout of writer's block on the horizon."

Danny whistles, and they sit in silence for a second.

"How's the hot boyfriend piece coming along?" he asks finally, breaking the tension.

"Still working on that." She laughs and then pauses. "I don't mean to be a melodramatic weirdo, but yeah, I guess I never really stopped long enough to ask myself what I really wanted out of this career, other than the validation of people I didn't really even know."

Danny whistles again and places his phone down on the table with a thud. "Well, this is more than I bargained for, Aristotle." She laughs, a bit of beer coming out of her nose, but he just stares at her googly-eyed like she's some sort of goddess.

"For what it's worth," he says, "I liked your latest article—the one about the wedding in Mexico City where everyone rode four-wheelers to the ceremony? I think you're a great writer. You've got a strong voice, very observant. Quite funny too, actually."

"*You* read my latest article?" She can't keep the shock out of her voice.

"It's not every day you meet a gorgeous New Yorker who works for *Bespoke*. I had to do my research," Danny says, and Christine can see he's blushing slightly under his scruffy beard.

There's a moment of nervous silence, and then Christine says, "Okay, I think it's time to tell me about your pertinent information."

"Well, if I'm going to tell you anything, you're going to have to let me buy you another drink." He leans in closer. She smells the warm beer on his breath and sees the twinkle in his eyes up close. A few honey-colored tendrils fall in his face.

"Only one—and only because I need information out of you," she says. Now it's Christine who leans in closer; if she's going to stay at this bar, she'll at least try to use her time wisely.

"Now, *tell me what you know*," she says with mock authority.

"Okay, I'll admit it, my 'pertinent information' might have been a last-ditch effort to get you to agree to drinks," he says. Christine feels a sting of annoyance at this. *Of course it was*, she thinks. *You're an idiot for falling for that*.

"But," he continues, "I do know a lot of Ballymoon lore that I think could provide an excellent *atmospheric* tone to your article." Now he has her attention. She props her head on her hands, eager to learn more about Ballymoon. Even though Danny claims not to know anything about a secret passageway hidden in the castle walls, she can't shake the idea that someone (maybe Seamus O'Reilly) is sneaking around unseen somehow and could be involved in this ever-evolving family drama.

"Go on," Christine encourages him.

"Gladly," Danny continues. "Ballymoon was last home to Ireland's High King Brian Boru. He was never supposed to ascend to the throne as the eleventh son, but many of his siblings died before him. Out of the ones who were left, he was the most qualified for the position. He became addicted to conquest and acquired more and more land for Ireland. Ultimately, it was his downfall. He ended Viking domination of Ireland and is widely considered one of Ireland's most prolific rulers." Danny flags down the bartender at the other end of the crowded pub.

"A controversial figurehead," Christine observes.

"You could say that—a proper mix of good and bad." Danny grins mischievously. "Sort of like the family you're wrapped up with this weekend—quite the controversial bunch from what I've read."

"Yeah," Christine mumbles. "To say the least."

He leans closer, his voice dropping to a whisper. "So, what's it been like hanging out with that lot?" he asks.

A wispy haired barkeep interrupts. "Another drink for ya's?"

"Another Guinness, mate," Danny replies.

"And what about your girlfriend?"

He smiles at Christine.

"Oh, I'm not his girlfriend," Christine says quickly.

Danny puts an arm around her shoulder. "Not *yet*, but she'll have another and then we'll ask her again." They both laugh, and Christine does her best to look perturbed, but ultimately gives in to another grin. His persistence is flattering . . . possibly even irresistible. A bevy of Irish step dancers take the stage where a DJ is now setting up. The music gets louder. She needs to stay focused.

"So, Gloria Beaufort's suite." Christine tries to steer the conversation back toward the tunnels. "I think it's called the Brian Boru Suite after the king you mentioned. Do you think those were his original chambers?"

"Sorry, what?" Danny leans his ear toward her. The pitter-patter of the dancers' steps and the house music make it impossible to hear anything. The bar is filling up, growing more crowded by the second thanks to the performers.

She tries again, this time louder: "The suite where they found Gloria Beaufort—they were King Brian's chambers?" Christine realizes her misstep instantly.

Danny pauses before answering. "What do you mean the suite where they found Gloria Beaufort?" Danny stares at her, his smiling eyes turning into a scowl.

"Did I say that? I just meant the suite where she's staying." The barkeep puts another beer down in front of her—one she clearly doesn't need. She's really got to pace herself.

"Christine," Danny says again, his voice serious. She doesn't say anything, just stares at her dark black Guinness, wishing she could dive headfirst into it.

Danny digs in. "I know you're hiding something. I saw the way you all looked at brunch, like you'd seen a banshee. I saw the conversation between you and Lyle after the rehearsal dinner. You can tell me what's going on. I want to help you." He puts a hand gently on her elbow. His touch triggers her emotions, and she promptly bursts into tears.

Finally, after a few large sips of beer and a glass of water, she tells him everything—about Gloria, about the Seamus note, the email, Ben and Raquel in the cemetery, Elliot screaming in the hall, Clementine's shoe lunge, Lyle's breakdown. The relief of being found out makes her want to collapse. Danny doesn't say anything for a full minute after she finishes. Then he puts his head in his hands and groans. Christine's whole body vibrates with anticipation. Will he turn her into the police? Is it all finally over?

Before Danny can say anything about her confession, his phone starts buzzing. He reaches for his pocket.

"It's my mom. I've gotta take this. She's been a bit under the weather." He gets up from the table abruptly with the phone to his ear. "I'll be right back. Don't go anywhere, okay? We'll sort this out." But Christine doesn't say anything; she just sits there in shock as he walks away, her face draining of color.

Because Danny's phone is sitting right there in front of her on the bar. And why would a hotel bartender have two phones?

CHRISTINE'S HEART THUMPS. SHE feels a prickle of sweat on her forehead, a ringing in her ears. She's going to be sick; she just knows it. The feeling of nausea that's come over her is crushing. She picks up the phone—the one Danny is currently *not* talking on—and looks at the lock screen. Of course it's password protected. All she can see is a sweet photo of a black lab and a text from "Ma." The phone he's left is clearly his personal one, which begs the question: Who is he talking to now? And why can't he speak to them on his black-lab-text-from-mom phone?

Danny is hiding *something*—and she's just told him *everything*. He could be the one who killed Gloria for all she knows. He could be the one sending her these cryptic notes! Just by sitting here, she could be in danger.

Christine is about to cut her losses and bolt when Danny comes back. The minute he sees her face, his smile disappears. His eyes dart to the bar, immediately realizing his mistake. Before she can get up to leave, he quickly rushes over and grabs her hand.

"Wait," he says. "It's not what you think."

"Really? What bartender has two phones, hm? Who the hell are you?" she demands.

"I'll explain," he says quickly. "But let's go somewhere more private." His eyes roam around the crowded bar.

"You're out of your mind if you think I'm going anywhere with you," she scoffs, and watches him try to think of a way out of this situation.

"Christine, you have to trust me," he says slowly.

"And why on earth would I do that?" she says. "If you don't tell me what's going on right now, I'll go to the police."

Danny lets out a sharp laugh. "In Ireland, they're called the Gardaí, love."

Christine tries another approach. "Fine, I'll tell the Gardaí and the Riptons." This gives him pause. He surveys the pub again, assessing the surrounding patrons, then glares at her, his dimples vanished, Irish smiling eyes nowhere in sight, his constantly cheeky grin now a hard line.

The man in front of her is a stranger.

TWENTY-FIVE

# THE COP

A Few Weeks Earlier
Cliffs of Moher

THE SALTY WIND WHIPS AROUND as the cop steps out of his beat-up red Mini Cooper. He stretches his back, cracking it in just the right place to release all the tension that built up on the long, pretzeled ride to the Cliffs of Moher. He needs to get a bigger car; the Mini is not suited to someone with his large frame.

He takes a sip from his to-go cup. A strong coffee and a long drive are good for the soul. He feels better now. Driving relaxes him, helps him turn his brain off. It's important in his profession to be mindless sometimes and let the brain rest. He learned this early on when he became a detective. The stimulation and brow-furrowing of looking for clues can cause you to miss what's right in front of you if you don't take a step back and relax. For him, taking a step back usually means taking some actual steps, so the cop suggested that he and his commissioner meet at the Cliffs of Moher instead of Colin's stuffy office for their meeting today. His boss had agreed—and quickly. Usually, Colin wouldn't go for such a breach of protocol. The commissioner's willingness to oblige his request was not a good sign.

The Cliffs are always a good place not to be bothered. Ireland's a small country—County Clare even smaller—and so he discovered (through one too many small talks in town) that there's no better place to *not* run into locals than the Cliffs of Moher. He and Colin can have a proper private chat here.

It's a gloomy day, but it usually is in Ireland, especially early in the morning. It could be as sunny as a Sunday over in town, but at the cliffs especially, it's rare to see even a patch of blue. The cop thinks that the constant gloom only adds to the beauty of the vista; the creamy gray sky and Aran Sea blend together, and he feels suspended between the earth and the heavens, perfectly balanced, right where he is supposed to be. A life lived outside the confines of an office is what drew him to the force anyway, and he likes being out in the elements surviving, hunting, discovering things—a return to the primal. He sees Colin's patrol car pull into view a few spots ahead of him and he trots toward it.

"Over here." His commissioner's familiar gruff voice cuts through the wind. He waves from the edge of the parking lot, pulling his windbreaker around his protruding belly. Colin definitely resents the choice of location for today's meeting—it's written on his frowning face—but the cop doesn't feel that bad. He knows Colin's doctor's been on him about his weight.

"Beautiful day, isn't it?" the cop jokes as he jogs over.

"Catch yourself on. This is the last time I agree to one of these new-fangled types of meetings. Next time, I'll see your arse in my office like everyone else." Colin grunts and hikes up his pants.

"All right, boss—you got it. Shall we?" He makes a sweeping gesture with his arm for Colin to lead the way down the path across the road toward the cliffs. There's only a smattering of poncho-clad tourists braving the elements today. They walk past them and up the narrow path along the edge of Galway Bay toward O'Brien's Tower.

"We got a call from New York PD through Interpol." Colin gets right to the point. The cop appreciates this about his boss. He doesn't dilly-dally.

"They think that one of the guys they're after has fled the country, and they have reason to believe he's here in County Clare," Colin continues. "Seamus O'Reilly—he's broken parole after doing twenty for armed robbery, money laundering, aggravated assault. Just a few of his greatest hits."

"Why do they think he's here in Ireland?" The cop takes another sip of his coffee and picks up his pace. Colin struggles to keep up.

"O'Reilly is a dual citizen. Born and raised here, left when he was a teenager and got involved with a major gang that works up and down the East Coast. He's wanted in connection with a man who was just reported missing. Some noteworthy photographer," Colin huffs, "but that's not all. There's a big twist with this one." The cop doesn't want to seem too eager to learn about this case—he has a gut feeling that Colin's going to make a big ask.

Reluctantly, Colin continues. "A tip came through connecting O'Reilly to the Ripton family, the ones hosting that lavish wedding over at Ballymoon in October. New York thinks that someone in—or close to—the family is involved with O'Reilly's gang. Have you heard of 'em, the Riptons?" Colin coughs, catching his breath as they reach the top of the hill where the tower is located.

"No, should I have?" The cop sighs, ready for Colin to just get on with it already. They peer out at the water, gulls crying overhead.

"A lotta quid." His boss whistles. "Billionaires, if you can believe it. Gloria Beaufort, the grandmother, started that beauty brand Glo. Kathleen's obsessed with the stuff. All overpriced crap in my opinion—everything smells like cotton candy and shite." The cop smiles; he always forgets about Colin's daughter, Kathleen. He's a fish out of water in the world of teenage girls, more at home among the likes of criminals and gangsters.

"So why do they think this crime ring is connected to a family of beauty moguls?"

"We're supposed to get an official briefing later this afternoon." Colin shrugs. "You know how these New York types are—they hold their cards close to their chest. But if you ask me, you don't become a tycoon like Gloria Beaufort without making a few enemies. I was told New York has it on good authority that there is a connection, and that O'Reilly will be in town for this wedding. It's not exactly clear what he has planned, but he certainly won't be a welcome wedding crasher." Colin pauses before continuing. "National Gardía's involved. This is a huge operation—O'Reilly is a real fecking bastard. And if he's somehow corrupted a person with access to a billion-dollar fortune, well, I don't have to tell ya how dangerous that is." The clouds start to disperse over the cliffs and the grandeur of the landscape comes into view.

"Is there a sketch of this guy? Mug shot?"

"We've got a picture of 'im, but it's rumored he's lost a lot of weight and changed his appearance, so not sure how helpful it'll be."

"Great," the cop scoffs. "Are there any theories of who he might have gotten close to in this family? Of which one of the lot is involved?"

"Not really. The tip was vague, but I'd have a look at Ben Ripton—the oldest grandson. He's been brought in multiple times for DUIs and drunk and disorderlies that dear ole gran's gotten 'im out of. Nobody else has a record. New York is digging into all of them now."

"So, what do you want from me, Colin?" the cop asks. The wind has picked up, the mist turning into rain. "Just ask already before we're blown out to sea."

"I need you to go undercover again." *There it is*, he thinks. *I knew it.*

"No," the cop groans. "You promised after last time, that was it. I need a break." He should have known there was a reason Colin agreed to go on a walk with him instead of forcing him to sit in his cigarette-smoke-filled office at the station.

"Listen, I tried to put up Fitzmaurice or Kennedy for the job, but they wouldn't hear of it. This came from the top, lad." Colin locks eyes with him for a beat, and he knows it's true. Colin wouldn't be asking if he didn't have to. He's a decent enough guy, a fair boss.

The cop takes a long sip of his coffee. He watches the foamy white mouth of the sea crash against the rocks. He has unfortunately impressed everyone with his latest undercover gig, and now it seems the powers that be want him to be anyone but himself—permanently. He doesn't know if he can do it again, but he knows he doesn't really have a choice. He resents the smugness he felt about his "gift" as an undercover agent. It's mentally and physically exhausting to be a professional liar.

"So brief me, then." He starts walking back toward the car, and Colin keeps pace next to him this time.

"You'll go undercover at Ballymoon—that's where they're hosting the wedding. It'll be a swanky affair, and you'll have a front-row seat." Colin says this as if the cop should be thanking him.

"Wow, when shall I expect my invitation in the mail?" Sarcasm drips from his words.

Colin ignores him and continues. "You'll get cozy with the family, find out where Seamus is hiding and who his inside guy is."

"Oh, is that all?" He knows he's being cheeky, teetering on the edge of getting Colin riled up, but his boss is asking a lot, and he's going to make sure he knows it.

"You'll have help every step of the way. I'll give you the full file back at the station, but there might be something to the local lore surrounding the castle. If walls could talk, ya know."

"What do you mean?" The cop has always been fascinated by the history of his country, by the impressive and almost mystical nature of Ireland's castles, kings, and queens. In another life, he would have liked to study Irish history at university somewhere.

"There's a legend that Ballymoon has a hidden passageway built into it. It was originally used as an escape route for Brian Boru. We think Seamus might be using the passageway to hide out and get around unseen. Hopefully, you find the passageway and then find our man." Colin opens his car door, relieved to be done with their grueling thirty minutes of exercise.

The cop breathes deeply, inhaling the salty air, preparing for his next role. "What's my cover?" he finally asks.

Colin grins. "Well, you always could pull a mean Guinness. How does the castle barkeep sound to you?"

TWENTY-SIX

# CHRISTINE

Friday, October 17, 2025
Evening of Rehearsal Dinner

DANNY'S NEXT WORDS ARE SO faint, she can hardly hear them.

"I'm an undercover officer. I've been investigating possible criminal ties to the Ripton family." Christine sits there blinking at him for a second, waiting for the punch line.

"You're serious?" she says finally. "You expect me to believe that?" Danny's eyes widen at her response—as if he has any right to be the shocked one in this situation!

"It's the truth. If you'd just listen—" he continues in his panicked whisper.

"Yeah," Christine sneers. "And actually, I should probably reintroduce myself. I'm not Christine Russo, I'm actually Mia Thermopolis, Princess of Genovia."

"Christine," Danny says sternly, "I can prove it."

"I'm not interested. Thanks for the beer." She makes a point of loudly getting out of her chair and storms out the front entrance of the pub.

Danny chases after her onto the busy streets of Limerick, but he's too late. She is already around the block, grabbing a taxi.

*Danny is a liar. He has been lying about who he is, about what he's doing here*, she berates herself, *and he's been trying to get close to you to get information. Did you seriously think he was into you?* Christine feels herself start to spiral into a tornado of anger, embarrassment, and fear.

Who can she even trust at this point? Not Lyle, not Danny—can she even trust herself? At every turn, she's been putting herself in more and more danger. She should have just stayed out of this, she should have just stuck to what she came here to do, which is write about designer dresses and cake flavors and custom cocktails. But it's too late, she is in too deep, knows too much. She thinks of the bride and Danny's vague statement about possible criminal ties. Danny didn't say it outright, but she knows whatever he's "investigating" has something to do with Seamus O'Reilly. She needs to warn Jane.

"Can you drop me off at Shenanigan's?" she leans forward to ask the taxi driver, remembering Elliot's mention of the after-party.

"Sure, love. The bar at the base of Ballymoon Castle, is it?" he asks. She nods in response. Hopefully Jane will still be there, and she can warn her that her ex-convict father could appear at any moment. The poor girl doesn't even know that he is *alive*.

Christine's mind cranks through possible scenarios. Danny didn't tell her anything specific about his case, but it doesn't take a rocket scientist to figure out that the Irish police—sorry, Gardía—got a tip that Seamus O'Reilly is prowling around Ballymoon . . . and probably has his sights set on his long-lost, soon-to-be-a-billionaire daughter. Seamus might have murdered Gloria. And if it's true about the passageway behind the castle walls, then nobody is safe. The taxi chugs out of town and barrels onto the highway toward the castle.

"Say, didn't I drop you off earlier?" Her taxi driver chuckles. "You're really getting around town today, girl-o." Christine looks up and catches the same crooked grin of the man who dropped her off at the rectory earlier that day, the same beat-up cap.

"Yeah," she says, and smiles, "I guess I am." She averts her gaze out the window, unwilling to make small talk under the current circumstances.

"It's a small world, isn't it?" He smiles back and turns up the radio, clearly picking up on Christine's antisocial vibes. She lets her head rest against the cold window as they breeze by passing headlights.

At least Danny provided her with valuable information, whether he wanted to or not. Christine now has all the confirmation she needs that Seamus O'Reilly is here, and he's dangerous. As for Danny's investigative flirting—well, it's certainly not the first time a guy has disappointed her, and unfortunately, thanks to the modern dating pool, it won't be the last. *You should have gone on a second date with the martini fingerer,* she thinks, and the consideration makes her want to throw herself out of the moving car. Thankfully, the cabbie pulls over by a tattered green-and-black sign that reads *Shenanigan's Pub* before she has the chance.

"Thanks for the ride. Hopefully next time, you take me to the airport." She sighs and slides her credit card through the taxi's card reader.

"Ah, homesick, are ye? I get it—try and have a laugh and a beer. That'll cheer ya up," the kind man says as she hops out. The sounds of the bass, clinking of glasses, and girlish squeals seep out onto the sidewalk.

Upon entering the bar, Christine is immediately smacked in the face with the smell of vodka. She worms her way into the main taproom, dodging twentysomethings in tiny tops taking very unnecessary shots, until she reaches the main room, where a small karaoke stage has been set up just opposite the overcrowded bar.

"All right, who's next on the mic?" a DJ's voice booms through the after-party. "Come on, come on—who's got a song for the bride and groom?" The crowd buzzes in response, every group pushing their drunkest member toward the stage. Eventually, a pudgy guy in black sunglasses and a backward Ballymoon baseball hat stumbles up and grabs the mic from the DJ.

"Okay! We've got a taker!" The DJ laughs as the guy starts fumbling through a screaming rendition of The Killers' "Mr. Brightside." Christine continues pushing her way through the mess of sticky, hot bodies.

Somewhere deep within the party, the music gets louder, the speakers pulsing. Christine feels her heart start to pound. How is she ever going to find Jane in this mess? A loud screech reverberates through the room, and Christine turns her head toward the stage, where a (slightly wobbly) Ben Ripton tries to pry the microphone out of Mr. Brightside's drunken hands.

"Whoa, whoa! We've got a challenger." The DJ tries to keep his voice light, but it's clear he's slightly unsettled by Ben's interruption. Mr. Brightside mumbles something that looks a lot like "fuck you, man," before his friends shuffle him off the stage. An awkward silence follows as the DJ tries to figure out what to do.

Ben grins and takes the microphone, tapping it. "Is this thing broken? Where's my song?" The feedback causes a few guests to cover their ears as the best man scowls at the turntable. Christine can see sweat glistening on the poor DJ's forehead before he ultimately starts the track and "Gold Digger" is blasted through the bar. The audible gasps that follow are drowned out by Ben's terrible singing, but Christine follows the inevitable turn of heads . . . that lead her right to Jane.

She is standing in the center of the room with Graham, a blank expression on her face. The groom, his face doubly red, leaves her to march toward the DJ's turntable. As the words "gold digger, gold digger, gold digger" ring unrelentingly through the bar, Jane holds her head high, turns on her heels, and exits the bar. Christine follows.

THROUGH THE STAINED-GLASS WINDOWPANES that frame the pub's back patio, Christine can see the bride, alone, staring up at the moonlit sky. Now that she has the opportunity to tell Jane what she knows, Christine's not sure what to say. *Hey, Jane, your dad is not actually dead. He's an ex-convict who's crashing your wedding weekend . . . and he may have also murdered your fiancé's grandmother!* She grimaces, her mind already showing her visions of Jane's inevitable "you're crazy" face. But she takes a deep breath and pushes open the door to the patio anyway. What choice does she have?

"Hey," Christine calls gently. The bride turns around and stares at her. Christine notices a lit cigarette dangling from her right hand. Her face betrays no signs of emotion, her lips in a hard line, brown eyes darkly serious. The bride doesn't look sad or angry or anything, really . . . She looks stoic, like a knight ready for battle.

"I didn't know you were a smoker." Christine tries not to sound judgmental. Jane honestly just does not give smoker vibes.

"I've been trying to quit," she says with a sigh. "But if ever there was a perfect moment to relapse!" She nods her head toward the party inside, toward Ben's embarrassing karaoke performance.

"That was so humiliating," Christine says, before quickly adding, "For him!"

Jane just shrugs. "It takes a lot to faze me these days."

Christine recognizes that this is the best opening she's going to get.

"I'm sorry, it must be so intense for you right now, with everything going on." She gives the bride a sympathetic half smile then plows forward. "You know, actually, I was hoping to talk to you about something." She tries to tamp down the tremor in her voice, clearing her throat before continuing. "About your dad."

Jane doesn't turn to look at her. Instead, she just stares out across the Ballymoon back nine and sighs as she puts out her cigarette.

Finally, she meets Christine's gaze, her eyes the inky black of an oil spill.

"I can't talk to you about my father," the bride says firmly. "Whatever you know about him, keep to yourself."

Christine is unsure how to respond to this. There's not a trace of shock or confusion on Jane's face.

*She knows about Seamus.*

But before Christine can press further, there is a loud thud from inside the bar. Both women turn and watch through the stained-glass window as Graham tackles Ben to the floor. Blood gushes from Ben's nose.

"Jane." Raquel peeks her head through the patio door. "We need you in here. There's a bit of a situation." She motions toward the fistfight.

"Coming," the bride calls to Raquel, who scurries back into the pub to relish in the drama.

Before she goes, Jane pulls Christine close, her cigarette-smoke breath hot on her face. Christine tries to step back, but the bride only grabs her tighter.

"I'm serious, Christine. Leave my family alone." Jane enunciates each word before pushing her away and disappearing into the bar.

TWENTY-SEVEN

# JANE

One and a Half Years Earlier
Charleston, South Carolina

THE BEST MEET-CUTES ARE SCRIPTED. *Just pretend you're in* Sleepless in Seattle, Jane thinks. She smiles politely at the security guard and makes her way into the Medical University of South Carolina's children's hospital. Her heart flutters up around the base of her throat as the elevator climbs to the sixteenth floor. With every ding, her breaths become shorter and sharper. She looks down at her burnt-orange ruffle skirt and vintage Frye boots. Her outfit brings her a bit of peace: she looks the part.

*I've done worse,* she tells herself, as if this will make her feel better. There was that time she pocketed the sapphire earrings at her friend Savannah's house. The time she almost got suspended in college for taking her RA's Lexus for a joyride. Jane cringes. That one was bad. She's lucky she never got arrested. This is how Jane rationalizes her behavior these days: by remembering what a shameless mess she used to be. Now her mess is artfully hidden. The elevator doors open. A pretty nurse with full red lips smiles and waves at her from a reception desk.

"You must be Miss Murphy. The kids are so excited to meet you. I'm Nurse Annie." She extends a hand of terra-cotta-colored shellacked nails in Jane's direction.

"Nice to meet you. I'm so happy to be here, even if I am a little nervous." Jane smiles, and Nurse Annie leads her down a sterile corridor. The smell of disinfectant floods her nostrils like cocaine. God, if only she had something to steady her shaking hands right now. A cigarette would be amazing.

"They'll love you. *The Very Hungry Caterpillar* is always a crowd-pleaser." *What a nice person Nurse Annie must be to work here in the service of these poor children and their families,* Jane thinks. She pictures her mother, also a nurse, dutifully caring for the seniors at Oak Bluffs and immediately feels bad about herself again.

"Are you okay?" Nurse Annie touches her back gently. Jane realizes she must look as sick as she feels.

"Oh, yeah. Like I said . . . nervous," she lies. Though it's not really a lie—she is riddled with anxiety. This is her chance to get out. Just one more con. Jane needs to escape, and soon. Her mom is starting to linger, calling her more often, planning more frequent trips to "check in." If her mom found out about the dark world her sweet daughter the art teacher has tumbled into, they'd both be irreversibly shattered. That can't happen. Jane can't let that happen.

Nurse Annie opens a door, and suddenly Jane is in the happiest saddest room that ever existed. Bright yellow flowers, rainbows, and smiley faces are plastered on the walls. A plethora of organized, shiny children's toys cover the floor and spill out of baskets. Big, bright windows beam in sunlight . . . but it's the faces that send Jane's heart falling down sixteen floors and spattering on the sidewalk. A room full of sick kids, smiling and clapping as she walks in. Oh my God, she is *such a bad person*. She wants to die.

It's not like Jane's going to do anything to these kids directly, but it doesn't stop her from feeling lower than dirt under a fresh manicure. Somehow, the cons she's done at her school, the posh South of Broad Simon and Friends School educating Charleston's next generation of elites, doesn't feel as bad as this. They were kind of asking for it, right?

With the pitiful salaries she and her fellow teachers made, who could blame her for getting scrappy for a bit more cash. If she wasn't working an angle there, someone else would be. Those kids will be fine. These kids will be fine too. It's the adults she's after. And then she clocks him, just off in the right corner chatting with a few of the parents: her target.

"Miss Murphy is here to read us *The Very Hungry Caterpillar*. Who's excited?" Nurse Annie gives Jane's arm a squeeze of encouragement as the room erupts in a gleeful squeal.

"All right, let's get the party started!" Jane flashes her whitest and brightest smile and sits upright in the small children's chair provided for her. A little girl, skinny and bald, with warm brown eyes, sits at her feet and looks up. *Look at this kid. You suck, Jane*, she thinks. *You suck you suck you suck.*

But she's still a damn good teacher. She's got that at least. She's going to give these kids the best reading of *The Very Hungry Caterpillar* they've ever heard. They are glued to her as she turns each page, mesmerized by every word. By the end, all the kids have joined in, and she has become so wrapped up in the performance that she momentarily forgets about him standing in the corner by the door, watching her, already besotted.

Jane closes the book, and the kids clap again. Now to seal the deal.

"Who would like a butterfly of their own?" A chorus of "me" fills the room as Jane hands out the pipe-cleaner butterflies she spent all night making. Nurse Annie told her candy "isn't preferred" because a lot of the kids were in treatment and not everyone could enjoy it, so this seemed like the next best thing. She is an art teacher, after all. She grimaces, wondering what her nineteenth-century Impressionism professor would think of her making pipe-cleaner butterflies.

Once all the kids say their goodbyes, with promises from Jane that she will be back very soon, it's just the two of them. She says sweetly, "Can I interest you in a pipe-cleaner butterfly?" Holding out the last one, she gives him her very best smile. She purposely made one extra, just to deliver this line. He grins, thrilled by her tenderness toward the kids, and her low-cut blouse probably doesn't hurt either. This is easier than it should be.

"Wow, now there is an offer I can't refuse." Dr. Graham Ripton takes the butterfly out of her hands.

"I'm Graham, the resident pediatric oncologist here," he says. "And you must be the lovely Miss Murphy I've been hearing so much about. I think Mandy Hudson is your biggest fan." His words are long and slow, with a Southern drawl that makes him sound confident and laid-back. And he didn't introduce himself formally as "Dr. Graham Ripton"—another win. He already feels personally connected to her.

"Oh, I don't know about that," she says, and grins.

"Mandy would beg to differ. She's been talking about your upcoming visit all week," Graham says with a wink. The breakfast burrito in Jane's stomach does a flip at the mention of her sick student. That's how this all began anyway. Mandy, a beautiful, giggly first grader who Jane absolutely adores (and it's worth noting that not all first graders are adorable), got very sick, very suddenly. Jane had taken to sending her books and care packages and visiting the hospital on occasion to check in on her. But when Seamus got wind of her hospital ties, everything got dark and twisted. Eventually, Jane was forced to use Mandy as an "in" to construct her casual run-in with Graham Ripton. Which is how she connected with Nurse Annie and ended up spending her Friday night making pipe-cleaner butterflies for sick kids as part of her "I'm a good person" disguise. She shudders with self-loathing.

Jane would like to say she doesn't know how she ever got involved in a life of crime, but she does. It makes sense. She has always known there is something a bit off inside her. She knew the thrill she got from stealing a bra at Victoria's Secret or copping a pair of earrings from a rich friend's house was not normal. She only took things nobody would miss, things that she pined for but didn't have the money to buy . . . Or so she told herself. But the truth is, she really loves the thrill of it. She loves looking into people's eyes after a theft, seeing that they are completely unaware of what happened, of what she did.

"I must have misplaced them," Savannah had said about the earrings.

"Oh, your purse probably set off the alarm." The salesgirl at Victoria's Secret had smiled, before her mom dragged Jane back into the store and demanded she apologize and return the black push-up bra she swiped off the sale rack.

Nobody ever thought it was her. It's Jane's superpower: her doe eyes, her slight frame, her timid and delicate demeanor. Nobody guesses that there is a streak of evil inside of her that she can't erase . . . even if she wanted to.

For a long time, she didn't understand why she had this gravitational pull toward a life lived on the fringes, a life of stalking, plotting, deceiving. But when she met Seamus last year, it all made sense. Seamus happened to be in downtown Charleston at the exact moment Jane was taking her class to a local art exhibit. It was one of those sliding-doors moments; she was at the right place at the right time. Or, more accurately, she was at the wrong place at the wrong time. He says he was immediately struck by Jane's similarity to his late mother. She was skeptical at first but agreed to meet him for a coffee. It was impossible to deny that they looked . . . related.

At that Starbucks after school, talking to Seamus, Jane felt like she finally understood the dark part of herself that she'd struggled with for years. She didn't tell her mom about the meeting—she couldn't. Maggie would insist she cut off the relationship immediately. All her life, Jane's mom told her that her dad had died in a car accident and she never questioned it. It's not like talking about him was off-limits. Jane just truly, honestly, didn't care. Maybe that's another sign that she's a bad person? Anyway, clearly Maggie hated Seamus so much she would rather her daughter think her dad was *dead* than have any sort of connection to him. Her mom would have wanted him thrown in prison again if Jane had told her about the meeting . . . like she did, according to Seamus, when Maggie was pregnant with Jane. Though, come to think of it, sending Seamus back to jail might not have been the worst thing.

Seamus, *Dad*—the word still sounds weird on her tongue—told her everything: about her mother selling him out, about his years as an inmate at Ridgeland, about the crime syndicate he worked for. And then, slowly, he brought her into the fold. Small jobs at first, easy money, but after six months, Jane was in deep. In the beginning it was fun, but as things escalated and escalated—it turned out that Seamus was much more devious than Jane. She had a bit of bad blood running through her veins, but he was a thoroughbred gangster. She wanted out. She needed to get out, she told him.

So the criminal operation that her father, and now Jane, were beholden to decided that she could do one final job and be done. A big job—they needed help maintaining one of their most prominent clients: the Ripton family, which provided their most lucrative income stream. Client relations were not going smoothly. There was a lawsuit brewing, the family was crumbling, and the gang couldn't risk being on the outs. They needed someone on the inside of the family that nobody would suspect of anything uncouth—someone like Jane. They needed Jane to marry Graham Ripton. He is her ticket out.

She doesn't believe they will ever really let her go, obviously. Once she does as she's told by draining Graham's trust fund and swiftly divorcing him, there will be something else. And even if she does somehow complete this job, who knows what the next one will be? It will probably be worse. Truthfully, Jane doesn't know if there is any way to get herself out of this mess. She puts the thought out of her head for now and smiles at Dr. Graham Ripton. She'll think of something. One step at a time.

"You hungry?" Jane asks. "I know a great deli nearby." She throws her canvas tote bag over her shoulder in an attempt to seem casual. Because, actually, she knows *his* favorite deli is around the corner, and she knows his go-to order (pastrami on rye, two slices of Swiss, extra pickle on the side), and she knows what he's reading now (*When Breath Becomes Air*) and she's ready to discuss it because *Oh my God, she's read-*

*ing that too!* And she knows where he plays basketball every Tuesday and what his favorite team is (the Knicks—he became a fan while in medical school at NYU) and she knows that he likes to spend Sundays with his grandmother, whom he adores (they play chess occasionally, and Graham is bad at it). And she knows that he's not perfect—that he doesn't always recycle all of his plastic water bottles and that he leaves the towels on the floor of his apartment for his housekeeper to pick up and that he often falls asleep to reruns of *Friends* because—as she's come to know—he doesn't have a lot of them as a workaholic. Honestly, it's amazing what you can learn about a person just from stalking them for a mere two months!

"I'm starving actually." Dr. Ripton runs his hands through his blond hair. He has the tired, weathered look of someone who wants to be taken care of the way he takes care of his patients. And Jane can be that person. She's been practicing.

TWENTY-EIGHT

# CHRISTINE

Friday, October 17, 2025
Rehearsal Dinner After-Party

BACK IN SHENANIGAN'S PUB, CHRISTINE watches as Jane drags her fiancé off his brother. Ben stumbles back, holding his face. A few friends rush to steady him, but Ben pushes them away and storms out of the bar. He bumps Christine on his way out, but she barely registers it, her mind still echoing with Jane's warning.

The party rapidly starts to dissipate, and even though the thought of spending the night alone in her hotel room sends a cold shiver down her spine, Christine feels her body giving in to the urge to rest. Her brain needs a break if she's going to try to decode Jane's involvement in all of this. She yawns loudly and pushes her way toward the door.

Shenanigan's is at the base of the Ballymoon property, a good fifteen-minute walk from the castle, which is no problem during the day, but at night, with a potential murderer on the loose, is daunting. Christine hurries to follow the group of tipsy guests down the woodland walkway behind the pub toward the castle. Mercifully, the path is lit with little streetlights to make the journey (slightly) less terrifying.

As she walks, Christine feels a sense of dread about what will inevitably happen at tomorrow's wedding. She thinks of all the times on the true-crime Netflix specials, when people say, "My life completely changed in an instant," and now she understands what they mean. She is not the same girl who woke up yesterday morning, giddy with excitement about her glamorous job. It feels like she's having an out-of-body experience, seeing the world through someone else's eyes. A full moon shimmers over the Ballymoon lough, and she stops to drink it in, a moment of stillness among the chaos. She doesn't even notice when a figure takes shape at her side.

"Such a gorgeous night, isn't it?" She jumps. In the twilight, it takes a moment for her eyes to recognize Raquel standing next to her.

"Sorry if I snuck up on you." Raquel laughs. "Honestly, everyone's so *jumpy* this weekend." Her green eyes mirror the reflection of the water. Somehow, even at this late hour, she still looks perfectly put together, her shiny curls bouncy, her face completely airbrushed, a fresh coat of bloodred lipstick framing her ultra-white teeth.

"Yeah." Christine forces a smile. "Wedding jitters."

"Right," Raquel scoffs, and it's clear to Christine that she's not buying it anymore.

Christine strains her eyes to see the gaggle of partiers ahead of her, but they've almost disappeared down the path. She starts walking quickly, and Raquel matches her pace.

"So, I saw you today," Raquel says casually, "crouching in the cemetery like Nancy Drew." Christine's pulse quickens, her cheeks flaming despite the cold night air. She doesn't say anything. She keeps walking.

"I figure you're probably looking for your next story, right?" Raquel sneers. "The press has just been having a field day with me lately, haven't they? It doesn't seem like I can do anything without being made out to be a slut or a homewrecker or whatever the sexist insult de jour is."

"We would never publish anything like that. *Bespoke* has standards," Christine says firmly.

"Sure." Raquel rolls her eyes. "Then what were you doing eavesdropping, hm?"

Christine doesn't say anything. She can't—she has no reason to trust anyone, and at this point she's best off just keeping her mouth shut.

They're almost at the castle gates; she can see the flickering torches that frame the stone staircase.

"Listen," Raquel says, and stops in her tracks just as they reach the edge of the golf course path. "I'm going to give you a tip, okay? A new lead that will blow whatever trashy article about an *alleged affair* with Trey Ripton you're planning out of the water." Raquel makes a dramatic gagging gesture as she says the words "alleged affair." Christine stays silent, a strategy that may be working for her. Raquel waits as the afterparty guests just ahead of them trickle into the castle and then she turns to Christine and whispers, "Glo is going down. There is a major lawsuit developing behind the scenes. They've been cutting corners on product development and they're being investigated by the FDA. Do you know how bad things have to be for a beauty company to be investigated by the FDA?" Raquel asks, and Christine slowly shakes her head no. Raquel pauses for dramatic effect. "Very, very bad . . . and I'm going to personally see to it that they pay for who they've hurt, for what they've done."

Even as they stand in the dark of night, it is now clear as day what Raquel is up to with Trey Ripton. She's gathering information to use against him . . . in court.

"You're going to testify," Christine whispers, eyes wide.

Raquel laughs. "Not only am I going to testify, I'm *finally* going to be taken seriously and on the world's stage. Then, when it's all over and all of Glo's loyal customers look at their empty medicine cabinets and ask, What now?, I'll launch Real Wellness by Raquel Williams."

"Your own line," Christine murmurs, baffled by Raquel's master plan.

"Cute, isn't it?" She tucks a curl behind one of her ears, her newly acquired aquamarine cocktail ring catching the moonlight just right.

"Why are you telling me all of this?" Christine asks, suspicious as to why Raquel Williams would confide in her of all people.

Raquel takes a step closer and sticks a French-manicured fingertip in Christine's face. "I don't want one more article out there insinuating that I am some stupid slut sleeping with Trey Ripton," she says through gritted teeth. "I'm *using* him to get information to take down a powerful company that's poisoning its customers. When I got in last night, all we did was have a few drinks. I asked him to share his 'advice' on running such a successful beauty brand. How he made it so *profitable*." She laughs. "Honestly, it was too easy. After his confession, and a few too many glasses of scotch, he promptly fell asleep on the couch in my suite. Clearly exhausted from clearing his conscience," she scoffs. "And not that it matters, but I'll have you know my mission has not required me to remove One. Single. Sock. Okay? Even if that's what he was after."

Even in the shadowy darkness, Christine sees the pain in Raquel's eyes.

The starlet's voice catches. "So, if you're going to write anything about me—write that." A strong breeze rolls across the golf course and Raquel wraps her cashmere cardigan around her shoulders before marching past Christine and up the red-carpeted steps, her sparkly stiletto heels dangling from her left hand like a pair of daggers.

Before she goes through the door, she pauses and turns around. "And be sure to mention Real Wellness in your article." She grins and disappears into the castle.

CHRISTINE PRACTICALLY RUNS TOWARD her suite, desperate to hide under the covers of her fluffy bed. Desperate enough even to call her mom and say that she was right about everything. That she is in *way* over her head. But there, sitting in front of her door, looking half asleep, is Danny—or *whoever he is*. He jumps to his feet the moment he sees her.

"What are you doing here?" she says coldly.

"Christine, I'm sorry I lied to you, but I'm just doing my job," he says in a hushed tone.

"You mean you're sorry I caught you in a lie," she says. "And then you lied to me again about being an undercover cop." She seethes.

"Shh, do not say that out loud," he snaps quietly. "I'm not lying about that—and telling you was a big risk for me to take, and I only did it because I didn't want you to think I was a total wanker."

"Well, mission *not accomplished*," Christine hisses back, digging through her clutch for her keycard.

"Please, if we could just talk," he starts, but she cuts him off.

"Why would I believe a word you say?" She glares at him. "Nobody here seems to be telling the truth about anything."

"Can we talk inside?" He motions to her hotel room. She thinks of what Raquel told her—of what it could mean for his investigation. And even though she doesn't fully trust Danny, the thought of being alone right now somehow sounds worse.

"You've got five minutes," she says, and with that, she unlocks the room and lets him inside.

CHRISTINE GIVES DANNY THE third degree, demanding to see his badge and real name, which she cross-references with his government-issued ID. She even checks it against a few of his credit cards for good measure.

"I promise, I just want to protect you," Danny insists. "That's my job, above all else. To keep people safe." She narrows her eyes at him, still unable to fully come to grips with the fact that the cute hotel bartender is actually an undercover cop.

"Now." Danny sighs and sits down on the couch. "Christine, I need to ask. Have you told me absolutely everything that's happened since you arrived at Ballymoon?" Danny uses his new professional voice, and she cringes thinking of when she snort-laughed at the bar and beer came out of her nose.

"Every detail is extremely important," he says with urgency.

Christine considers this. She considers telling him about Jane, about Raquel, but something stops her—she is too tired to think straight. She needs some time to figure out how the pieces all fit together. Could Raquel have murdered Gloria, so there would be less competition for Real Wellness by Raquel Williams? There is no doubt that it will be *way* easier to take down Glo now that Gloria Beaufort is gone. And what is Jane hiding? Besides, of course, that she knows about her convict father's presence this weekend. She's definitely involved in all of this.

"I need to sleep," Christine says finally, sliding her feet into a pair of Ballymoon slippers.

"Okay," Danny replies desperately. "What if you take a quick nap and then we have a coffee and a proper chat about everything?" Christine rolls her eyes and goes to plug in her phone, only to realize her charger is unplugged . . . and so is the hotel alarm clock. In fact, the entire nightstand has been moved.

*That's odd.* She steps back, assessing the room further . . . that's when she notices that the four-poster queen bed has also been moved, and significantly—it's a good two feet from where it used to be.

Danny notices her puzzlement. "What is it?"

"Help me move this bed," she says. He quickly joins her, and they push it against the far wall.

"Somebody's been moving the furniture around," Christine says. She and Danny get on their hands and knees, both of them clearly thinking the same thing: the tunnels.

Danny pushes down on the floorboard between them. It moans. They both jump back; he pushes on it again and it groans louder. Christine notices that this particular block of floorboards does look slightly different; they're not as close together as the rest of them. Cautiously, Danny tries to lift a board up, and to their surprise, three more boards lift with it. They've found a disguised door. And behind it, a set of stairs leads into a dark underground passageway.

TWENTY-NINE

# GRAHAM

Saturday, October 18, 2025
Wedding Day

WHY DID HE PUNCH BEN like that in front of all his guests? That's not like him. He doesn't snap like that. Graham moans and rolls over in bed, his arm flopping to where Jane would normally be, but of course she's not there. For tradition's sake, they agreed to separate rooms the night before the wedding, even though they live together. But if he's being honest, Jane's barely been present at all this weekend. The charming, bubbly girl next door that he met at the children's hospital has been replaced by a silent, aloof woman that he barely recognizes. At first, he thought it was prewedding nerves, but then Gran . . . and now . . . Well, he just doesn't know anymore. Rubbing his eyes, Graham sits up and turns on the bedside light.

His phone glows on the end table, and he picks it up, already dreading seeing the time. It's 4 a.m. He has to try and get at least three hours of sleep, but it seems virtually impossible to relax at this point. He keeps thinking about Gran, about her lifeless body hidden somewhere in the bowels of this castle. He thinks of his brother's hurtful words on the dance floor, of his fiancée's callous and somewhat annoyed reaction to his display of chivalry.

Did he rush into things too fast? He fell in love with Jane because she seemed so—it sounds bad to admit but—simple. The polar opposite of his messed-up family. But after this morning, not even his relationship with Jane seems uncomplicated anymore. She's a part of them now, a fly trapped in the ever-growing Ripton family web. Trying to sleep is pointless. So instead he scrolls through endless Instagram stories of friends and family arriving at the castle; he likes and comments and tries to persuade himself that the tiny squares of happy people toasting his wedding at this five-star hotel are his reality, and not the hell he's actually living.

Graham hears a knock at the door. He waits for a beat. Another knock, this time louder. Reluctantly, he pulls himself out of bed, grabs a discarded T-shirt off the floor, and looks through the peephole to see who it is. Ben.

"Hey, man, bring it in," Graham says, opening the door and wrapping his brother in a bear hug.

"I'm so sorry," Ben sobs. "I didn't mean what I said. I don't even really remember what I said, actually."

Graham's brother looks more wrecked than usual. His blazer is ripped, his belt buckle hangs unclipped from his dirty grass-stained khakis, and his eyes are bloodshot.

"Jesus, what happened to you? Well, besides the obvious. Sorry, dude." Graham winces when he sees the black-and-blue blotch forming under Ben's right eye where Graham took a crack at his already shattered brother earlier.

"She's gone, Graham. She's gone. I messed everything up," Ben moans. Graham feels the painful reality that the inevitable has finally happened. Ben's talking about Lyle. She's finally left him.

"Come in here, let's not wake up half the castle." He leads Ben into the hotel room. Graham throws him a water bottle from the mini fridge that he drinks all in one go. Whatever hangover Graham is feeling right now, Ben's is at least ten times worse.

"What do you mean she left?" Graham asks calmly. He stands opposite his brother, who sits on the edge of his unmade bed.

"When I got back to the room, her stuff was gone. Miles was gone." Ben crushes the now emptied water bottle.

"Why would she leave so suddenly the night before the wedding?" Graham asks.

"She got a different room for her and Miles. She said that it was too volatile for him to stay in the same room as me. With my drinking." His eyes fill up again. "But I know it's over. She won't even look at me. She thinks I have something to do with Sebi's disappearance, but I don't."

"She didn't leave you, Ben. She just got her own hotel room. You can still fix this. Flowers, a vacation, cut back on the booze . . ." Even as Graham says the words, he's not sure if he believes them.

"God, it's ironic, isn't it?" Ben spews. "I'm in trouble because my wife thinks I might have done something to the guy she was cheating on me with. Why is it always *me* who gets blamed for every fuckup?"

"Why does she think you have something to do with the Sebi thing?" Graham assesses his brother, memorizing his body language, trying not to miss a single detail of what he says or how he says it. Because even though Graham loves Ben, he has reason not to trust him. Ben pauses before responding. His next words are so faint, Graham can barely hear them.

"Somebody told her I was at the Lumina event last month. I was in the background of some pictures." He doesn't raise his head to meet Graham's eyes.

"Did you lie to her about where you were that night?" Graham rubs his hands over his face. Suddenly, he's tired and he'd like to get those three hours of sleep.

"Why would I *tell* her I was going to confront the guy she was sleeping with? I just never told her that we blew off the baseball game," Ben spits. "But I didn't have anything to do with Sebi's disappearance . . . You know that. You were at the event too—you can corroborate my story that I went straight home, that was it." He looks at his brother, his eyes wild. "You know I just went there to intimidate him. Sebi was sleeping with my wife—I was entitled to tell him off!"

It's clear he wants Graham's validation, but he can't quite give it to him. "Ben," Graham says with a sigh, "I want to help you, and you know I will do everything in my power to protect you, but you tricked me into going to that event to begin with. I thought we were there to recruit sponsors for the Grow 2 Glo Gala, but we were really there so you could fight some sleazy photographer." Graham rolls his eyes. "Not to mention, we missed the Yankees winning in the bottom of the tenth."

"I know, and I've apologized for all of that," Ben murmurs. "I needed to see him. To tell him to stay the hell away from my family." Ben launches himself off the bed and paces the hotel room. "I'm innocent. You know that." He points at his brother.

Graham doesn't like what he's insinuating. "What's there to be innocent of, Ben?"

Graham continues calmly, "We don't know if anything even happened to Sebi. He could be on a trip or have lost his phone or something." The words sound even more pathetic as he says them out loud.

"Seriously, Graham. I mean, come on. He left all his stuff in that hotel room. Nobody's heard from him in weeks." Ben sits down again, this time on the tufted ottoman at the base of Graham's bed. "But regardless, you know I did not do anything to him." He adds quietly, "I didn't *kill him*."

"You stayed at the event longer than me. I came back to the hotel room alone, and when I woke up in the middle of the night, you were not there." Graham is not letting him off the hook. He can't. Ben's whereabouts that night remain suspicious, and he needs to know what his brother is hiding.

"You found me right outside the room, passed out," Ben pleads. "I just—I was just outside."

"I found you passed out on a bench outside *the hotel*. You could have been robbed, or worse. But that's beside the point. The fact is, you weren't in the hotel room on the last night that anyone saw Sebi." Graham crouches in front of his brother now. He's shaking, the reality of how this all looks finally dawning on him.

"Where were you, and what were you doing?" Graham demands.

"I've told you, I don't know, man. I blacked out. Don't you think I wish I knew? But I did not hurt Sebi. I swear to you. And honestly, I bet whoever did was probably the same person who hurt Gran. There's got to be a connection." Ben looks up at his little brother helplessly. "Someone is trying to destroy us from the inside. Don't you see?"

"If you blacked out, how can you be sure you didn't hurt him?" Graham presses. "How do I know you didn't black out and hurt Gran too? Maybe she said something about you going to rehab again and you just lost it. It's happened before, Ben! Remember the time you lunged at her when we were trying to check you in at Passages?" He watches his brother's face struggle to conceal the hurt inflicted by his words, but now Graham is angry. He leans in.

"And what the fuck is going on with Grow 2 Glo, by the way? The charity's finances are a shit show and *you're* the treasurer. Have you been stealing money again? For drugs?" Graham feels his voice edge toward a shout, but it's not an unfair accusation. It's the unspoken truth. He's seen the books and he knows what Ben has pulled in the past. Addiction is a terrible, unrelenting demon.

"How can you say that? How could you think I'm such a fucking monster? First Lyle, now you too."

Graham senses his brother nearing a full-on breakdown, and he feels a wave of empathy come rushing in now that he's said his piece. Ben is his family. Despite it all, he loves him. They can fix this, all of it.

"I'm sorry," he says softly. "I shouldn't have been so harsh. I choose to believe you're a good guy. I choose to believe that all this shit is just one big, horrible coincidence. But you see how this looks, don't you?"

His brother doesn't say anything but gives a slight nod of his head.

"Once we get through this weekend, we will sort it all out, but you need to get help. Like serious help." Graham puts a hand on Ben's shoulder.

"I know," Ben says meekly. The groom pulls his brother in for another hug, but his mind is elsewhere. He's thinking about finding him on that park bench outside the Beekman Hotel, momentarily thinking he might be dead, shaking him awake, screaming, about to dial 911 when he finally opened his bloodshot eyes. That's when Graham noticed the dark red stains on Ben's oxford shirt.

THIRTY

## CHRISTINE

Saturday, October 18, 2025
Wedding Day

DANNY GAPES AT THE OPEN trap door at the base of Christine's bed. They both know what they're looking at.

Danny shakes his sandy mop of hair. "I didn't think it was true," he murmurs to himself.

"So you *did* hear rumors about a secret passageway. I knew it," Christine scoffs, but Danny doesn't reply.

Then, she has a sudden realization. "This might be how someone got in to leave me that note." Her body trembles with fear at what could have happened while she was sleeping in here alone.

Danny pulls out his phone flashlight and peers down into the passageway. "I'm going down there. If I'm not back in one hour, call this number—"

"No way I'm staying here alone!" Christine whisper-yells. "I'm coming with you." She is seriously freaked out and does not want to be by herself in this creepy room. Plus, she wants to know what is going on down there. Something is pulling her toward unraveling this mystery; it's like the messed-up version of Taylor Swift's "Invisible String."

"No, you're not. It's too dangerous. And there is nothing down there that would ever make it into the glossy pages of *Bespoke*," he says, trying to lighten the mood.

"Honestly, I don't think I am going back there after this weekend," she says. The truth of her words hit her with their full weight. How could she go back to her normal life after this? If by some miracle she doesn't get fired, would she even *want* to go back to her normal job after this? She has watched an ultrawealthy family unravel before her very eyes in the most grotesque way possible—during what was supposed to be one of the happiest weekends of their lives. It has made her reconsider all the weddings she covered before this; all the fighting and money-grubbing and dysfunctional relationships that happen behind the scenes that she ignores because her job is to spin it and sell it to the world as some sort of gold-plated fairy tale. She doesn't know if she can do it anymore, if those are the stories she wants to tell.

"I'm coming," Christine declares.

"No, you're not." His voice makes it clear that this is not up for discussion. Christine watches as he places a foot on one of the wooden steps, and then another and then another. She follows him.

"What are you doing?" he snaps.

"I said I'm coming! Want me to scream and alert everyone to this discovery?" she hisses. *As if* she's going to let this guy tell her what to do. She's the one who discovered the passageway to begin with!

"Unbelievable," Danny grumbles. "You know I could get fired for this?"

"Join the club," Christine replies.

"Just stay close to me, okay? You don't want to get lost down here." Christine nods and hurries down the last few steps to meet Danny.

As they make their way into the dark abyss, it becomes clear that this passageway hasn't gotten much use in the last millennium. The dust makes her cough, and whatever she is stepping in—warm and wet—is seeping through her castle slippers. She regrets not having the foresight to put on sneakers.

The farther they go, the more Christine realizes that this was a bad idea. She's the girl in the horror movie who went into the basement as everyone watching at home screamed, "Don't go into the basement!" How did she become that girl?

They slowly walk down the narrow corridor. The walls are the same stone as the outside of the castle and lined with dusty sconces, sans torches, unfortunately. A small hole on the right side of the wall catches her eye. A crack between the stones is allowing a streak of light to seep into the tunnel. She puts her eye up to the hole, and her breath catches in her throat. Staring back at her is someone's (very messy) hotel room. They are literally inside the castle walls. She thinks of the missing jewelry and knows, without a doubt, that someone has been using this system to steal from and spy on the guests.

"Shit," Danny says, dropping his phone and fully enveloping them in the darkness. He stumbles around trying to find it on the nasty, damp floor. With the flashlight now out of commission, Christine's other senses are heightened and she is certain that she hears the patter of footsteps coming toward them. The sound echoes faintly from the other end of the historic corridor.

*Tap, tap, tap.*

"Do you hear that?" Christine grabs Danny, her heart pounding as she blinks into the blackness, afraid to breathe. Danny, apparently having found his phone, turns his flashlight back on to reveal that the source of the tap is just a leak from the ceiling. Christine is shaken.

"Okay, I changed my mind. I think we should get out of here," she says, cursing the bravado that brought her down here in the first place.

"I think we've nearly reached the end. I want to see a little more and then I'll take you back." They walk a few more minutes in silence.

Along the way, Christine peers through more stone cracks. First, she looks into what must be Lyle's room, where little Miles sleeps peacefully, then into the drawing room, and then they hit a wall, possibly the end of the tunnel. Christine bangs on it. Solid stone through and through.

"But that doesn't make any sense," she says. "How do we get out of here? If this really was an escape route for the king, wouldn't it lead outside somehow?" Danny shines his flashlight all around the walls. The light lands on a small door no more than four and a half feet tall. It's barely visible and would be easy to miss, as it was clearly designed to match the stone.

"Clever king," Danny says, and pushes on the door, revealing a small room. They crawl inside and stand up. Christine looks around and sees a cot and some men's clothes on the floor. She stops dead when she sees the jeans. She immediately recognizes them: the muddy, heavily patched pants of the groundskeeper she ran into yesterday.

"I saw him. I saw a man in jeans like that when I was on the path that leads to the garden—on my way to meet with Maggie before the rehearsal dinner."

"Are you sure?" Danny whispers.

"He popped right out of the bushes. He said he was the groundskeeper, but wouldn't a hotel groundskeeper here be in uniform?"

Danny ponders this. "Yeah most of the groundskeepers wear uniforms—except for the head groundskeeper, Eddie. I usually see him in jeans almost identical to those every day. But we can confirm when we get out of here."

They stand in silence for a moment; then Danny picks up the jeans and riffles through the pockets, producing a wallet. He flips through it.

"Got him," he says smugly.

"What? What is it?" Christine walks over to get a look at what he's holding.

It's a credit card with the name Sebastiano Giovanni clearly printed on it. Danny uses his phone to snap pictures of the wallet, the jeans, and the rest of the room. Under a pile of old blankets, he finds a fake passport with Seamus O'Reilly's photo and the name Harold Green. Christine stands by, her mouth hanging open. She was right—Seamus O'Reilly has been sneaking around inside these castle walls. *But why would he leave me a note to look into him? It doesn't make sense.*

"I want to see a photo of that groundskeeper and compare it to Seamus's mugshot," Danny says matter-of-factly. He's lost in thought, his brow furrowed, as he documents their findings. His hand wavers slightly as he shines the light around the room. The air in the small room is akin to that of a musty attic. Christine can't believe someone's been sleeping down here.

And then she feels it . . . the subtle whoosh of air behind her. She spins around just in time to see a shadow disappear back down the corridor.

They're not alone.

## THIRTY-ONE

# SEAMUS

September 6, 2025

SEAMUS O'REILLY WAITS FOR THE call. His body is tacky with sweat—a damp layer of nerves and dread. He looks in his rearview window; the guy is passed out in the back seat of his stolen Toyota Corolla. It barely took anything to get him stumbling out of that Lumina Tequila event. His eyes had locked on the Uber sticker in the car's window, and all it took was a slight wave from Seamus for him to fall into the back seat. Two minutes later, he promptly passed out from the drugs.

It was like clockwork. Was it too easy? Seamus wonders. He thinks about the street cameras. Could they catch his face through the tinted windshield? Did they have technology that could do that now? For a brief moment, he considers bailing on this job. Just getting out of the car, going to his parole officer, and confessing everything, but he shakes himself out of it. It's too late for that.

Cracking his back like it's a glow stick, he releases the knot of energy bottled up inside him. In the side mirror, the man reflected back at him looks a good ten years older than he actually is, almost unrecognizable after his stint at Ridgeland. Seamus would venture to guess that most people wouldn't recognize even a family member after ten to twenty in that place. Even though he's been out for a few years now, the two decades Seamus spent eating powder-based white bread (if one can call it bread), lighting up cigarettes, and giving himself pen-ink tattoos has left him feeling... well, let's just say not like the best version of himself.

But when he finally watched the prison gates clank shut behind him instead of in front of him, Seamus didn't even hesitate. He went right back to Mac without entertaining the possibility that working for the crime syndicate that put him away in the first place wasn't the best plan. The thought of starting a new life—a better life—never even crossed his mind. His phone vibrates and he looks away from the mirror. Speaking of his boss.

"Hey, Mac," Seamus answers. "I've got him. It must be easier to get drunk adults into a fake Uber than it is to give kids candy from a white van these days. Might see if I can steal a taxi over in Limerick." He chuckles, but his boss doesn't reply. The loud breathing on the other line is a bit disconcerting.

"Get rid of him," Mac snarls.

"I thought the instructions were to scare 'im, pay him off?" Seamus glances back at his captive.

"The instructions were to handle it, and I am telling you how to handle it," Mac says sharply. The guy moans and fidgets in the back seat. He might be coming out of it—is that even possible? The drugs Seamus gave him were borderline lethal. Seamus's heartbeat quickens.

"I have to be careful," he whispers. "I'm on parole."

"O'Reilly," Mac says with a sigh, "let's not lose sight of the big picture here. We've got a major job coming up—your final act of service. The wedding is in just a few weeks. Once that is settled, you'll be retired. This is the last thing we need to handle before Ireland." Mac continues in that cheery singsong voice reserved only for preparing Seamus for the worst of jobs. "This guy Sebi has been digging. He has it out for the whole family. Now imagine if this bastard got wind of our plan—we'll be finished. We've come too far to let him trip us up," Mac insists. "Think of Jane."

*Jane.* Seamus remembers when he first saw his adult daughter two years ago, not long after he'd reconnected with Mac's organization. She had been leading a pack of students out of a local art gallery. He'd done a double take. *Could it be?* The sight of her rendered him motionless. There in front of him was the reincarnation of his late mother. The same dark hair, the same deer-in-headlight eyes, the same smile. Even the way she carried herself was like his mother, Maura: she was frail and slightly hunched, always making herself smaller, always disappearing into crowds.

He knew what his mother's physicality really meant, though, and it was a great advantage. Maura got away with everything because the world barely gave her a second glance. An overlooked woman can be lethal with the right training. The Maura look-alike noticed him staring and quickly shuffled the children across the street.

"You're not going to believe it," he said to Mac later, "but I just saw my mother's ghost. It had to be . . ." He'd trailed off. After a beat, Mac's mouth melted into a slippery smile, and they put the pieces together. Seamus had just seen his grown daughter. He didn't know it then, but at that moment, he'd planted the seed of Mac's master plan.

Her name was Jane Murphy. They found out all about her quite easily. Everything was on the internet these days. He watched her whole life unfold by clicking through Instagram pictures. High school prom, graduation caps, college dorms, first apartments. Beach vacations to Fort Lauderdale that turned into weekend jaunts to New York City. He watched her cheap kitchen-sink bleached-blond hair return to its natural raven black, with an extra gloss. He watched her style evolve from ill-fitting jean shorts and neon tees to chic Parisian black trousers and expensive jumpers. Jane had developed a taste for the finer things in life. They could use this to their advantage.

It hadn't been hard to bring Jane into the fold. She told Seamus that she needed time to process meeting him first, but after a while it became clear that she shared his DNA. She wasn't some squeaky-clean do-good art teacher. No, not in those shoes. Jane wasn't fully interested in forming a relationship with her long-lost father, but she was interested in making a little cash on the side. She'd broken a few rules in her day, given Maggie a run for her money. Like father like daughter, Seamus laughed to himself. Genetics always win in the end.

"Seamus," Mac barks, "are you there? Stay focused."

"Right." Seamus lets out a deep breath. "Right you are. I'll handle it."

"Good," Mac says. "I can always count on you. Thank you for your undying loyalty."

Seamus feels his chest swell with pride. Mac's smooth talking has never—not once—failed to work on him. After the wedding, Mac's enterprise will be permanently hitched to the Gloria Beaufort money wagon through Jane. Then Mac will see to it that Seamus gets his new identity, and he'll live the life of Riley—the life he was always meant to live. America, as it turns out, wasn't for him. Seamus envisions being back in the verdant land of his youth, living in a quaint cottage overlooking the sea, or a cozy flat in Dublin. He imagines his daughter—rich! Married to a billionaire! A happy life ahead for them both. Good things come to those who wait.

"Let me know when it's done." Mac hangs up the phone. Seamus sighs and looks in his rearview mirror at the guy, who is fully passed out now, his body limply hanging off the back seat. The name Sebi makes him roll his eyes—a pretentious name, perfect for a pretentious prick. Sebi barely even looked at Seamus when he sold him the drugs earlier. He just stood there in his expensive-looking jacket, handing over crisp bills like he was peeling off paper towels. Seamus feels jealousy simmer inside him. Why hadn't he been born into a life that was so effortless? Not only had he come into this world broke as a joke, but he'd also lived his best years in a cage.

He drags Sebi's limp body out of the car. It's hot and swampy in this area of Long Island, a dark, moonless night. They've used this spot to get rid of people before. Bodies just melt into the earth here, never to be discovered. Seamus pockets Sebi's wallet before tossing him into the murky water. Maybe Seamus'll do a little online shopping. He watches the body sink into the swamp. Sebi's limbs don't even twitch in protest, like the useless spoiled brat that he is. *At least it'll be a painless death,* Seamus tells himself.

When he gets back in his car, ready to drive away, he sees a flash of light behind him. It's gone so fast that he convinces himself he's just being paranoid. But later, as he tosses and turns trying to fall asleep—well, he could have sworn what he saw was a pair of car headlights, and he can't shake the thought that somebody might have followed him . . . and watched him toss a body into the Long Island marsh.

## THIRTY-TWO

## CHRISTINE

Saturday, October 18, 2025
Wedding Day

"I THINK I SAW SOMEONE," Christine says quickly. Danny grabs his phone and shines its flashlight out of the little room hidden in the castle walls.

"Are you sure?" he demands, his flashlight illuminating the empty passageway.

"Yes. I felt someone behind me and then I saw a shadow disappear there." She points back down the corridor. "I'm positive."

"I'm calling for backup," Danny says, looking at his phone, but of course: zero bars.

"Let's get out of here, *please*," Christine pleads, regretting ever searching for this creepy, musty ancient escape route.

"There has to be some way for whoever is staying down here to come and go from the castle as they please. Your room can't be the only entry or exit point." Danny shines his flashlight closer to the walls, giving the cobwebs and filthy grime a spotlight they certainly don't deserve. Something catches Christine's eye. Just past the cot, there's another faint outline that could be a second door.

"Look over there." Christine points at the outline and then crosses toward it, Danny on her heels. The door is sticky, but it's definitely an exit. As they push on it, they can hear the hinges give slightly. After some effort, the door swings open, and they fall straight into . . . the Snug?

A stunned Neil nearly drops the glass he is polishing.

"Hey, mate, careful there. That's the crystal," Danny says, brushing himself off.

"Sorry, uh—you surprised me. I didn't know there was a closet back there," he stutters, fumbling to pick up the glass. Neil looks them up and down, and Christine is ready to die of embarrassment. She knows how this looks. Neil thinks they were hooking up in the closet.

"Yeah, well, um, there is. A little secret." Danny winks. "Keep this between us, yeah?" Neil blushes. A shameless move on Danny's part, but it's a good cover.

Danny looks at his watch. "Gosh, is it six a.m. already? The big day is upon us. I'll be down and ready in a few minutes, Neil. Sorry for the holdup." Danny closes the hidden door and moves a bar cart in front of it. After a few awkward seconds that seem to stretch into hours, Neil carries a tray of polished glasses out of the pub, leaving them alone.

"I can't believe we've literally been up all night," Christine groans, picking tunnel debris off her sleeve. Danny looks pale and a bit frazzled as he pulls up the Ballymoon staff directory on his phone. Christine catches a glimpse of herself in the pub's brass mirror—she looks equally tragic.

"Okay," Danny says, "let's see if you recognize Eddie as the guy in the muddy jeans. He's worked here as the groundskeeper for over thirty years, so there's no chance he's living a double life as Seamus O'Reilly. Hell, I don't think he's ever left County Clare!" He thrusts his phone at Christine. "Is this who you saw?"

Christine studies the picture on the screen. Eddie Olsen is a kindly-looking older gentleman with sparkly eyes and smile lines. Christine is pretty sure that she recognizes him as the man she saw on the path. Plus, the more she thinks about it, she's almost positive he didn't have any tattoos. In Seamus's mug shot, he has an unmissable snake tattoo slithering up his neck. If the man she saw had that, she would have remembered it. Her heart sinks.

"Yeah." She sighs. "I think that's him. Sorry, I just got caught up in it all."

"There are lots of muddy jeans in Ireland." Danny gives her a defeated smile.

"True," Christine musters.

"Given what's just been discovered," Danny says in a low voice, "I'll be needing access to your room."

They quickly head down the hall and shut the door to Christine's suite behind them. When they see the state of the suite, they freeze. It has been put back together, the open tunnel latched shut. Another single tented piece of paper sits on the edge of the bed. Somebody else was in here while they were in the tunnel. Christine reaches for the note, but Danny holds her back, insisting that he do a thorough sweep of the room first. Finally, when he's deemed that they're safe (and alone), Christine picks up the piece of paper.

"What does it say?" Danny asks as he inspects her closet thoroughly for any other secret entrances.

Christine whips her head around. "It says who killed Gloria Beaufort—and how to catch them."

THIRTY-THREE

# SEBI

September 6, 2025

NOTHING SAYS *I'VE GIVEN UP* quite like slamming consecutive shooters of Skol Vodka outside a CVS at a quarter past midnight and—wait for it—on *Bleecker Street*. The irony of his location brings tears to Sebi's eyes and a gurgled laugh to his throat as he fishes around in his jacket pocket for his final shot. He rolls it around in his palm, the liquid sloshing as if asking, *Will you? Won't you?* He will and he does. The sharp burn of the alcohol instantly invigorates him. He takes a deep breath and shoves his hands back into his jeans pockets. It's an unusually cool night for September in New York City.

He has a decision to make, and he's never been particularly good at decision-making—hence the shooters—but he's finally settled on it: he'll do whatever it takes to destroy the Ripton family. He walks down the street, swarms of overgrown teenagers—baby adults—stumbling around, cackling and shrieking, or sitting on the curb eating slices of pizza. He scoffs, bitter and jealous, wishing he could be drunk for fun and not drunk because he needs the liquid courage.

*I don't deserve this*, he thinks for the one millionth time. He should be on a date with his girlfriend—well, now his ex-girlfriend. Maybe in another life, they'd be drinking martinis at the Monkey Bar or sharing an Aperol spritz at a bar in Positano. Perhaps they'd even be on a yacht in the Mediterranean or tucked into a cabana somewhere on St. Barth's. He shakes the thoughts loose, his dark curls bouncing from side to side.

He has a plan—not a good one, but one that feels soulful and righteous and suited for his love-scorned state. Tomorrow, he has a meeting with a reporter at the *New York Times*. He's going to go on the record and spill everything he knows about the Riptons—the lawsuit, Gloria's blackmailing, everything. The more vodka he drinks, the better the plan sounds.

He's almost at Gusto's, where he'll shoot a promotional event for Lumina Tequila and try to act like he's having a great time. At least between the flashes of his camera, he will find one hundred pretty girls and endless drinks to help him forget, even if only for a few hours.

A shriek from across the street makes him jump. A burly twenty-something picks up a tiny brunette and throws her over his shoulder. Just dumb kids. Sebi's body nearly vibrates with the pulse of the music coming from the nightclub next to him. *Is this a mistake? Should I go home? Should I get a good night's sleep before the interview? Really figure out exactly what I want to say?*

"You all right, lad?" He feels a hand on his shoulder. He turns around to see a wiry older guy looking at him with concern. He's wearing a baseball cap and a worn leather jacket. It's hard to get a look at his face, but it's also hard to miss the serious tattoo on his neck. *Is it a python?* Sebi tries to get a better look. He's always loved body art.

"Yes, fine. Fine." Sebi pulls his light jacket around him tightly as the breeze picks up. The man smells putrid, like onions and sweat.

"Right." The smelly man raises an eyebrow in a way that conveys he does not believe him.

"Anyway, you, uh, look like you could use an upper," the man says with an Irish lilt and reaches into his pocket. He pulls out a little white bag and taps it with his finger. Sebi looks at the bag longingly. He really *could* use an upper.

"How much?" He reaches into his pocket for his wallet.

"Two hundred. Good deal because you look like you could use something." The guy laughs and pats him on the back. Despite his hard-core tattoo, he has a friendly face, like a little leprechaun drug dealer. Sebi hands him the bills then takes the plastic bag. The guy scurries off as Sebi saunters into Gusto's. He makes his way to the bar area, looking for the event coordinator, when he hears a familiar voice over the thumping music. He stops and turns around to see Ben Ripton taking shots at a high-top table by the door. He locks eyes with Ben.

*"Merda,"* he mumbles before turning away. There is no reason for Ben Ripton to be at a Lumina promo event, yet here he is. Sebi clutches the little white bag, desperate to get its contents into his system.

"Hey." Ben rushes toward him. "Hey, asshole."

"Ciao," Sebi musters, and then, as expected, Ben lurches toward him. Sebi has to let Ben hit him—it's only fair. He stumbles back for show, but it was a weak punch. Ben stumbles back too, but probably because of all the drinks he's consumed. As he hits the floor, so does his drink, sending shards of glass everywhere. Sebi tries to help by picking up the broken pieces, but Ben lunges at him again, cutting himself in the process. Now there is blood on his shirt and hands. A few of the bouncers rush toward the scene and pull Ben away. Sebi takes his opportunity to get out of there, fleeing down a back staircase and into the red lights of the dance floor. He hears the ragged voices of a younger generation belting out some new Charli XCX song. He longs to be one of them again, to rewind time, to go a different route, to never have even met Lyle Ripton.

Finally, he reaches the bathroom. It's empty besides a couple making out in the corner. He goes into a stall, takes out his little white bag, cuts the powder with his credit card, and snorts it all up. He feels his lifeblood surge with energy—for a second, he feels unstoppable.

And then, well, he doesn't remember anything after that.

# THIRTY-FOUR

# CHRISTINE

Saturday, October 18, 2025
Wedding Day

CHRISTINE TAKES A SHOWER AND slips into the silky pink bridal pajamas that Jane gave her for the "getting ready" portion of today's events. Initially, she was so excited to be included in the intimate wedding-day ritual, but now she is dreading it. She just wants to decipher the latest note, which is playing on a loop in her brain. She comes out of the bathroom in her skimpy pajamas, and Danny raises his eyebrows.

"Just—don't say anything." She glares at him. "Elliot is making me wear them in case I end up in the background of any pictures." Danny throws up his hands in mock surrender, and Christine picks up the note and reads it one more time:

*I have taken care of Mac, Gloria's murderer. After seven o'clock, call the police. Trust that I am on your side.*

"Who the hell is this Mac person? Could it be a code name for Seamus?" Christine asks, slumping onto her bed and covering her face with a pillow. Her eyelids feel heavy. She's going to need about fifteen shots of espresso today.

"It could be a code name for anyone," Danny murmurs unhelpfully.

He takes the note from Christine and rereads it himself. "But I don't think it's Seamus. Why would he tell us to call the police?" Danny pauses before continuing. "I think we can afford to take the calculated risk and assume whoever is sending you these messages is trying to help. I think we should do as they say." He turns the note over, checking the back—again—for any hidden clues or meaning.

"But Seamus is probably the only one who knows about the passageway besides us," Christine presses.

"As far as we know," Danny reminds her.

"I think he's been snooping around in there—and using it to steal things too," Christine asserts. "I bet he stole Maggie's necklace and Raquel's earrings. They both told me at the rehearsal dinner their jewelry was taken."

Danny sighs. "I agree, but let's try to stay in the present moment. I'm going to catch Seamus and whoever this Mac is and then you'll get the answers you're after. I'll send this note off to the lab for fingerprinting."

Christine folds her arms over her chest.

Danny crouches down next to her. "You and me—we're on the same team, right?" His eyes crinkle again as he smiles at her. "And after seven o'clock, this'll be over and you'll be on the next flight out of here, back to New York. Just hang in there a bit longer."

She nods but can't shake the twinge of annoyance she feels toward him for not taking her help seriously.

"But why wait until seven o'clock?" she presses—she can't help it. "It just feels like a long time to wait to make some arrests."

Danny sighs and stands up. "I'm assuming the sender picked seven so that everyone will be back at the castle. It will be easier to make arrests that way, harder for anyone to escape." Danny is more thinking aloud than speaking to her at this point, but Christine doesn't care—at least he's providing a tiny bit of insight into the police investigation. She slides her cardigan over the revealing pajamas and puts on a fresh pair of squishy Ballymoon hotel slippers. She thinks about seeing Jane again after her chilling warning last night and freezes.

"Wait, what about Jane? Maybe she's Mac. Maybe that's why she was so hostile toward me last night." Christine feels her heart rate start to pick up again.

"That's for me to worry about," Danny says tightly. "You go to the ceremony. Act as you normally would at this type of event. My unit is taking over. You need to stay out of this—for your safety." Danny shoots her a look.

"Fine, fine," Christine huffs. "I'll just enjoy my time mingling with suspected murderers. Don't mind me, waltzing into certain death." Christine puts on a swipe of lip gloss and flashes him a fake smile.

"I won't let anything happen to you," Danny says seriously, and their eyes meet. She feels her heart flutter slightly . . . She believes him.

Danny quickly clears his throat and looks away. "We can't tip off this Mac person, and since we have no idea who that is at the moment, you have to be cautious around everyone. Just promise me you'll do your best not to draw any attention to yourself, okay?" he pleads, and Christine nods again.

"I'm going to head out. When this is all over, I feel like you owe me another drink after running out on me last night." He winks and ducks out of her room before she can object. She smiles to herself, comforted by the brief glimpse of Danny the bartender. *Maybe it wasn't all a cover*, she thinks.

Then Elliot's text screams through the screen: WHERE ARE YOU? GLAM IS STARTING. Her smile disappears. She grabs her bag and shuffles down the castle hallway. *Glam will be good*, she tells herself. *It will be a welcome distraction.* Everything in life is always more manageable after a fresh manicure.

THIRTY-FIVE

# CHRISTINE

Saturday, October 18, 2025
Wedding Day

IF CHRISTINE WAS AT ALL focused on her coverage for her article, she'd make a note to describe the spa at Ballymoon as "dungeon chic." But all she can think of as she wends her way down the staircase into the underground sanctuary is whether someone is watching her through the cracks in the stone.

Most of the castle has been meticulously preserved in all its old-fashioned grandeur, but the spa could just as easily be situated in a chic Tribeca warehouse. The walls are painted a creamy ecru, and the modern furnishings in funky shapes and shades of beige give the space a futuristic feel.

"Hi, Christine, how'd you sleep? I hope you weren't up all night writing." Raquel winks. "Have a mimosa!" The brunette beauty hands Christine a coupe glass brimming with orange juice and champagne. *Could Raquel be Mac?* Christine thinks, warily accepting the glass. She certainly would have had motive to get rid of Gloria—she made that crystal clear last night.

"Morning, ladies!" She snaps herself out of it, her voice coming out an octave higher than usual. "Everyone looks gorgeous." The other three bridesmaids give her a range of dismissive smiles. Christine recognizes all of them from various features in *Bespoke*: Alison Hunter (founder of the frilly dress line Hunter Haus, where a cotton shift starts at six hundred dollars), Lily Weisberg (the much younger second wife of celebrity chef Jerry Weisberg, controversial creator of some meat-only diet), and Paige Van Lier (distantly related to the Rockefellers and likely in massive credit card debt given the number of European vacations she's taken this year). And they all have one thing in common: they're Lyle's friends, not Jane's.

"Help yourself to some breakfast," Elliot says curtly. He nods in the direction of a giant buffet table at the far end of the room. The spread is fit for an Oscars after-party—complete with a teeming chocolate fountain. Christine's heart beats quickly in Elliot's presence. Maybe she wrote him off too quickly after his outburst aimed at Gloria on Thursday. He could definitely be Mac. She pushes the thought out of her head. *Act normal*, she reminds herself.

"Chocolate?" Christine grins. "On her wedding day preceremony? This couldn't have been your idea." She helps herself to a perfectly flaky croissant. Why not? If something goes wrong today, she doesn't want to regret *not* having the croissant. She briefly considers the look Sandra would give her if she saw her indulge in carbs, and then she takes a big bite.

"Of course it wasn't my idea. I can't even look at chocolate without feeling my face puff up," Elliot quips. "But it was a must-have request from the bride." He signals to the glass of green juice he's holding. "But I am forcing her to drink this."

The crystal has *Jane* etched into it. "Personalized Waterford crystal glasses—nice touch." Christine takes a few pictures of the over-the-top detail. She's overdue responding to Sandra, so she sends her a picture of the personalized glasses, along with a text: Everyone's going to die when they see these photos.

"What's your name, love?" A chic woman with a hoop nose ring and bouncy high pony grins at Christine over her clipboard.

"Oh, I'm just here to observe. Not a bridesmaid. The pajamas were just a gesture from a thoughtful bride." Christine tries to make eye contact with Jane, but she seems set on ignoring her. The bride, Raquel, and her bevvy of blond bridesmaids in pink silk prance around the room as the wedding photographers capture every girly giggle with a flash. Jane looks completely at ease, not a worry line of stress on her face about what her formerly thought-to-be-dead ex-convict father might be up to at this moment. *Very Mac-esque behavior,* Christine notes. She fidgets in her pajama shorts, wanting to be anywhere else.

"Well, we're quite overstaffed—fancy any treatments?" Nose Ring offers. Christine looks around; there are at least five estheticians standing by the spa entrance.

"Come on, then." Nose Ring winks. "Treat yourself to a mani-pedi at least."

"Oh fine, why not." Christine smiles, and the woman leads her over to a glorious massage chair. The morning proceeds in an eerily normal fashion. From the classic "champagne pop" photoshoot to Jane's teary-eyed hug with Maggie, everything flows seamlessly. But every time a bridesmaid shrieks—which is about every thirty seconds—Christine jumps a little in her chair.

"Are you all right, love?" the manicurist asks after she's redone her right thumb two times. "Can I get you a cup of tea?"

"No, no. I'm fine, just ticklish," she lies, before sinking deeper into the massage chair. Christine watches as Jane is tanned, sprayed, shined, painted, glossed, and fawned over.

"Are you sure you don't want that tea? Your hands are icy, it could warm you up." The manicurist massages her hand with some delicious citrus-scented oils. *Will this woman stop asking her questions?*

"Oh no, seriously, I'm fine. Thank you." Christine admires her glossy red manicure and tries to sound flippant. A hush falls over the room. Jane has just stepped into the dressing room—ready for her put-on-the-dress moment. On muscle memory, Christine pulls out her phone, ready to record the big dress reveal. Jane has kept her final dress decision a major secret. It is the one part of the wedding that she didn't let Elliot sink his teeth into.

"Okay, ladies." Elliot puts a hand on the dressing room door. "Are we ready to see our bride?" The girls cheer. The wedding planner has that undeniable look of someone who really and truly loves their job. The look of joy on his face makes Christine realize suddenly that she actually doesn't feel the same way anymore.

"Here she is!" Elliot makes a point to open the door with agonizing slowness. The videographer and photographer start snapping and out walks Jane. The bride beams in a gorgeous cream-colored high-neck gown that's cinched at the waist. A long train billows behind her that Christine imagines will be a nightmare to bustle. The gown has to be Stella McCartney—very different from what Christine thought she'd go for, but now she can't imagine her wearing anything else. Her hair somehow strikes that perfect balance of elevated and effortless, held up in a slightly wispy, shiny bun. She's glowing.

"Oh, Jane," Raquel whispers. "You look perfect. Just perfect. We need to get Gloria for pictures—she has to see you," Raquel exclaims as she hugs her. Christine steals a glance at Raquel. The comment seems genuine.

"We told you a thousand times already, she's too sick," Clementine says, her voice sharp. She doesn't exude even a hint of grief or unease regarding Gloria's absence. *Maybe Clementine is Mac.* The champagne bubbles turn to acid in Christine's mouth.

"Is Lyle ill too? Where is that girl? I can't believe they're missing *this*. I mean, seriously, take some DayQuil and get down here." Raquel tries to keep her voice light, but it's clear she is trying to figure out what's going on.

"She's running late," Clementine says crisply.

"And if Gloria is so sick, shouldn't a doctor be called? I mean, she's getting up there—even a cold can be serious at her age," Raquel continues, not ready to let this go. But Clementine pretends not to hear her, and instead busies herself by applying a bright pink lipstick in the mirror.

"Okay, people," Elliot interjects. "Time to take the bridal portraits in the garden." With a clap of his hands, the bridesmaids and glam supervisors ready themselves to go outside. Raquel begrudgingly falls into line. The group exits the spa through a barely there glass door and up a not exactly heel-friendly set of stone steps. As they step into the sunshine, Elliot pulls Jane aside.

"Now, just a reminder about the outfit change schedule, since we have three fabulous postceremony looks. The cocktail dress you'll slip into immediately after church photos, that'll be easy. Then I'll grab you to change into the dinner dress around six, just before guests sit down to eat, and finally, the fireworks dress—"

"I'll change into the fireworks dress right after the mother-daughter dance," Jane says quickly. "It's way more comfortable than that long dinner dress."

"Great." Elliot jots down the note on his clipboard. "Now, don't worry about a thing. Today is going to be beautiful. You're a vision. Graham is so lucky." Elliot squeezes Jane's hand.

The bride smiles. "What's there to worry about? Everything is going to be perfect." She struts away from Elliot.

Then Christine sees it—and she's shocked that she didn't recognize it sooner, after all the weddings she's attended, all the couples she's dissected over the years.

Jane isn't in love with Graham.

Christine can see it now, in her eyes, in the way she ignores all mentions of him, in the way she jerks her head a bit to the left every time he leans in for a kiss, in the way she shied away from him during the emotional rehearsal dinner speech. Jane is cold and calculating, and undeniably up to something—*a carbon copy of Gloria Beaufort.*

# THIRTY-SIX

# GLORIA

September 6, 2025

IT'S JUST AFTER MIDNIGHT. GLORIA awakes in Southampton to the sounds of her cell phone vibrating, but she wasn't really sleeping anyway. She doesn't sleep much these days—doesn't see the point. Who knows how long she's got left. Might as well sleep when you're dead, as the saying goes. Plus, she's got unfinished business—time is of the essence. Manipulating Trey was one thing, but outright *stealing* from her, *disobeying* her. The nerve. *After everything she's done*—she takes a deep breath. *Stay calm*, she reminds herself. She's going to fix this. All of it.

Gloria sits up in bed. She answers her phone and skips the pleasantries. "What did you find?"

It's not the first time she's hired a private investigator to look into a man who's lost her trust . . . but it's certainly the last.

THIRTY-SEVEN

# CHRISTINE

Saturday, October 18, 2025
Wedding Day

CHRISTINE LEAVES THE GROUP IN the garden to go get herself wedding ready, which she does in record fashion. Normally, she'd have blocked off three hours for her usual preparation ritual, but now she is just desperate to limit her time alone in her suite. After twenty scattered minutes of half curling her hair and half steaming her dress, she meets the rest of the guests in the lobby of the hotel to be shuttled to the church, looking like a performer on *Saturday Night Live* who ran out of time during their quick change. She tries to keep to herself and focuses on admiring a portrait of Queen Gormlaith in the historic halls. There's something about the painting that looks familiar to her, but she can't pinpoint what it is.

"Beautiful dress." Clementine walks up behind her. The mother of the groom is wearing an olive-green one-shoulder gown in a silky fabric that ripples like a mossy lake as she walks. But in true Clementine fashion, she has put her own spin on the classic look: a wacky headband with sparkly silver prongs sticking off it, making her look kind of like an alien.

"Oh. Thanks," Christine mutters distractedly. The structured, strapless metallic Ellie Saab number is a loaner from a colleague and meant to mimic a knight's armor (an ode to the castle), but now she wishes that it was made of *actual* armor.

"All right people, let's move it, move it!" Elliot's gold bangles rattle. "We wouldn't want the shuttle to leave without you!" Christine can't meet his eyes; she is so unnerved by his peppiness and commitment to the facade that everything is normal. Sensing this, Elliot pulls her aside.

"I know it's all bizarre," he says quickly, "but it's almost over. I spoke to Trey, and the family has already come up with a perfect plan to keep this whole Gloria thing out of the press and keep us all protected: suicide." Elliot looks at her like she should be relieved. "So you can relax a little. Enjoy the party! Get the juicy scoop for your article." Christine forces herself to look at him. They stare at each other for a moment in silence.

"Elliot," Clementine calls, "one of my talons has fallen off! It's a fashion emergency."

"Coming," Elliot replies. "Lighten up, Christine! Have a martini. Or two!"

She turns away from the wedding planner and takes one final look at the painting of Queen Gormlaith. Her gaze is powerful yet playful, an unsettling combination—just like Gloria Beaufort's. She turns around and yet another set of unsettling eyes meet her own: Graham Ripton's.

She gasps, putting her hand to her chest to calm her heart. "You snuck up on me." *Get a grip, Christine.*

"God, sorry," he blurts out. "I was just admiring the portrait." Graham's eyes take in the Irish queen, while Christine's eyes take in him. The groom looks like he just stepped off the pages of *Bespoke*, in a custom Armani tux and Gucci loafers, his hair perfectly coiffed, his handsome face clean-shaven.

"It reminds me of her, don't you think?" Graham says softly.

"Yeah." Christine smiles sadly. "I was just thinking that, actually." The groom runs his hand through his hair.

"Really, Christine," he says, and sighs, "I'm so sorry about all of this. You've been such a professional this weekend. We're so grateful. I can assure you that your career will take off once this is all behind us." Graham's words stick to her like slime.

She musters a weak "Thanks." Sweat starts to prickle in her armpits. Of all the people that could be Mac, Graham was pretty low on her list . . . until that comment. *Does he really think I'm worried about my career trajectory anymore? After all this?* But then she remembers the whole Grow 2 Glo drama. This is her chance to ask him about it. She just needs to dig deep and find the words.

Outside the window, the skies open up again. Christine and Graham watch as guests scurry onto the limo buses to head to the church ceremony. Elliot and his staff scramble to hand out white umbrellas embroidered with Jane and Graham's wedding crest.

"Wow, what a downpour." Graham whistles. "Nobody puts a show on like Mother Nature, right?"

Christine feels her breath catch.

"Gran said that to me just yesterday. It was our last conversation together, come to think of it." His eyes fill with tears, but he inhales deeply, keeping them at bay. "Anyway, see you over there." Christine watches him jog out into the rain, her mouth agape.

She is stuck, her feet glued to the floor in front of the portrait, her mind immediately flashing back to her exchange with Gloria at the Bespoke Ball a couple weeks ago . . . Because the groom has just repeated her own words back to her.

THIRTY-EIGHT

# GLORIA

September 28, 2025
The Bespoke Ball, New York City

"MOM, PLEASE LET ME HELP you." Trey reaches for his mother as the door to her black Town Car flings open, exposing them, once again, to the unrelenting glow of camera flashes. *The irony!* Gloria thinks. *Trey offering me his help as I try to fix the mess he made!*

But she just tuts. "Nonsense, I'm fine." She pulls her hand away, glaring at her son. She loathes how the minute someone her age starts letting their gray hairs show, middle-aged people feel the need to step in as unrequested caretakers. Gloria is not on her deathbed yet—and she is determined to exit her town car with the help of only her cane. Gloria Beaufort does not show weakness. Especially not now.

"Gloria! Gorgeous! Over here! You look amazing." The flock of photographers shout at her as she makes her way across the red carpet and toward the steps of the Metropolitan Museum of Art. She takes a deep breath—the stairs will be a challenge, but she purposefully chose a light, gauzy look for this year's Bespoke Ball. This year's theme is "Stormy Weather," paying homage to Chanel's latest collection, inspired by the classic Etta James song. And it's safe to say Gloria captured the theme perfectly. Her ethereal silver gown by Dior, meant to mimic the shade of an approaching storm, feels like practically nothing at all on her gaunt frame. It was a safe choice for fashion's biggest night of the year—but she needed something that she could easily walk in. As walking at all is proving to be a challenge for her these days.

Before her eyes even have the chance to adjust to the flash of the cameras, they're off her and onto it girl Raquel Williams, who's just behind her on the carpet. The tall twentysomething, famous for her stunning curls, is wearing a gown that is clearly supposed to look like a puff of white clouds but looks more like something a toddler created by gluing cotton balls all over the duvet. *Probably Giambattista Valli,* Gloria scoffs bitterly. Her days of wearing dramatic contraptions more akin to performance art are behind her.

At her age, Gloria has decided that she'll let her jewels do the talking. And tonight, they're singing. She's wearing a pave-set pendant necklace featuring a fifty-karat sapphire surrounded by twenty karats of tiny glistening diamonds, to represent the eye of the storm, of course. Her emerald-cut diamond earrings could each be a sizable engagement ring, and her wrists are wrapped in her signature collection of diamond and sapphire tennis bracelets. She's a walking insurance nightmare.

Gloria struts the carpet without giving a single interview or comment—dismissing the few intelligent reporters who've clocked her insane jewelry instead of falling prey to Raquel's louder ensemble. She makes a beeline for the steps while her family trails behind her, lapping up compliments from the ogling reporters, probably divulging more than they should about the details of their private lives. She hears her daughter-in-law, Clementine, attempting to explain to someone from E! News how her bubble gum–pink and sherbet-orange chiffon catastrophe of a dress somehow fits the theme.

Lyle is the only one who seems to have any restraint when it comes to chatting with the media. She's wearing a pale blue Givenchy gown hand-sewn with thousands of Swarovski crystals and a tiara that shows the swirl of tidal waves in an assortment of blue jewels. Her stylist borrowed the piece from the country of Monaco, and it's rumored the tiara once sat atop the head of Princess Grace, but she ultimately found it too gauche.

Lyle's facial expression is stony and unsmiling—which is actually a perfect reflection of the Stormy Weather theme, but that's probably just a coincidence. Come to think of it, Gloria can't remember the last time she saw Lyle smile. She sighs, feeling a prickle of guilt about Sebi—about the inevitability of what's to come. It's a pity he got caught in the cross fire of her bitter battle with *Mac*. She scoffs at the stupid nickname.

Gloria trudges her way up the steps without even breaking a sweat. She's always had a one-track mind when it comes to accomplishing her goals. She grins, looking around to see if anyone noticed the impressive feat for someone in their mid-eighties, but nobody even bats an eye. Of course they haven't; she's gone to great lengths to try to hide her deteriorating condition.

Once she's inside the museum, she observes the scene. It takes a lot to impress her these days, and let's just say the aesthetic of this year's Bespoke Ball is . . . not Sandra's best work. The longtime editor in chief at *Bespoke* is losing her touch. The lighting is too dark and too blue, making it hard to see anything at all, but what she does notice seems tacky and too on the nose: raindrop chandeliers, tables in the shape of clouds, flowers in unnatural shades of blue and gray. Frankly, the whole room is ghastly. These events used to be dignified and restrained, like state dinners, but now they're like tacky high school proms planned by new-money Instagram influencers. Gloria immediately asks to go to her table. She'll need to have a word with the board about this calamity—it's time for Sandra Yoon to be put out to pasture.

"Right this way, Ms. Beaufort," says a flustered assistant in a tight black dress and chunky headset before leading her through the room. Gloria settles into her chair and prepares herself to hold court there this evening, but first, she needs a drink. She's about to signal to the waiter to bring her a glass of champagne, when a young woman appears before her holding one. She's wearing an elaborate—possibly Chanel?—pale green off-the-shoulder puff-sleeved gown of duchess satin, and her strawberry-blond hair is covered in a thousand tiny golden butterfly clips. Her face is hidden by an elaborate mask that Gloria thinks is meant to mimic a swirl of wind and autumn leaves; it perfectly frames her bright hazel eyes.

"I know a 'I need a glass of champagne' look when I see one." The woman grins and hands Gloria the bubbling glass.

"Thank you," she says with a laugh. "Have we met? Forgive me if I don't recognize you under that fantastic mask."

"I don't think so. I'm Christine Russo. It's a pleasure to meet you." She holds out her hand for Gloria to shake, which she does cautiously.

"And you look amazing too, Ms. Beaufort. Like a human hurricane." The woman smiles.

"I will certainly take that as a compliment." She laughs again.

"As you should." She sits down at Gloria's table and extends her glass for a clink. Gloria racks her brain trying to place Christine Russo. She must be *a somebody* at the magazine, or this woman certainly wouldn't be drinking champagne and chatting with someone of Gloria's stature. She's probably somebody famous's daughter or niece. Her laugh and cute nose sort of remind her of Gwyneth.

"I'm surprised we haven't met. I'm good friends with Sandra, so I attend a lot of events," Gloria says. She takes a sip of champagne, her intrigue growing.

"I'm relatively new," the woman says quickly. "I work for *Bespoke Weddings*." She must be a nepo baby, Gloria concludes.

"The predivorce parties division," Gloria says, and smirks. "Chin up, darling. I'm sure they'll promote you out of there soon." She pats her arm and gives her a wink.

"Ha!" Christine snorts, almost spitting up a bit of her champagne. Gloria would normally find this disgusting, but this girl somehow makes it appear charming.

"I actually really love it. I get to go to all of the year's best parties!" she says. "And weddings are such fascinating stories to write about. Fashion, style, setting, mood—they're all pivotal parts of any good piece, really. I'm having a blast covering them."

Gloria cocks an eyebrow, amused by her ingenuity. "That's a very positive take," she replies. "I see you're not yet jaded." A waiter walks around and offers them slivers of crispy rice topped with seared tuna and jalapeño. The girl takes one, but Gloria refrains. She doesn't have much of an appetite these days.

"Definitely not," the woman says, then crunches down on her hors d'oeuvre. "I'm still very enamored by everything." Christine throws open her arms dramatically.

"The cynical view would be to say that weddings now are ridiculous and unreasonably extravagant—a flagrant and gross display of narcissism and wealth. A complete deviation from what was once a holy sacrament. And that *Bespoke Weddings* serves it all up on a silver platter only to remind people of what they will never have. It's all a charade, a tragic performance, a costume party, a *spectacle* with no real meaning," Gloria spits out, and puts down her glass, motioning to the party at large. "Sort of like this."

*How will she respond to that?* Gloria wonders. As of late, she's been thinking a lot about her own lavish and somewhat morally ambiguous existence. About what to do regarding the hard truths she now has to face at the end of a long life . . . about her own family, about the company she keeps, the choices she's made.

But the woman doesn't skip a beat. "Oh, but don't we all *love* a spectacle? Isn't that what brings people to the altar to begin with? Because they saw something *truly spectacular* in someone else?" She takes a sip of her champagne before continuing. "Sometimes the world can feel so dark. Why not highlight a little sparkle if you can? And sure, *Bespoke Weddings* certainly surpasses *a little sparkle*. The weddings we cover are definitely the supernovas among the stars, if you will—but we cover those weddings as a way to inspire people, not dishearten them. At least, that's my goal."

Gloria's eyes twinkle. "Well, my grandson's wedding next month will *certainly* be a supernova."

"That's for sure." The woman grins. The party starts to fill up around them.

"Now you must tell me about what you're wearing." Gloria grins, knowing she won't be disappointed.

"So glad you asked!" She claps her hands together. "It's Chanel—meant to reflect the fierce femininity of the natural world . . . I love the idea that even though traditionally God is always referred to as 'Him,' humanity has always assumed that it is a woman who controls the elements, who summons the stormy weather—the hurricanes and thunderstorms and tsunamis—and then, She is the one that clears it, planting and nurturing the seeds of new life. She is the beginning and the end, the destroyer and the creator, wreaking havoc some days, growing flowers the next. It's so on the money for the female experience, isn't it? The wrath, but also the love! The beauty, but also the brokenness! The dizzying power! The absolute drama of it all!" She raises her glass and grins. "I call the look: Nobody puts a show on like Mother Nature!"

The woman's eyes flit toward the museum entrance. "I see your family is just arriving, so I won't keep you. It was really great meeting you, Ms. Beaufort. And congratulations on the upcoming marriage of your grandson, Graham. I know it's going to be *thee* supernova of the year. If I was given the chance to cover it, I guarantee it would be presented to the world as such." The woman lifts her champagne. "To Mother Nature," she adds in conclusion, and they clink glasses before she disappears.

"Who was that?" Clementine asks as she nears the table. "She certainly didn't understand the theme." Gloria doesn't have the bandwidth to have a conversation with her daughter-in-law, so she decides to take the opportunity to guzzle the rest of her drink and ask for another.

The rest of the party is a buzzy, bubbling blur. Gloria's head throbs from the champagne and the dull conversation. Everyone else she speaks to pales in comparison to the woman with the butterfly clips, in wit, in charm, and honestly, in costume. But she can't remember her name—she lost it somewhere between her fourth and fifth glass of Veuve.

"Gloria, you look ravishing." Sandra Yoon approaches her, everyone around Gloria parting like the Red Sea. She gives Gloria a chaste kiss on the cheek. "That necklace is ungodly good." Gloria ignores the compliment, her foggy brain unsure of what to say to Sandra's fire-engine-red Schiaparelli mini gown (honestly, does the theme even *matter* to anyone anymore?), so instead she seizes the opportunity to ask about the girl.

"I had the loveliest chat with one of your employees," Gloria slurs, teetering in her pewter Prada kitten heels; her steady diet of strictly alcohol and no food has caught up with her. Sandra's severe black bob starts to rock back and forth in her blurry vision.

"Really?" Sandra's voice pitches up an octave. "Then please tell me who I should promote. Was it Eleanor? She really killed herself to make tonight a success." Sandra looks in the direction of the girl in the headset who escorted Gloria to her table.

"No, someone higher up than that," Gloria says dismissively. "But I can't remember her name. She was wearing a gorgeous green dress. Chanel, I think. Her hair was covered in butterfly clips." The name is on the tip of her tongue—something middle class like Kristy or Kathleen. No, neither sound quite right, Gloria thinks.

"It's not ringing any bells, but we must figure out who it was!" Sandra turns behind her, where a woman wearing a black headset loiters in her jet stream. "Monique, have Christine send me over the list of senior editors in attendance tonight. She should be outside at the door checking guests in," Sandra says, and Gloria's eyes light up with recognition. *Christine*—that was her name. But something stops her from declaring it out loud.

"Oh, didn't I tell you?" Monique says to Sandra. "She's sick, poor thing. At home with the stomach bug. Olivia is at the door instead." Sandra frowns at this.

"Let me know when you find out who it is," Gloria says, and tries to keep the excitement out of her voice. "I am going to turn into a pumpkin if I don't make my exit soon." Sandra nods and gives her another air kiss before leaving her. As the night has descended into loud laughing and deafening music, Gloria makes her way toward the exit.

"Gran, let me help you to your car." Graham trots up behind her. She smiles at him—her charming, gorgeous poster boy of a grandson in his Tom Ford navy and black tux. She'll let him escort her out of the event; with him on her arm, nobody will pay attention to her shriveling figure and sallow cheeks. As the pair make their way to the bottom of the Met steps, another woman with a headset holding a clipboard comes rushing up to her.

"Ms. Beaufort, it's started raining outside. Let someone escort you with an umbrella—" But Gloria just continues on down the stairs, waving her off. She doesn't mind a little rain.

"Thank you, but no need. It's just a quick dash to her car." Graham smiles at the woman graciously, and she melts into his grin. He tends to have that effect on women, especially when he's solo. Jane refused to attend tonight's event and Gloria can't hold it against her. This isn't Jane's crowd. Plus, she rather has her hands full with all of her *elaborate* wedding planning, Gloria would imagine. Her *supernova*.

A lightbulb turns on.

Her brain is flying fast now, a plan taking shape in her mind . . . snowballing bigger and bigger as plump raindrops explode on her evening gown, marking it with permanent water stains, but Gloria doesn't care.

"What's got you in such a good mood?" Graham jokes when they reach Gloria's town car.

"You know I love discovering new talent." She gives her grandson's hand a quick squeeze and closes the car door before he can ask any follow-up questions. Smiling to herself, she has only one thought before she drifts off to sleep:

*Nobody puts on a show like Mother Nature.*

## THIRTY-NINE

# MAC

Saturday, October 18, 2025
Wedding Day

MAC LOOKS OUT THE WINDOW. It's pouring, but as the saying goes, rain on your wedding day is good luck. And Mac feels lucky indeed. Who wouldn't feel lucky after successfully turning an almost career-ending oversight into a fully funded retirement plan?

Mac is a people person, a dealmaker if you will. So when the president of Broadway Manufacturing approached him at the annual Grow 2 Glo Gala a few years back, insinuating that there would be kickbacks if Mac could broker a deal for them to get the Gloss Drops contract . . . he didn't think twice. It was too easy!

Mac's oversight, of course, was having to involve the wildly incompetent Trey Ripton in his plan. As always, Gloria's son proved himself to be a liability. When Broadway Manufacturing offered some ideas for cutting costs to up the profit margins on Gloss Drops, Trey didn't even blink before saying yes. He didn't do his due diligence, he didn't listen to his team . . . That was his fault as CEO, not Mac's fault for bringing him an opportunity.

Unfortunately, Mac saw the writing on the wall for Gloss Drops; he heard the whisperings Trey chose to ignore. And he knew he had to get ahead of whatever was coming because, well, it didn't sound like it was going to be good . . . which is how his retirement plan started to take shape. There was no way he was going to lose his hold on the family fortune.

At least when they started meeting with lawyers, Trey didn't out Mac as the one who connected him with the ethically questionable manufacturing company . . . although Gloria figured it out pretty quickly. But she was too late. Plan Inside Man was already in place. Jane had the ring—the wedding was imminent.

And today, on this glorious day, it will all be solidified in the eyes of the law and the church. Mac takes a sip of strong Irish coffee and watches the storm clouds roll in over the hills. Unfortunately, the tranquil scene is interrupted by a ping from the burner cell: O'Reilly.

Mac reads the text: Are you awake? Can I have a wash in your room? It's dusty as shite down here. Ah, Seamus O'Reilly, always the wordsmith. Mac hates that business requires associating with *swine* like O'Reilly, but it can't be helped. At least he's sleeping in the bowels of the castle where he belongs, scurrying through the walls like a rabid rodent, siphoning away jewelry and cash from unsuspecting guests, biding his time until the wedding is over. Mac would have finished him off sooner if O'Reilly hadn't reconnected with his daughter, Jane. What a stroke of luck that was for O'Reilly, connecting with his grown daughter in Charleston as Mac was starting to consider the advantages of marrying a mole into the Ripton family.

"A little help here!" Seamus O'Reilly calls from the closet.

"Oh, Jesus," Mac groans, and helps open the hidden door. In addition to Jane, the secret passageway that lurks inside the castle walls was O'Reilly's only other helpful contribution to the plan; it made Ballymoon the perfect choice for the wedding by allowing for Mac to keep tabs on all the family members and Jane—they wouldn't want her to get cold feet. O'Reilly had known about the hidden tunnels of Ballymoon since his youth. Growing up in County Clare, he and other mischievous boys would use the tunnels to sneak into the castle hotel and commit petty theft.

"Today's the big day!" O'Reilly laughs, dusting himself off. "My little girl's getting married. Boy, I remember when she was this big— Oh, wait, I don't, because I was in the slammer! We'll make sure Miss Maggie pays for that. I scared her good when I tossed that rock through the window the other day, but that was nothing compared to what's coming next." O'Reilly rubs his small hands together. The ex-con's official responsibility for the wedding weekend was to be Mac's eyes and ears in the castle walls, to let his boss know if anyone caught even the slightest whiff of their plan—but it was clear O'Reilly had spent the better part of the weekend torturing the mother of the bride.

"Don't get too excited. It's not over yet," Mac responds as Seamus makes his way to the bathroom. He does need a shower. On top of being a serious liability, the man reeks. The rock was way out of line and could have easily led to an investigation that jeopardized everything. And the sprinklers during the rehearsal dinner—Mac feels a headache coming on just at the *thought* of the sprinklers. When Mac confronted Seamus about the idiocy of his "pranks," he just said he was going stir-crazy.

"What did you do with Sebi's wallet?" Mac calls into the bathroom.

"I still have it on me—down in the dungeon with the rest of the loot I snagged this weekend, including the Saint Christopher medal I took back from the bitch. I can't wait to see the look on her fecking face when she sees me here."

Mac rolls his eyes. "We went over this. Maggie's not going to see you. It's too risky. You need to leave her in the past. It's time to embrace your future," Mac lies.

"I know, I know," O'Reilly grumbles. "I've got my eye on a nice flat in Dublin overlooking the River Liffey."

"Sounds lovely." Mac smiles. O'Reilly won't be renting any waterfront flats, despite what's been promised. He won't be making it out of this weekend alive. No, he sealed his fate when he sloppily killed Sebi without realizing Gloria Beaufort had someone tailing him the entire time. Mac just can't risk getting rid of him now—not until Jane is married off. No need to upset the apple cart, as the saying goes.

"Did you talk to your daughter today?" Mac asks him. They have to be careful and send Jane on her honeymoon in the Seychelles without so much as side-eye from anyone.

"Yes, everything is all settled. The wedding will proceed as planned," he says.

"Good." Mac gets dressed, putting on each piece of wedding garb with ceremonious care.

A knock on the door. Right on time—Elliot is always prompt. Mac admires that about the wedding planner.

"Hello, Elliot," Mac chirps, and quickly joins the wedding planner in the hallway. Hopefully he can't hear the shower running in the bathroom.

Elliot smiles over his clipboard. "Good Morning, Father Kenneth! Your car's ready for you. Here's a program."

"Beautiful," Mac replies. He always likes seeing his name etched in gold: *Father Kenneth McEntyre, wedding officiant.*

The Ripton and Murphy families
request the honour of your presence
at the marriage of

## Jane Nicole Murphy

and

## Graham Beaufort Ripton

Saturday, the eighteenth of October
two thousand twenty-five
at three o'clock in the afternoon

St. Frances of Clifden Cathedral
County Clare, Ireland

Dinner and dancing to follow
at the Ballymoon Castle Hotel

Black tie

FORTY

## CHRISTINE

Saturday, October 18, 2025
Wedding Ceremony

SEVERAL GUESTS ARE USHERED OFF multiple coaches and into the parking lot of the cathedral. Despite the rain at the castle, the sky is bright blue at the church. Two Elliot Adler staffers dressed in all black and wearing headsets start handing guests "ceremony survival kits" in beautiful leather tote bags embroidered with Jane and Graham's crest.

"A survival kit . . . Good God, what could I possibly need for an hour-long ceremony, a flare gun?" some uppity silver-haired woman sneers. Christine takes a survival kit, knowing it's probably just Advil and mineral water, but the irony is not lost on her: a flare gun might be needed. She checks the inside of her bag to reveal that it was made by Louis Vuitton. Ahead of her, two teenagers dressed in sexy cutout dresses that are far too mature for their ages unveil the contents of the kit for their TikTok followers.

"Omigosh, how *cute* is this? Jane and Graham coconut water. And—wait, is this a limited-edition Sony digital camera? So retro," squeals the brunette with shiny hair down to her butt.

"They literally gave us all Tiffany Lock bracelets—look," the smaller girl in neon green says. She holds up a long talon and shows off her bracelet to her friend's iPhone.

These lavish perks, which would have once made Christine herself giddy, now somehow make everything seem more dystopian. She walks up a rose petal–lined path and through a whimsical man-made flower arch. Once at the cathedral doors, she is asked by a large unsmiling man to turn off her cell phone. She nods, but he stops her and looks down at her purse expectantly.

"Oh, you need me to do it right now?" Christine asks.

"If you wouldn't mind." He gives her a forced smile, which is somehow more unsettling than a frown. After turning off her phone under the Phone Warden's watchful eye, she takes a thick ceremony program from him and shoves it into her purse, along with her cell. But once she in the cathedral and out of view, Christine quickly turns the phone back on. What if Danny calls her? Obviously, he didn't tell her the details of his unit's operation to catch Seamus and Mac, but she assumes that he'll update her if they're in custody before 7 p.m. She needs to be reachable.

Taking a quick peek at her screen, she sees only one notification—a fraud alert from her bank, mistakenly flagging a purchase she's made in Ireland. She'll sort it out later. She puts her phone away and surveys the cathedral.

Christine is immediately floored by the abundance of white roses. The whole place is filled with them; the entire length of the pews and the altar are lined with the delicate flowers in various shades of cream. Mentally, she tries to tally the cost. *Roses aren't even in season right now!*

The blinding floral blanket is such a stark contrast to the gloomy, Gothic structure that she saw at the rehearsal yesterday, one can hardly believe it's the same space. Christine takes a minute to drink in what's in front of her, but after looking around, she notices that a majority of the guests' necks are craned upward. She follows suit and then gasps.

The once Michelangelo-inspired ceiling has been turned into an intricate floral installation, again sporting Jane's and Graham's names written in gold-dusted flowers. Christine listens to the excited whispers of the guests as they gawk at the display.

"How do you think they even did that?"

"Did the florists survive this installation?"

"I didn't even know gold roses existed!"

By contrast, Christine is consumed by an intense awareness that underneath the thick layer of cream and gold, everything is black and gray. She shivers, keeping her eyes peeled for the Riptons . . . and all the potential Macs in her midst. Every time she hears so much as a loud laugh, her heart leaps out of her chest.

Christine turns her attention to the altar, where members of the Berlin Philharmonic are tuning their instruments. She knows this is the Berlin Philharmonic because *Page Six* published an article a few months back saying that the orchestra had been paid quite handsomely to perform at a billionaire's wedding. Gloria must have been that billionaire. The guests are being gracefully ushered to their seats as the musicians start playing George Gershwin's *Lullaby* for strings.

The notes flutter through the space, and Christine half expects butterflies to be released into the church at any moment to complete the Disney-ride-come-to-life vibe that Elliot's going for. She takes a few obligatory photos and videos to send Sandra out of habit before she settles into her seat and crosses her legs to keep them from bouncing in anticipation. At this point, she knows there won't be any *Bespoke* coverage of this wedding at all—not after the cops show up. But Christine jots down a few observations anyway. Even if *Bespoke Weddings* doesn't cover this, eventually someone has to report what happened here. Maybe her notes will be helpful.

A thunderous organ starts to play from the balcony, and everyone sits up straighter in their seats. The clack of stilettos echoes throughout the cathedral as a gorgeous auburn-haired woman walks up to a microphone in front of the orchestra. Christine recognizes her from somewhere. She combs through the filing cabinet in her brain to try to place her. The auburn beauty takes a delicate hand and smooths out her extravagant hot pink gown, flashing a smile so big it almost causes her cheeks to disappear completely as she looks out at the throng of wedding guests or, Christine supposes, her audience.

The beehive hairdo in front of Christine whispers to her elderly husband, "That's Eloise Wright."

"Who?" he says too loudly, and leans closer to his wife's waxy red lips.

"Eloise Wright! The operetta star from *Britain's Got Talent*." She rolls her eyes and pulls an ungodly fox fur closer around her shoulders. "Honestly, Howard, keep up."

A hush falls over the crowd of three hundred and fifty as Eloise Wright clears her throat and starts to sing "Ave Maria," accompanied not only by the organ but also by a slew of violins. The rest of the orchestra sits back.

The pews creak in unison as all the guests shift their body weight toward the aisle for a glimpse at the wedding party gathered at the back of the church. It's about to begin. Graham walks down the aisle looking like Prince Charming, the part he was born to play. Clementine is perched on his arm, beaming. Christine notices her tight grip around the sleeve of his suit, reluctant to give up even a small part of her golden child to anyone else.

The groomsmen follow next, processing one by one like they're on *The Bachelor*. Christine notices unaccompanied female guests lean forward and wet their lips. The makeup team did an excellent job covering up Ben's black eye. Only a slight glimmer of plum is visible if the light catches him just right. Once the groomsmen are displayed in front of the altar like an Olympic team of gold medal winners—which, in most ways, they are—the bridesmaids glide into view.

Shiny-haired women in glossy pink dresses shimmy down toward their male equivalents, each one looking more perfect than the next. All the girls are grinning, except Lyle, who looks like she's in a funeral procession. Christine's heart goes out to her; this has to be the last thing she wants to be doing right now. Raquel processes last, stunning in a champagne-colored dress paired with delicate gold Canfora stilettos.

Once Raquel joins the rest of the flock, there is a moment of silence as the orchestra and Eloise collect themselves for the main entrance. A cello starts to delicately play an acoustic version of Adele's "To Make You Feel

My Love," and tears are flowing in the church before Jane even comes into view.

While the rest of the guests catch their breath as she glides down the aisle, Christine draws in her breath for another reason. Just outside the doors of the cathedral, behind the bride, a slight man with leathered skin loiters by the party buses. It's her taxi driver. The man who dropped her off at the rectory and then *again* at Shenanigan's Pub. From the back of the car, she couldn't see his full profile, or she would have clocked the snake tattoo crawling up his neck. It's Seamus O'Reilly.

Her heart thumps loudly as Seamus slithers quickly out of view. Jane and Maggie continue to process down the long aisle, clearly unaware of Seamus's presence behind them. The bride smiles as Maggie leaves her at the altar with her fiancé, and Graham tears up. Christine watches the bride's eyes land on something at the back of the church, and she knows that Jane has seen Seamus too, if only for a second. Christine turns back again but can't spot him through the throng of guests.

*Is someone going to grab him? Are there cops outside?* Christine waits with bated breath, but nothing happens. Even though she knows they aren't supposed to arrest Seamus until after everyone is back at the castle for the reception, she can't help but feel like the cops have missed their chance.

She turns back to face the front of the cathedral and watches as the nuptials proceed. Jane and Graham put on a good show, both laughing and crying like this entire wedding isn't about to go up in flames. They do traditional Catholic wedding vows, Eloise wows with a few more songs, and the rings are presented.

"And now . . . by the power vested in me, I pronounce you husband and wife. Graham, you may kiss your bride," Father Kenneth proclaims, and everyone claps, but Christine can't bring her hands together. She watches the couple exit the church, swept away by the cheers and camera flashes and happy music. She feels as if she's having an out-of-body experience. The sweet elderly woman sitting next to her touches Christine's arm.

"Wasn't it a beautiful ceremony, dear?" she says in a thick Southern accent. "Father Mac always performs the most beautiful weddings."

Christine freezes and whips her head toward the woman. "What did you say?"

The elderly guest blinks through her false lashes. "Father McEntyre, the priest, he did a beautiful job. Are you all right, honey?"

Christine doesn't respond; instead she rushes out of the cathedral and texts Danny:

I know who Mac is. It's Father Kenneth.

A text bubble briefly appears . . . but he doesn't reply.

FORTY-ONE

# CHRISTINE

Saturday, October 18, 2025
Wedding Reception

THE BUS RIDE BACK TO the castle after the wedding ceremony is one of the longest rides of Christine's life—not only is she distraught, having *finally* laid eyes on Seamus, but she also has to try to call her credit card company while a horrific mash-up of "Who Let the Dogs Out" and "Barbie Girl" blares through the bus speakers. Turns out, that notification about fraudulent charges was related to her taxi rides with Seamus! And he's racked up *quite* the bill on her credit card over the past twelve hours.

Once she's dealt with her credit card, Christine allows herself to start processing the fact that Father Kenneth is Mac. In hindsight, it seems obvious. The press release! Of course he'd be the one to murder Gloria—he was pissed off she cut him out of Grow 2 Glo, which he was probably using to steal money from her or for other nefarious purposes. *Did Gloria find out? Is that why he got rid of her?* There are still so many unanswered questions.

As she clip-clops off the bus in her chunky platform heels, she scans the Ballymoon grounds for another glimpse of Seamus or Father Kenneth, aka Mac, but instead she spots a woman clutching a thick cardstock sign with *Christine Russo* written on it.

"Hi, everyone, gather round, gather round, please," the woman says, corralling Christine and six other guests into her area. She introduces herself as Felicity from Elliot's staff, their "table leader." Felicity is a broad-shouldered woman who looks more suited to being a bodyguard than a personal butler (which is essentially what a table leader is, Christine assesses). This is a new one for her—and she's seen a lot of over-the-top weddings.

"Welcome, Table Eight!" Felicity's Brooklyn accent is as thick as a slice of mozzarella. "Jane and Graham matched you all together for the evening based on the personality quiz you filled out upon receiving your invitation. We trust you'll all have much to chat about." The table leader tucks the sign under her arm, and Christine takes a moment to size up her new forced friends. The crew includes the two teenagers in the neon dresses, the uptight elderly couple from church, and a chic young couple who look incredibly offended to be included in their group of rejects. The woman's slicked-back bun, massive diamond studs, and matte mauve lipstick imply that once out of earshot, she will go up to Felicity and insist, "There must have been some sort of mistake."

A low rumble of thunder vibrates through the throngs of guests as the gray sky turns a purplish black.

"Well, let's get a move on before we're struck by lightning," Felicity jokes nervously, and proceeds to lead her band of misfits through the castle.

"Thank God they didn't opt for an outdoor reception," Slick Bun tells her date. "I keep refreshing the weather app, but it's just supposed to *pour* all night. They're saying there might even be flash floods."

"I hope our flight tomorrow isn't delayed. These destination weddings are such a nightmare," her overly gelled date says, checking his Omega Speedmaster watch as if he already can't wait to leave the reception that hasn't even started yet.

Even though these people are a bit painful, Christine is just grateful not to be at Father Kenneth's table. She can't believe she didn't suspect him earlier—everything about him feels off now, from his fake tan to his designer clothes. But it's not over. Looking at her phone, she realizes that it's only four o'clock. The police probably won't be making any arrests for hours.

"Welcome, everyone," Felicity says, opening the door. "Please enjoy the cocktail hour and know that I am around if you need anything at all. Cheers." She ushers the guests down a dark staircase lined with a light installation that changes color with every step. The teens squeal, right at home in this fluorescent horror show straight out of a Berlin nightclub. Roaring remixed jazz music beats through the speakers. At the bottom of the stairs, a giant glowing bar sign reads, *Welcome to Jane & Graham's Drinks Dungeon.* The vibe is ultramodern and very youthful—a complete departure from the old-world glamour of the welcome dinner.

"They turned the castle dungeon into their drinks reception. That's a bit . . . dark, no?" Slick Bun says with a laugh behind her. *You don't know the half of it,* Christine thinks. But once inside the event, the vibe, she'll admit, is cool. The lighting is moody and the whole "dungeon" is adorned with velvet lounge furniture in various maroon and navy jewel tones, with shiny brass cocktail tables interspersed. The floral arrangements are restrained in this space. They're all dried flowers mixed with birch branches in low gold vases. The lighting installations wrapped around the dungeon bars make them glow like warm candlelight and *almost* make Christine forget that this space used to house tortured prisoners . . . if she didn't feel like one herself in this very moment.

She wonders where Danny is. Her stomach tightens remembering her unanswered text, but she tries not to overthink it. He's got to be careful; she understands this. Still, she checks her phone again, the minutes ticking by slowly.

Under normal circumstances, a wedding cocktail reception can feel unbearably long, but knowing she's in the presence of dangerous criminals in a foreign country only adds to the slow passage of time. She looks for Seamus in the swarm of rich and important people, but there's no sign of him. However, she does spot Mac in his priestly garb, making small talk with a few elderly guests, and decides the best thing she can do is keep a discreet eye on him.

But first, she needs some liquid courage. Christine looks around as staff dressed in velvet tuxedos carry decadent drinks that fizz, pop, and sparkle in crystal glasses of all shapes and sizes. Some drinks even ooze fake smoke. Christine grabs something the waiter calls a Hazy Jane and takes a sip to calm her nerves. The drink is perfection: a hint of lavender paired with the smoothest barely-there vodka and a dash of sweet champagne fizz.

"This is delicious," Christine says to her tablemates, most of whom are just loitering near her. Felicity stands against the wall, starring out at the party but making eye contact with nobody. One of the stringy neon girls aggressively swirls her Hazy Jane with a cocktail straw and declares, "I had better on Harbour Island." She shrugs her skinny shoulders and discards the drink on a nearby table.

"There they are!" someone hollers from across the room. An eruption of clapping and whistling begins, and everyone positions themselves for the ceremonious "raising of the iPhones" to capture the married couple's entrance.

Jane and Graham stand perfectly positioned at the top of the stairs, looking the part of happily married couple. Jane drops jaws in a fully crystal flapper-style dress that drips off her willowy frame. A whisper from one of the neon teens, who Christine has learned is aptly named Alexa, confirms that the dress was made by Swarovski himself and is rumored to be valued in the six digits.

The bride parades down the staircase, basking in the Instagram-friendly ambiance, careful not to topple over in her six-inch Valentino pumps. Like everything at this event, the lighting has been expertly designed by Elliot's on-staff social-media guru to make sure it is optimal for guests to post pictures and videos, which they are doing en masse at this very moment. So much so that the professional photographers and videographers are struggling to get angles of the bride and groom during this Instagram-photography amateur hour. At the base of the staircase, a waiter presents the couple with two shot glasses and pours from a bottle of Don Julio 1942. They down the shots, and the crowd goes wild. Then Graham lifts his bride into the air for a well-timed kiss, and on cue, a club remix version of the Black Eyed Peas "I Gotta Feeling" bursts through the surround-sound speakers. Jane and Graham begin their dance, parading over to the DJ booth set up in one of the dungeon cells, where they don matching white headphones and the photographers clamor to capture their "DJ wedding moment." The bride swishes her hips, sending the crystals on her dress whirling with a Gatsby-level sparkle. Graham picks her up again and spins her around for the cameras. Finally, the cringey choreographed moment comes to an end . . . just as Christine's phone lights up with a text from Danny.

All good here. Keep it up on your end. Almost at the finish line, the text reads. She nearly drops her drink in relief that he's responded. He and his unit are going to arrest them. It's only a matter of time. She scans the room until she locates Father Kenneth standing near the bar and laughing at something Trey says. He makes eye contact with her and smiles. She can't help it—she smiles back and raises her glass. *They're going to catch you*, she thinks.

At the top of the stairs, an elderly man in a dapper tuxedo appears. With the flick of his wrist, he starts to ever so slightly ring a small gold bell. The chatter in the room dies down to a dull murmur as the tiny bell tolls.

The gentleman clears his throat, then says, "If you will all kindly join me in the great room. Dinner is served."

## FORTY-TWO

# CHRISTINE

Saturday, October 18, 2025
Wedding Reception

FELICITY LEADS HER POSSE BACK up the staircase, everyone gossiping about what luxurious ludicrousness awaits them at dinner in The Great Room. Christine watches the way each guest holds up their iPhone to capture each ornate sign, fancy drink, and ridiculous floral invention they pass along the way. Sandra has been begging her for content, but Christine can't bring herself to keep the facade up any longer. She doesn't have any energy left to comment on tablescapes and goodie bags. The opulence is starting to grate on her in a way she didn't think was possible a few days ago. She just wants it to all be over.

The group passes a giant stained-glass window featuring a portrait of King Brian Boru just as a giant tree branch slams against the colored glass with the force of an eighteen-wheeler. Everyone gasps as a hairline fracture zig-zags down the King's stoic face.

"I'll let management know about this," Felicity says clearing her throat. "Please, everyone if you'll follow me." Begrudgingly the group continues with her down the hall as the wind howls outside.

Felicity stops in front of the entrance to the great room. It is literally sparkling. A giant crystal chandelier that serves as a high-end disco ball is reflecting off every surface, while elegant linens in various shades of ivory and white grace the tables under the castle's silver cutlery and green-and-gold china plates. A long banquet table in the center of the room features nothing but naked taper candles, a bold and cool choice that unfortunately reminds Christine of the welcome dinner setup and the fire that followed. There are also no windows in the ballroom, which adds to her unease.

The room would be worshiped by the society world for its elegance and restraint . . . if it wasn't for the orchids. The flowers are *everywhere*, hanging from the ceiling and climbing up every pole, the bar, and even the sides of the stage. It's clear they were supposed to be a dramatic touch, but it feels more like the room has been overtaken by an invasive species.

"I hear Gloria Beaufort had a hundred thousand dendrobium orchids flown in from Thailand, just for this room alone. They stole the idea from Jay-Z and Beyoncé's wedding," Alexa whispers to her neon-green-clad companion.

"Oh my God . . . it's so sad she isn't here to see this. It's beyond gorgeous."

"I know, it's such a bummer that she's sick. I was hoping to get a selfie with her. Becky, take my picture." Alexa thrusts her phone into her friend's hands.

Word of Gloria's "illness" has finally made its way through the wedding, Christine notes. She checks her phone for more info from Danny, but he's gone silent again. Where are the police? Why isn't this all over yet? How is she supposed to eat a five-course meal under this sort of duress? Her stomach churns at the thought.

As Felicity ushers their group toward table eight, Christine notices an earpiece in her ear for the first time. She does a double take, then tries to see if any of the other table leaders have an earpiece. It's hard to tell from a distance, and it's not out of the norm at an event of this size and scale for the staff to have that level of technology for communication, especially if Elliot is in charge. But still . . .

"Here we are, everyone." Felicity motions to a table with a large cursive ice sculpture of the number eight in the center.

"Oh my God, that is so sick." Alexa's friend uses a long talon to poke at the ice sculpture. Christine can feel Felicity's body tense up next to her.

"Let me know if you need anything." The table leader gives a slight bow and disappears.

Christine watches as Father Kenneth takes his seat at the family table near the dance floor. He leans back in his chair and lets a waiter fill up his wineglass. He definitely doesn't look like he's going anywhere—he also definitely doesn't look like he's about to be arrested.

"Red or white, miss?" She looks behind her and finds Danny smiling, two expensive-looking bottles of wine in his hands.

"White, please," Christine says as casually as she can.

"We've got a gorgeous 2019 Château d'Yquem Sauternes from the Bordeaux region of France, or—"

Christine cuts him off. "That sounds great." She jumps as a drone camera buzzes over their table. Panicked, she looks around to see if any of her tablemates notice, but they're still enthralled, taking photos of the ornately decorated ballroom.

Danny fills up her glass to the brim and leans in. "You're doing great," Danny whispers in her ear. "Almost at the finish line." He brushes Christine's arm and makes his way around the rest of the table filling up glasses. She marvels at how much he seems like an *actual* professional server. He doesn't skip a beat as he moves among the seasoned staffers who float around the room. Christine takes a big gulp of her wine as a thought nags at her: *Danny's really good at lying.*

## FORTY-THREE

# MAC

Saturday, October 18, 2025
Wedding Reception

MAC ENJOYS HIS GLASS OF red wine, leaning back in his chair with triumph. He's relaxed; everything is going as planned. Jane and Graham are married. The paperwork is signed—it's done. He only has to string O'Reilly along until the couple is safely on their honeymoon. Then O'Reilly will have a little "accident." Maybe a car crash? A drug overdose? After botching Sebi's murder, O'Reilly deserves whatever is coming his way. Mac grips his glass, thinking of the moment Gloria had confronted him with the photos of his dim-witted crony last month.

"First, you convince Trey to sign with that idiotic manufacturing company to produce those toxic Gloss Drops behind my back, and now this?" she'd said. "I don't pay you to *kill*."

Gloria slid the oversize images across her desk, her face pinched with anger. Photos of Sebi getting into O'Reilly's car, photos of O'Reilly dumping Sebi's body into the marsh. In her images, he can see O'Reilly's face clear as day—and the Saint Christopher medal that dangles around his tattooed neck. Mac doesn't even bother denying the fool works for him.

"Yes, it's exactly what you pay me for," he hissed back. "To do your dirty work. How do you think I make your problems, as you say, disappear? You think it's as easy as paying people off? How do you think I got rid of your husband?"

Gloria's face had gone white. And with that, it was over. His words couldn't be unsaid.

Mac didn't regret the bold-faced admission of guilt. Gloria should know what had been done to preserve her company; what he had done from the very beginning of their relationship to assure her future success. She liked to act like she didn't have any help, or do anything unsavory to get to the top, but she did. She wasn't better than him. In most ways, she was *worse*.

Gloria should have thanked him. But she never said thank you. Not even once. Mac *always* said thank you. Mac was polite. He repented for his sins. He taught about forgiveness and kindness and faith. He ran her nonprofit—sure, he might have siphoned some money from it, but he still coached the volleyball team! For free! And he dedicated his life to God—well, kind of. But he dedicated more than most people did, okay? He wasn't the first person to join the church for personal gain. He wasn't the first person to weaponize religion. People had done *much* worse than him over the years. How dare Gloria sit across the table and judge him after what he'd done for her!

"J-John died of heart failure," Gloria finally stuttered. "I came to you for advice, for counsel, and you thought . . ." She trailed off. Mac watched as her world caved in, her eyes darting around the room, the lies she told herself fizzling out. Gloria had come to him, to the church, to try to figure out what to do about her good-for-nothing husband. He was making a mockery of their marriage. His business ineptitude was ruining her budding company. She didn't have anywhere else to turn, so she turned to her faith.

Well, actually, her exact words had been "Does God do murder for hire?"

Mac knew she meant this as a joke, but he'd seen the seriousness in her eyes. He felt the hatred and hurt trapped in her heart, heard the desperation in her voice.

And Mac's a businessman.

He saw an opportunity, and he seized it. Getting rid of Gloria's husband was his first job for the young beauty tycoon. Their relationship had taken off from there. She kept coming to Mac with her problems, and Mac, like a magician, would make them disappear. It was a classic don't ask, don't tell policy.

"There are a lot of drugs you can give someone that mimic heart failure," Mac had said, his lip curled into a snarl. "What? You thought it was just divine intervention? That's a little convenient, no?" Mac pointed a finger at her. "I know you, Gloria. You're a lot of things, but you are not stupid." His body flooded with relief after finally saying his piece, but Gloria looked genuinely wounded. Which only made him angrier. *Classic rich people*, he thought, *pretending they don't know what it takes to keep their rosy reality intact.*

Mac knew he'd lost Gloria the moment he stormed out of her office after that blowup. But final confirmation came just a few weeks later at the Grow 2 Glo Gala, when Gloria announced to the world that Graham would be the sole inheritor of her charity's executive chair. A role Mac had been promised for years, further fueling his fury; he had made that charity what it was today—and he planned to continue using it as his personal cash cow once Gloria passed. Of course, it was clear that Graham knew something was up that night at the gala. He had already started looking at the books, wondering where some of the donation money had gone. But luckily, Graham's mind had gone straight to his derelict brother. Naturally, Mac encouraged this theory. It didn't matter, though, because at that point, his grand plan was already in motion. Pretentious self-righteous little Graham didn't realize it then, but he was stuck right in the middle of it, an unassuming cog in Mac's machine—his future wife, Mac's willing accomplice.

Mac always knew it was possible that Gloria could cut him off at any moment. He knew how she operated—and he had put his contingency plan in place for just this reason, a surefire way to maintain a hold on the family fortune, no matter what: Jane. Through Jane, Mac would have easy access to Graham's trust fund—which he planned to swiftly drain. He'd also be able to use her to manipulate Graham's decision-making as executive chair of Grow 2 Glo. A two-for-one deal!

Yes, his new retirement plan was simple: marry Jane to the Riptons and then wait for the inevitable... Gloria's death. It was just basic math. At eighty-five, the sand in Gloria Beaufort's hourglass was running low.

All he had to do was make sure they made it through the wedding weekend without Gloria figuring out the connection between him and the bride. But that turned out to be easier than expected, because somebody killed her! Divine intervention once again!

Now, with everything tied up in a neat bow, the wedding done, the paperwork signed—Mac can just relax and enjoy a gorgeous party while sipping expensive wine. He brings the chalice to his lips and thanks God as a glass clinks at the end of the head table.

"Attention, attention." Ben bangs on his champagne flute. "We're about to begin the most God-awful part of any wedding: the best man speech." A trickle of laughter.

"First, I'd like to say a heartfelt congratulations to the new Mr. and Mrs. Graham Ripton." Claps and whoops vibrate throughout the room.

Ben continues. "I'd also like to thank our grandmother, Gloria Beaufort. She isn't feeling well this evening"—Mac notices Ben's eyes shift downward briefly—"but she was instrumental in planning this beautiful night for you all and in keeping our family together. So, cheers to you, Gran. Thank you!" Ben raises his glass, and all the guests including Mac follow suit, but the priest's eyes are glued to the figure lurking in the shadows behind Jane and Graham's sweetheart table.

*Goddamnit, O'Reilly.* He had been given implicit instructions not to come anywhere near the wedding today, and this is the second time he's disobeyed orders. Mac feels a hot flash of rage pass through him. He slams his glass down on the table. A few people turn their heads in his direction.

The best man clears his throat. "Jane, welcome to our crazy family.

From what I've seen so far, you're going to fit right in. Cheers to the happy couple." The mic spews out a high-pitched screech, and the room collectively winces in discomfort.

Elliot, the MC of the evening, takes the mic. "Thank you, Ben, for that touching toast," he starts, but the microphone cuts in and out. "Sorry about that." Elliot taps the mic head, and a faint crackle echoes through the speakers—and then . . . the mic dies.

"Tech malfunction!" Elliot screams, cupping his hands around his mouth. "Happens to the best of us!" He laughs manically. "Now, if everyone could take a pause from their appetizer course, Jane and her mom will share a mother-daughter dance." The room begrudgingly puts down their forks and migrates to the dance floor while Elliot cuts into the orange-haired staff boy, who quickly flees from the room, presumably in search of a new microphone.

Mac follows the shadow of Seamus skulking around the edges of the party, just out of the light. Thanks to Elliot's ambiance expertise, the room is dim and sultry. It's hard to make out the people sitting next to him, let alone someone trying to prowl around unnoticed. The lights get even darker and a spotlight illuminates Maggie and Jane on the dance floor. The band starts to softly play Whitney Houston's "I Will Always Love You" as the mother and daughter smile and cry. Jane is practically sobbing.

Billowing smoke from Elliot's strategically placed fog machines starts to encircle the dance floor as the women muddle their way through the song, the videographer circling the dance floor like a shark. Mac momentarily loses track of his crony, but about twenty seconds into the music, he hears someone whispering "Psst, psst!" behind him. He turns around to see O'Reilly lurking by the doorframe. He waves desperately for Mac to join him.

Mac searches the crowd for anyone who might notice him slipping away, but luckily all of the guests are focused on the dance floor. He makes his way to the exit. Then he sees the bartender heading directly toward them, his hand at his waist. It looks like he's going for a gun. Mac should have known there might be law enforcement in their midst; he got too cocky, too comfortable. But O'Reilly should have flagged this. It was the entire point of him being here this weekend—to keep an eye out for infiltrators like this one while Mac kept up appearances with the family.

Mac locks eyes with the bartender as O'Reilly quickly strides to the corner and flicks off the panel of light switches . . . enveloping everyone in complete darkness.

FORTY-FOUR

# CHRISTINE

Saturday, October 18, 2025
Wedding Reception

THE LAST THING CHRISTINE SEES before the lights go out is Danny practically running toward the exit sign at the back of the ballroom. She forces her way through the crowd, trying to get to the exit. Cell phone lights start to illuminate the dark room, making it easier for her to navigate the sea of people.

"Christine! Wait!" a familiar and angry male voice shouts from behind her amid the chaos. She pretends not to hear as she makes her way toward the door, but she can feel him following her. And once they're in the flickering lights of the castle foyer, there is no avoiding him.

Ben grabs her arm. "We need to talk. In private." He pulls her around the corner and down a long, dimly lit hallway. Her heart starts to pound.

"Let go of me." Christine tries to free herself from him as he hustles her down the corridor. He doesn't respond, instead just stares blankly ahead and tightens his grip on her arm. His eyes are bloodshot, the stubble on his chin two days past scruffy. "What do you think you're doing?"

The hallway lights flicker again, adding to the eeriness. Christine has never been in this part of the castle before—it looks forgotten in time. The mahogany wood floors are worn and scuffed, and the doors that line the walls do *not* look like hotel rooms. *Maybe this is the old staff quarters?*

she wonders. Once they're alone, Ben lets her go, almost pushing her away in disgust.

"I knew you couldn't be trusted," he spits at her. She can smell the stale whiskey on his breath.

"What are you talking about?" She backs up, genuinely confused by this bizarre accusation. She needs to get out of here. She needs to find Danny. The arrests should be happening, like, right now.

"This," Ben practically screams, thrusting his phone at her. She squints to read what's on the screen. It's a *Daily Mail* article . . . "Glo Is in the Dark" by Christine Russo. Her stomach drops. She's dumbstruck. She didn't write the article, but there it is with her name on it.

"It's quite the hit piece. Linking my family to Sebi's disappearance." Ben scrolls through the article. "Insinuating that a target was put on him because he knew sensitive information about Glo that would be damning in an upcoming lawsuit. I'll admit, I am impressed by the tale you were able to spin. If I didn't know it was completely false, I'd believe it myself." He steps toward her, forcing her back against the wall.

"But that's the problem," he continues. "You've killed us in the media. *Everyone* will believe your fabricated lies." His eyes are cold, his cheeks flushed with anger. In her bones she knows that there will be no reasoning with him in this state, but she has to try.

"Ben, listen to me. I didn't write that. I swear. I—I think I'm being framed," Christine says breathlessly.

"I'd like to believe that, Christine. But you know I can't. What's next? You're going to tell the world what happened to Gran? I can't have that." He moves closer to her. The alcohol stench becomes more putrid, and she can see the dark emptiness in his eyes. She is completely alone. There is not a hotel staffer or guest in sight.

It's time to run.

Pushing Ben out of her face, she sprints farther into the staff quarters. Ben chases her, but she's got a bit of a head start, and as she winds down the hall, she sees it—a maid's closet propped open with a mop bucket.

Bolting inside, she slams the door, shoving a broom under the handle. She hears Ben rattling the handle on the other side.

"Fine." He laughs sharply. "You want to spend the rest of the night in a maid's closet? Be my guest. But you can't hide in there forever."

She tunes him out, frantically feeling the walls for any loose bricks or hidden levers. The floor is cement, so the castle walls are her only hope. Christine spots a slightly wonky-looking brick behind a shelf of Clorox and Lysol products and pulls on it. She gasps in relief at the sound of gears starting to crank. The brick works as a lever, and she feels an ancient door opening, coming back to life for the first time in probably centuries before her very eyes. But then it stops opening. She pulls the lever harder—it's stuck; she throws her body weight against what she thinks is the outline of the door, and it gives way, a stretch of darkness laid out before her. Christine is back in the tunnels . . . only this time, she's alone.

*The only way out is through.*

She takes a deep breath, hikes up her gown, and plunges into the heart of the castle.

## FORTY-FIVE

# NEIL

Saturday, October 18, 2025
Wedding Reception

NEIL STOMPS DOWN THE CREAKY wooden steps into the basement. The castle groans around him, pummeled by the gale force winds the forecast predicted would hit this evening. The weather probably won't let up until this awful set of Americans are in the air and out of Ireland; it's like his country is literally trying to flush them out. Neil closes his eyes. *By Monday, this will all be over*, he tells himself for the fortieth time today. But for now, he has to hope and pray that he can find some sort of backup microphone to appease Elliot the Tyrant.

The wedding planner's whisper-bark rings in his ears as he searches the basement. "Fix this! Now!" Neil shudders. These people are all too much—too much money, too much pressure, too many snapping cameras, too many refills of champagne that costs more than what he makes in a month. It's all just *too much* for a minimum-wage part-time job. He's exhausted. Ballymoon used to be a slightly sleepy, fun place to work; now he feels like he's wandered onto the set of some crazy American reality television show.

Finally, Neil stumbles upon a cardboard box containing a tangle of cords and what looks like—wait for it—a microphone. He could cry at the sight of it. *Thank God.* Neil slumps against the wall in relief and looks at his watch; while he's down here, he might as well take a fiver.

He brings up Snapchat on his phone and takes a picture to send to a few of his friends and his latest crush, Marigold Foley. His hair looks good in this light, more of a muted red. He filters out his freckles, and frowns slightly, craning his neck upward so he looks a bit bulkier. After a moment of deliberation, he captions the shot "On break." *Simple, accurate, shows I've gotta job. Check, check, check.* With a click, the picture is blasted out to his contacts.

Desperate for a few more minutes before he has to go back up and clear dirty plates and refill wineglasses for people who should have been cut off hours ago, he looks around the basement. In the corner, near an industrial refrigerator, there are a few giant white canvases covering up some lumpy unidentifiable objects. They almost look like ghosts. The sheets probably conceal some old castle artifacts . . . Perhaps there is even something under there that would impress Marigold? A medieval sword or a knight's armor? It wouldn't hurt just to take a peek.

Neil works his way over and pulls off one of the canvas sheets and a cloud of dust along with it. Coughing, he shines his phone flashlight and gasps. It's a very lifelike statue of Queen Gormlaith chiseled out of stone. Her fiery red locks must have once been painted tomato red, like Neil's own hair, but now they've been weathered into a muted rust color. She's holding a sword in one hand and a rust-colored heart in the other, and Neil realizes why this statue has been pulled into the basement and covered up. Besides the statue being beat up and in need of a full restoration, the heart she's holding is cracked completely in half, with one side missing. So he will *definitely* not be sending a picture of this to Marigold. Unless he wants to be brought into mandatory psychological counseling at school.

He covers up the statue and is about to hoof it back up the stairs when he sees a thin line of light shining out from the base of the utility refrigerator. *That's weird,* Neil thinks. Management won't be thrilled to know there's an old fridge down here hiking up the electricity bill. He should unplug it—but first, he'll make sure it's not in use. *God forbid, Elliot's storing like one thousand raspberry-filled lemon cupcakes down here or something*, he thinks, and his stomach rumbles. *Though come to think of it, if he is, he might not notice if just one is missing.* Neil pulls the latch, but there is a padlock on the fridge. He looks at it and realizes whoever placed the lock forgot to set a code, leaving the fridge unlocked. "Idiot," Neil snorts. He clicks it open with ease and pulls the door open. An icy blast sends him stumbling back before he takes a few steps forward to peer in. The frost clears, and his eyes land on a pair of shriveled shoeless feet sticking out of a large black trash bag. Not a raspberry-filled lemon cupcake in sight.

Neil is only sixteen.

Neil is *not* paid enough for this.

So, understandably, Neil screams.

FORTY-SIX

# SEAMUS

Saturday, October 18, 2025
Wedding Reception

"O'REILLY," MAC WHISPERS THROUGH THE dimly lit halls. "Wait." But Seamus doesn't wait; instead he picks up his pace.

"What is going *on?*" Mac growls, grabbing him by the back of the collar and yanking him into a corner and away from the large castle window letting in streaks of moonlight.

"It's over," Seamus says quickly. "I've been trying to get a hold of you all afternoon. I even came to the church. One of the bartenders is with the Gardía. I overheard him on the phone through the cracks in the stone, *calling for backup*."

"Yes, I pieced that together," Mac says hotly. "How did you not figure this out until *today?*"

"I don't know." Seamus's mind flashes back to all his antics from the weekend, including, most recently, his taxi card-reader scheme. He didn't do as much keeping watch as he was instructed to do. Discovering the bartender had been a fluke. "What should we do?"

"We need to get the passports from my room and get out of here," Mac commands, and throws himself against a wall, pulling O'Reilly with him just as a dozen cops swarm the lobby and run up the historic grand spiral staircase. They crouch behind a rogue bellman's cart piled high with suitcases. Through a small crevice, Seamus can see the pudgy blond hotel manager standing with a red-headed kid with a blanket over his shoulders. Other staffers loiter, curious about what's going on.

"There's a body in the basement," the redheaded kid trembles, "down those stairs there. In the fridge." A few of the officers run down the stairs. *They found Gloria.* Seamus feels his heart racing in his chest. A few cops trot down the main staircase into the lobby.

"We found the gun and, uh, you won't believe what else in Suite 405," a young cop tells a heavyset man who must be the boss. "Go see for yourself, Commissioner." The commissioner huffs up the stairs with backup at his heels.

Mac looks at him wide-eyed. They're both thinking the same thing: Suite 405 is Mac's room. But Seamus is confused . . . Mac doesn't have a gun in the room. Neither of them had anything to do with Gloria's death—though he wishes they could take credit for it. The honor of getting rid of the old bat went to someone else who she pissed off, and their plan just happened to benefit from it.

Clearly somebody's trying to frame Mac, but there's no time to think of who—and there's no going back for the passports now. They're close to the pub. If they can make it to the passageway, they might be able to get out of here.

Seamus leans in and whispers to Mac, "Follow me."

FORTY-SEVEN

# MAC

Saturday, October 18, 2025
Wedding Reception

"HURRY UP." O'REILLY'S PANICKED VOICE echoes through the cavernous castle walls. But Mac is too old for this. He feels himself giving up. He should have killed O'Reilly when he had the chance. It's fitting that the deadweight he's been carrying around will be what finally does him in. Mac doesn't have a plan anymore. The plan is foiled. The police have found a gun and God knows what else in his room. He's clearly been set up—but by *who*? Certainly not O'Reilly.

At least the buffoon figured out how to get them out of the castle through the passageway. The system leads to the boathouse overlooking Ballymoon lough. It's their only chance at getting out of here. If they can get to one of the boats docked there, they can make it across the lough, flag down a motorist, and then . . . hop on a flight? He hasn't gotten that far.

Mac stops to catch his breath and runs through more potential options in his mind. Then it comes to him. *Could I possibly pin the whole thing on O'Reilly?* Mac's a smooth operator, so maybe the cops will buy it. Maybe he can make it worth their while . . . He can offer information on another murder. Come to think of it, he can offer valuable information on *multiple* murders and crimes. He could give up his whole book of business—say Seamus O'Reilly has always been the mastermind.

Yes, Mac is a walking gold mine of information for the authorities. Sure, he's in his mid-seventies, but he's heard what the hipsters are shouting from the rooftops: "Know your worth!" When he finally catches up with O'Reilly, Mac puts his new plan in motion.

"What do we do now?" O'Reilly is sweating through his cheap white dress shirt.

"Take us into that boathouse," Mac demands.

"Right, right." O'Reilly shines a flashlight on the grimy tunnel wall to reveal an ancient ladder that leads to another trapdoor. Water leaks from the ceiling, so presumably they're near the lough—or, more likely, under it.

"You first," Mac offers, and O'Reilly greedily climbs up the ladder. Mac closes his eyes and listens. He hears, just barely, the soft patter of feet coming down the tunnel after them. That damn bartender-cop must have discovered the tunnels too. But no matter—this could work out perfectly with Mac's newly formed plan.

"Are you coming?" O'Reilly asks.

"Yes. As fast as I can." Mac takes his time putting his feet on the ladder.

"Can't you go any bloody faster?" O'Reilly whines. He looks down the ladder at Mac, his ratlike eyes glowing in the dark.

"I'm trying," he snaps. The footsteps get louder. *Come on, move it, faster.* Mac wills the cops closer just as O'Reilly grabs him and pulls him up onto the boathouse floor.

"Help, help!" Mac yells. The bartender-cop looks upward before scaling the ladder himself, a few other officers trail behind him. Mac watches O'Reilly's mind try to compute what's happening, but his gears seem to be shifting even more slowly than usual.

"Freeze! On the ground, hands behind your head." The bartender-cop points his gun in their direction. Mac and O'Reilly throw their hands up.

"Help! This man's kidnapped me! Thank the Good Lord you found me." Mac falls to his knees.

"What are you doing?" O'Reilly whispers. All Mac can muster in response is an exasperated shake of his head. Then their eyes meet and O'Reilly's face hardens into stone.

# FORTY-EIGHT

## SEAMUS

Saturday, October 18, 2025
Wedding Reception

TOO MANY PEOPLE HAVE UNDERESTIMATED him. Too many people have wronged him. Mac, who he'd stayed loyal to all these years, *who he went to prison for*, has betrayed him. Now Seamus understands that his boss purposely stalled going up the ladder, acting like he didn't know how to put one foot in front of the other. But what Mac didn't realize is that by doing so, Seamus had a chance to formulate a plan of his own. In the time he was waiting for Mac to haul his arse up the ladder, he surveyed the room and spotted numerous jugs of fuel lining the walls of the boathouse. Just before the cop made it up the ladder, he managed to unscrew the top of the jug closest to him.

As the cops slowly work their way into the boathouse, shouting at them to get down on the floor with their hands behind their heads, Seamus kicks over a container of fuel, which emits a strong smell of gasoline. Now, instead of complying with the police, he slides his lighter out of his shirt pocket.

"Hands where I can see them!" the bartender-cop shouts, seeing what he's up to, but it's too late. The flame is already in Seamus's hands.

"Don't come any closer. I'll do it—I'll blow this whole place up!" Seamus's voice trembles. Will he do it? Is he capable?

"He's lying," Mac screams from the ground. "This was all his idea. I'm done protecting him. I'll make a deal."

"Seamus, we need you to put that lighter down. We can talk about this. We can work something out." The bartender-cop keeps his voice calm and steps forward, the wooden boards of the boathouse groaning under his boots.

"Why would I trust you?" Seamus eyes him, and his hand trembles on the lighter, trying to spark it.

"You can trust me. We just want to talk, to sort this whole mess." He takes another step toward Seamus.

"You're not listening to him, are you?" Mac shouts. "That man is a liar." One of the Gardía puts a boot on Mac's back and he yelps.

*Yeah, that's right, go to hell, Mac,* Seamus thinks. It's Seamus who stands his ground. It's Seamus who can't be stopped. It's Seamus who will go out in a blaze of glory.

"You know what? Forget it. I—I don't want to live anymore. I don't want to rot in a fecking jail cell. Not again." He closes his eyes. The cops share a look.

"O'Reilly, so help me, God—don't do it," Mac croaks. Danny moves in on Seamus, but he's too far away to reach him in time.

Seamus clicks the lighter again.

Nothing happens.

He clicks once more, but she's on him before he can click a third time.

# FORTY-NINE

# CHRISTINE

Saturday, October 18, 2025
Wedding Reception

AFTER THE POLICE ARE DONE taking her statement, Christine walks back up the hill toward the gawking guests on the front lawn. Her absolutely trashed heels dangle from her hands, and a heavy wool blanket is draped across her shoulders. Even though it's not technically "over" yet—the Gardía have informed her she won't be leaving Ireland anytime soon—Christine knows that on the most fundamental level it really *is* over . . . and partially, at least, because of her.

Once Christine entered the castle walls through the supply closet, she heard Seamus and Mac's voices echoing through the passageway. She followed them, a few paces behind, lurking in the shadows, careful not to alert them to her presence. When they entered the boathouse, she found another staircase that led into the boathouse by way of the walls instead, allowing her to watch the drama unfold through the cracks in the stone, directly behind where Seamus stood.

Heart in her throat, she had been waiting, watching, ready to make her move if needed . . . and when she saw Seamus start to flick the lighter, instinct took over. Christine pushed through the passageway entrance into the boathouse and jumped on his back, tackling him to the ground before he even knew she was behind him. She grins through her chattering teeth at the memory of her heroic moment, her body still pulsing with adrenaline. The bad guys have been caught; Gloria's murder has been revealed; the heaviness that has hung over her this weekend has loosened its grip . . . And has been swiftly replaced by Christine's desire to write down this story, to try to understand what happened here this weekend—what it means, and how she fits into it all.

But she'll start that project another day—after she hugs her mom and eats fifteen chicken tenders and sleeps for twelve hours in her own bed. For the time being, she just focuses on her walk up the hill back toward Ballymoon.

"Christine!" she hears Danny call, and turns to see him running to catch up with her. She feels her heart leap a little. "Wait up," he huffs.

"Shouldn't you be in better shape, considering you're a secret agent or whatever?" she jokes. Danny grins as he jogs toward her, his dimples prominent, his Irish smiling eyes glistening like blue pools in the bright moonlight. A few leaves fall from the large oak tree behind him, like pages turning in a book.

"If memory serves me correctly, you still owe me one more pint." The outline of the castle shimmers behind them amidst the scattering clouds—the calm after the storm.

"Really? You're serious?" She laughs. "Haven't I done enough for you and your investigation at this point? I think—"

Danny doesn't let her finish her sentence though. Instead, he grabs her by the waist, pulling her in. She looks into his deep blue eyes, and he stares back at her in a way that makes her whole body melt. They stay like this for a moment, drinking each other in, before (finally!) her lips meet his . . . just as a flurry of green and gold fireworks explode overhead.

And as the world around them sparkles, Christine feels the first bud of a new beginning bloom inside her.

# FIFTY

# LYLE

Saturday, October 18, 2025
Wedding Reception

LYLE IS NUMB. SHE SITS on the terrace, a blanket around her shoulders, her toddler son somehow sleeping in her arms. A police officer tells her Sebi's body has been officially identified. After she hears those words, she zones out, the officer's questions becoming a faint static in the distance. She won't speak; she can't find any words at the moment. She just hugs her son as tightly as she can. Miles opens his eyes but doesn't stir or squirm; instead he burrows closer to his mother.

Down at the boathouse she can see Seamus O'Reilly and Father Kenneth getting cuffed and thrown into the back of a police car. Lyle always had a weird feeling about the priest, always thought he was around too much, too involved in the family's business. Knowing what she knows now, she shudders to think of him baptizing Miles. Closing her eyes, she nuzzles her son. Hopefully he doesn't remember any of this.

A crowd of guests have gathered on the castle terrace behind her, murmuring and watching the arrests, unamused by the fireworks display that is somehow still going on as planned even after the police raided the wedding reception.

"Look! Aren't the fireworks gorgeous? No, look up here, not down there." Elliot's voice cracks as he tries to redirect the guests' attention away from the arrests. Lyle watches an officer put a hand on the wedding planner's shoulder, and he brushes him off. The officer grabs him more forcefully, and Elliot starts to bicker with the cops, demanding to speak to a lawyer. Lyle turns her attention back to the fireworks finale.

A colorful array of gold, green, and white sparkly lights explode overhead. And then the grand finale booms.

The words *Cheers to new beginnings! Love, Gloria* blaze across the night sky, spelled out in tiny golden stars. Lyle covers her mouth as the words dissolve in the air. She can't help it . . . She starts laughing. The poor boyish-looking officer she is with backs away from her slowly, his eyes searching for another, more senior member of the force to step in and help.

"You don't see?" Lyle laughs. "You don't see what this means?" The cop shakes his head.

"It's Gloria. It's *Gloria*." Lyle's laughs descend into sobs. Then she feels Ben's arms around her, and she allows herself to be comforted by him. *He didn't kill anyone.* It's a low bar, but it's also the one good thing to come out of this evening, and she's going to cling to it and to him. She hears Graham's voice cut through the crowd.

"Will someone please explain to me what's going on? Where is Jane?" The one person everyone has overlooked: the bride. It will be hours before they can confirm it, but Lyle already knows in her bones that Jane Ripton is long gone.

FIFTY-ONE

# JANE

Friday, October 17, 2025
Morning of the Rehearsal Dinner

JANE PULLS THE DOOR SHUT behind her and locks it. She closes her eyes and leans against the wall, willing her heart rate to come down. She picks the glittering earring up off the floor and puts it in her pocket. Nobody will notice it's missing. The familiar thrill of being bad runs through her like a shot of espresso, and she feels like herself again.

"Gloria?" she calls into the room. "Are you decent?" Jane rounds the corner into the main room. The Brian Boru suite is gorgeous. It's named aptly after Ireland's most successful high king and richly furnished in gold and red hues, with ornate wallpaper and antique furniture that looks like, if Jane touched it, someone would yell, "Don't touch that!" Their wedding planner, Elliot, had initially saved this room for Jane and Graham, but Graham had insisted Gloria get it, because she's paying for the entire weekend. Honestly, Jane is kind of glad not to be staying here. The room is a bit creepy, lacking some of the modern touches found in the newer suites. She hears a running faucet in the bathroom squeak off.

"Just a minute," Gloria calls. Jane's whole body starts to tremble with the words that will come out once Gloria exits the bathroom. She takes off her engagement ring in preparation.

"Hello, Jane." Gloria comes into view. Jane is momentarily taken aback;

the elderly woman is bare-faced, not a lick of lipstick or a touch of mascara in sight, wearing a nightgown and robe—a stunning silky set, probably vintage Dior. But frankly, Jane has never seen Gloria look so human.

"Sorry if I woke you. I can come back later," she rushes to say, turning toward the door.

"Nonsense, I asked you to come and this is a perfect time. Please, take a seat." Gloria ushers her into the suite's seating area, which faces a window overlooking the lough. It's still dark outside, but the harsh black of the night before has started to melt into a dull gray. Jane gives Gloria a moment to get into her chair. She is moving slowly these days but will not accept any help doing basic tasks.

"There," Gloria says finally, and it's all Jane needs to hear to spill her guts out. She doesn't want to live like this another minute.

"Gloria, I need to give this back to you." She holds out the engagement ring. "I don't want it anymore. This has all been a big mistake. I need to tell you—" Jane stops talking when she sees the curl of Gloria's lip, the twinkle in her eye. *She already knows.*

"You know what I'm about to say, don't you?" Jane already feels lighter and collapses back in her chair.

Gloria tuts. "Put that ring back on your finger and then we'll talk."

Jane does as she's told.

"Now," Gloria begins, "tell me what happened. Start at the beginning."

And so she does. Jane opens the floodgates of her subconscious and tells Gloria everything. She tells her about her urge to commit petty crime from a young age, finding out about her father, Seamus . . . about Mac. How she teamed up with their crime ring to infiltrate the Ripton family through a marriage to Graham. How Mac planned to use her as a puppet to drain Graham's trust.

How she's bad, broken probably, but that Mac and Seamus are evil. And how she has grown so fond of Graham, how she can't hurt him like this or live a life of never-ending scheming and betrayal. How, when Mac had Seamus kill Sebi, they'd gone too far, and she realized that the life she was signing up for would put her in constant danger—if she lived at all. How she is exhausted. How she's done, even if it means death.

Gloria nods, and Jane waits for her face to express surprise at any of the bombshells she just dropped, but it never does. They sit in silence for a moment, but then Jane has to ask—

"How did you know that I was working for Mac?"

Gloria sighs, that knowing twinkle returning to her eyes.

"When I saw the pictures of his hoodlum getting rid of Sebi in the marsh, it all crystalized. I was able to track down plenty of images of—what's his name?—Seamus, and well"—Gloria smiles sadly—"you're his spitting image! All I had to do was hold your pictures side by side, and I had a feeling. It was simple to figure it out from there."

*Of course*, Jane thinks. She'd been struck by her likeness to her father when they first met too.

"But how did you figure out that Seamus was working for Mac specifically? That he wasn't just some random criminal who killed Sebi in a drug deal gone bad or something?" Jane presses. Gloria smiles at this and then slowly reaches into the pocket of her robe and pulls out a Saint Christopher medal, placing it on the table between them. It's identical to the one Seamus wears, to the one Maggie wears, and Jane realizes . . .

"Father Kenneth's signature gift," Gloria spits. "He's not as subtle as he'd like to think he is."

"Wow," Jane says finally, and takes a breath. "Well . . . I understand you have an obligation to protect your family and have me arrested or killed or whatever."

"I don't have people killed," Gloria snaps, like a rubber band against raw skin. "It's lazy, messy, and honestly . . . it's classless. That's all Kenneth, or *Mac*, as you call him. Though, I suppose, maybe on some level, we've had a don't ask, don't tell policy. But that's my mistake. I'll have to live with it, or die with it, I guess." Gloria shakes her head and taps her fingers on the cherrywood table between their two chairs before continuing.

The elderly woman's voice quivers. "A few weeks ago, I confronted

Father Kenneth about disobeying my orders and having Sebi killed instead of just paying him off. I found out that he killed my ex-husband."

Jane can't help it—she gasps.

Gloria takes a sharp breath. "Anyway, once he made his confession to me, on top of Sebi and a whole *host* of issues in relation to Glo and my nonprofit that I won't bore you with—I have decided I want him gone." She pauses and looks Jane dead in the eye. "And you're going to help me."

Gloria gets up and struggles over to the closet, where her luggage lies open. She grabs a manila envelope off the top and pulls a pistol from the suitcase. She picks it up with a small white cloth. Jane watches her walk back toward the sitting area, her mind moving like molasses. She should be nervous, but she just feels groggy.

"You're in a pickle and I can help you get out of it. You want to get out of this, right? You want to get rid of Mac's hold on you?" Gloria asks, and Jane nods in response.

"Good, we have a shared goal." Gloria opens the folder. "Now, you're going to have to do exactly as I say. First, you're going to kill me."

"What?" Jane almost shouts. "Gloria! I can't do that."

"A little gallows humor—relax." Gloria chuckles. "*I* am going to kill me, but the cancer's got a good head start." She shows Jane the inside of her handkerchief. It is spattered with blood.

"I can't let you—" Jane starts, but Gloria interrupts.

"Oh, please. I've lived a good long life, and I don't want to waste away. I want to go out with a bang." She laughs, and Jane jumps. "And not only that—my death, and the mystery of it, are integral to your escape and safety. Do you understand?" Jane doesn't know what to say, but she feels her stomach drop. She knows that whatever Gloria has plotted is likely the only way that she can make it out of here alive and get away from Mac.

"I am going to shoot myself with this gun, but I know how to make it look like someone else did it. Everyone will think I was murdered . . . and you"—she points to Jane—"will say you found me dead; I've already made the room look like there was a bit of a tussle. I've given myself defensive wounds." She shows Jane bruises on her neck and wrists.

"But why?" Jane starts, but Gloria holds up a hand.

"We don't have much time. Let me finish. It is vital you hear the plan in its entirety. My family, upon finding my body, will try to cover it up. I know them. I'll let you in on a little secret—they're on the verge of losing the business, losing control. Money—well, *losing* money—it makes people crazy. They will try and hide my death for as long as possible. And that's where you come in. You will follow my instructions and feed Christine Russo information."

"Christine? The girl from *Bespoke*?" Jane's stomach lurches at the thought of her life being in that tiny airhead's hands.

"Stop interrupting," Gloria barks. "She's smart—she'll help you. You will go through with the wedding. This is how we catch Father Kenneth and put your father back in jail where he belongs. You have to trust me."

"But Graham," Jane squeaks. "I can't."

"Don't worry about Graham, he'll be fine. He needs to toughen up." Gloria opens the folder on her lap. Inside are three typed pages. "Now, in here is important information for you and a set of instructions. You'll need to guide Christine with tips about Father Kenneth's crimes. Do your best to linger by her and keep her on the right track. Elliot will have her full agenda if you need it. The idea is for *her* to be the one to put together what's been happening with Father Kenneth and alert the police, so you don't have to get involved and incriminate yourself in the process. I've done as much as I can to ensure your success, but I'm trusting you're smart enough to handle the rest." She flips to the back of the folder. "At the end of this, you'll find a new identity, passport, and plane ticket—everything you need for a fresh start. I've scheduled my helicopter to pick you up Saturday night at seven p.m. So be ready."

"Gloria, I don't understand." Jane's eyes are filled with tears. "Why would you do this to your family? Why are you going to such great lengths to help me?"

Gloria tuts. "I want to help you because you're smart and ambitious," she says, "and when I played you in chess, I saw so much of myself at your age. I hope things can turn out different for you than they did for me. I hope I can give you the opportunity to make better choices, keep better company." Now Gloria's eyes are misty. She pauses before continuing. "I want to set you free. That's what my legacy is about now: a fresh start. For you and for my family. My money is dangerous in their hands. They're all intertwined with Mac now, embedded in a life of crime, knowingly or not. I brought him in and so, before I go, I need to take him out."

"But you don't have to do *this* . . . these games, this psychological torture. If you put your family members in this position, teasing them with notes, with a fake murder—people could go to jail. Lives will be ruined."

"And you didn't have to steal my diamond earring off the floor when you walked in here," Gloria scoffs. "Don't bore me with your convenient conscience now. What fun is that?"

That shuts Jane up.

"I never claimed to be an angel. But I'll tell you one thing: at the end of my life, when I should have turned to God, when I needed him most, he turned out to be a fraud . . . just another man I couldn't trust." Jane watches the old woman's eyes get teary again. "So I'm going to put what's left of my faith in myself instead. And I'm going to direct my final act." She laughs. "It'll be a real showstopper. I'm going to really stick it to Father Kenneth, because I want to *win*. I think you can understand that." She looks at Jane knowingly, but the girl is still confused.

Gloria stands up. "Now, there is a silencer on the gun, but once it goes off, I want you to hide it in Father Kenneth's room. He won't be looking for it. Use the hidden passageways in the castle walls to get around unseen, to give Christine clues and keep tabs on her."

Jane's cheeks redden slightly.

"Don't give me that look. You didn't think I found out about the passageways? I have to imagine it's the reason why the wedding is here in the first place," Gloria says. "Now, I've done a lot of the heavy lifting here for you. It's been a busy couple of weeks. I've already sent a tip to the Irish local forces, so there will be someone keeping an eye on the wedding this weekend, and I've written a hit piece that will drop on Saturday night that should really twist the knife." She smirks. "Hell, I even went as far as to preplan my funeral arrangements."

Jane stares at her, dumbfounded, unsure of what to say.

"I laid out as much as I can for you here. Copies of my will, photos that might be useful." Gloria places the manila folder on Jane's lap. "But you'll certainly have to improvise on occasion. And one more thing." Gloria reaches into the pocket of her dressing gown and produces the marble queen from her chessboard back in Charleston. Jane's mind flashes to the game from the first night they met. Her cheeks prickle with embarrassment. *She knows I let her win.*

"A bit of advice: never disgrace the board like that again." She places the chess piece in Jane's hand and chuckles softly. "Don't be afraid to win, no matter who you piss off in the process. That is how I amassed my fortune, how I built Glo from nothing—by never playing it safe. By being bold and sometimes, when it was necessary, being bad. What's the saying? Nice guys finish last? Anyway, I'm counting on you to win here, above all else. I think you've got what it takes—and by that I mean: I trust you'll do *whatever it takes.*"

Jane squeezes the chess piece. She can't let Gloria go through with this. "Gloria, this is psychotic. Just disinherit your kids, report Father Kenneth to the authorities—"

"If I do that, you'll die—you know that, right? Or, best-case scenario, spend most of your life in prison," Gloria retorts. "Now let me do this for you, and for my family, so you can all start over. And let me do this for *me*. I've had a marvelous time plotting my grand finale." She smiles, but Jane catches the slight quiver in her voice.

"Gloria." Jane stands up cautiously. "I'm asking you not to do this."

"Be careful . . . you don't want your fingerprints on this gun. Use the cloth when I'm done." Gloria points the gun at Jane with shaky hands and Jane is forced to sit down and watch as Gloria turns the gun on herself. Jane's vision starts to blur, black spots popping in and out.

"Life is full of hard choices, Jane. Sometimes you only get to choose between bad and worse. I've made my choices . . . and now you get to make yours. Now, please, look away."

But before Jane can protest, Gloria Beaufort goes out with a bang.

# EPILOGUE

# JANE

Two Years After the Wedding
Istanbul, Turkey

IT'S A BLISTERING DAY IN Istanbul. Jane has already sweat through her linen pants and head covering, but she doesn't care. She grins widely as she shoves her way through a crowded marketplace and into a post office. It's her last day on the job. After she drops off this letter, she's officially free—her debt to Gloria Beaufort paid in full.

It's been eighteen months since Christine Russo's op-ed, "A Killer Wedding," was published by the *New York Times*; she regaled the world with wild tales from the wedding weekend from hell that Jane herself narrowly escaped. Gloria's instructions were clear: wait until the zeitgeist had moved on before sending Christine this final letter—the last item on her postmortem to-do list. Now, with court proceedings finally wrapped up, Father Kenneth and Seamus behind bars, Glo shuttered and Gloria's fortune dismantled and dispersed among the plaintiffs in Glo's lawsuit, Jane knows the time is right.

"Is that all?" the postwoman huffs behind the kiosk in a thick Turkish accent. "Do you mind please stepping to the side?"

But Jane can't move—she stares blankly at the envelope addressed to Christine Russo as the woman casually tosses it onto the mail pile.

"Hello?" the woman says, her voice tinged with annoyance. "Speak English?"

"Yes, sorry." Jane shakes herself out of the trance. She hadn't realized a line had formed as she stood there staring at the last thing tying her to Gloria Beaufort, to her past. She moves out of the way, bumping into the man behind her as she does so.

"Sorry," she says again, quickly helping him pick up his packages. Then she stumbles outside in a daze. The Middle Eastern sun beats down on her head, but Jane feels chilled to the bone—transported one final time back to that October weekend at Ballymoon. Sprinting through rolling green fields when she was supposed to be changing into her sequin-studded fireworks dress, the hum of Gloria's helicopter becoming louder and clearer with every step.

*A shadow floating through the tunnels . . .*
*A spy peeking through the cracks in the stone . . .*
*A trail of clues . . .*
*A few close calls . . .*

In the end, it had been thrilling, hadn't it? Living so close to the edge? Jane looks around and then reaches into the pocket of her linen trousers, pulling out the wallet of the man behind her, that familiar charge pulsing through her body.

*There's really no better feeling in the world . . . than getting away with it.*

Thursday, October 16, 2025

Dear Christine,

As I write this, the captain has just announced that we are "approaching our final destination," and I can't help but laugh at the irony. Final destination, indeed. At least it is for me. The long and short of it is, I'm dying. I haven't told my family about my diagnosis, and I don't plan to. But let me just say, lung cancer is a real bitch. And the rest of them better get used to flying commercial.

    I spent the better part of my life building an empire and the latter part watching my family destroy it. The whole thing has been exhausting, if I am being honest. I'm ready to be done. And how fitting—no, how poetic!—that I am coming back to the country that my great-grandparents fled so long ago for my final rest. I have nothing left to conquer. I've had a good run. You have to know when to leave the party, right? And when to crash it . . . But you already knew that.

    Still, I have a little bit of drama left to savor. The longest, healthiest relationship in my life has been with the melodramatic. So naturally, I have painstakingly planned my finale. If you fail to plan, you plan to fail—that's my motto. Ever since the doctor gave me the "a few months at best" talk—just before our chance meeting at the Bespoke Ball—I've been thinking of how my story will end, and who will tell it. And when I met you, it all became clear.

    I've decided that I am going to end my life and change my legacy for the better. Starting by repaying the victims of Glo's wrongdoings with my fortune. This will be my service to society and to my family. Father Kenneth will go to jail and all the money will be gone. The money has ruined my family, spoiled them to the point of no return. I should have given it all away earlier, but, well . . . hindsight and all of that. Plus, I do love money. I don't want to live without it, and I shouldn't have to. It's mine—and I'm taking it with me.

I am not a perfect person. I have done a lot of things that people might find . . . uncouth. I have hurt people I love in my quest for power and success. But for the most part, I'd say it was worth it. And by the way, I didn't personally kill anyone or do anything horrid like that. I just play to win . . . It's not my fault that most people play to not lose.

Maybe God will cut me some slack for turning Father Kenneth in. Perhaps She will appreciate the gesture of putting a bad guy behind bars—especially a criminal masquerading as a man of the church.

Anyway, the point of this letter is to clear a few things up for you. At this juncture, I am assuming you know that I have weaponized Jane to help me execute my plan. The girl is scrappy and tough—and she's smarter than she lets on. If I were you, I wouldn't try to track her down again after you get this letter. As you're probably aware, she can't be trusted. I figured her game out quickly, though. She played me in chess the first time Graham brought her to meet me. Actually, she hustled me in chess. But in that moment, playing a worthy opponent for the first time in decades, I rediscovered a piece of myself that I'd long lost: the chip on my shoulder, the tiny niggling feeling of something to prove—to Jane and to myself—that I've still got it. That nobody needs to let me win, that I'll always be able to win on my own. Part of my final act, trusting Jane, well, I had to leave some of that to chance. But if you're reading this, I'd say the plan was a raging success.

And as for you, Christine Russo, well, you are the other part of my scheme:

The girl who snuck into the Bespoke Ball against her boss's wishes and shamelessly pitched herself to cover my grandson's wedding.

The girl who said, "Nobody puts on a show like Mother Nature," and inspired me to summon this woman-made storm, to give my family a second chance once I'm gone.

You are sharp and observant, with a bright future ahead—and exactly the sort of person I want to tell my story, to tell the world who Gloria Beaufort really was. Maybe you can call my story *Fifty Shades of Rouge*? I think that's good. Feel free to use it.

Anyway, apologies for the messy handwriting; our plane is really bobbing and weaving on the descent. I can feel the raindrops pelting us. The captain said it would be a bumpy landing, but I don't mind. I find it thrilling, actually. A smooth landing is an unmemorable experience. But a bumpy landing . . . you're on the edge of your seat the whole time, heart in your throat, wondering: What will happen next? And when you finally land—if you do—well, that's a flight people will remember, isn't it?

Gloria

## ACKNOWLEDGMENTS

WHERE TO BEGIN? IT FEELS unfair that there is only one person's name on the cover of this book! First, I must thank my brilliant editor, Liz Stein, and my fantastic agent, Elisabeth Weed. I think I will have to name my first-born child some variation of the name Elisabeth in order to repay my debts to you both.

Elisabeth, thank you for plucking me from obscurity and giving *A Killer Wedding* its wings—I'll be forever grateful to Martha Otis for connecting us! Liz, thank you for making my story soar. I learned so much from you over the last year and enjoyed every minute of it. I'd also like to extend a massive thank-you to Liate Stehlik and the entire William Morrow/HarperCollins team. You really know how to make a girl (and book) feel special.

To Michelle Weiner, my film rights agent at CAA, and Jenny Meyer, my international rights agent. Thank you both for representing me and advocating for *A Killer Wedding*.

To Kristen Bozzone Armstrong, Katie Hogan, and everyone at Cheree Berry Paper & Design, thank you for bringing the fabulous Ripton/Murphy wedding to life by designing the invitation suite of my dreams. Brides everywhere, take note!

To the best parents a girl could ask for, thank you for your unwavering support of all of my creative endeavors since, well, forever.

Mom, thank you for believing in me even when I didn't. I couldn't have been luckier to be raised by such a creative, strong-willed, and optimistic woman—with impeccable taste, I might add! You are the best mom-ager a crazy theater kid like me could have ever asked for. Also, you win: thanks for never listening to me when I said, "Don't tell anyone I am writing a book, it's embarrassing."

And to Dad, the original storyteller in our family (see currently unpublished: *The Boy with No Christmas Boots*)—thank you for giving me my love of sarcasm and my obsession with Ireland. But mostly, thank you for teaching me to work hard and to never ring the bell. When you took a break from reading World War II nonfiction to read the first draft of *A Killer Wedding* and said, "It sounds like a real book!" I knew I might have something here.

Many thanks to my sisters, my best friends and the reluctant stars of my basement theatrical productions; to Georgia, whose reading of this book in itself is a miracle given that she hasn't read anything but medical textbooks since 2019.

And to Victoria, our family tastemaker, whose opinion and approval matter more to me than is probably healthy. Thank you for being one of my first readers. If you didn't like this book, I probably would have lit it on fire.

To Aunt Lula—my fairy godmother *and* my first editor. Thank you for always being in my corner and always showing up for me in every way possible. Our family is so lucky to have you.

To Martha and Ann—like I said, I am so glad my mom ignored me when I asked her not to tell anyone about this book! Thank you both for all your efforts to help me make this dream come true.

Thank you to my wonderful in-laws, Beth and Jim. I am so lucky to have married into the Robinson clan, who share my affinity for big laughs, extra dirty martinis, and a good mystery.

To Gerard Bradford, Jimmy Fallon, and all of my *Tonight Show* peeps! Hilarious, talented, and kind GOATs who taught me so much about comedy, storytelling, and the importance of making people laugh. Except for Adler, of course.

To Christina Noval, Priany Hadiatmodjo, Annie Sizemore, and the entire NBCUniversal Page Program team. Being an NBCPage was my first dream come true and I will be forever grateful for the opportunities, connections, and lifelong friends that this wonderful program gave me.

To Amy Spicer, Tom Dodd, Kim Weems, and everyone at the Lake Placid Center for the Arts. I was so lucky to be taught by so many talented educators growing up. You all helped me hone my skills and gave me the confidence to pursue a career in storytelling.

To Bonnie Monte, Karen and Jeff Kirby, and the wonderful Shakespeare Theatre of New Jersey—another amazing place filled with literary fanatics and creatives who I was lucky to learn from.

To our ninety-seven wedding guests! Thank you for not murdering *me* and bravely stepping out into the post-Covid world to attend our thrice-rescheduled destination wedding in Ireland . . . And, of course, thank you to my husband, Tom; a man who's probably wanted to murder me on many occasions. I finished this book for two reasons: 1.) Because you said I couldn't talk about it anymore unless I actually started writing it, and 2.) Because what else was I supposed to do while you were up so late, working so hard? Thanks for letting me turn our special day into a cheeky, fashion-forward whodunit, for supporting my big dreams since the moment we met, for fact-checking my incorrect use of common phrases (we found the Rubicon!), and for being my perfect match. I can always count on you to make me laugh until I cry . . . or turn my cries into laughs, depending on the day.

Also, sorry for always leaving my coffee cups in precarious places. I promise to try and not do that going forward. (Narrator: she would, in fact, do that going forward.)

Anyway, it's time to guzzle some champagne! I love you all.

# ABOUT THE AUTHOR

JOAN O'LEARY holds a bachelor of arts in English with an emphasis in creative writing from the University of San Diego. She spent many years working in the entertainment industry, starting as an NBCUniversal page and most recently as a producer for *The Tonight Show Starring Jimmy Fallon*. *A Killer Wedding* is her first novel.